PRACE FOR THE LA

PRAISE FOR THE LA...

"I love Lexi Blake. Read *Ruthless* and see why."

—*New York Times* bestselling author Lee Child

"Smart, savvy, clever, and always entertaining. That's true of Riley Lawless, the hero in *Ruthless*, and likewise for his creator, Lexi Blake. Both are way ahead of the pack."

—*New York Times* bestselling author Steve Berry

"*Ruthless* is full of suspense, hot sex, and swoon-worthy characters— a must read! Lexi Blake is a master at sexy, thrilling romance!"

—*New York Times* bestselling author Jennifer Probst

"With *Ruthless*, Lexi Blake has set up shop on the intersection of suspenseful and sexy, and I never want to leave."

—*New York Times* bestselling author Laurelin Paige

"The love story that develops will touch the hearts of fans . . . A welcome and satisfying entry into the Lawless world."

—RT Book Reviews

PRAISE FOR THE NOVELS OF LEXI BLAKE

"The sex was hot and emotionally charged in many beautiful ways."

—Scandalicious

"A book to enjoy again and again . . . Captivating."

—Guilty Pleasures Book Reviews

continued . . .

"A satisfying snack of love, romance, and hot, steamy sex."

—Sizzling Hot Books

"Hot and emotional."

—Two Lips Reviews

PRAISE FOR THE PERFECT GENTLEMEN SERIES
BY SHAYLA BLACK AND LEXI BLAKE

"Hot and edgy and laced with danger, the stories in the Perfect Gentlemen series are just that—perfect."

—*New York Times* bestselling author J. Kenner

"While there are certainly incendiary sex scenes at the top of this series opener, the strength is in the underlying murder and political mystery."

—RT Book Reviews

TITLES BY LEXI BLAKE

THE COURTING JUSTICE NOVELS

Order of Protection

THE LAWLESS NOVELS

Ruthless
Satisfaction
Revenge

THE PERFECT GENTLEMEN NOVELS

(with Shayla Black)

Scandal Never Sleeps
Seduction in Session
Big Easy Temptation

ORDER
of
PROTECTION

LEXI BLAKE

JOVE
NEW YORK

A JOVE BOOK
Published by Berkley
An imprint of Penguin Random House LLC
375 Hudson Street, New York, New York 10014

Library of Congress Cataloging-in-Publication Data
Names: Blake, Lexi, author.
Title: Order of protection / Lexi Blake.
Description: First edition. | New York, New York : Jove, 2018. |
Series: A courting justice novel ; 1 | "A Jove book."
Identifiers: LCCN 2017053744| ISBN 9780399587467 (paperback) |
ISBN 9780399587474 (ebook)
Subjects: | BISAC: FICTION / Romance / Contemporary. | FICTION / Romance / Suspense. |
FICTION / Contemporary Women. | GSAFD: Romantic suspense fiction.
Classification: LCC PS3602.L3456 O73 2018 | DDC 813/.6—dc23
LC record available at https://lccn.loc.gov/2017053744

First Edition: June 2018

Printed in the United States of America
1   3   5   7   9   10   8   6   4   2

Cover design by Alana Colucci
Cover photo: Couple © Claudio Marinesco / Ninestock
Book design by Kelly Lipovich

ACKNOWLEDGMENTS

I would like to thank everyone who helped make *Order of Protection* possible. Thanks to my assistant and all around Girl Friday, Kim Guidroz; to my incredible editor, Kate Seaver, and the team at Berkley; and to Merilee Heifetz and Writers House. I would be remiss if I didn't acknowledge some experts who were willing to read this book to make sure I didn't screw up too much. Thanks to Jennifer Zeffer, for providing the forensics and DNA information, and Margarita Coale—my personal lawyer and all around legal guardian angel—for explaining that lawyers don't sleep with their clients and still going along with me anyway.

ONE

MARTHA'S VINEYARD,
MASSACHUSETTS

Henry Garrison sat on the back-porch steps, looking out at the Atlantic. The waves were calm at this time of day, an endless beat that once had been the rhythm of his childhood. The sky was darkening, a storm coming in with savage quickness. It was one of the things he'd always loved about this place. One minute the sky was perfect, and then some terrible storm would roll in, and thirty minutes later the world was back to flawless again.

If only his life had turned out to be so quick to change. Oh, it had gotten shitty fast, but the cleanup afterward seemed like it might take a lifetime.

He let the coffee cup he held warm his hands and concentrated on the beach. When he looked out over that sand, he could practically see his grandfather walking. The old man who'd raised him had walked the shoreline every single day, combing the beach he'd known for decades as though he would find something new. He would show back up with some shell or sand dollar like it was a treasure.

Damn but he missed that old man.

Sometimes he didn't though. He was happy his grandfather hadn't lived long enough to see the complete wreck Henry had made of his life. Along with his daily walk on the beach, Alistair Garrison had sat right here on this porch and read the *New York Times* every single morning while sipping his two cups of coffee. Never more, because that would be too indulgent.

Control and discipline, my boy. Those are the keys to life.

Yeah, his grandfather hadn't lived long enough to watch his only grandchild, the golden boy, fall from grace because of booze and arrogance. He hadn't had to watch as the New York Bar had nearly taken away his ability to practice law. He hadn't been alive to witness the downfall of his grandson's made-for-the-tabloids marriage, and Henry was sure as hell happy he hadn't been alive to know that his precious house was being put on the market to pay off a never-ending series of bills he'd run up when he'd been married. He'd bought cars and houses and other shit he didn't need.

Most of which he didn't even own anymore. He'd had to sell almost everything to simply keep his head above water. He'd blown it all on booze and luxury vacations and clothes with price tags that would have made his grandfather roll over in his grave.

Henry gripped the coffee cup with both hands, willing himself to stay out here on the porch and not go back inside the small but beautifully decorated bungalow. That had been his grandmother's doing, and he reminded himself that he was happy she hadn't witnessed his tragedy either.

He'd been packing up the closet in the smaller of the two bedrooms when he'd found a wooden box containing a lifetime's worth of photos. They were black-and-white and color. Some had been professionally done—his father's army photo, his grandfather's wedding portrait, Henry's Harvard graduation portrait. Some had been from the various cameras his grandfather had used over the years.

There had also been a Bible with a pressed white rose in it. His mother's.

Pictures of the dead. Pictures of people who'd smiled and had lives, and then they were gone and he was left behind.

But those bittersweet memories weren't what had prompted Henry to practically run out of the house.

Nope. It had been the small bottle of Scotch he'd found. There had been almost half the bottle left. He'd looked at that liquid gold and known exactly how it would taste, how it would smell, the way it would burn down his throat. He'd stared at it and figured he could get three decent glasses out of it. He could go to the kitchen, grab one of the crystal tumblers his grandmother had been proud of, and sit and toast all that death.

He'd dropped the bottle on the carpet and walked out of the house. He'd walked to the small café two blocks from the beach and ordered a large coffee and told himself that he could keep the monster locked in that room. He would simply sell the contents of the house along with the structure.

The problem was, the monster didn't live in the bottle. The monster was with Henry always.

His cell trilled, and he practically breathed a sigh of relief. Work was something he could deal with. Work was an addiction he could sink into. He set the cup down and answered the call. "This is Garrison."

"Hey, buddy. How's the packing going?" David Cormack's voice came over the line, a steady sound that soothed Henry. There was something about the ex–NFL star turned lawyer that Henry found oddly calming. David never flipped his shit, never got angry or emotional, but managed to also never seem cold.

David's whole world had turned upside down, all his hopes and dreams burned to cinders, and all he'd done was find a new dream.

Henry would bet that not once had David ever had a drunken

screaming argument with his wife in the middle of a Manhattan restaurant with a phalanx of reporters documenting every moment for posterity.

Of course, David was a widower. He didn't argue with his wife at all.

"I'm getting through it. I only got in yesterday. I'm going to pack up anything personal and let the movers take the rest." He wasn't going to talk to David about the fact that he was on the back porch hiding out from a bottle of Scotch. David had enough to deal with. "Did the kid get in all right?"

The kid was named Noah Lawless, and he was the only fucking reason Henry Garrison was still going to be able to practice law in Manhattan. After his disastrous divorce, he didn't have the influence or the cash flow to keep up his private practice. Manhattan's best criminal lawyer had become a has-been, and only his connection to the incredibly powerful Lawless family was saving him this time.

Once upon a time, he'd defended Riley Lawless's future wife from embezzlement and fraud charges. Not that she'd needed much defending, since she'd actually been innocent, but getting Ellie out of jail had apparently endeared him to the clan, and when he'd needed help, they'd been amenable. They were funding him for the time being. They were also his only real client.

Of course, that meant doing Drew Lawless, the family patriarch and head of their multibillion-dollar company, a massive favor and taking on his baby brother as a freaking junior partner. But a desperate man did what he had to do. Noah wasn't coming in as an associate, the way he should. He had his damn name on the door.

"He's not as bad as you think." David knew how reluctant Henry was to take on an entitled kid. He'd dealt with enough rich pricks to last a lifetime.

Despite the fact that he was sitting on one of the world's most affluent islands, he hadn't grown up wealthy. The house had been built by his boat captain great-grandfather back in the 1920s and passed down the line. His grandfather had been a fisherman, and his father had gone into the military. After his father had died, Henry had grown up here as a townie. It had only been later on that he'd turned into an overprivileged asshole of a human being.

"I think he's probably pretty bad, so you're not giving me a lot of confidence." Henry wished he hadn't stopped smoking. No more smoking. No more drinking. No more random, meaningless sex. Being virtuous was starting to get to him. He needed a good murder case, and soon, or he wouldn't know what to do with himself. "The kid went to Creighton Academy. They're all rich jerks who never worked a day in their lives."

"He's not what you would think, and you know his background. He practically raised himself. I like him. And he's damn good with computers," David said, his enthusiasm coming over the line.

"I would think he should be." The Lawless family money was built on technology. 4L Software was known for innovation. "I don't know why he didn't go into tech in the first place. He could be working at 4L."

"Maybe you don't know him as well as I do. Read the files I send you every now and then. Or at least pretend to. He used to be a hacker, and it got him into some trouble. Things got violent, and he wants to stay as far away from that world as possible. When he went to college, he liked the law classes he took, and here he is."

"Yes, big brother bought him a law firm." And two partners. There was really no way around that. "I'm sure he's also got a multimillion-dollar penthouse. I'm sure he'll be supereasy to deal with."

"Can the sarcasm, please," David admonished. "As I was trying to explain, he's worth more than the cash he's bringing in, and he is very helpful. The network went down, and he got it up and working long before the IT guy I called managed to get to the office. By the way, we could use an in-house IT guy."

They could use a lot of things they weren't going to get. "Find me his salary in our budget and we'll talk. Until then, the Creighton kid can do it, apparently. How did the meeting with Keillor go?"

Greg Keillor was a Wall Street businessman accused of murdering his business partner. The police believed he had one hell of a motive. A quarter of a billion dollars was worth killing over in a lot of people's minds. It was exactly the kind of case Henry liked to sink his teeth into. High profile, tons of billable hours, a client who could pay his freaking bill. Yeah, he wanted in on that. He'd been back in New York for less than a year, and most of his cases had been small-time. He'd done a couple of pro bono, mea culpa, I'm-still-a-beast cases, but it was time to move back into prime time.

"I'm sorry, man. Keillor decided to go with Dustin and Klaus." There was something tight in David's tone.

"What did he say?" If this had been three years ago, Keillor would have been begging to have the Monster of Manhattan as his attorney. Henry Garrison would have been the first number he called. Henry would have been the one to make sure the case was worth his time.

Unfortunately, this was today.

"It doesn't matter," David insisted.

"It matters to me." He should let it go, but he couldn't. Now it was almost more real than it had been before, because now he wasn't simply Henry Garrison, Esquire. He was a member of Garrison, Cormack, and Lawless. He'd brought himself down. How much harder would it be to bring them all down? After all, he hadn't meant to do it the first time.

"He wasn't interested in a lawyer who was more scandalous than he was," David replied, his tone wry. "See? He's a massive ass if he thinks divorcing your actress wife is more scandalous than beating his business partner to death with a polo mallet. Also, might I add that he was a shitty polo player and that was the most action his mallet ever saw. I don't want him as a client."

That was David. He looked to the silver lining. "You need to think about this, man. I know we've been friends for a long time, but you might do better on your own."

It was an argument they'd had many times since the night his old friend had come to him and offered to start up a law firm. Henry had pointed out that no one wanted an addict, who couldn't even keep a wife, as a lawyer.

David had pointed out that no one would want a washed-up jock, who hadn't been known for his brains, as a lawyer.

"Stop. There's no going back now. We're in this and we're a team. And you know it's not all bad," David quipped. "This office is small but spectacular. Drew Lawless knows how to pick real estate. The view impresses the hell out of everyone. I've already got two clients, and one of them is the Missiles. We should be rolling in dough soon, because you know how those athletes can be."

He sighed in relief. David had been trying to get on as the Manhattan Missiles' lawyer on retainer for months. It was a secret no one liked to talk about, but many professional sports teams kept criminal lawyers on retainer just in case. They wouldn't be rolling in dough, as he'd said, but that retainer would keep the lights on. And it was a serious win for his friend. "Good for you, man."

"Yeah, well, the new GM is an old friend of mine," David admitted. "But you're the one who told me half this business is who you know. Speaking of who you know . . . there's a rumor floating around that a group of New York–based reality stars are hanging around

Martha's Vineyard for the end of the summer. No cameras. Apparently this is vacation time, so they might be willing to talk."

He groaned. That was not a world he wanted to set foot in. He'd been around the elite of the entertainment world, and they were bad enough. Reality shows were pretty much the bottom of the barrel. "Absolutely not."

"Come on. You know that's a gold mine," David countered, his voice going low. It was the same tone he used when trying to get a jury to see his point. *Look at how sensible I'm being. Don't mind the facts. Isn't my voice soothing?* He had to admit it. David had that shit down. "And it's publicity, Henry. You're the one who taught me getting your name out there is half the battle. This would be a great way to announce you're back and you're not afraid of anything. It's work just waiting to happen. They always get in trouble. It's actually a part of their career paths. If their ratings stall, they get arrested and do an apologetic media tour. That group has been going for more than five years now. They're all about to hit thirty, and that's geriatric on their network. Rumors are it's going to get canceled soon. One of those kids is going to do something stupid, and we could be the lawyers who get paid for mopping up the mess."

The thought made Henry's stomach churn. He glanced out over the beach. It was peaceful. So unlike his former life. At this time of evening, the families had gone in for early dinners and the only person he could see was a woman jogging toward him from the east side of the island.

She was brave, because that storm was moving in even faster than he'd thought. There wasn't much the way she was going. No shops unless she made a turn and jogged into Edgartown proper.

"I'm not getting back into that life—even as the janitor," Henry replied. "Besides, after the way I left L.A., I don't think there's a studio or a network around that would recommend anything with my name on it."

That had been the real mistake. He'd followed his bombshell actress wife out to La La Land, and that's where it had all gone to hell. He should never have left the East Coast. God, there were pictures of him in douchebag V-neck T-shirts and skinny jeans. What had he been thinking?

He'd come back to New York with his tail between his legs and a big decision to make. Keep the home he'd grown up in or the Manhattan condo that impressed potential clients. In the end, there had been no other logical choice. The Martha's Vineyard property was worth even more than the condo, but he couldn't practice out here. Oh, he was perfectly licensed to practice in the state of Massachusetts, but there wasn't much to do. The worst thing that happened out here was someone's Maltipoo violating the dog-doo rules.

Unfortunately, the murders were few and far between.

"Think about it," David said with a sigh. "I know you hate the fact that you have to climb the ladder again, but it won't take as long this time. New York is different than L.A., and you know it. That Harvard degree means something here."

So did his public meltdowns. They had been scandal fodder in L.A., but they were serious here in New York. New York lawyers were serious. They did not make headlines for anything but winning cases. "I'll think about it."

He wouldn't, but he owed the lie to David. He glanced up again, and the jogger was getting closer. She was pretty, from this far out. Not the type he'd gotten used to in L.A. Thank god. This woman looked healthy. Nice breasts that not even her sports bra could force to be still. They moved in a way that let him know they weren't made of silicone. Her blond hair was up in a ponytail, leaving her face exposed. She wasn't all angles and planes. There was a softness to her even as she jogged along.

He heard the first rumble of thunder and saw her glance up at the sky.

"All right, then," David said with a long sigh. "I'll let you go, but seriously think about what I said. That chick Brie Westerhaven alone could bring in millions if she's anything like her dad. And I seem to remember there was a best friend. Some superskinny heiress."

"Yeah, I know who you're talking about," he replied. His ex-wife, Alicia, had been obsessed with *Kendalmire's Way*. It was a reality show about the über-rich and idiotic. One of the "stars" had been a woman named Taylor Winston. "She was the Billion-Dollar Baby."

When Taylor's parents' yacht had gone down in a storm on their way to Bermuda, there had been only one survivor—a baby found floating in a life vest. The newspapers had called it a miracle, and Taylor Winston had inherited a multibillion-dollar fortune before she'd turned two. Too bad she hadn't used it to get an education. He knew little about her and didn't want to know more.

The woman jogging by him was probably a local. She was too healthy to be a model. She was at least a whole size six, and in that world she would be plus-sized. Those breasts wouldn't fit in designer wear, and she was wearing a plain T-shirt, cutoff sweats, and old-school Ray-Bans. Her sneakers were nothing special. There was none of the blingy designer crap the wealthy and desperate-to-be-seen wore. And this was a quiet beach. No cameras or gawkers.

He nodded her way, giving her a friendly smile. He didn't recognize her, but then he'd been gone for nearly twenty years. Maybe he could visit some old acquaintances during this last two weeks.

Or maybe he should get his ass back to New York. "Are you sure you're all right with me taking this time?"

"Stop, Henry. Take it. This is the last time you'll get to be in that house, and you'll regret it if you don't pack it up yourself," David insisted.

And regret was one thing he didn't need more of. "Have I told you how much I appreciate you?"

The old Henry had appreciated nothing. The new Henry wasn't going to make the same mistake.

"Never. But you could let me win the next time we play golf," David suggested.

"That will be the day." He hung up, feeling a bit better.

And then even better, because the blonde smiled back at him and he was damn near knocked over by those sweet dimples. She was soft and sexy and . . .

Clumsy. She hit something in the sand and went flying.

He let the phone drop and got off the steps, racing toward her. He'd saved many a woman from tripping in five-inch heels on the streets of Manhattan, but this was his first sneaker rescue. She was facedown in the sand when he got to her. It was shitty and super-male of him, but he couldn't help but notice that she filled out those sweats. Her backside was gorgeous and curvy.

She didn't move.

"Are you all right?"

"It depends. Is this a weird anxiety dream?" She stayed down, her face inches from the sand. "Because then I'm sure I'll be okay. I'm nervous about starting grad school in a couple of weeks, and you could be a stand-in for all those professors at Duke who are going to be grading my work soon. So if you'll turn into a walrus and start singing, my work will be better."

Oh, he liked a quirky girl. It was absolutely where drunk-ass, too-rich-for-his-own-good Henry split from the Henry he'd been when he'd lived here. The blond hair and curves were nice, but the weird sense of humor was what really did it for him. "And if I'm nothing more than a guy sitting on his back porch?"

"Then I'm planning on lying here until you go away, and then I'll slink off and never come back again."

He didn't want her to slink away. She might be the most interesting thing that had happened to him in a long time. What would it be like to sit with a normal woman for a few hours? A grad student. Didn't get more normal than that. "There is a third option."

"I'm listening." She turned her head slightly, and he could see her lips starting to curl up.

He knelt down. "You could let me help you up and take a look at your ankle."

"Are you a doctor?"

"Lawyer."

She groaned and let her head sink back to the sand. "Nope. I'm staying here. Can't deal with lawyers. This is my home now."

"Well, your home is going to get awfully wet in a few hours when high tide comes in. How about I promise not to throw any legal crap your way and you let me ice that ankle before it swells, and then you can decide if you want to become a mermaid." He didn't usually bring random women inside his childhood home. Hell, he hadn't brought them back even when he'd lived here.

But he wanted to talk to her. She was intriguing. Even more now that he realized she was a weirdo.

She glanced up at him and frowned. "Sure you're not a ridiculously hot figment of my imagination?"

That was another plus. She had terrible taste in men and likely no idea who the hell he was. "One hundred percent real." He could guess at what made her skittish. "And you should know that I found your swan dive charming and attractive. Now let me get you inside. It's going to rain soon."

She groaned. "Yep, that's what my nana said. She won't let me live it down if I come home looking like a drowned rat. Is it all right if I ride it out?"

"Anything for a fellow townie."

She pushed up and winced as she got to one knee.

He held out a hand and helped her up. "I'm Henry Garrison, by the way."

She smiled, and those ridiculously adorable and yet sexy-as-hell dimples showed up. "Winnie Hughes. But please call me Win. Not that the nickname is applicable today. It's nice to meet you. Actually, the ankle's not too bad. It's mostly my pride and the fact that if I don't get in before it starts raining, people are probably going to see way more of me than they want to. I was so sure it wouldn't rain that I picked a thin white T-shirt. That's what I get for rebelling against authority."

He felt the first drop of rain hit his head and managed not to keep her outside longer. He wasn't going to be some leering stranger. After all, he wasn't that far out from his divorce. It had only been six months since he'd signed on the dotted line, and he wasn't about to be the idiot who threw himself back into the ocean after nearly drowning.

She was a townie, and he was going to miss the hell out of this place, so he would play nice.

Also, for the first time in hours, he wasn't thinking about a drink. "Come on. Let's get inside."

The sky chose that moment to open up and bring down a deluge. Win squealed in a wholly feminine way and ran for the porch. Henry followed her, thankful because he knew he was going to make it one more day.

That was all he could ask for at this point.

⁓

Taylor Winston-Hughes took the tea from her gentleman savior. Outside, the rain beat against the roof of his small house. Her clothes were in his dryer, and she wore a way-too-big-for-her Harvard T-shirt and pajama bottoms she'd had to tie around her body. Her hair was in a towel, and she was absolutely certain she looked ridiculous.

Naturally, she looked like a crazy person and he was a gorgeous god of a man.

"Thanks." She looked up at him, hoping she wasn't drooling. He was an actual man and not a boy in designer clothes. She would bet he didn't spend all day checking his Twitter or starting flame wars with other celebs. "So you live here? I haven't seen you around."

She'd been on the island for six months. Six months since she'd gotten back from Sweden. Six months since she'd hugged her counselor and walked back out into the world. Would Helena be proud of her that she hadn't even hesitated to ask for sugar for her tea? Real sugar. And she was going to eat one of those cookies he'd put out, because they looked really good and her life was going to be about joy now, not fitting into some tiny piece of fabric and having the world celebrate her for not eating.

"I used to," he admitted, holding out the plate. He smiled at her. "Don't get excited. I didn't make them. Actually, that's something to be excited about, because I'm a terrible cook. I got them from the bakery in town."

"Christina's." She knew the place well. She took one of the snickerdoodles. "I love that place. She makes the best madeleines."

He put the plate down and sat across from her. "When I was a kid, the place was run by her mom, the original Christina. Though she answers to the name, the woman who runs it now is actually named Dawn. I went to high school with her. Never thought she'd come home to run the bakery. I believe she left the island the day after we graduated with dreams of becoming the next great country singer."

Win shuddered slightly at the thought. She knew too many desperate artists. Her house was full of them right now. It was why she'd gone for that jog despite the weather. If she'd had to listen to one more complaint from Brie's overly injected mouth, she would have screamed. "Yeah, I think that sounds horrible."

Henry shrugged. "I suppose when you're young it all seems like a good idea."

"Somehow, I don't see you dreaming of fronting a band." There was something serious about the man, even when he was smiling. "When I was a kid I wanted to be a zookeeper. Then I got a real whiff of what it smelled like and I shifted my dreams."

He laughed, a deep, rich sound. "I can see where that was a wise move. My grandfather was a fishing boat captain."

She fought back another shiver. Though she couldn't remember the accident that had taken her parents' lives, it was embedded deep in her subconscious. She could get on a boat, but it bothered her. The storm bothered her, too, which proved how far she'd come. Now she found dealing with Brie and Hoover and Kipton was far worse than a potential storm. "I'm not big on boats."

"But you live on an island."

She did now. She could tell him about the Manhattan penthouse or the pied-à-terre she kept in Paris. She could mention the manor house outside London or the mansions in Bedford, Malibu, and Palm Beach, but she kind of liked being a townie. "Let's say I'm working on getting over all my hang-ups. So you grew up here?"

She didn't want to talk about herself. She'd spent way too much time doing that. If she could spend a day as Win Hughes, she would count it as a victory. She was trying her hardest to leave Taylor Winston-Hughes as far behind as possible.

"I did. This house has been in my family for a couple of generations. The Garrisons have lived on Chappaquiddick since long before it became associated with the Kennedys."

Her eyes went wide. "I left the main island? Wow. I got on to one of the trails and started following it. I wasn't thinking."

He had to laugh. "Haven't been here long, have you?"

"My nana moved here ten years ago." Right after Win had left for college. Right before she'd fallen in with the ridiculous crowd and wrecked her life. Mary Hannigan had been her nanny all Win's life, and when Win had moved, she'd decided to take over running the house on Martha's Vineyard. She'd wanted a quieter life, but Win suspected she'd mostly wanted to be rid of Win's uncle.

After the last year, Win had wanted nothing more than to find home again, and for her, it wasn't a place. Home was a person, a person she shared not a drop of blood with. "I kind of screwed up my life, and now I'm living with her until I start grad school. Typical millennial, you know. Almost thirty and still searching."

"Well, I'm moving toward forty and I still don't have it figured out. I think it's a human thing." He sat back. "I miss my grandfather. You're lucky to still have family. I'm afraid I am the last of my line."

She gave him a short smile. She was fairly certain it didn't reach her eyes. "My family is very small and not warm. My parents died when I was young, and I've been raised by my uncle ever since. Not that he had much to do with me. He was busy running the business my dad left behind. It's been me and Nana for as long as I can remember."

It wasn't like she was going to see Mr. Gorgeous again. She was leaving for North Carolina in a couple of weeks, and according to him, he was selling this place. There wasn't any real reason for her to explain the complexities of her life to a stranger. Actually, he might be a nice diversion before she threw herself into her studies.

She needed a diversion. Brie constantly trying to get her back on the show was proving to be stressful.

It was obvious to her this man had no idea who she was, and she liked it that way. Especially since she knew exactly who he was. Henry Garrison, former Manhattan attorney turned Alicia Kingman's latest victim. She'd heard he'd gone into rehab after leaving L.A., and she believed it. He looked good and seemed calm and centered.

He was exactly the kind of man she could spend some time with. But once they were both back in New York, their paths wouldn't cross, since she was staying completely out of social circles as much as possible from now on. There would be her charity work, but since they'd never bumped into each other before, she had no reason to think they would again.

The house rattled with the next clap of thunder.

"You all right?" Henry asked.

"I don't like storms much either." She'd almost gotten caught in this one. This part of the island wasn't filled with houses and shops. It was stark and beautiful and isolated. It was why she spent so much time here, though she was usually on the Edgartown side of the beach. She glanced at the window. Lightning blanketed the sky.

"It's okay." His voice was deep and rich. "It's hurricane glass, and this isn't a hurricane. It's a nasty storm, and from what I read on the weather site when I went to make the tea, it's going to last a couple of hours. We should talk about what that might mean."

It would be dark by the time she could start back. "I can call a cab. Well, maybe."

"I'll drive you back. I have a Jeep up here, but there might not be a road left," he said. "The beach often floods. In fact, if you'd been here a couple of years ago, you wouldn't have been able to get lost like you did. Norton Point Beach went underwater for eight years. It could do the same tonight, though it shouldn't last quite that long."

Oh god. She was stuck. "Is there a motel?"

"Not close, and again, I wouldn't drive around as long as the storm is going. My nearest neighbor is about a mile to the east. I could try to get you there if you're worried I'm a serial killer who waits for his victims to fall while jogging by."

When put like that, it didn't seem at all likely. Also, she was fairly certain he meant her no harm. She had some friends who knew Alicia, and they had nothing but good things to say about her fourth victim . . . husband. Alicia Kingman was a tornado who swept up men and tended to drop them again in a place that had been devastated. She kind of understood that. "If you don't mind, could I stay for a while?"

"I would not mind the company at all," he said, his voice warm. "I'll be honest. I've been lonely for the last couple of days. Going through all my grandparents' things has made me melancholy, and I forgot how isolated it is out here."

He was packing up his childhood and looking forward to an uncertain future. Yes, she definitely understood that. How long had it been since she'd been around a real man? One who cared about something beyond his Instagram followers and how his hair looked? There had been a guy in Sweden, but she'd had to focus on herself and getting healthy.

It would be nice to spend an evening with a man she could talk to. "Thank you. I'll call home and let them know I'm safe. Do you have a landline? My cell isn't getting service."

"Of course." He stood up. "It's in the den on the desk. I'm going to head into the kitchen and pray I can heat something up for dinner."

"I'm pretty handy in the kitchen. I'll be right there. I can pay for my room and board with my culinary skills." She'd grown up in Nana Mary's kitchen, helping her make meals and learning how to bake.

She'd relearned how to eat, and oddly, it all seemed new again. New palate. New girl.

New woman. She wasn't going back to being a girl again.

"I'll see what we have." He grimaced. "Besides frozen dinners for one. We might be choosing between frozen mac and cheese and Salisbury steaks. You might prefer the storm."

Oh, she knew that wasn't true. "I promise. I can come up with something good."

He pushed open the door that led to the kitchen. "I'll hold you to that."

The door swung shut. Damn, that man was fine. He was roughly six-two, with ridiculously dark hair and blue eyes. Had he been wearing glasses she would have called him Clark Kent. He did have a jaw of steel. Something about a cut jawline did it for her. Broad shoulders and a fit body rounded out his status as a complete hottie.

She was never going to call him a hottie, but he was.

She picked up the phone and dialed the number to the landline at Hughes House. She'd been forced to memorize it as a child. Nana Mary hadn't wanted her out playing without a way to contact her, but she'd also wanted her to have some freedom during those summer months.

"Winnie?"

Only her castmates from the old show called her Taylor. She was Win to her real friends. She'd been Win to Brie for years before that stupid show. The fact that her childhood friend now exclusively called her Taylor said a lot about where they were. "Hey, Nana."

She couldn't bring herself to call the woman Mary.

A long sigh came over the line. "Thank god. I was worried. You've been gone so long." Her accent was strong, proving how emotional she was. "I was about to force those lazy boys of yours to get off the sofa and go and look for you."

Hoover and Kip? She would bet they'd spent the afternoon playing video games and taking selfies. "Please don't. They rarely drive themselves and won't have any idea how to handle a car in this weather. They would kill someone. I'm fine. I'm at a friend's house, and I might stay here if the weather doesn't break."

"A friend?" There was no small amount of suspicion in her voice, but Win couldn't blame her. After all, she hadn't been smart in choosing friends before. "I didn't realize you still had friends on the island."

She had a couple of acquaintances, but any real friends she'd made during those childhood summers had left the island long ago and were out in the world making lives for themselves. "All right. He's a new friend. I met him recently, but he did save me from becoming a land mermaid. He's got a place on Chappaquiddick. I must have wandered over here."

"The closest house to those trails is the Garrison place." Mary was quiet for a moment. "Are they renting it out, or is the son there? I know the grandfather passed a few years back, but the son was a nice boy. You were a bit too young to remember him, but he was extremely polite."

It was funny that was what she remembered, since it wasn't his reputation now. However, Win knew sometimes reputations weren't earned. "Yes, his name is Henry and he assures me he's not a serial killer."

"Did he say that? Because that's what I would say if I was a serial killer."

"It was a joke. He's nice, and he offered me the phone so I could tell you where I am. Hardly the actions of a man about to murder me." She had to smile because at least someone gave a damn. "I'll call you in the morning, and I'm sorry I left you with guests. I promise I'll get rid of them as soon as possible. Once they figure out I'm not coming back on the show, they'll move on and find someone else."

There would be a line waiting to take her place.

"Don't worry about it, love. But Brianna is here and she's insisting on speaking to you," Nana said, her voice going professional. There was barely a hint of her Polish accent now. "And your uncle is here. He managed to fly in before the storm hit and he's staying for a few days. He wants you to sign some paperwork for the foundation."

"All right. I need to talk to him about the fund-raiser, too. The good news is, I've got everything ready and the invitations went out months ago. I need to wrangle a nice check out of him and then the pocketbooks should open up." Her uncle wasn't a cold man. He simply wasn't great father material. He'd done right by her in a way though. He'd given her Mary and ensured that Mary had everything she needed to be a mother. He'd allowed Mary to make all the decisions, and he'd shown up from time to time and sent lavish gifts for her birthday. She certainly didn't hate her uncle. They'd managed to get closer since she'd grown up. He simply hadn't known what to do with a child, which was odd since he'd had one of his own. Not that he'd spent time with his son either. "I'm going to talk to him about taking over the foundation. I want to be more than a figurehead. I can do more than plan a fund-raiser."

"Once you have your master's degree, he won't be able to argue with you," Mary said. "And he'll have to deal with you once you turn thirty. You'll be his boss then. He won't be able to treat you like a child."

She didn't like to think about it, but it was true. She would come into her inheritance when she got married or turned thirty. The marriage thing hadn't happened, but the birthday was inevitable. She'd been assured nothing had to change, except she would sign more paperwork. "Don't even tease him about that. I have no idea what I would do if Uncle Bellamy didn't take care of the business. I want to concentrate on the foundation, not on making cash. Tell him I'll be there as soon as I can, and maybe don't mention I'm at a strange man's place."

While he wasn't the most involved of guardians, he could be a bit on the protective side. The last thing she needed was her uncle calling down a bunch of PIs on Henry Garrison. He'd had enough scrutiny for a lifetime.

"I'll be silent as the grave, love. Here she is."

"Jesus, Tay, where are you? How could you leave me stuck here? This place is supposed to be all luxurious and shit, but it's superdull. I can see an ocean back in L.A." Brie's voice was like nails on a chalkboard after the soothing ease of Henry's.

"Then you should go back to L.A. I'm stuck on Chappaquiddick, and I won't be back until the morning," she explained. "Don't even try to go out in this. No clubbing tonight. They won't be open in this storm."

"What the hell am I supposed to do, then?"

Win looked over the bookshelves in front of her. They were built-in and ran the length of one wall. There were some pictures, but the shelves were mostly used as they had been intended. The owner of this home loved books. She ran her fingers over the spines. *The Complete Works of Herman Melville. Mutiny on the Bounty. In the Heart of the Sea.* There was definitely a theme going. But there was also a shelf of legal-looking books, and she found another with Jane Austen and Charles Dickens.

"Read a book," she said to Brie.

Laughter came over the line. "That's funny. I guess I'll give myself a facial or something and post it online. And you know I'm not leaving. I'm going to help you with the fund-raiser, and we have to meet with Sully next week."

Win knelt down, looking at the bottom shelf, where the paperbacks were. Oh, those told a tale. There were a bunch of split-spined Stephen King books down there, along with novelized adaptations of big Hollywood sci-fi films. Michael Moorcock and a Dan Simmons. And a thick stack of comic books. Nerd. He'd been a nerd.

Somehow that made him even hotter.

Was she actually thinking about seducing the Monster of Manhattan?

Could she? He'd been a gentleman up to this point, but he'd also definitely been flirting with her.

"I'm going to be happy to see Sully, but I'm not coming back to the show. He doesn't want me back." Sullivan Roarke was the producer of *Kendalmire's Way*. He was a genuinely lovely man. He was the one who'd been kind enough to fire her. He'd also sent her to Sweden, and every week that she was in the clinic a lovely new bouquet of flowers had been delivered with a note wishing her well.

Getting fired was the best thing that had ever happened to her. She would love to see Sully, but she would never work with him again.

"You're wrong. He knows how important you are and what your story line would mean to the series."

"Story line?" It always made her a little nauseous to think about the fact that her life was some kind of story line to entertain people.

There was a pause that let Win know Brie was still capable of some form of subtlety. "Win, you went through something rough."

She'd gone through anorexia. "I'm good now. Hell, some people would even say I'm moving toward heifer status."

The bitchy mean girls would definitely say it. If she put herself back on the Internet, the trolls would have a field day with her. She wasn't afraid of them anymore, but she also no longer needed their approval.

"Don't say that about yourself," Brie said, her voice more emotional than Win could ever remember.

It was good to know that under all that Hollywood chic, Brie still cared. "I wasn't saying it about myself, but other people will. Going through what I went through is precisely why I can't go back to that world, Brie. The first thing the producers will say is that I would look better on camera if I lost a few pounds. Nothing serious.

No more than five pounds at most. A single dress size. And they'll be right. I did look better on camera."

"You're beautiful now, Win."

Tears pierced her eyes. "That's the first time you've called me that in years."

"Because I don't want to screw up in public. Look, I'll back off for now, but you could show young girls that they don't have to be a size zero. I know I'm a freaking caricature of myself now. I do get that, but I remember who I am underneath it all, and if you come back, I will defend you. I love you, Win. I don't say it often enough, but I admire you. I wish I could be more like you."

"You are the toughest chick I know, Brie Westerhaven," Win said with a smile. "You don't need to be anyone but your own fabulous self."

Brie chuckled over the line. "Yeah, well, we tabloid babies have to stick together. You safe where you are? Because I can come get you."

"I'm good. A white knight saved me from the storm. I'm going to sleep on his couch." She found a bunch of old board games.

"On his couch? Is he hot?"

"Yes, he is, but he's also not the type who parties it up. I think I really will be on the couch tonight."

"*Every* man is the type to save a pretty girl and have her pay him back with her sweet, sweet body." Brie was right back to her usual role—dirty sprite. "I like this, Win. Handsome man saves innocent woman and requests her body as payment."

"I'm hanging up now." She wasn't going there. "Good night."

She hung up the phone and pulled out a battered edition of Clue. She remembered that game well.

There was the sound of pans clanging and a low growl of masculine frustration.

She needed to fix that if she was going to have any chance of not sleeping alone. Perhaps if she fed the beast, he would be in a more affectionate mood.

Or she could accept that she was going to pass a pleasant but passionless evening with a nice man. She shoved the Clue box back and pulled out Monopoly. Not as much fun, but given what was happening in her life, it was the safer bet.

She carried it with her as she made her way into the kitchen.

After all, she didn't need to play a murder game. Not after Stockholm.

She glanced outside, at the lightning flaring along the sky.

At least for tonight, she seemed to be safe.

TWO

Henry stared out at the storm and wondered if he was a complete idiot. It raged outside, off and on all evening. There had been an hour right around midnight when he'd thought he might be able to get her home.

Such a coward.

She'd saved him from a boring microwave dinner by putting together a nice stew from a bunch of stuff she'd found in the cupboard and freezer, and then from boredom by playing a rather ruthless game of Monopoly. The lights had gone out sometime around eight, but his grandparents had kept the place stocked with candles and flashlights. He'd sat with her for hours, listening to the storm and the sound of her voice.

He'd been tempted to try for her house when the storm had quieted, but the sky had opened up again and the lights that flickered briefly had turned back off. He'd given in to the inevitable.

When the time had come to go to bed, he'd offered her the guest room, making sure the sheets were changed. Guest room? He supposed that was what it was now, but for years it had been his.

He'd finally managed to get a girl into his room, and here he was watching the storm.

Damn but she was sweet. She'd talked about her plans for grad school over dinner. She wanted to work for a nonprofit. Wanted to "give back to the world." Naive idiot. And yet he'd sat there and listened to her without pointing out all the fallacies of her assumptions. It was odd for him. He tended to view normal conversation as an argument to win. *Oh, you think the sky is blue, buddy? Prove it, and while you're at it, why do you think you know enough to even comment on something as scientific as the upper atmosphere?* Yeah, he could be a dick.

But not with her. Something about the way she talked, the passion in her voice, made him wonder if he'd ever been that young and enthusiastic. He'd watched her as they'd played, utterly fascinated with the way her face lit up when she landed on a good space and how she frowned when she had to pay up. Her honey-blond hair was pulled up in a ponytail, accentuating the features of her face. The candlelight warmed her skin, but even without a drop of makeup she'd been the single prettiest woman he'd laid eyes on in years.

She was not for him. No way. No how. She was a twentysomething do-gooder grad student with obvious stars in her eyes. He had no doubt he could have kissed her and eased his way into bed with her. She'd even turned her lips up right before he'd stepped away, and there had been shy disappointment on her face as she'd closed the door between them.

He was too old for her. Way too old. Oh, the difference on paper might be less than a decade, but in experience he was ancient to her baby bird.

He'd liked how she looked wearing his T-shirt, enjoyed the fact that she'd been dependent on him for food and shelter and clothing. The possessive caveman in him had threatened to make an appearance, and wouldn't that have shocked her feminist sensibilities? He'd sat there and wanted to pull her into his lap, let his hands wander under the shirt, cupping those luscious breasts. He'd been able to see himself teasing his hands under the waist of the sweats that were far too big for her, easing down until he could find that warm, welcoming place at the apex of her thighs.

And then she'd say something about how she'd volunteered at a Swedish orphanage when she'd visited the country.

Winnie. Even her name was saccharine-sweet. She was not his type. His type was obviously crazed harpy actresses who ran through men like they did money. Or New York models who looked good in print and had nothing to say of any substance.

He did not need an innocent social-justice warrior who still thought the world could be saved.

So why was he brooding over her?

Because until that moment when she'd closed the door, he hadn't thought about drinking all night. He'd forgotten about the bottle he'd found and concentrated on her.

Now he was thinking about it again.

Being in this house made him realize how far he'd fallen. How much he'd aged since he'd run along the beach with his grandfather.

Had he really been the kid who'd sat at the kitchen bar, eagerly awaiting the moment his grandma would tell him the cookies were cool enough to eat?

He wasn't going to drink.

Maybe.

What would it truly hurt if he drank one more in honor of his grandfather? That Scotch had been one of his grandfather's only indulgences. When he thought about it, it would be rude to pour it out. And was he truly an addict? Or had it all been the scene he'd found himself in? He'd never had a problem before Alicia. It was all about her.

She was the reason he'd spent thirty days in a ridiculously expensive Palm Springs rehab center talking about feelings he didn't really have and doing yoga he didn't need to do.

How could he know unless he tried it again?

How was he supposed to socialize without alcohol? It was everywhere in the city. At every party and fund-raiser. Who trusted a lawyer who couldn't handle his liquor?

One drink. That was all. If he could take that one drink and put the rest away, he would know it was all bullshit.

Please don't stand up. Don't walk into that room and take that first drink. You know where it leads to.

He was pathetic. That whiny voice in his head would go away if he took the drink. He'd done his good deed for the night. He'd allowed the sweetest fish he'd caught in a long time to swim right back into the ocean. He hadn't dragged her to his depths and used her to forget everything he'd done and every crappy thing to come.

He deserved that drink.

Be a fucking man and call your sponsor. It's not even midnight in L.A. He'll be up.

But his cell wasn't working, and the landline had finally gone out, too.

The universe was pointing the way. All roads led back to that little bottle.

He didn't mean to stand up, but he did. He didn't mean to start down the hallway, but he found himself there. He wasn't going into his grandfather's study. No. So why was his hand on the door?

A massive crack of thunder made the walls shake, and he heard a terrified scream.

Win.

Without another thought, he turned and raced to the guest room door. Thankful to find it unlocked, he threw it open, ready to confront whoever had made her cry out the way she had. Adrenaline coursed through his body, heightening his senses.

She was alone. No one else was in the room, but the covers had come undone and she was thrashing on the bed, moaning and pleading with some unknown attacker. Her eyes were closed, but it was obvious she was caught in a nightmare.

Henry took a deep breath. "Winnie? Win? Wake up, sweetheart. You're having a bad dream."

She gasped as though trying to breathe. Her hands came up to her throat.

He knelt on the bed. "Win, it's time to wake up."

What the hell was she dreaming about? Her body was completely stiff, every muscle fighting like someone was holding her down.

"Please wake up." He wanted to reach out, but he wasn't sure what was happening. Wasn't it dangerous to wake someone in the middle of a dream? Or was that sleepwalking?

Her eyes flickered open, and she sat straight up in bed, still clearly in the grip of fear. A light sheen of sweat covered her forehead though it was perfectly cool in the house. She looked around as though desperate to figure out where she was.

"You're in a house on Chappaquiddick Island." He kept his distance despite the fact that he wanted to haul her into his arms and promise that whatever had happened to her wouldn't happen again. It was so fucking unlike him, but the instinct was right there. "You got caught in a storm. My name is Henry, and I'm not going to hurt you."

She was still for a moment, and then she took a deep breath and chuckled, a shaky sound. "I didn't lose my memory, Henry. Just my damn mind. Did I scream?"

"Louder than the thunder." He was the one taking a deep breath now.

Even in the low light, he could see the way she blushed. "I'm sorry. I did not mean to wake you up. I don't like storms. I had a bad incident on a boat in a storm once."

He didn't buy that. "It looked like you were trying to get someone off you."

She shivered lightly. "It was just a dream. I'm sorry I woke you up."

This was the moment when he should stand up and tell her it was all right and walk away. He would close the door and . . . go back to staring at the storm? Go back to the office and finish his slow descent?

"I wasn't sleeping," he admitted. He didn't want to leave her.

She moved closer, letting the sheet fall away. "Did I keep you awake?"

"Nope. My deep desire to drink my life away kept me awake. I'm six months sober, and when I was cleaning out the study earlier, I found a bottle of Scotch. It was why I was on the back porch when you came running up the beach. I was scared to be in the house with the Scotch. I forgot about it for a while, but after you went to bed, it was still here. I've spent the last couple of hours trying to decide if I was going to give in or not. I was just about to lose that fight when you screamed. Consider your nightmare to be my salvation for the night." He would be honest with her, let her know how shitty a choice he was—even for a night. She hadn't moved away from him, and the intimacy of being on a bed with her, the rest of the world held at bay by the storm, was getting to him. He needed her to make the decision to turn away this time because he wasn't sure he could do it again.

Honesty was the only thing that could keep him sober, and he wasn't being honest with himself before. Somehow, now that he was in a room with her, it was easier to be honest. She needed to know who she was dealing with—an alcoholic who had wrecked his life and was trying to put the pieces back together. Not a good bet if she was looking for something stable.

"I don't think you should do that," she said quietly. "I ate the cookie today. If I ate the cookie, I think you shouldn't have the drink."

She'd said it so seriously, he had to wonder. "What does that mean?"

"It means alcohol isn't the only thing a person can get addicted to." She turned her face to his, eyes somber in the low light. "Sometimes a person can get addicted to hurting herself. I know that sounds silly, but it *was* an addiction."

He softened, his focus shifting back to her. It was easy to forget that some scars ran deep, unseen beneath the smooth surface presented to society. Some scars were hidden behind sweet smiles and innocent eyes. "You hurt yourself?"

She sat back against the headboard. "In a way. I wouldn't eat. I got addicted to people telling me how pretty I was because I was thin. And even later, when they would tell me I looked horrible because I'd lost so much weight, I didn't believe them. I would say 'haters gonna hate.' I was in Sweden because they have an amazing program to deal with anorexia. They taught me how to eat again, how to properly see myself as a whole human being. But you know what we started with?"

"Talking." He knew exactly what she meant. He'd been through it. Maybe she wasn't as young as he'd thought. Maybe she needed more than a gentlemanly distance. "You have to make a connection with the people around you, or it won't ever work. You have to make real, honest connections."

"You can't be an island." Her hand reached out, sliding over his.

"I was dreaming about something that happened to me about six months ago. I was attacked, and a man nearly strangled me to death in an alley. Only the fact that a couple of kids came out of a night-club and were looking for a shortcut back to their car saved me. I can't stop thinking about it, and I don't know how I'm going to get through the night if you don't kiss me."

There was nothing he wanted more than to kiss her, to lay her out and make a fucking feast of her. But he needed to not be the shit he'd been in the past. He needed to think about someone other than himself. "Win, I don't know if that's a good idea."

She slipped off the bed and walked to the window. "Sorry. I didn't mean to push you. I'm good. It's not the first time I've had that particular dream. Won't be the last. Just a little PTSD. Damn, it's still coming down, isn't it?"

He'd stepped in it. This was the world now. Before he'd been sure of his place, sure he was the master of his universe. Now he fumbled on a daily basis. It had been easier to not give a shit. "Win, you don't know me."

"I said it was okay. I'm not normally this aggressive. You do not have to worry. I won't jump you or anything." There was a tremble to her voice that let him know she was getting emotional. "I think I'll go and make some tea, if that's all right with you. Do you want some tea?"

He needed to stop being so damn wishy-washy. "I want to talk to you."

"I might need a minute."

If he gave her a minute, they would be back to polite. She would pull out Connect 4, and he wouldn't find out if she could want him in an honest way. "Win, I'm an alcoholic. I'm divorced, and it wasn't some thoughtful conscious uncoupling. It was nasty and ugly. I'm a lawyer who doesn't give a shit if his clients are guilty or not as long as they have the money to pay me. I have gotten off people who probably went back out into the world to do terrible things, and I'll probably do it again because I believe in this system. It's imperfect, but it's better than anything else. And I'm too old for you."

She snorted, an oddly amusing sound. "I'm not some shrinking virgin. I'm twenty-nine, and I've been around the block a couple of times and with some men I wish I hadn't ever gotten into the car with. How old are you? Forty?"

He winced. "Thirty-seven."

Her lips curled up, and it was worth the blow to his ego. "Well, you don't look a day over forty, and that's a pretty nice age for a man. You think you don't deserve such a young, hot chick?"

Thank god she was teasing him again. He'd hated the way her shoulders had slumped when she'd thought he'd rejected her. But still, he had to be honest. If he was going to do this, she would get the new Henry. "I think I could hurt a woman like you if I'm not careful."

"Then be careful with me, Henry Garrison," she said, moving closer to him. "And I'm a big girl. I can make my own decisions and live with them. I would like to spend the night with you. It doesn't have to last beyond tomorrow. I'm not asking to be your girlfriend. I'm asking you to help me get through the night, to help me get that nightmare out of my head, so I can feel safe for the first time in months. It's been a long time since I felt safe."

That he could do. She moved in close, right between his legs, and he reached up and cupped her face, holding her still as he looked into her eyes. So much fucking innocence. He didn't care what she'd been through. She was way too young for him, but she'd said yes and he wasn't a saint. Not even close. "Be sure. I might want more than one night. I'm here for a few weeks. I could use this. I could use some time with you."

It wouldn't work long-term. When he finished up and got back to the city, he wouldn't have time to spend with her, and she deserved that. He would be knee-deep in the sewer again. It wasn't a place he would take her, but he could be what she needed here.

"I could use some time with you," she replied. "You're right about a few things. I haven't ever been around a man like you. The men I've been with have been boys who cared more about their images than they did about pleasing me. I think it might be different with you. I know you're trying to scare me off with all that 'I screwed up my life' stuff, but I get that. You can't make me run, or I would run away from myself. Tell me if you can make me forget about everything except what you're doing to my body because tonight that's all I want."

Oh, he could do that. He might not be able to feed her soul, but he could work her body all fucking night long. He could stroke her and make her scream out his name, and when she did, he would feel like himself again, like he was worthy.

His whole body started to warm, his brain softening. Yeah, this was exactly what he needed. This was one indulgence he wasn't going to feel guilty about because he'd given her every single way out and she hadn't taken it. She was here. She wanted him. He'd been honest and open, and she was offering herself up like some sugary-sweet treat he'd been dying to taste.

He was done waiting, done asking. He had all the permission he needed. She wanted a night where she thought about nothing but his tongue on her, his cock inside her? He could make that happen. He stood up, his body coming into contact with hers. Henry lowered his mouth down, brushing his lips over hers for the first time.

He actually thought the words. *For the first time.* What the hell was that? He let it go because he was incapable of thinking in the moment. He wanted to feel, too. It had been so long. So long since he'd allowed himself to sink into another human being this way. Since he'd forgotten anything existed but her silky-soft skin and the way she shivered in his arms.

God, he'd gotten married and divorced, but he hadn't had a true lover in years. He'd had a woman he slept with, but not one he let go with. Not one he was himself with.

He brushed his lips over hers again, not feeling the need to hurry at all. He didn't want to rush a second of this. They had all night. They had until the storm cleared, and that could take a while. Until then, he had nothing to do except bring her pleasure. He'd come from a long line of fishing boat captains, men who'd charted the ocean. He would make a map of her, learning her every plane and angle, every curve and line of her body.

He kissed her over and over again. He let his hands sink into her hair. So much hair now that it was freed from the utilitarian ponytail. Soft and yet thick and strong, her hair was like silk against his skin.

She sighed, and her body brushed against his. He could feel her breasts and the hard points of her nipples as they came into contact, nothing but the thinnest of T-shirts between them.

Lightning struck outside, but it almost seemed as though it had hit his body, giving him an energy he hadn't felt in forever. Electricity seemed to crackle between them, mimicking the storm outside. He deepened the kiss, running his tongue over her plump bottom lip. Her arms came up around his shoulders, and she let him in.

Something about the way she moved against him, trusting and eager, made the caveman come out again. A feeling of savage possession surged through him, and he dominated her mouth. He took over and let the kiss go from sweet to carnal in a heartbeat. His tongue found hers, rubbing and playing.

She gave as good as she got, not merely allowing him to overwhelm her but holding her own. Her arms tightened around him, and he could feel her nails grazing his skin as she ran her hands under his shirt and along his back.

He needed more. He wanted to feel her against him, nothing between them.

"How long has it been? I don't care about anything you've done before, but I want to know how slow or fast I can go this first time." He whispered the words against her lips before diving in again.

Those nails of hers dug in lightly, barely enough to make him shiver and tighten his hold on her hair.

"A while," she replied, utterly breathless. "A year or so, and like I said, it wasn't anything special. I had a boyfriend, but he wasn't interested in anything more than getting off. I thought that was normal. I've heard a rumor it's not."

Oh, she was right up his alley. Smart and sassy and unafraid to challenge him. He wasn't sure who she'd been before that she'd accepted scraps, but he was crazy about the woman she was now. He kissed his way along her jawline. "I don't intend to get you off, sweetheart. That's too juvenile a word for what I'm going to do to you."

He needed to slow down, but he wasn't about to explain. He wouldn't lose her to insecurity again. She needed to know exactly what she deserved from a lover.

"What's the right word?" Win asked, her body moving with his like they'd done this a thousand times before. A gentle tug on her hair, and she was offering him her neck.

He kissed his way up to her earlobe, whispering softly, "The word I want you to think about is 'fuck,' but I mean that in the best way, in the sweetest, most intimate terms. First I'm going to kiss every inch of this gorgeous body. I'm going to use my lips and tongue and, yes, I'll use my teeth to get you ready. When you spread your legs for me, I'll make a meal of you until you scream. I'll get my mouth on your pussy, and I won't leave until I've had my fill. I won't leave until you're wet and slick and you beg me to fuck you."

"Okay. Perfect. You should do that."

"Does that sound good to you?"

"Yep."

The fact that she seemed barely able to talk did something for him. Her body moved restlessly, her hands touching and cupping the muscles of his back and shoulders like she couldn't bring herself to stop. He licked along the shell of her ear, eliciting a shiver from her, and then he gently nipped her earlobe.

She gasped but didn't try to move away from him.

"Tell me what you're thinking about." He wanted to be damn sure she wasn't thinking about anything but him.

"I'm thinking about you doing that thing."

They had to work on her vocabulary. He turned her in his arms so her back was to his front and her delicious ass was pressed to just below his cock. He was already hard and ready, but there was no way he was letting his cock take control of this. He wasn't giving in until he'd done everything he'd promised her. "Which thing is that, sweetheart?"

She leaned back into him. "All the things."

He eased his hands under the Harvard T she was wearing as a nightshirt. Her clothes had dried earlier, and it seemed she'd found her undies again. He skimmed over them—enough time for that later—and brushed over her belly, moving toward her breasts. "I'm going to need you to be more specific, Win. What do you want me to do to you? Tell me. Say dirty words with that sweet mouth of yours."

Her head fell back against his shoulder, making her breasts swell in his hands. They fit perfectly. Not too big. Not too small. Just right. He could cup them and make sure every part was cuddled by his hands. "This is nice. Touching my breasts feels good."

He would have to make himself plain. He rolled her nipples between his thumbs and forefingers, easy at first. "Your breasts are beautiful, and they feel like heaven in my hands. I can't wait to see them, but you didn't say anything dirty. Does my dirty talk bother you?"

"No. No. I like it," she admitted. "I think it's sexy. I wouldn't have said that before, but coming from you it's sexy."

"Because you know I can back it up and I'm not spouting random filth. I'm going to use my dirty mouth to get you hot and make you forget. It should tell you how much I want you. I've been polite so far. I've been a gentleman, but that's done, and now you get the bad boy."

She shook her head. "Man. You're a man, Henry. I should know. I've been around far too many boys. You want dirty talk? I'm not good at it, but I can tell you what's going through my head. I can tell you why I fell this afternoon. I tripped because I was far too busy looking at you to maintain any kind of balance. I took one look at you sitting on that porch, and I wondered if you would take your shirt off and go for a swim. I wanted to see you. I thought maybe if I hid, you would dump the shorts, too, and swim in the nude like the gorgeous sea god you are. That's what I was thinking."

"Sea god?" It was funny, but once he'd known these waters better than anyone. He'd had a skiff he'd learned to sail on, and when he'd been old enough, he would take it around and pretend to be a pirate. "I don't know about that, but you would have made a good mermaid. I think you should let me take this off you."

She went still, and for a moment he was afraid he'd lost her, but finally she let her arms drift up. Henry pulled the shirt over her head, unveiling gorgeous skin. He could see her in the mirror of the dresser. The room was dark, though lightning illuminated it every few moments. He stepped back and lit a candle, wanting to see her better. The candlelight played over her skin.

How could she ever have thought she was less than perfect? He stared at her for a moment, taking in the graceful lines of her body. "You're beautiful. Don't let anyone tell you different. You're gorgeous, and I'm lucky you said yes to me tonight."

Her eyes caught his in the mirror. "It can be hard to feel that way. I hope you're real, Garrison, and that you don't turn into something else in the morning."

Because she'd likely met a lot of men who did. Hell, he might have been that ass in the past. He moved in behind her, letting his hands find her arms to run up to her shoulders. He eased her long hair to one side, giving himself access to her neck. She smelled like the soap from her shower. It was his soap, but something about it on her skin made it seem feminine to him. "I'm too tired to change on you. The problem you're going to have in the morning is I might want more."

He was already thinking about it.

She leaned back, bringing their bodies together like neatly fitting pieces of a puzzle he hadn't thought to solve. "You would change your mind if you understood what my life is like. It's complicated."

Her life was difficult? Somehow he thought he could handle it. "We're not thinking about that tonight. Stay with me. Be with me."

He cupped her breasts again and was satisfied when she said yes.

～

Win couldn't breathe, but it was a good thing. She didn't need to breathe. All that mattered was the feel of Henry's hands on her body.

What the hell was happening to her? It wasn't like she was a virgin. She'd had plenty of sex, some of it meaningful, most of it futile. She'd gone to bed with men for the wrong reasons. She'd looked for love and affection when she should have understood she would get neither if there wasn't a deep connection.

Of course, she hadn't understood how connected she could feel to a person until Henry Garrison had wrapped his arms around her and held her close, whispering truly filthy, beautiful words in her ear.

Henry kissed the nape of her neck, sending a delicious shiver down her spine.

Stay with me. Be with me.

The words he'd said warmed her. She wanted nothing more than to hide away, to be the girl on the beach he'd helped out. As he began a slow worship of her body, she wished the storm would keep up for days.

Arousal flooded her system as he cupped her breasts again. She wasn't sure how he managed it, but somehow Henry's hands on her breasts were more erotic than all the sex she'd had before.

Because he needed her for something more than an orgasm. Because he was a man and not some lonely boy.

Because he'd been brutally honest about where he was in life and what he needed. A distraction. Some women might protest, but Win needed one, too. A distraction and some kindness.

Not honesty. Not from her. He had no idea who she was because he wasn't the kind of man to watch superficial reality junk TV.

She shoved the guilt away. There wasn't a place for it anymore. She wasn't that girl, and it didn't matter that her one-night lover didn't know her every secret. All that mattered was getting through the night, getting the image of that masked face out of her head, the feel of those hands around her throat . . .

"Stop it," he said, his voice harsh in her ear. "I don't know what's going through your head, but I don't think I would like it. I can see I'm going to have to try harder."

He turned her, and his mouth was on hers again. That was what she needed. She couldn't think when he was kissing her.

Her breasts brushed against his chest, the soft cotton of his T-shirt rasping her nipples. Her whole body felt alive as his hands slid down her back and cupped the globes of her ass. He hauled her close, rubbing against her.

"Tell me you want this," he demanded before running his tongue over her bottom lip.

That was an easy command to follow. She wanted this more than she'd wanted anything in a long time. "I want this."

But he needed something, too. Something she hadn't given him. It was weird to talk during sex, but maybe that had been her problem before. Sex had been furtive and silent, something to get through so she would have the solace of another body in bed with her. Henry wanted to connect. One of the ways he was trying was with words.

He wanted dirty words to get him hot, to ensure they were on the same page.

"I want your mouth on me." It wasn't hard when she stopped thinking about it. What did she honestly want? Past all the niceties. Past what was polite and correct. What did she want right this second? Shouldn't she be woman enough to ask for it? All her life she'd been taught to be polite and thoughtful and never to ask for anything because she'd been blessed with the material possessions of the world. Damn it. She needed more, and she was done pretending. "I want you to suck on my nipples, Henry. I want you to lick them and play with them."

A savage, sexy grin lit his face, and he dropped to his knees in front of her. "That I can do."

He leaned forward, and her vision went hazy as he sucked a nipple into the warmth of his mouth. She let her hands sink into his hair. It was a tiny bit on the long side and she loved the way she could tangle her fingers in it, holding him where she needed him to be. While he lavished affection on one nipple with his mouth, he rolled the other, tweaking her slightly. It sent a shiver through her, that bite of pain rushing to her pussy.

She'd never been so ready in her life. "Henry, let's go to bed."

"When I'm done." He switched to her other breast, licking and lavishing pleasure on her.

Her body wound tight. "Can't you be done now?"

She'd never begged for a cock before, but then she'd never felt need like she did now.

He bit her, a gentle but firm lesson. "I'll be done when I'm ready and not a second more. You said you've gone to bed with boys before. Well, I believe it." One hand trailed down and skimmed over her underwear. "I'm not taking you until you're ready, and while this might be nice and slick, it's still not ready for me. Not until you're soaking wet and can't take a second more will I take you. I'm going to make this last all night long. Do I make myself clear?"

Her nipple throbbed with a pleasant ache that made her whimper. He was in charge. She could handle that. The truth was, she didn't know what she wanted besides pleasure, and he seemed perfectly capable of giving that to her. "Yes, Henry."

"Excellent. Keep saying that. 'Yes, Henry.'" He licked her aching nipple, a slow drag of his tongue as his eyes remained fastened on hers. "Those words will get you far."

"Yes, Henry." She liked saying them. Oh, she wouldn't let him take the lead in everything, but he was the expert here.

The idea of spending weeks in his bed caught in her brain. She had years of work ahead of her. A few weeks of sex might be what she needed before she gave herself over to finally learning how to run the foundation her parents had left her.

And maybe the business, someday.

His fingers found the hem of her undies and started to drag them down. She was going to be completely naked in front of him. God, she hadn't been naked in front of anyone since she'd been in treatment. She knew she wasn't as thin as she'd been, but there was something about the way he was eating her up with his eyes that made it impossible to find the will to be self-conscious. He didn't have a problem with her body. He liked it. He thought she was sexy.

She was healthy, and that was what was important. She was alive. She was alive and with him and in the moment, and that was all she needed for now.

When he pulled her undies down to the ground, she stepped out of them without hesitation. It didn't matter that she was naked and he was clothed. There was something sexy about it. He hadn't been able to wait. He wasn't attempting to show off his body so she could tell him how hot he was. He was interested in seeing her, touching her, tasting her.

She nearly screamed when he dropped his head lower and put his mouth on her pussy.

His hands held her hips. "Hold still."

How was she supposed to hold still? She gritted her teeth against the wave of pure sensation that washed over her as he kissed her mound and then ran the tip of his tongue over her clitoris.

Her body threatened to go off then and there, but she held out. She needed more. He'd been right to hold out. Every slow lick of his tongue brought her closer and closer to the edge of a precipice she'd only thought she understood. This was higher than she'd ever been before, and the fall was going to be all the sweeter for it.

"Get on the bed. I want you on the edge, feet up and knees wide." He got to his feet, tugging the shirt he was wearing over his head and tossing it away.

Oh, her lawyer liked to work out. Damn, that was one perfectly sculpted chest. With lightning flashing behind him and thunder cracking through the room, it wasn't hard to see him as a fallen angel. He merely lacked the dark wings that would spread out from his shoulders and enfold her.

She couldn't help but place a hand on his chest, running it down to his defined abs. "You're beautiful, too, Henry."

He reached for her hand before it could move lower. He gripped it and brought it to his lips with a shake of his head. "Not yet. I have to take care of you first. It's been a while for me, too. I don't want this to end too soon. And I need you to wait for a minute. I have to get something."

She grinned. "No condoms stashed away in here?"

A grimace furrowed his brow. "There might be one or two, but they're remnants of my optimistic youth. Lie down like I told you, or when I get back, I'll tie you up so I can make sure you stay where I put you."

He strode out of the room. *Tie her up?* The thought didn't scare her the way it should have. Still, she might not be ready for all of Henry's kinkiness. Not yet. She climbed on the bed and caught a glimpse of herself in the mirror.

She looked . . . good. Her hair was messed-up, her body flushed with arousal. She wasn't a size double zero anymore, but her breasts looked round and pretty.

They'd taught her more than how to eat again. They'd taught her to look at herself in a different way, to value herself.

She wasn't that girl who had gone on TV trying to find a place for herself. She was the girl who made a place for herself through hard work and self-acceptance. She was the woman who could take on a challenge and care about herself even if she failed.

"Yes, you're awfully lovely."

When she looked up, Henry was standing in the doorway, leaning one broad shoulder against it.

"I don't look at myself a lot these days," she admitted. "I'm trying to value myself for something more than my looks. I'm trying to value myself at all."

"And I need to value someone else," he admitted. "We're quite the pair. Lie back. Let me take care of you."

He stood at the end of the bed, looming over her like a decadent dream. She lay back, willing to let him take control again. It was good now. This wasn't a choice she'd been backed into because she couldn't handle it herself. She was stronger now, and giving over to Henry was about pleasure.

She could use a little more of that in her life.

Her eyes nearly rolled to the back of her head as he settled in and she felt the long lick of his talented tongue.

Win gripped the sheets of the bed, holding on for dear life as he took her higher and higher. He didn't hold back. He did exactly what he'd said he would. He made a meal of her, and it was clear that Henry had been starving for a long time. Win wasn't sure how long she lasted, lying there and letting the waves crash over her, but before she knew it, she was going over the edge in a way she never had. Her body seized, holding for a single second before releasing. She shook in the wake, and then Henry was moving over her.

Even as she came down from the orgasm, she watched him shove his sweats off his hips and reach for the condom with trembling hands. He managed to roll it over his cock, and then he was shifting, moving himself between her legs.

"Tell me it's okay." The words sounded tortured coming from his mouth.

How could he think she would turn him away? Likely because it had happened. Likely because his marriage had screwed him over in so many ways. "Please, Henry. Please, I need you. I need more."

She expected the arrogant smirk to hit his face again, but there was nothing there but his own honest need.

"I need more, too. Take me." He pressed against her.

Win wrapped her legs around his lean waist as he filled her inch by inch. She loved the way he stretched her, the connection she could feel. Win watched him as he worked his way in. That magnificent jawline of his was tight, and his hands gripped her hips, holding her down.

She tilted her pelvis up, and he groaned as she took him. All the way.

"I'm not going to last." The low growl of his voice cut through the thunder.

"You don't have to." She was perfectly satisfied. Her body still hummed with the orgasm he'd given her before. She reached up, putting her hands on his arms, completing the circle their bodies formed. Dirty words. He liked dirty words. Somehow he made them not so dirty at all. "Fuck me, Henry. You promised to fuck me hard, and I'm going to hold you to it."

"I knew you would be trouble the minute I saw you," he said with a chuckle. "Well, I wouldn't want to let a lady down."

He pulled back and slammed in. He held her close, finding a rhythm she caught in an instant.

He fucked her over and over. This was what he'd meant. There was no other word for it, but it wasn't nasty. It was connection. It was primal and pure.

She gave up all thought and let instinct take over. She found herself rising again, her body ready and primed for another fall.

Win didn't want it to end, but before long she felt the pressure build to a crescendo and she called out his name. Henry's head fell forward, and he lost that perfect rhythm, fucking her until he held himself tight against her, pumping out the last of his orgasm.

He fell forward, kissing her neck as he gave her his weight.

They were quiet for a moment, the rain hitting the roof. Her blood pounded in time, a leisurely languor.

"Sleep with me." The words were whispered against her neck, his arms around her.

"I thought I did."

"Sleep with me."

Stay with me. That was what he was saying. It was more intimate than the sex. It was comfort he was asking for, and the sweetness of it pierced through her. "Yes."

He cuddled against her, and she fell asleep to the sound of the rain, warmth all around her.

THREE

Henry woke to warm sunshine on his face.

And a definite lack of warmth in his bed. He slid a hand over the pillow where Win should have been and frowned. The pillow was cool, the sheets she would have slept under tossed back. Had she disappeared with the storm? He knew they'd talked about getting each other through the night, but that didn't mean she had to run out on him the minute the sun came up.

He sat up, listening for the shower running. The door was open and the light off.

He was surprised at the depth of disappointment he felt at waking up alone. Shouldn't he be relieved? Old Henry would have been. He didn't even have to give her a ride home. It would have been a win-win for his old selfish asshole persona. Now he wondered how she'd gotten back and if he would see her again. He didn't know where she lived, except that it was somewhere on the main island.

Damn it. Was it even safe for her to walk back to Edgartown? It had rained a lot the night before. Would she think she could wade across? The currents could be deadly.

He shot out of bed, reaching for his sweats and his cell phone. He glanced at the screen and saw that someone had called. He had a few messages, but he would have to deal with them later. He shoved the phone in the pocket of his sweats. He couldn't call her because he didn't have her damn number. How had he not asked for her number?

How far had she gotten? He picked up his shoes. He could at least see if she'd gone toward the beach or out the front of the property.

He was in the hallway when he heard the soft sound of television news playing in the kitchen. It had been a quirk of his grandmother's. She liked to cook and watch her stories, so the small TV had never been taken out of the kitchen. Now the sound wasn't soap operas playing, but morning news hosts discussing the storm and its aftermath.

He pushed the swinging door open and there was Win, back in his Harvard shirt, wearing it like the sexiest nightie he'd ever seen. The shirt hit her at midthigh, and she had nothing else on, leaving her legs and feet, with their bright-blue toenails, on display. She didn't have polish on her fingers. Her fingernails were utilitarian, but those toes were vivid and feminine. She'd pulled her hair up and looked ridiculously young, still without an ounce of makeup on. She was stirring something in a bowl and had the oven turned on and a muffin pan out.

She looked right standing in his kitchen.

"Yeah, I thought you would be like that."

She turned, her eyes going wide. "I didn't know you were awake. I hope it's all right that I poked around the kitchen."

"You can poke around anywhere you like." There were no secrets in this house. Now if they'd been in Manhattan, he would have told her to stay out of his office. He had client files there and wouldn't want her accidently seeing them and breaching confidentiality. Everything was open here.

"What did you think I would be like?" Win asked.

He should keep his distance, but he couldn't. He dropped his shoes and closed the space between them. Something had happened the night before. Something different. He wasn't sure he trusted it, but he knew he wanted to explore it. He leaned over and kissed her. "I knew that I could do dirty, filthy, glorious things to you and it wouldn't even start to get rid of that innocent look in your eyes."

"I don't feel innocent, Henry," she said with the cutest wrinkle of her nose. "I'm actually quite sore."

He couldn't help but laugh because she'd dropped her tone like she didn't want anyone to hear. He hugged her close. "Sorry, sweetheart. You'll get used to it."

Her chin tilted up, resting on his chest. "I will? I thought this was a one-night thing."

It was supposed to be. He was supposed to ship her off with a kiss and thanks for getting him through a rough night. There was only one problem with that scenario. He didn't want to do that.

He liked her. A lot.

"I'm here for a couple of weeks before I have to get back to real life." He smoothed back her hair. "How about you? How long do you have until you have to report to Duke?"

"I've got a few weeks," she said. "I wouldn't mind hanging out with you while you're here. You could show me your favorite parts of the island. I could show you mine."

He kissed the tip of her nose. "Deal." He groaned as he heard his cell phone trill. "Ah, did I mention coverage is back? I think I liked it better when it was all out. No cell phones. No electricity. I liked roughing it last night."

She stepped back. "You only think that. When you woke up without coffee this morning, you would have been sad."

"How do you know I even drink coffee?" He was a two-pot-a-day addict, especially since he'd given up the liquor. He could drink coffee all damn day long, and the heavenly scent hit him as Win turned and poured him a cup. She'd made him coffee. There was something deeply intimate and domestic about the act that reminded Henry of how long it had been since he'd had anything like it.

She offered it up to him. "I'm excellent at deductive reasoning. There's very little in this kitchen. It's obvious you don't place a big emphasis on food, but there's a five-pound bag of French roast. I also guessed you take it black since there's no cream. Do you want sugar?"

His day was looking up. He shook his head. "Nope. This is perfect. And you would be shocked at the emphasis I can place on food when someone else is cooking." He was hungry. How long had it been since he'd been honestly hungry? A long time. He would handle the phone call and then they could eat and maybe they could take a walk on the beach, see what damage the storm had done. There was something peaceful about the beach after a storm, as though it needed to make up for the violence of before. Or he could ignore the world entirely for a day or two. He was supposed to be taking a little time. He glanced down at his cell. It was David. He could call him back later. "What are you making?"

She glanced up, a wooden spoon in her hand. "Muffins. They're pretty plain though. I did find some chocolate chips, so we're eating like we're in grade school."

"There's nothing wrong with chocolate chips, woman." He leaned against the table, watching her cook. "They make the best cookies."

"How long have you been here?" she asked as she started to spoon the mix into the muffin pan.

He shrugged. "Three days."

"Do you believe in vegetables? How about fruit?" She shook her head. "You're going to have to buy groceries if I'm going to feed you."

"Done." How long had it been since he'd eaten anything but takeout or something he could microwave? "There's a little grocery about two miles from here. Even if the beach is washed out, we can get there by Jeep. Not the greatest selection, but you can make it work. I have faith in you."

She was about to say something when there was a knock on the door. Her eyes widened, and for a moment he would have sworn she looked scared.

"Hey, it's all right." He put a hand on her shoulder. "It's probably one of the neighbors. We check on each other out here."

He would need to walk the beach and make sure his elderly neighbors had come through the storm all right. His grandfather would have had his head if he didn't.

She stood up taller, her shoulders going back. "It might be my uncle. I told my friends where I was last night, and I wouldn't be surprised if he found a way to make it over here. Henry, we should talk about something."

"Hello? Henry, you here?"

He closed his eyes. Damn it. He knew that voice well. That voice should be back in the city. "It's not your uncle. That's my partner. His name is David, and apparently he's worried about storms and good with locks. Unless I forgot to lock the door."

It was actually pretty easy to forget out here.

The door swung open, and David strode in. He sighed as he saw Henry. "Thank god. I thought something happened to you."

He wasn't alone. A kid walked in behind him. Kid? Noah Lawless was twenty-eight years old, but there was something about his movie-star good looks that made Henry think of him as a kid. He'd graduated top of his class at Yale and done a two-year associate gig at one of Manhattan's top legal firms. "You really need better locks. Who knew David picked locks? I told him it was probably something trivial." He caught sight of Win standing by the stove. "Or something incredibly important that we shouldn't have interrupted. Hi, I'm Noah. Sorry to intrude."

He held out a hand that Win took and shook, her pretty mouth frowning.

"I should go get dressed." She winced as she looked up at him. "I'll call my friends. They can come get me if you need to work."

That was the last thing he wanted.

"I do not need to work and you don't need to do anything at all except finish our breakfast." He kissed the top of her head. "These guys will be out of here in no time at all. Come on, David. Let's talk out in the living room." He held the door open. "Noah, you can come, too. And maybe someone can explain why you're here."

He winked Win's way but could easily see he would be in for a lecture about proper introductions and etiquette. He would take it—after he'd gotten rid of their impromptu guests. "We don't have enough food for them, sweetheart. You're right about the fact that I'm not properly stocked up." He nabbed his coffee. "Also, I don't even like them."

"Henry, that was rude," she whispered.

"Yes," he said. "They should have called."

He let the door close before she could follow up on her argument.

"Should have called? I called about fifty times," David pointed out. He turned and walked down the hall. "I left several voice mails. I know that the storm last night caused some coverage to get lost, but you should have called back before now. What the hell is happening? You never ignore your cell."

But he'd been smart enough to silence the fucker the night before. He'd known service would come back at some point, and he hadn't wanted to get interrupted. Not when they'd been having sex, and not when he'd been curled around her and sleeping.

Funny how he'd enjoyed the latter as much as the former.

"I didn't want to wake up Win," he admitted.

"Win?" Noah asked. "Is that her name? She looks oddly familiar. I can't place her though."

"I doubt you've met her. She lives out here." The last thing he wanted was Win getting to know the younger, less-dark-and-snarky, hadn't-fucked-up-his-whole-life-yet Noah Lawless. She was about the same age as Noah, and who really hated a billionaire's brother? Henry hadn't met the woman yet who counted that on the con side. "Please explain to me why you're here. I don't get it. David is an old worried mother hen, but we've barely talked to each other."

"He needed a pilot," Noah replied. If he'd even noticed Henry's irritated tone, he didn't show it. He was busy looking around the living room as though cataloging the place for later study. "And a plane. I provided both."

Naturally. The kid got better and better. "Well, now you can see I'm perfectly fine and you can go."

"I didn't come out here to see if you were fine." There was something about the dark look in David's eyes that made Henry stop.

"What's going on?"

"It's Alicia. She gave an interview to *Rolling Stone*," David began.

"And she's going on the morning talk shows talking about how your marriage fits into her new movie role as the abused wife of an alcoholic." Noah finished laying it out, no real sympathy in his voice. "I've already drafted a cease and desist, but David won't let me send it off without your approval."

His stomach dropped. She'd done what? "We have a confidentiality clause."

He'd insisted on it. Oh, he'd known damn well it wouldn't stop her from talking to her friends, but he'd thought it would shut her up when it came to the media. It was one thing to have a bunch of rumors hanging around. They would go away after a while, a new controversy taking over the news cycle once he was no longer in the immediate public eye. The one thing that could keep him there was Alicia herself.

"And I'm invoking it," Noah replied.

"The trouble is she doesn't name you," David explained. "She talks about the great love of her life and how hard it was to let go of the man she loved when she lost him to booze and other women."

"I never cheated on her." Not once. Not even when he'd realized she was sleeping with her director. "And I certainly never hit her. Never."

His stomach was in knots and his brain went right to where he didn't want the fucker to go. He wanted a drink, and not coffee.

"I wanted to tell you before you turned on the TV and saw it for yourself. She's using you to try to up her chances during awards season." David paced the floor. "She's being careful about not naming names."

"Doesn't matter." If she didn't name him, there would be plenty of on-air personalities who would. "It'll get out."

"Or I can explain things to Ms. Kingman." Noah finally turned. "That is, if you'll allow me to act as your lawyer."

"David is my lawyer." He trusted David.

"I think in this case we should let Noah handle it," David suggested.

He shook his head. He wasn't sure there would be any way to handle it. Yes, they had a confidentiality clause, but everyone knew there were a million ways around it. And if he sued her, he'd out himself as the man she was talking about and keep the headlines going. "Noah is new and doesn't understand the subtleties. He's a baby and I need a shark. I need someone subtle and not some mewling infant lawyer who will likely make the problems worse."

David winced. "Well, don't mince words, brother."

"You know I never do." It was one of his problems in life. He turned to Noah, who had a placid look on his face. "I have nothing against you."

"You shouldn't since I'm the reason you have a firm in the first place," Noah replied quietly.

Maybe he did have some problems with the kid. "And I'm the reason anyone with a half a brain will take you seriously. How many cases have you tried? Ten? Twelve? I've tried five hundred and forty-two and lost exactly ten of those. While you were playing around on your brother's dime, I was hustling and building a reputation. There's a reason they call me the Monster of Manhattan."

"Yes, I believe they're throwing that around on the talk shows this morning, too, though in a different context." Noah sat down on the sofa. "And while I was playing around on my brother's dime, I was also learning from him. If you think you're ruthless, I don't know what you would call my brother. Oh, just because he doesn't feel the need to bare his fangs all the time like you do doesn't mean he doesn't have them."

"Will you please listen to the kid?" David urged.

"How about we stop calling me a kid," Noah replied.

"He wants to send her a cease and desist." It was ridiculous. "Do you honestly believe she's going to get a little piece of paper in her hand and stop talking? Nothing is more important to that woman than winning an Oscar. If she thinks selling me out will help her chances, she will do it without a single regret."

Why had he thought anything would change? She would trot him out every time she wanted some sympathy or to punish him for not being what she needed. The woman didn't know what she needed, but she did appreciate punishing those she felt had failed her. It would be this way the rest of his life. He would be the brute who had pushed around America's sweetheart and made her cry. No one would care that she matched him drink for drink, screaming match for screaming match, that he couldn't even play her game when it came to infidelities.

He wished the storm had never passed. He could be safe and warm in bed with Win. He could have rolled her over and had her again, making love to her over and over until they didn't have the strength to do it anymore and they simply lay there in each other's arms. Happy and sleepy and satisfied.

Win. Who was watching TV. Win, who didn't even know who he was. Not really.

He stalked out of the room and slammed open the door to the kitchen. Win was standing there, staring at the TV. Of course she was. His face was plain as day on the screen. They'd used a photo where he was in a suit with a bolo tie, wearing sunglasses and looking like the world's biggest douchebag. Alicia's stylist had forced him into that, saying she wanted him to stand out. He was smiling, but Henry knew that dumbass grin. He was drunk, and if he'd taken the sunglasses off, his eyes would have been rimmed with red. He stopped, listening to the national morning personalities discussing his life like they fucking knew something about it.

"Well, she's being coy about names, but it's obvious to anyone who knows the story that she's talking about her fourth husband," the bleach blonde with fake everything said with a shake of her head toward her slightly less fake, younger brunette colleague. "Henry Garrison's violent temper and problems with alcohol are widely known."

The brunette tried her best to look somewhat intellectual. "I agree, Brandi. She was very young when she married her first husband. Her second husband was an extra on the set of her first movie. The marriage lasted roughly three months. That hardly fits the narrative Alicia Kingman is telling. And while she was married to a producer for five years, nothing compares to the passionate and dangerous marriage to the volatile New York lawyer. I, for one, was shocked she married him in the first place. I guess we all love a bad boy."

He reached over and turned the TV off. Well, that had been a short relationship. "We should talk."

Win looked shocked, like she couldn't quite believe what she'd seen. It was time to play this properly. He wasn't going to get his quiet weeks with her. He was going to get to fight it out in the press, and it would be ugly and nasty and there would be no peace for him. He sure as fuck wasn't going to even try to drag someone like Win into his world. "Something's come up with work and I'm going to need you to leave. I'll call a cab. Or actually, my law partner can drop you off."

"You want me to leave?" She asked the question like she didn't quite understand the words she was saying.

"Like I said, something came up." He hated how cold he felt, but it was time for distance. It had been one thing when he'd thought he could spend a week or two with her and she would get out of it unharmed.

"Is it about Alicia Kingman?" She asked the question quietly, more than a hint of sympathy in her tone.

"She's my ex-wife and she's none of your business." The last thing he was going to do was discuss the apocalypse that had been his marriage. She didn't need to think any less of him than she likely already did. How long had she been watching? Alicia was an excellent actress. She probably cried as she haltingly talked about how much she'd loved him. She cried beautifully. Then her voice would crack slightly when she explained she'd had to find the strength to love herself more.

It was her go-to move when she wanted to elicit sympathy.

Win's hand went to her hip, her shoulders going back. "All right. I can deal with that. I didn't intend to ask about your past at all, so it's fine, Henry. Nothing those anchors said this morning makes me not want to spend time with you. They take some tiny piece of information and blow it up. I know how gossip works."

She knew nothing at all about his life. He was surrounded by children who thought they could swim in deep waters while still wearing water wings. "You know absolutely nothing and if you did I wouldn't have spent time with you at all. If I'd thought for an instant that you had connections to that world, I wouldn't have touched you. I wanted to get as far away from that world as possible. It's why last night happened. You're as far from my ex-wife as I can get."

"Am I?" She'd gone stiff, her natural grace leaving her.

He didn't want to hurt her, but it might be the best way to explain things. He'd acted out of character. He wasn't the guy who fell for a woman over the course of a single night. Hell, he didn't fall for anyone at all. He enjoyed women—their company, their ideas. But he wasn't about to sell his soul to one. "Yes. And that's why I did something I shouldn't have done and took you to bed last night."

Her eyes narrowed. "Is that how you're going to play this? You were only attracted to me because I'm the opposite of your gorgeous Hollywood ex-wife?"

Damn it. He couldn't let her think that. He couldn't hurt her like that. "That's not what I meant. You know I think you're beautiful. Trust me. I don't find anything at all attractive about that woman. I have no intention of ever getting involved with anyone at all in that industry again. And I won't involve you. It was a nice night and I'm grateful, but I need to get to work, and that means you need to go."

A single brow rose. "Ah, we're switching it up, then."

This was not the sweet Win he'd met last night. Oh, he'd seen a little sass under her sugar, but this was different. This woman was assertive, and damn if that didn't do something for him, too. "What are you talking about?"

"We've gone from trying to push me away because the attraction wasn't real. I think you realized how much that would hurt me and backed away," she allowed. "You should be glad you did that. Now we're moving on to the excuse that you're merely protecting me from the horrors of your everyday life. I'm a big girl. I know I seem to have this innocent thing going that does something for you, but I'm not innocent. I've been through plenty of bad crap and I know when a man is embarrassed, when his pride is hurt."

He chuckled but there was no humor to the sound. "You think I have any pride left at all?"

She held her hands up in obvious defeat. "Fine. I get it. You need some time, but I'm coming back tomorrow."

Where had this stubbornness come from? He'd kind of expected her to run the minute she had the chance. Now she was coming back? "That's not a good idea. I won't be here."

"Then I'll have gotten in a nice workout. But I bet you will be here because, once you calm down, you're going to realize that whatever is happening with your ex means nothing to me."

"That proves exactly how innocent you are."

She rolled her clear blue eyes. "I'm getting sick of that word, Garrison, and if you open the door tomorrow, I'll show you how not innocent I can be. I've got a couple of weeks before I'll be shutting down everything except my studies, and I intend to spend them in bed with you getting as much sex in as possible because I'm about to be in for a long dry spell. Now, if you'll excuse me, I have something I need to do before I leave and give you some space."

He shifted, trying not to let her see how her words had affected him.

"Space isn't going to solve this." Why wasn't she listening to him? "I won't answer that door."

She simply turned and walked out. When she returned, she was dressed in the clothes she'd worn the day before, right down to her plain white-and-blue sneakers. The one change was what was in her hand.

The Scotch bottle he'd found.

"I'll take this with me. If you want to ruin six months of sobriety, you'll have to buy some yourself." She walked toward him, going up on her toes, and before he could move, she'd brushed her lips against his. "Goodbye, Henry Garrison. Don't miss me too much. I'll be back."

Before he could move? He didn't want to move. He wanted to turn the clock back so she wasn't leaving at all. And, damn it, she was right. He was embarrassed. The feeling sat in his gut, poisoning his thoughts. But just because she was right about his motivations didn't change the fact that he couldn't bring her into his hell. If he didn't find a way to shut this down, there would be reporters and photographers. They would figure out where he was and drag the whole damn island into it.

He hated the thought of Win trying to deal with paparazzi who would drag up every detail of her life, shove it all under a microscope, and put the worst spin on it possible.

It wouldn't matter if she came back because he wouldn't be here. He would go back to the city and face this all there. He wouldn't bring a bunch of reporters to this quiet island his grandparents had loved. He would go back to his beautifully decorated, completely soulless apartment and try to forget about Win. She would find someone else to take care of her pre–grad school needs. It wouldn't be hard. Any man with eyes and a working dick would happily hop into bed with her and spend every waking moment inside her before she had to leave.

He kind of wanted to kill that man. And that wasn't like him either. Win was doing this to him.

Win. Damn it. She couldn't walk home. Anything could happen to her.

He strode out of the kitchen and down the hallway in time to see her striding out the door.

He stepped out on the porch. "Wait, and I'll drive you."

She turned briefly, though she didn't stop putting space between them. "No need. I wouldn't want to waste a good exit scene. And look at that. The beach is all free and clear. You know, sometimes storms come along and they seem fierce, but you wake up the next day and the sun is shining again. Would be silly to let a temporary storm keep you from enjoying something good. I'm going to jog home and have a nice breakfast. Take the muffins out in fifteen minutes."

He didn't want her to go. The need to keep her was an actual ache in his chest. "I can't see you again."

"That will be your misfortune, Garrison. You promised me a couple of weeks. I believe that was an oral contract, Counselor. I'll hold you to it. You should think about that. You don't want to meet me in court." She turned and started down the beach.

"She's a pistol," David said, a smile on his face as he watched her jogging down the trail. "I can see why you turned off your phone. I would have, too. Not your usual."

"My usual is a man-eating terror in Louboutins. I thought I would change it up and see if I could get out of a one-night stand fully intact." He heard the words come out of his mouth, but it was all bluster. One-night stand? At least he could try to be honest with himself. He watched her until she disappeared down the trail that would take her back to Edgartown.

He wouldn't see her again. Couldn't. Alicia had made sure of that.

"Give me a couple of minutes and I'll pack up. I'll call a moving company when I get back home. They can finish up here." He wouldn't see this place again either. It was a remnant of a life he'd left behind a long time before. It had been a mistake to come back. Coming back here had made him soft when he needed to be hard. He should have handed it all over to a real estate agent and pocketed the cash without a single look back.

"I don't think that's a good idea. Noah and I talked about this on our way here." David sat down on one of the two Adirondack chairs where his grandparents used to sit and watch the waves roll in. "The minute you step onto the streets of Manhattan, reporters will be all over you."

Yes, that was the problem. But David wasn't counting on how persistent those suckers could be. "Do you think they'll stop looking for me? They won't. They'll figure out I'm here soon enough and then the island will become a chaotic mess, all thanks to me. The good news is, Manhattan is already a chaotic mess. I can't make it worse."

"They won't find you because, after I'm done, they won't be looking for you." Noah stepped out on the porch.

He would give it to the kid. He was confident in his own abilities. "I told you. I don't want you on this. If David won't handle it for me, I'll deal with it myself."

And he would find a meeting. The minute he got off the plane, he would head to the nearest sad-sack gathering of pathetics he could find and sit and remind himself why he couldn't drink.

Mostly right now he couldn't drink because Win had taken the only liquor he'd had. She'd walked right into his grandfather's study and stolen his damn Scotch.

Because she wasn't going to leave him with the monster. Because even though he'd been a dick to her, she hadn't left him without a fighting chance.

She wasn't as delicate as he'd thought.

"Unfortunately, I'm not going to be able to allow you to deal with this yourself." Noah sat down as though he owned the place. Entitled brat. Though there was something powerful about the younger man, something that had to come from his self-confidence.

"Allow me?" Self-confidence would only take a person so far. He wasn't about to let himself get pushed around by what amounted to a third-year associate. "You think you run this firm? The last time I checked, I was the managing partner."

"Please," David said. "Can we drop the testosterone level? I can't stand you two beating your chests and roaring at each other. It's too early in the morning."

"I'm not being some crazed alpha male," Noah replied. "I'm telling the pure, unadulterated truth, and he needs to hear it. I've put a lot of money into this venture and I did it because I believe in Henry Garrison. I believe I can learn something valuable from him. He's shaking my belief right now."

Awesome. Now even the associate doubted him. "Your brother put the money into this venture."

"No." Noah was firm on his point. "I sold a good quarter of my 4L stock to fund this. I sold it to my family, but I sold it, and it's my cash funding us right now. Drew merely bought us the office space. And before you say anything about how the stock was given to me, understand that 4L was based on my father's ideas and philosophies. I am my father's child. You think you know what a gold digger can do to a man? Meet my mother. Oh, I'm sorry. You can't meet her. I was there when she died. She died because at the time she was attempting to kill me and my brother. You can't win in a woman-done-me-wrong fight, Garrison. I have the mother of all stories, and yes, that was a terrible pun. Luckily, I also have an amazing sister and three wonderful sisters-in-law who taught me what it means to be a family. I want this firm to be a family. Maybe that makes me naive, but it's true."

He looked to David, who sent him his sad-puppy-dog, please-give-me-this-one look. Damn it. He should never have gone into business with a friend. He should have figured out a way to practice all by himself, where no one talked about families and he owed no one. "All right, what's your plan?"

"It's already in motion." Noah glanced down at his phone. "Ah, there it is. Now I don't even have to file any paperwork. Your ex-wife released a statement through her publicist explaining that she wasn't talking about you when she gave that interview. She apologizes for any confusion, but the relationship she was referring to happened when she was a young woman. She is very sorry for any worry it caused her ex-husband, who is one of the kindest men she knows."

Henry felt his jaw drop. "What?"

David was looking down at his phone as well. "Damn, Noah. You scared the piss out of her, didn't you? She described your marriage as brief and passionate, but never once violent. Look at that line. 'Henry Garrison is nothing short of an amazing man, and I hope the press will leave him alone to continue his important work serving the citizens of New York.' Who wrote that for her?"

"I did," Noah said, his fingers texting. "Did you think I would leave anything at all to chance?"

"What did you do?"

Noah looked up and grinned, though this time it was a grin of pure joy, and he looked like the kid he was. "Never file a lawsuit when a simple phone call will fix things. Who said that, I wonder?"

"I did." He'd used that line of wisdom when he'd taught a few seminars for undergrads. "Work smart, not more, when dealing with a criminal case because the client's life and their financial future are on the line. It adds up quickly, and even if the outcome is good, the client can end up ruined. The court doesn't pay an accused man's legal fees simply because he's innocent."

Noah pointed at him. "That's the Henry Garrison I believe in.

You talk a good game, man, but you actually give a shit about the people you defend."

Sometimes. Sometimes it was all about the game and winning. "Are you going to make me guess?"

"It's all about who you know and how you use your resources," Noah replied. "That was not you. That's my brother. He taught me a lot, too, and one of the things he taught me was, if you need to hit someone, hit them where it will hurt the most and make sure they understand that if they get up and try it again, you'll put them down for good. You get one chance with my brother. Well, in business. He's not that way at all with his family and friends."

He was starting to get the picture. "You threatened her career? Does your brother own a production company?"

"He has large investments in several," Noah explained. "His wife is a journalist, but she recently started publishing some fiction as well. One of the stories she wrote a few years back about drug cartels was used as the source material for a movie that everyone knows is going to be up for best picture. It's only natural that Drew would meet with some people, maybe put some money into the film's Oscar campaign. But my brother is also kind. He knows that not everyone has as much influence as a woman like Alicia Kingman. He explained that he would be willing to fund any actress up against her. And maybe talk to the Academy about funding some of their good works, too."

Drew Lawless was one hard-core son of a bitch. "As long as Alicia doesn't become one of them."

Noah shrugged. "There's always a price when it comes to business. Sometimes it's money. Sometimes it's influence. Here's another thing I learned from my brother. No one fucks with my family. Like it or not—like me or not—we're going to be together for a while, and I won't let anyone drag you down if I can help it."

What the hell? He couldn't quite believe what Noah was saying, but he wasn't a stupid man. Stubborn, yes, but he knew when to let go, too. He looked to David. "I'm sorry, man. He's my lawyer now."

David's head fell back and he laughed. "I'm glad you get that. I hired him, too. The great news is, he comes with a plane and he can fly it."

Henry held a hand Noah's way. "Thank you. I'm sorry I was a complete ass. It was more about . . . well, Alicia knows how to get to me."

Noah shook his hand. "It's okay. I know it's an odd situation, but you'll find I'm willing to work my ass off to make this firm everything it can be. And I would have been pissed, too, if I had to run off that hot chick."

The hot chick who swore she'd be back tomorrow. Would she? Or would she get home and remember what a dick he'd been and write him off?

David stood up. "All right, then. Our job is done. Why don't we get some breakfast, and then Noah and I will head to the city and you can get back to packing and all the other things you were doing."

"I didn't get her phone number," he admitted. Some player he was.

"What's her last name? I can find that for you. I can have her phone number, address, any arrest records, pretty much all the information you would need to know about her," Noah offered.

"Don't you dare." He wasn't going to sic a former black hat hacker on her. "I know everything about her I need to know. She's sweet. She can cook. She's going to grad school in a few weeks in another part of the country. We were spending a little time together. Two old townies hanging out until we get back to the real world."

David sat back, looking out over the ocean. "You're right. It doesn't seem quite real here, does it?"

Time slowed down on the island. The world seemed gentler here, gauzy and simple. "It does. It was a great place to grow up. Sometimes I wish I had never left this island."

Noah slipped his cell in his pocket. "You know what? I need to call the airport and make sure we've got the all clear. Someone is going to have to do a check on the plane. I think I'll take the rental car and go into town for a while. David, I'll pick you up around noon."

So Noah was kind, too. It would be nice to talk this whole thing out with David. He needed to talk in order to purge some of the poison, but he couldn't do it around someone he didn't know. Well, not someone who wasn't in a meeting.

He didn't even need to talk about Alicia. He needed to talk about this place and what it meant to him.

"Thank you, Noah."

The younger man nodded. "Not a problem. Hey, maybe I'll find my own hot chick in town and it will all be worthwhile. Don't forget those muffins."

Within ten minutes he was sitting on the porch with his best friend, a cup of coffee in one hand and some muffins on a plate between them.

It wasn't high-powered and impressive. It was normal and good, and he started to relax again.

"Tell me about your grandfather," David said, watching the waves roll in.

Henry sat back and started to talk.

FOUR

Win slipped in the back door, happy that it wasn't locked. If it had been only Brie and the boys here, the house would have been locked up until late afternoon, but Mary kept strict hours. She got up every morning at seven and walked on the beach to get some exercise. It was nine now, so she would be working on breakfast because she had guests.

Win thought of them that way. Though technically she owned the house, it was Mary's chosen home, and that made Win a guest. Her nana always took care of guests.

Win sighed at the smell coming out of the kitchen. Bacon. If there was bacon, there would be pancakes. Her stomach rumbled, and she took a silent moment once again to be grateful for that small blessing. When she'd been sick, she'd gotten past hunger. Hunger was proof that she was still alive, that she could live a normal, healthy life. Hunger was proof that she'd beaten back her demons, and she could do it again if she needed to.

What was Henry's proof? Was there some singular thing he could point to that made him feel like he'd gotten through the fire? She'd tossed the Scotch bottle into the first public trash can she'd found, but the problem would always be around for Henry. It would be there every time someone asked if he wanted a drink. It would be there in every bar he passed.

Stubborn man. If she'd had her way, she would still be with him, still have had his back, but he had to play the martyr. She eased out of her shoes and walked from the mudroom into the kitchen. "Morning."

Mary turned and frowned. "You could have called."

She winced. "I called last night."

"Well, you should have called again this morning, especially after all that terrible news with that wretched woman." Mary walked over and put her hands on Win's shoulders, looking at her with serious eyes. "Is he all right? Tell me you didn't see that news story and run out on the poor man. I've told you time and time again that men are sensitive creatures and you can't use them for sex."

Nana Mary also had quite a dark sense of humor.

"He's out of sorts, but I suspect he'll get over it. And I didn't use him for sex. It was a mutually beneficial experience."

"I did not need to hear that." Her uncle walked into the room in his usual casual wear. He wore slacks and a button-down, sans jacket and tie. It was the most relaxed he ever got, but then he did run a multibillion-dollar firm. "Please tell me you didn't find some sad townie to bed down with. My darling girl, we've talked about this. You have to be careful."

Yes, she'd heard this a million times before. She had to be careful who she was friends with because they could use her. She had to be careful who she slept with because the minute any human heard the name Winston-Hughes they turned into ravaging money-hungry beasts. At least, according to her uncle they did. "I assure you, my sexually satisfying one-night stand is not going to cost you a dime. I promise."

He shook his head as he poured himself a cup of coffee. "Again, not something I needed to hear. Do you have any idea how I long for the old days when I could marry you off to some deserving man of my choosing and not have to worry about you again? I'm grateful I only managed to produce a single boy."

Her cousin. Trevor. He was a massive ass, the embodiment of perfect privilege. "Now, see, there you go, Uncle Bell. His sex life costs you all the time. Between the hookers and all that other stuff I'm not supposed to know about, you've spent a ton of cash on his defense attorneys alone."

She hated Trevor. He brought out the worst in her. He had ever since they were children. Trevor's hatred of her had been the reason she'd spent so much time in boarding schools.

"Defense attorneys?" Brie strode in wearing nothing but tiny boxers and a tank top that was far too small for her. She yawned as she strode up to the coffee maker and grabbed a mug. "What did Trevor do this time? Oooo, or are we talking about the hot lawyer Win did last night? I got the skinny from Mary."

Win winced but her uncle's ears perked up. "Lawyer? He was a lawyer? Well, perhaps we should meet the lad if he's got an actual viable degree. Don't look at me like that, Win. I'm excited. You usually bring home idiots, like those two sleeping it off on my pool table. Actors and DJs. Scratching records and wearing massive earphones is not a career path. Do I need to remind you of your poet period?"

She'd dated some men who wouldn't score high on the eligible-bachelor board. "Like I said, it's nothing serious."

"And speaking of the idiots you date, tell them I expect that pool table to be paid for. Drool and vomit don't come out of felt," her uncle said.

Brie's eyes rolled. "Yes, Daddy Dearest. I'll handle it. I told you last night that the film crew will pay for it because we got some good footage. Of course, it would work way better if our sweet Win would agree to go on camera."

"Not happening. My reality TV career is totally over." She sat down at the table more out of habit than desire. She wanted to make a plate and run up to her room, but Mary had taught her manners, and those included eating with family.

"A mature decision, Winnie." Her uncle sat at the head of the table. "And one that befits the future head of the Winston-Hughes Foundation. I'm proud of you, you know."

She didn't want to admit it, but his words did make her sit up a bit straighter. Bellamy Hughes wasn't a bad man. Yes, he was ridiculously rich and had some arcane ideas about poverty, but he'd been good to her. "Thanks, Uncle Bell. I've been trying to explain to my bestie that once I start at Duke, I won't have time to film anything at all. Do you really think they want to film me studying and going to classes?"

Brie groaned. "It's why you should defer. You're almost freaking thirty, Win. How long do you think you have before you're some over-the-hill chick who has to pump out kids to keep people interested?"

Which merely proved Brie didn't understand her. "I don't want people interested in me."

"Brie, darling, you're a sweet girl but you don't understand," Uncle Bell began. "You see, we're serious money, and that means we have a duty to our name and our honor. Your father made his money playing a guitar and snorting cocaine. It's perfectly acceptable for you to show off your assets to earn cash. It's not for Win. Win needs to honor her family name and her parents."

Brie's eyes narrowed. "Yes, her parents. Who she never actually met. Her name. That means so much more than mine. You're an asshole, Bellamy. Take that and shove it up your old-money anus."

Brie stood up, grabbed her mug, and walked back out.

Bellamy sighed. "She's a high-strung one, that girl. Win, you would do better to find other friends. I know she's been around since you were a kid, but she's also gotten you into a lot of trouble. Now tell me about this lawyer."

She needed to go talk to Brie, but it might be better to give her a few minutes to chill. Brie could take things badly, and she could transfer her anger at Bellamy straight back to Win. It had happened often enough. At least the boys were apparently still sleeping it off, or it could be worse. "He's a lawyer. I like him. That's all."

"He's Henry Garrison, a nice young man who grew up in these parts," Mary stated helpfully. "You knew his grandfather. He was on several of the governance boards for the island back in the '80s and '90s."

Her uncle's eyes went wide. "Are you talking about the Monster of Manhattan?"

She didn't like that term. "He's certainly not a monster."

He was actually quite sweet, and she hoped he'd remembered to take out the muffins or he would go hungry. Unless he was already on his way back to Manhattan, and then she likely wouldn't see him again. She knew she shouldn't be so invested after one night, but she couldn't help how she felt.

Bellamy went still and then a massive smile crossed his face. It was his evil-genius smile. That's what Win called it. "You slept with Henry Garrison. We could use that. I never could get him to rep Trevor. He said he was uninterested in college-boys-gone-wild cases, but if he's interested in you, we might be able to get him on retainer. After all, Trevor is no longer in college."

"Yes, he got kicked out," Win replied with no small amount of satisfaction. "So now it would be entitled men gone wild. I don't think Henry would be interested in that either."

Her uncle frowned her way. "You could be nicer to him. Trevor, not Garrison. It seems to me you've been nice enough to Garrison. How long have you been seeing the man? Tell me you don't have anything to do with his ex-wife's current media tour bashing him. Because the last thing we need is gossip. The fund-raiser is in a few weeks. I can't have paparazzi in front of the building. If we're going to have a mob, I'll move the entire thing. I don't want those terrible people anywhere close to our home."

There would be a postgala reception for the foundation's biggest donors at the Winston-Hughes penthouse. The entire five-thousand-square-foot penthouse would be done up like a Gilded Age salon, and there would be a midnight buffet. She'd already lined up a couple of Broadway stars to entertain, and the booze would be flowing freely.

Not the kind of place she could take Henry. Although the guest list would include the movers and shakers of New York, there would also be an L.A. element there. Her uncle tried to keep it toned down, but there would be producers and a couple of directors. They had deep pockets, and she had to do everything she could to raise money for the foundation that had been her mother's life's work.

"I didn't have anything to do with that." She glanced at the clock. It had likely been long enough and Brie would be calming down. "Apparently his ex-wife is trying to build her Oscar campaign. And I told you. I met him last night. It's not a serious thing."

"It is if you slept with him," Mary said. "You don't sleep around."

Bellamy nodded. "Mary's right, dear. Are you sure you're ready for a relationship? It hasn't been so long . . . well, it hasn't been long since we thought we would lose you."

"I'm good, Uncle Bell. And the thing with Henry is nothing more than two consenting adults spending some vacation time together. Don't look for anything deep." Though she'd never felt connected to another person so fast, he'd made it plain that he wasn't interested in having a relationship past the next few weeks. The good news was, she wouldn't have to explain her past to him. She could enjoy being around him and then they would go their separate ways.

Not every relationship lasted forever.

"Besides, the last time I talked to the man he was planning on heading back to the city to deal with the crap from his ex." Maybe that would be for the best. She'd talked a good game, but did she want to open herself up to that kind of rejection? Wasn't it dangerous?

Mary placed a plate in front of her. "Oh, she's already taken care of that. She released a statement. Apparently she wasn't talking about him at all. It was very cordial. I knew she was a nice girl under all that makeup. So much makeup these days."

"She apologized?" Maybe he wouldn't leave.

"Oh, yes. It was a mix-up. She wasn't talking about Henry at all. Like I said, his grandparents were proud of him. Always talking about how he graduated from Harvard. He made it off the island, though there's nothing at all wrong with staying on the island. The island is nice."

But it wasn't where Henry would live. He would need to be in the city. He would be a different man there. And she was a completely different person than she'd been before she'd gone into the hospital.

"Well, that's nice." Her uncle nodded Mary's way as she put a plate in front of him. "Now if you could call an exterminator and get rid of the rodents in my house, everything would be all right."

Win groaned because she understood what he was saying. "I told them they couldn't film any more here. They're looking for a rental that will work."

Not that they'd been looking hard. Brie was using scouting locations for the next season as an excuse to come here and try to get Win back on board. It wasn't going to work, but it was hard to tell her oldest friend that she didn't want anything more to do with the life she'd worked hard to build.

"You know you're doing the right thing," her uncle said quietly. "You got out before that lifestyle could kill you."

Mary's hands came down on her shoulders, and she felt her kiss the top of her head. "We almost lost you."

"It won't happen again." Win was resolute about that. She'd put everyone who loved her through hell, and all because she'd let other people push her until she'd broken. She was stronger now, able to see herself more clearly.

Bellamy sat back. "See that it doesn't. I've lost far too many family members. I know Trevor isn't your favorite human being in the world, but the two of you are all I have. And it was hard for him to have to share his father after your parents died. I coddled him far too much and then I went into mourning for my brother. Well, just know that I hate the fact that there's distance between the two of you. It was my fault. You should have been like brother and sister."

But even she knew that sometimes brothers and sisters didn't get along. Especially when one of them was psychopathically entitled. "I'll try to be more patient with him."

She would try to stay as far from him as possible. Once she was safely ensconced at Duke, she likely wouldn't see her cousin for anything but holidays.

"That's all I can ask." He picked up his fork. "Now let's have a nice breakfast and then you can deal with your friend. I know you want to run after her right now, but she's a spoiled child and that would be rewarding her bad behavior. Tell me about the gala plans. I got the email you sent but I wanted to discuss some of your seating arrangements. Mary, please join us. I don't want you fussing around and getting yourself tired out over those ridiculous friends of Win's. They can have cereal if they don't care to keep proper hours."

Win agreed with him when it came to Hoover and Kip. They were vultures and they didn't deserve Mary's excellent pancakes.

But she was getting worried about Brie.

Still, she started to talk as she ate, discussing the upcoming gala with her uncle and the woman who had been a mother to her. She relaxed and for a moment forgot to worry about Henry.

~

An hour later, she found Brie sitting on the beach. She wasn't hard to find. Brie was a goth girl, and she kind of stuck out in her leather mini, ripped fishnets, and combat boots. Her hair was casually messy, though Win knew it took Brie a good twenty minutes to get it to look like she'd just rolled out of bed. She walked up the dune, avoiding the beach grass that swayed with the wind.

"You okay?"

Brie didn't look up. "I'm sitting on a beach getting sand up my crack. I'm not okay."

Win dropped down beside her. It was quiet this late in the summer. She could see a fishing boat in the distance. Soon all the tourists would be gone and the island's population would shrink. The year-round residents would hunker down for the winter.

The island was a lot like her life. People seemed to come in and out for brief seasons. Tourists who merely wanted an experience. Very few stayed, and for the first time in her life she realized that was all right. She'd spent much of her life seeking approval, trying to make up for the fact that she'd lost her parents and spent most of her youth in boarding schools. She'd sought to build some kind of a family, but now she knew she couldn't force that.

But Brie had been around since they were kids. They'd been sent to the same boarding school and had stuck together from fourth grade through graduation. It was hard to leave Brie behind.

Even when she was a massive bitch. Even when she kept trying to pull Win back to a place she didn't want to go.

"You know how my uncle can be." She sighed and leaned back. "He's on the stuffy side."

"He's an ass and a complete hypocrite."

She wasn't going to argue with Brie. Brie believed everyone who didn't agree with her was a hypocrite. It was one of her favorite words, along with the word *literally*—which she misused constantly. "He's leaving in a few days. He only came out to make sure I have the gala plans firmly in hand."

"You always have them in hand," Brie replied almost sullenly. "You're supercompetent. You even handled the gala during the years when we were filming. That had to be hard. And you wouldn't even let us show it."

Because her uncle wanted nothing to do with reality TV. "I told you the East Coast is nothing like L.A. Those old-money families are serious about their image. They wouldn't come if they thought there was a film crew."

"Their loss." Brie wrapped her arms around her knees, laying her head there. "You know you don't need a graduate degree."

They'd been over this before. "I told you, people will take me more seriously if I have one."

She'd wrecked her reputation by spending three seasons on a reality show that had made her look like a walking, talking party machine. She'd looked shallow and vapid, but then she'd allowed herself to sink into that lifestyle because she'd wanted to be known for something beyond how her parents had died.

"They'll take you seriously when you take over the company."

Brie turned back to the ocean. "It's yours, you know. What's old Bellamy going to do about it? You come into your inheritance in what? A year?"

"Yes, but I'm not ready to run Hughes Corp." She might never be ready. "I'll take over as the CEO of the foundation. My uncle does a good job with the company."

"He's used you all these years. Can't you see that? He kept you around because if he hadn't, he would have lost everything."

She turned, looking at her friend. What was she talking about? "Kept me around? What do you think he would do with me? Kill me?"

Brie's face flushed, but her jaw formed a stubborn line. "Nothing. But without you everything would have gone to charity. That's all I'm saying. You brought him an enormous amount of wealth and power that he didn't have, and he should understand that it's your right and not his."

Somehow she thought the board of directors might disagree. One day she would have to make a decision about taking over the company, but it certainly wasn't going to be any time in the next decade. Her parents had left it to her, and part of taking care of it and all their employees was being realistic about her abilities. She wasn't ready, and the good news was, she didn't have to be, no matter what Brie said. "I thought you wanted me to come back on the show."

"I do, but I also think he's taking advantage of you. Everyone thinks he was such a good guy for taking you in, but he shoved you away as fast as he could. He only kept you around so he could have the money."

"He's not . . . Like I said, he'll be gone soon." She didn't ask what she wanted to. *How soon will you be gone, Brie? Because I'm not enjoying this visit. Because I would really like to get back to my suddenly interesting sex life.*

"Good, because the film crew will be back tomorrow." She shook her dark hair. "Don't look at me like that. They've rented another house for us on the other side of the island. Your precious privacy will remain intact. It's a solid week of shooting and then we'll be gone."

She hated how hollow her friend sounded. "I know you don't understand, but I can't do it anymore."

Brie shrugged. "Hey, being a star ain't for everyone."

She would have taken issue with the word *star*, but it would have only started a fight. "I know how much the show means to you."

"Our ratings are sinking," Brie said quietly. "They almost canceled us last season. We'll never get back to that first year."

She had to point out a few facts to Brie. "That first season was a hit because crazy Marcy was in love with you and tried to kill Hoover. I believe I might have mentioned that she was insane."

Marcy had been a wannabe fashion designer, and Brie had been her muse in the first season of the show. Shortly after Marcy had been sent to jail, the show blew up and they needed someone to fill Marcy's spot. Brie had begged and begged, and finally Win had given in. But it had been the backstory of a crazed love triangle that had raised *Kendalmire's Way* up from the multitude of reality shows about the rich and entitled.

Nothing truly scandalous had happened since then. Oh, Brie had gone from perky blond model to goth princess trying to form a girl punk band, and she and Hoover got into trouble every now and then, but there hadn't been anything as juicy as the murder attempts. Not until Win had nearly died.

How long had Brie thought she could get by as a young, hip urbanite trying to make it in various careers? "We're almost thirty. You started the show when you were twenty-two. The party scene was cool in the beginning, but now . . ."

Brie stood, turning on her. "But now what? But now I'm too old to get drunk and sleep with douchebags? I think a bunch of house-wives might disagree with you. Just because you want to play this charade out doesn't mean the rest of us can't live authentic lives."

"Authentic?" She was getting sick of being the bad guy. "You think filming your life makes it authentic? How many times have you and Hoover broken up? Like five or so? I was there for the last one. It took you ten takes to get the tears right. Some authentic life. You haven't cared about him in forever."

"Well, it's better than giving in to the man and doing something as boring as grad school. You gave in."

"I didn't give in, Brie. I nearly died."

She rolled her eyes. "Such drama. You got a little too thin. You looked good. So what if you didn't want to eat. Do you have any idea how many women would kill to look like you did?"

Oh, she was done with Brie. Decades of friendship had just gone down the toilet because she wasn't risking her health for anyone ever again. She stood up, going toe-to-toe with her former best friend. "I weighed eighty pounds when I went in. Do you have any idea what kind of damage I did to my heart? I'm healthy now, but that won't go away. I might have taken years off my life because I was trying to look perfect on camera and you want me to feel good about it? You want me to feel good that there were little girls who wanted to look like me? I was a skeleton. I was nothing, and it's women like you who encouraged me every step of the way. Get out of my house, Brie. Take the boys, and I don't want to see you again."

She started to turn, but Brie reached out. "I'm sorry, Win. God, I'm sorry I said that." Tears shone in her eyes, and not the fake kind. Brie's face had flushed and there was a quaver to her voice. "I can't believe I said that to you. There are things going on in my life I can't talk to you about, and they are seriously turning me into a complete bitch. I love you. God, you're the only real friend I have."

Win stopped because there had definitely been times when Brie had been all she had, too. They'd started to drift apart. The show had brought them back together, but not in a good way. "I love you, too. But I don't know that we fit together anymore."

"Because you know what you want to do with your life and I have no idea? I'm not the only one, you know. When we were growing up, they promised us the world, but the world turns out to be a pretty shitty place."

"You have unrealistic expectations of it." That had always been Brie's trouble. "I know you don't want to hear this, but it's time you stopped thinking that you're going to have this fabulous career because your dad was a rock star. Not many people get to be rock stars, but have you thought about producing? Or working for a label? You have a brilliant ear. You could find bands and help them."

"Find bands? Like I'm going to be some twit who works A and R?"

"You would be good at it."

Brie rolled her eyes. "Of course I would." She sighed. "I've been thinking about asking Sully if I could direct some of the scenes I'm not in."

That was such a step forward. "That's amazing."

"Yeah, well, I'm worried. Hoover tried it and he ended up breaking a superexpensive camera because he wanted to prove he was steadier than a Steadicam. He was filming from the back of his motorcycle and crashed. Idiot."

That sounded like Hoover.

"Hey, Brie! Taylor!" Speaking of the devil. Hoover had just walked out of the house wearing nothing but a pair of board shorts and his sunglasses. "We're going shark hunting."

Brie shook her head. "He's going to die one day."

"And then the ratings will probably go back up," Win pointed out.

Brie smiled for the first time that morning. "And then we retitle the show. *Brie's Way.* I like it." She started down the dune. "What are you doing, you moron? Put that spear away. You're going to kill someone."

Win breathed a big sigh of relief. At least they would be occupied.

And she could work on seducing one stubborn lawyer.

FIVE

Win stared at the selection of cheeses. Though the grocery store was small, the luxuries it offered were plentiful. Because of the clientele, it was well stocked when it came to wine and cheese. She was skipping the wine, but cheese and crackers seemed like a good idea.

She should have talked more about food with Henry. She wasn't sure if he was a play-it-safe sharp-cheddar kind of guy or the go-for-broke organic-sheep's-milk-with-dried-blueberries type.

It was the little things that tripped a girl up.

She had a couple of steaks and some veggies. He seemed like a meat-and-potatoes kind of guy. Did he like fish? Seafood? She had a couple of nice dishes she made with shrimp.

What was she doing? She'd known this guy for two days and he'd told her to stay away. Why was she here trying to figure out what to cook for a man who claimed he didn't want her around at all?

It had been that look in his eyes. It hadn't been there long, but when she'd turned from the TV and caught him watching his ex-wife degrading him in front of the world, there had been a hollowness she couldn't stand. It was like he was staring at something he couldn't believe. She'd seen that look before. She'd seen it when she'd stared in a mirror and hadn't recognized the woman looking back at her.

How could she leave him in a place she knew was so lonely? How could she not even try?

"Fancy meeting you here."

She closed her eyes and tried to smile when she turned around. "Hey, Hoover."

Hoover Kendalmire was technically a good-looking guy, but there was something almost too perfect about his features. Of course, they had been cosmetically perfected. He was under thirty but he'd already had two nose jobs and a chin implant. In addition to daily workouts, he did regular lipo and routine Botox.

He looked like someone had carved him from plastic and he might melt if the heat got to be too much.

And yet she remembered when he'd been just a dumbass kid in love with Brie and willing to do anything to be a star. Except now that Win was older and saw the world through a different lens, she knew he hadn't been trying to be a star. He'd merely wanted attention of any kind. His father, like her uncle and Brie's parents, had shipped him off to boarding school. Unlike Win, Hoover had often been left there even for holidays. He'd acted out for attention and he was still doing it years later. Good, bad—it didn't matter as long as someone was looking at him, talking about him.

It was what motivated Brie. It had motivated Win for a long time.

"Hey, Taylor." Kipton Keever stepped up next to his best friend, giving Win a long once-over. "You're looking . . . healthy. Good. Healthy."

She forced a bright smile on her face. "Gee, thanks."

He looked like he did way too much coke, and not the sugary-drink kind. Kipton was superskinny, and he liked his girlfriends that way, too. He was one of the people who'd cheered her on the thinner she'd gotten. He'd hit on her when she'd gotten under a hundred pounds. She could still remember how he'd told her she was beautiful then and tried to kiss her.

Then he'd called her a bitch and a tease when she'd pushed him away.

Yeah, she was happy to not have to deal with him anymore. This was what she'd learned. She had to value herself, and that meant cutting out people who filled her life with negativity.

His opinion didn't matter. His opinion was meaningless in her life.

It was a mantra she said over and over until her negative thoughts passed.

Hoover slapped Kip's chest. "Dude, you know you're not supposed to talk about that. Go get the protein bars I need. I'll meet you at the cashier."

Kip flushed slightly. "Sorry. Didn't mean to be a dick. Just thought that at one point you were like . . . goals. Good to see you, Tay."

He trotted off. Well, as fast as he could while wearing supertight skinny jeans.

"I'm sorry," Hoover said. "He can't help it. He is a dick. It's part of his personality, but I think that's why people love to watch him. They're always waiting to see what dick thing he's going to say or do next. And you know, he makes me actually look pretty good."

"I suppose that's a reason to keep him around," she admitted. Goals. She'd been "goals" when she'd weighed next to nothing and her heart literally couldn't keep up with her body. Yeah. Goals. His opinion didn't matter. It didn't fucking matter more than her life. More than her soul.

It doesn't matter. Those words settled deep inside her, warming her.

"He's also got a contract. You know we're down a cast member. There's definitely no getting rid of him now," Hoover said, looking down at the cheese. "But the new house is seriously pimped-out. Pool and hot tub. We've got three bars. Brie's closet is getting some designer-wear upgrades as we speak. You should come and see it."

"And do a guest appearance? I can't." Had Brie sent him in? She could sometimes be persistent.

He glanced up. "Nah, you don't have to do that, Tay. Win. I meant Win." He chuckled a little. "I got used to calling you Taylor, but you look like Win again. Have I ever mentioned I'm glad you got healthy? And don't listen to Kip. He's crazy. You look good, girl. I was worried about you for a while."

Again she smiled, but she hated this. She hated anyone talking about her looks. It was too hard to deal with, too difficult to know when praise was being used to manipulate her.

Except for Henry's. When Henry had told her she was beautiful, she'd believed him. There had been honest need in his eyes. Need for her. Maybe she was fooling herself, but she'd felt the way his hands had shaken slightly as he'd reached for her the first time, the way he'd nearly inhaled her. He couldn't lie about that. He'd wanted her in a way no man had wanted her before. He hadn't wanted her money or the connections her uncle could give him. He hadn't wanted to come on the show or get an introduction to her more famous castmates. He'd met a woman on the beach and he'd wanted her because she could make him feel good.

"Thanks, but I'm better now." She was. She could handle all of this. A quiet confidence took hold inside her. It would be all right because she was strong and she wouldn't let go.

"I can tell. I think it's pretty cool. I know I'm a trendy asshole. I've had pretty much every plastic surgery known to man so I can be as perfect as I can, but I think what you did was right, Win. You're stronger than the rest of us. It can be hard not to give in to expectations. Have I mentioned that to you? How much I genuinely admire what you managed to do?"

She was startled because that was the smartest thing that had come out of his mouth in years. "It is. And, no, you hadn't mentioned it. I came back from Sweden and everyone kind of pretended nothing happened."

It hurt at first, but she'd realized she needed to stand on her own.

His cheeks flushed slightly. "Yeah, I felt bad about that, too, but I wasn't sure how to handle things, you know? Do I pretend nothing changed because for me it didn't? I still feel the same way I did before. Well, maybe not. Like I said, I think a little more of you than I did before, but either way you're my friend. It took guts to walk away. I know I can't."

She shook her head. "I was faced with a choice, H. I could walk away or I could die. It wasn't guts that moved me forward. It was fear."

"Don't sell yourself short. Facing your fears is hard. God knows, I try not to." He gestured to her small cart. "Is all this for the new guy?"

"It's only dinner." She wasn't sure how she felt about the less douchey Hoover. When he wasn't around Kip or Brie, he was somewhat relatable. "Nothing serious."

"And he's the lawyer guy? Henry something?" Hoover asked.

"Henry Garrison. He's a criminal defense attorney in Manhattan, but he was raised here on the island. His grandfather died a few years back and he's finally getting around to selling the house." He had to. They'd talked a bit about it the other night. He had to sell the bungalow that had been his childhood home because he'd pretty much lost everything in the last couple of years. He was starting over and that meant getting rid of a cherished part of his past.

"Yeah, I've definitely heard the name," Hoover said. "I'm surprised he's hanging with you. Isn't he like old and shit?"

Hoover needed to face some truths. "He's not that much older than we are, dumbass. How are you going to handle not being in your twenties anymore? Because that is going to happen no matter how hard you try to keep it at bay."

He frowned and then ran a hand over his forehead as though testing it for wrinkles or lines. She could have told him it was perfectly smooth. "When I turn thirty, I'll declare that thirty is the new twenty and move on, but beyond the dude being old and his career being superboring, I'm wondering why he's hanging with you. Not because you're not a cool chick. You are, but he recently got out of a relationship with an actress. The rumor is he hates her and the whole Hollywood scene."

She felt her skin flush. "I'm not in that scene anymore."

"Yeah, but you were." His eyes flashed as he seemed to get it. "You haven't told him. Is that a good idea?"

She'd thought about this all damn day. "I'm not that girl anymore. I've presented him with exactly who I am now. I'm a grad student who intends to work for a nonprofit."

"A nonprofit funded by a billion-dollar corporation you own."

She didn't think of it like that. "My family owns it."

"Oh, I'm certain that's how your uncle talks it up, but I think both he and Trevor know exactly who owns that company. You know he's going to figure out who you are eventually. Henry, that is."

She wanted badly for him to not find out, wanted to be Win and not some reality star who couldn't handle the pressure, and definitely not the Billion-Dollar Baby. The press had followed her all of her life, had defined who she was, comparing her to her parents and other heiresses. Always judging her. "I'm a grad student who's going to work for a nonprofit. That's all he needs to know. It's the truth.

The other stuff makes everything complicated when it doesn't need to be."

"Hey, it's your love life," he said. "Though you should probably be warned that I heard your uncle talking about him. You know you hear a lot when people think you've got no brain. Well, and when you pretend to be passed out somewhere."

"My uncle was talking about Henry? He just found out about Henry. What could he possibly have to say about him?" She'd been surprised at her uncle's easy acceptance of her kind-of-crazy, maybe-would-last-longer-than-one-night stand. He tended to be critical of any man in her life.

And utterly accepting of any bimbo Trevor brought home. It was a nasty double standard.

"Kip and I snuck into his office to raid his bar before we left." Hoover made a face that plainly explained his feelings. "The network is trying to make us drink branded shit. I don't care what they paid for advertising, that Scotch they're making us drink tastes like shit. I switched it out for your uncle's fifty-year. He's so old he won't notice. His taste buds have to be like dead, right?"

There was the douchebag. Her uncle was barely sixty and he would definitely notice the difference between the thousand-dollar bottle of Scotch he nipped into at holidays and special occasions and the blended stuff from the company that sponsored the show. "I promise nothing, Hoover. If he comes after you, you're on your own. Okay, you stole Scotch and that's when he was talking about Henry?"

"Yeah, we heard him coming down the hall at the last minute and Kip got out in time, but I played passed-out so I wouldn't get caught. I kind of draped myself over that big chair in front of the fireplace. I've found if you look relaxed enough, they'll believe you're totally passed out. He kicked me a couple of times, but my muscles are stoked, if you know what I mean."

She didn't. "What did he say?"

"He was talking to someone on the phone about the fact that he didn't like some lawyer sniffing around you. Does he really sniff you? 'Cause that's kinky."

She bit back a groan. "Of course not. It's a euphemism. And you must have heard him wrong because he was excited I was seeing someone who wasn't in the entertainment industry."

He'd mentioned it again at dinner the night before, asking if she planned on seeing Henry again.

She'd lied and said no because she didn't want her uncle siccing anyone on Henry, and that was something he could do. He'd done it before. He'd been known to send private investigators to look into her dates, and he didn't hesitate to present her with reports that showed how awful men could be. She did not mention to Hoover what his or Kipton's own reports had said.

Hoover shrugged. "I know what I heard. He said he didn't want a lawyer around you. Maybe it's because he's the dude who divorced that hot piece of actress ass. Damn, man. Who would do that? That woman is on fire and her style is so on fleek."

"Well, at least three men we know of didn't think she was so hot." She shook her head. It didn't matter because her uncle was on his way back to the city and he didn't need to know about her affair with Henry. It would be over in a few weeks, and honestly, she kind of liked the fact that she would have something private for once. If she could keep Hoover's mouth shut. "I guess my uncle is being careful. Did he say if he was going to do anything about it?"

"I'm not sure who he was talking to. He sounded irritated, but he said something about how it would all be over soon because you were going to Duke and there was no way a guy like the lawyer dude would do some kind of long-distance thing. He said you would fuck him out of your system and get back to what you're supposed to do."

Her stomach turned at the thought. "He put it like that?"

"Well, he said something about things playing out emotionally and how distance would fix the problem, but I think you're totally going to fuck him out of your system."

At least her uncle hadn't put it that way. "Well, good for me. I should probably go and start my seduction."

"With cheese," he said, picking up a wedge of cave-aged Gruyère. "Go with this one. It's nice and nutty, and pretty much everyone likes the taste."

She took it out of his hand. "I've never seen you eat cheese that wasn't on pizza."

He slapped his abs. "Dairy's hard on the six-pack, but I know what I like. And I don't tend to actually eat the pizza. Not more than a bite or two for the camera. Come by the new place and I'll make sure the camera crew knows not to film you. But you should totally come and watch. Brie and I are scripted to have a big blowout over Kipton and then we start talking about getting married. You know how hard the fans 'ship us."

There were a surprising number of fan fiction sites dedicated to Hoover and Brie. Some writers made them sound way deeper than they actually were. Win had read a couple and been moved in a way the actual couple had never moved her.

Which was precisely why she felt her jaw drop. Brie and Hoover had been "on camera only" for years. "Tell me you're not going to marry Brie for ratings."

He smiled but there seemed to be no humor behind it. "People get married for worse reasons."

"Name one." She couldn't. Anything would be better than marrying for TV ratings.

Hoover's nose wrinkled in distaste. "To have kids. That's one. They're pretty gross. Not sure why people do that, but don't worry. This is a long-term story line. It's not playing out tomorrow or anything. This shoot is only a week, and it's going to be a special before the actual season begins. The season is going to be off the hook. Kipton's going to get with Brie's new bassist and cause all kinds of trouble."

"Sounds like fun." It sounded terrible. "I'll make sure to tune in."

"But you're never coming back." It wasn't a question. He held his arms open. "I'm going to miss you, Win. But I understand. You get out and get as far away as you can."

She hugged him, knowing it was unlikely she would see him regularly from now on. For years she'd had this weird family, but it was time to move on. They had been deeply dysfunctional, but there had been companionship there, too. "Any chance you'll ever take over your dad's company?"

"And run the stock into the ground?" Hoover grinned and stepped back. "Not a chance. The minute I say a damn thing about being interested in management, the stock takes a dive. No, I have to respect what my father built. Besides, I'll have a much better shot at keeping my trust fund well stocked if Stepmom Number Four knows I have zero interest in running anything but my liver into the ground. My stepbrother and stepsister are being groomed to take over. They both graduated top of their classes at Wharton. So fucking boring. I've agreed to not fight her and she'll continue to make it rain."

It sounded like a hollow life. "I hope you find something that makes you happy, H."

He shrugged as he reached for a six-pack of carb-free beer. "Happiness is a state of mind, Win." He started down the aisle but stopped and turned again. "And, hey, watch out for Brie. She's been weird lately and I think it's got a lot to do with you."

"What do you mean?"

"I don't know. She's weird. Secretive. She disappears and lies about where she's going. I wondered for a long time if she and Kip actually had something going. Maybe they do, but I don't know. He's usually not a good liar, even when Brie is excellent."

She did not want to get dragged into drama. Certainly not Brie's rotating bedrooms. She'd known Brie and Hoover had been on the outs for a while, but she couldn't see her picky bestie with Kipton. "What does that have to do with me?"

"Timing, I guess," he offered. "And a feeling. After you left she started doing some weird shit. She was pissed that you were gone."

Win knew exactly why Brie had been angry. In Brie's mind, everything in life should be shared on camera, and Win hadn't seen things that way. "She thought I should play out the story line for the cameras. I disagreed."

Hoover was quiet for a moment, as though thinking the problem through. "Maybe, but most of us understood what you were going through. Not many people fought you leaving the show. Not even Kip. Brie did, but I don't know how serious she was about it. She and Sully had some shouting matches, and I thought for a while that he would shut the show down. Then she went away for a few days, and when she came back she was cool again. Said it didn't matter that you were gone. Said she'd found another way to make some cash off you. That's the part that worries me."

Win rolled her eyes. At least one mystery was solved. "It's okay. That threat has already passed. She wanted to do a fashion line. She talked to me about it after I came home. She said my personal truth would sell clothes. She'd gotten together with some dumbass designer who thought my size eight was a plus size and that she could use my eating disorder to sell clothes. Obviously, I turned her down."

Hard. And was ready with a lawsuit the minute the insensitive bitch tried to mention Win's name in her ads.

No one was using her pain to sell clothes. She would use it to help people, to open herself to others like her, but she wasn't selling this piece of herself. Not ever. That pain, that insecurity, was sacred because it had led her to healing. She had learned to honor it by not allowing others to pick at it, to use it.

"That explains things," he said. "Although I still think Brie's keeping secrets. Anyway, it probably doesn't matter. I know we're in our last seasons. We might get one or two more specials out of this, but there's always someone richer and younger willing to do even worse shit to get on the air. I wanted it to go smooth, to relax and enjoy the rest of the ride, but I don't think Brie is going to let that happen."

"If she thinks her career is going down in flames, she'll try to make them count." It was part of who Brie Westerhaven was, always had been. When they'd been younger, Brie had been a force of nature, protecting her friends with a ruthless will. In the last couple of years, she'd started protecting herself in the same way.

"Well, I'll watch for that and you watch your back, too. She's not always nice when she talks about you. I know you two are besties and all, but she knows you've moved on, and when Brie feels like someone's leaving her behind, she can get nasty." Hoover stepped back. "Have fun with the lawyer dude. Do I still get an invite to the big gala thing?"

"As long as you play by the rules." She'd had them in place ever since she'd started bringing her friends along.

"No cameras. No groupies. No drama." He winked her way. "Got it. As long as I get some of those little tart things Mary makes, I'll be happy. Peace out, my sister."

Those were the new rules of her life. No drama.

Was she creating drama by going after a man who would likely hate her if he knew who she was? It wouldn't be fair of him, but it was the likeliest outcome of Henry finding out who she was.

It would ruin their time together.

Two whole weeks in a place where she could be exactly who she wanted to be. Two weeks with the most fascinating man she'd ever met. Two weeks of pleasure before years of hard work.

What could it hurt?

She picked up the last of her items and paid for her groceries. She was doing this.

When she walked outside, she noticed Hoover and Kip hopping into a ridiculously expensive convertible that had almost certainly been expensed. That was when she noticed her Jeep. She kept a Jeep here on the island. It was the best car for moving around on the beach. It wasn't the most expensive of vehicles, and she liked the fact that it was a normal car that didn't cry out for someone to look at it.

Except it did now because there was a long mark down the driver's side of her car. Someone had dragged a key all the way from the front to over the back tire.

Fucking Kipton. It had to be him. It was why he'd smirked her way as they'd driven off.

She was well rid of that group. Hoover could be all right, but he would also have waved this off, saying it didn't matter. He would say Kip was just Kip and he hadn't meant anything by it, and hell, she had more money than she knew what to do with, so what was the problem?

She settled the groceries in and hopped into the driver's seat. It didn't matter. Kip was an asshole and she was out of that world for good.

She backed up and started toward Henry's, promising herself that she wasn't doing anything but spending some time with a man who needed someone to talk to. And to do other things with.

She wasn't lying to him. She was exactly who she said she was.

She stopped at the light, an eerie feeling skimming over her. Like she was being watched. It was an instinct, probably one more sensitive after what had nearly happened to her in Stockholm. Win glanced around, trying to see if there was anyone odd on the streets, but she saw nothing out of the ordinary.

Deep breath. And a second. She closed her eyes and forced herself to center before taking the turn that would lead to Henry's.

And hopefully to a few weeks of peace.

Henry sealed the box and marked it. *Books.*

He would have them shipped back. He knew he should donate them or leave them here as part of the package along with the furniture and kitchen stuff, but there was something personal about his grandparents' books that had him packing them and making them ready for transport.

He glanced up at the clock. Two thirty P.M. Somehow he'd expected Win to show up bright and early this morning. He'd woken up and made a pot of coffee, and he'd gone over all the ways he would explain to her that this was a bad idea.

Because it was still a bad idea.

Alicia might have given in to Noah and Drew Lawless's blackmail, but she would be back at some point. Then there was the fact that he dealt with unsavory clients on a daily basis. He took on high-profile cases and often got dragged through the mud along with the client.

There were plenty of people out there who hated him. Loathed him and despised the very fact that he existed and cheered if he failed. He was used to it. Sweet little Win was not and would be horrified.

So he was going to tell her how amazing their night together was and then turn her down gently.

Except she hadn't shown up and that bugged the hell out of him.

She'd been the one to claim she would be here despite the fact that he'd told her not to come. She'd told him she didn't care what he thought.

It was perverse, but if he'd had her number, he might have called and said a few things about setting expectations and then not meeting them.

He started another pot of coffee. This was completely foolish. She'd put some distance between the two of them and realized how little they had in common. At least one of them had some sense.

The scent of French roast hit the air and he realized he was procrastinating. He was putting off the moment when he had to step back into the city and face the music. He would have to work his ass off to find anyone who wanted to hire a lawyer with his tarnished reputation. It didn't matter that his addiction issues had never cost a client a dime. The perception would be there, and perception was over half the battle in life.

He should pack up tonight and leave it all to the agent. It's what he should have done yesterday, but he'd enjoyed spending time with David, showing him places on the island and telling him stories.

It was time to go home now. Time to forget about pretending to be someone he couldn't afford to be anymore. Time to put away thoughts of quiet and peace and get back to being the Monster of Manhattan. That was the only way he was going to survive.

The Monster of Manhattan didn't give in to urges. He plowed through all problems with a single-minded, ruthless intent. The Monster didn't need attention, though he tended to get it. Attention didn't matter to the Monster. Money mattered. Power mattered.

He would get them both back.

The Monster certainly didn't need some do-gooder in his bed. He would select a woman, rationally discuss his needs with her, and pay her for her services, whether they be as a plus-one to gatherings or as a body in bed. That was how he would view it. Transactional.

Transactional was safe.

So he was going to stop being such a whiny asshole and be grateful that Win had some sense.

A knock broke through the quiet of the house.

He practically ran for the door.

He opened it and there was Win, standing in the soft light of the afternoon, her hair up in a ponytail. She was wearing denim shorts and a blousy, feminine shirt. She had a bag of groceries in one hand and what looked like a duffel in the other.

"I know you said I shouldn't come back, but you're wrong and I'm going to give you all my reasons why."

He didn't care. She was here. He walked straight up to her and cupped that pretty face in his hands and kissed her for all he was worth.

Fuck transactional. He wanted something real for once in his damn life.

When he came back up, he was rewarded with a soft look in her eyes, her lips curving into a small smile.

"No arguing with me?"

He did have some problems they should discuss. "You're late."

Her smile went brilliant. "I had some things to clear up. I thought if you didn't mind, I might stay with you for a few nights."

He took the bag of groceries out of her hand and led her inside. "I think that sounds like a great idea."

"This is way easier than I thought it would be," she admitted. "Have you had lunch? I could whip up some sandwiches and we could have a picnic."

He stashed the grocery bag in the fridge. She set down her duffel, and that made it much easier to scoop her up and into his arms. "I know exactly what I want for lunch."

Her eyes went wide, but she didn't struggle at all. Her arms went around his shoulders as he carried her to the big bedroom.

It had been cozy in his old room, but he needed more space if she was going to live here with him for a few weeks.

He stopped at the edge of the big bed he'd had brought in after he'd inherited the place. It was the only room he'd redone, with the thought of spending long weekends with his friends up here. He never had managed the time, but now he was happy he'd spent the cash to do it because he could share it with her.

The last few weeks of being Henry before going back to the real world.

He set her down on the bed and pulled his shirt over his head. He wasn't playing around this time. That was for later. It had been entirely too long since he'd had her.

He needed her.

He knew it was something he should question, even be slightly afraid of, but he didn't care in the moment. All that mattered was she was here and he could put off any thoughts of letting her go for a few days. He could sink into her.

She was his reward for every crappy thing he'd been through in the last couple of years.

"Take off your clothes."

She stood up and he could see her nipples had gone hard under the light fabric of her blouse. "You're quite bossy today."

He didn't want to scare her away. "I'm sorry. I'll slow down. How about take off your clothes, please?"

She wrinkled her nose. "I think we can dispense with the niceties. I like you dirty, Henry. I wouldn't have said I would like to get ordered around by any man, and if you try it anywhere outside of sex, I'll fight you on it."

His cock pulsed in his jeans. "You like it. You like when I take control."

She nodded, pulling her blouse over her head and letting it drop to the floor. Smart girl. She wasn't wearing a bra. "Somehow it makes me feel wanted."

"I've thought about you every single second since we've been apart. Even when I was sleeping. Let that make you feel wanted."

Not that he wouldn't take control. It had definitely done something for her. Her skin had flushed a pretty pink and those nipples begged for his touch.

She kicked off her flip-flops and her hands went to the waistband of her shorts. "I haven't stopped thinking about you either. Henry, my life is so fucked-up right now, but I'm working on it."

He shook his head. "No. No thinking about the past or the future. I'll talk to you, baby. I'll spend hours and hours trying to help you sort out anything you want, but not today. Today we're letting it all go."

He needed to let it go, needed to be in the moment with her.

"I can do that." She tossed aside her shorts and undies and stood in front of him.

What did it cost her to do that? He'd meant what he'd said. There hadn't been a waking moment in the past day and a half he hadn't been thinking of her. When the Internet had come back up, he'd looked up her eating disorder, tried to understand what had motivated her downfall. It was surprisingly close to what had led to his own. Fear. Insecurity. The weight of the fucking world. He had no intention of making her wonder what he thought of her beauty. Not for a second.

"You're so fucking beautiful, Win."

"When I'm with you, I feel that way." She reached out for him. "It scares me a little. I don't want to be this wrapped up in what someone else thinks."

But a woman like her would never be happy as an island. She needed people who cared about her, who she could throw her vast caring and love into. "Don't. I won't hurt you. Not for anything."

"I'll hold you to that." She wrapped her arms around him and went up on her toes, pressing her lips to his.

His body lit up. Electricity sparked through him, a sensation he'd only experienced with her. It was new and thrilling and he didn't want it to end. He wanted to feel this way forever.

Forever would only last a few weeks, but he intended to make the most of it.

He kissed her, slowing down now that she was here and naked in his arms. He let his tongue play leisurely with hers, stroking and stoking the fire between them.

He let his hands move along her body, loving her smooth skin and the slender curves. How she'd ever thought she was less than gorgeous, he had no idea. "I love how you feel against me. You fit perfectly."

She shook her head. "I don't like that word."

Perfect? He kissed her forehead and worked his way down. Had that been her problem? She'd felt the need to be perfect? He'd learned long ago that it was nothing but a word. There was no perfection in the world, and he was okay with that. Perfect things couldn't be trusted. "You feel right against me. Is that better?"

She leaned over and kissed his throat, warming his skin wherever her hands or body or lips touched. The connection was a vibrant, physical thing with this woman. "Yes, I like that better. Perfect is a problem for me."

"No perfection, sweetheart," he promised. "Just what feels right. You feel right." He ran his nose along her neckline, gently pulling on her hair so he had access. "You smell right." He ran his tongue over the shell of her ear. "You fucking taste right to me."

A shudder went through her and her eyes went soft. "I think I should see if you taste right to me."

Now he was the one shuddering. "I think you should. I think you should make sure you like my taste."

She dropped to her knees in front of him, her fingers working the fly of his jeans. His cock strained, testing the limits of the denim and the cotton of the boxers he wore. She drew both down gently. He watched, not touching her as he let her explore. He'd done the same to her previously, touching and licking and enjoying every part of her body. He wanted her to know him, too.

Win took her time, easing his jeans and boxers down. He was barefoot so it was simple to step out of them, and then he was as naked as she was, and it was . . . right. That really was the best word to describe how he felt. It was good and right to be naked in the middle of the afternoon with her.

She stroked his cock, taking it in one hand and pumping experimentally. He bit back a groan and forced himself to remain still. He wasn't going to make her go faster. This was her time, and she needed to know that no matter how bossy he could get in the bedroom, he wanted her to enjoy it all, to feel comfortable.

He'd never thought of sex this way before. When he'd been in college, it had been enough to get a woman off and take his own pleasure. After he'd gotten his practice up and going, sex had been a simple physical need. With his ex-wife, it had been a battlefield.

He wanted something different with Win. He wanted to know her body as well as his own, to figure out what made her sigh with pleasure and what got her so hot she couldn't stand another minute without him.

Lovers. He wanted them to be lovers. He'd had partners, but now he wondered if he'd ever honestly had a lover.

She studied him, brushing her fingertips over his dick and making him fight to stay still. After a few moments of touch, she leaned over and gently licked the head of his cock.

"I don't know," she said, glancing up with an impish grin. "I think I'll have to try more to be sure."

"I think you should be very sure." He enjoyed playing with her because there was zero thought in her head of gaining anything. He could see it in her eyes. She wasn't playing him. She was having fun, offering him connection and intimacy and pleasure. He let his hands find the silky wheat of her hair. "Don't give up until you know for sure."

She leaned forward and sucked the head of his cock into her mouth. He was surrounded by warmth, the sensation going from his dick to sizzle its way up his spine. He forced himself to focus, staring down at her as she settled in.

"You feel so good, sweetheart. I hope I taste as good as you do because nothing compares to you." He pumped lightly into her mouth as her hands found his ass, squeezing.

Her tongue whirled, and she worked her way down his stalk until he was completely inside the heat of her mouth. She sucked hard and then worked her way back until her teeth lightly scraped the tip of him.

His eyesight was going a little on the fuzzy side. Between the hot tug of her mouth and the way her hands were cupping his ass, he wasn't sure how much more he could take. He was a man who could normally last for long hours, only giving in when he wanted to. He had no such control with her and it didn't bother him. It made him feel young again, like all of this was new.

"You have to stop. I'm not going to come in your mouth. I want inside you." He'd dreamed about being inside her again.

"But how can I be sure unless I get a good taste?" She licked him again.

Oh, he was only playing that game to a point. He tugged gently on her hair. "Be sure later. Later, I'll let you suck me dry. Hell, we'll have a contest. I'll lie down and you can get on top of me and we'll see who can make whom come first. I'll eat that sweet pussy of yours and you can have at my cock. We won't stop until we're both screaming. But get up here now. I need to kiss you again."

He helped her up, pulling her back into the circle of his arms and kissing her. His cock pressed between their bodies, vibrantly aware of what was to come. He wrapped her hair around his hand, tugging lightly to expose her throat. He kissed his way down. He let go of her hair and lifted her up so he could get to her breasts. Such pretty breasts, the nipples all perfect and pouty and waiting for his attention.

He sucked a nipple into his mouth as he carried her toward the bed. His heart thudded in his chest, reminding him of exactly how alive he was. The rest of the world seemed a bland black and white. When he was with Win, it bloomed into gorgeous Technicolor.

He settled her on the bed and couldn't help but stare at her for a moment. He loved her like this, naked and without a single inhibition.

She stretched out, her arms welcoming him. "Come here. I'm cold without you. Though you should probably grab the bag we left in the front room. It has something we need."

Oh, she thought he'd been a pessimist, had she? He moved to the side table. "I bought a box of condoms. I was hopeful you would show back up."

She frowned, the expression utterly adorable in his eyes. "You could have told me. It would have saved me an uncomfortable transaction at the drugstore. The clerk there knew me as a kid. He gives a great judgmental face, and he used the store speaker system to ask for a price check."

"He winked my way and told me to have fun," Henry admitted, taking one out. His hands shook slightly, but he was resolute.

"Well, we know who's buying the condoms from now on," she shot back.

"And we know who's supplying all the desserts." He knew exactly what he wanted before he got to the main course. He was always disciplined, but this time he was having his sweet first.

He dropped down to his belly and moved between her thighs.

"You're going to kill me, Henry," she said breathlessly.

He had no intention of killing her, but a little torture could do a soul good. He put his mouth on her pussy, making a feast of her. She whimpered and moaned under the onslaught, but he held her firm, keeping her open for him. Everything about the woman was sweet, from her smell to the taste of her arousal to the way she clenched and shuddered as she came.

Only when she'd relaxed, every drop of pleasure wrung from the orgasm he'd given her, only then did he force the condom on and join their bodies together.

He gave her his weight as he started to thrust inside her.

Henry kissed her while his body moved, connecting them in every way he could. His tongue found hers, playing as they fucked. Her arms surrounded him, holding him tight, and it wasn't long before her nails bit into his back as she came for a second time.

It was all he needed. He let go, allowing himself to fly as high as he could. The orgasm flashed through his system, warming his whole body and making him shake with pleasure.

Pure bliss. And he had her all to himself for two whole weeks. He wouldn't think about the future or mourn the past. He would wrap himself in the pleasure of the present.

He rolled over and cradled her to him. "Now we can talk about food."

She sighed and laid her head on his chest. "You're cooking it, buddy. I'm exhausted."

He couldn't help but laugh. "Hey, as long as you stay with me."

"I only brought a couple of days' worth of clothes," she admitted.

He rolled her over, getting on top of her again. "You won't need clothes."

He kissed her and vowed to make this a memorable couple of weeks.

SIX

NEW YORK CITY
TWO AND A HALF WEEKS LATER

"Hey, Garrison. Nice to see you in the office early. It's always good for the boss to be the first one in." Margarita Reyes smiled as she leaned against the doorjamb. She was a lovely woman with a chic style. She always had a sunny smile and made the absolute best tacos he'd ever eaten.

She was also one of the most ruthless lawyers he'd ever met. Behind all that feminine energy was a woman who genuinely enjoyed confrontations and won more than her fair share of them.

They were lucky to have her working part-time here.

"It's good to be back." He said the words without true enthusiasm. He hadn't come in because he'd been eager to get to work. It had been hard to sleep since he'd gotten back. He tossed and turned, and at some point after four in the morning he would give up and get ready for the day.

"Was the island nice?" Margarita asked.

The island would likely haunt him for the rest of his damn life.

Between his childhood and the weeks he'd spent with Win, he would always have left a piece of himself there. "It's lovely there this time of year, but it was past time to get the place packed up and sold. I never get out there anymore and won't have time in the future. I've already got a full-price offer on it. Do you mind checking the contracts for me?"

She held up a thick stack of papers. "Already done. Your admin let me take a look at them."

Margarita specialized in mergers and acquisitions. She typically worked in Austin with 4L as Riley Lawless's right hand, but she was fascinated by criminal law, so she now split her time between 4L and Garrison, Cormack, and Lawless, with her boss's permission. She'd proved a boon in these early months. It had been her work that had brought in their first high-paying clients.

He took the contract from her hands. It was a bittersweet thing. He now had the cash he needed for his buy-in, but he'd lost the one place in the world where he'd truly felt at home.

What was Win doing today? Now he couldn't think about his childhood home without seeing her there. He'd spent two weeks with her, two incredible weeks. She'd helped him pack up the personal items, but mostly they'd spent their time either picnicking on the beach or walking around the island hand in hand or in bed. They'd talked for hours. They'd found a happy routine of waking up and taking a shower together, and then planning their day over breakfast.

And then it had been time to come home.

He'd kissed her goodbye, then gotten on a plane.

He hadn't said that he would see her again. He hadn't asked her to call. He'd let her go. That had been days ago and his gut was in knots because he had no idea where she was or what she was doing. If she had everything she needed.

It was ridiculous because he knew she was in Durham, North Carolina. She hadn't called him, but she'd sent a couple of texts, including one with a picture of her buying books in a brightly lit college bookstore.

Though he'd read each text, he hadn't replied because he wasn't sure what to do.

He'd made his decision. It was best to leave this alone. He wasn't used to vacillating. It was logical to end the relationship and move forward, but he couldn't seem to cut her off completely.

Why couldn't he get that woman out of his head? "So you checked into the buyer?"

A single brow rose above Margarita's left eye. "I made sure they're legit. I didn't know you wanted a dossier."

He shook his head. It was better not to know. "I don't. As long as they have the money and there's nothing funny about the contract, I'll sign it."

Margarita stared at him for a moment, as though trying to figure him out. "Are you sure you want to do this? You know Drew Lawless will give you the time you need to pay him back. He's not a bad guy."

No, Lawless was a good guy, but Henry couldn't handle owing anyone. Not money. Not favors. It was a pride thing, instilled in him since childhood. He sat down and quickly signed the papers that would set the sale of the house in motion. "No, I want this. Once the money comes in, I'll transfer the million into the company account."

It was his portion of the buy-in. Up until now Lawless had floated them along, but it was time to pay up. If he was going to lead this firm, he needed to have skin in the game. A million dollars' worth of skin, in this case.

Margarita took the papers. "The sale is going through a law firm. They're a big one and mostly practice corporate law, but I've been assured it's a private sale and the buyer intends to use the property as it is."

So it would likely be a vacation rental or getaway for some wealthy businessperson. He didn't want to think about some stranger sitting in his grandfather's office. "It doesn't matter. I appreciate your help. Did you come in for the board meeting? We've actually got clients to discuss, thanks to you and David."

"I'm in town for a few weeks. I've got a couple of open issues I'm working on with the New York office. I'm also representing 4L at the Winston-Hughes Foundation gala tonight," she explained. "I've got a Valentino gown and everything. I'm taking David with me, though I might have to force him into a tux. I thought we could troll for business together. You know there's nothing like a meeting of the East Coast's wealthiest to find someone in need of a good lawyer."

"I passed. I was surprised to get an invite, but I'm fairly sure it would be a mistake to go." He hadn't even considered it. It would have been one uncomfortable party. "Too many celebrities. I assume my ex-wife was invited. Isn't the heiress some dimwit reality star?"

Margarita shrugged. "I don't pay much attention to celebrity stuff. I think the daughter did a TV show for a few years. I remember hearing something about her having a breakdown and leaving the show. And yes, Alicia is going to be there. Another reason David and I are going. We want to make sure she understands that not bad-mouthing you includes doing it in person."

"Please don't tell her hello for me." He shuddered at the thought and was glad his partner didn't mind putting on a tux and mingling with the rich-and-bored set.

He sat down in his chair, ready to get back to the never-ending paperwork that came with a new firm. He had associates to hire. Hopefully. He had a thick stack of applications, but god only knew if any of them were up to his standards.

"David told me you met a woman while you were on the island."

He bit back a groan. "David is a gossipy old lady."

She grinned. "Yes, he is. I think the NFL taught him that. I walked in on him and some of his old teammates the other day and I swear they were gossiping like hens. But that's not the point. David said you seemed happy with her. He also said when he asked about her now, you wouldn't talk."

Because it was over and he tried to focus on the future and not the past. It was the only way to get through life. "It was a vacation fling, nothing more. There's nothing to talk about. She's got her life and I've got mine."

And it was damn lonely. He'd sat in his wretchedly expensive condo and stared at the news on the television, half-heartedly eating whatever he'd picked up from one of the fast-food places around him, wondering if she was doing the same thing hundreds of miles away.

Less than five hundred miles. He'd looked it up. Durham was about an eight-hour drive from Manhattan. Less than two hours on a plane.

"That's a shame." Margarita stared out the floor-to-ceiling windows. "David said she seemed nice."

He didn't understand why David couldn't keep his mouth shut. "David didn't really meet her. And she is nice, which is precisely why I should let her lead her own life, far from my madness."

"Madness? That seems like hyperbole."

He gestured at the mess of files around him because it wasn't. It was the truth. "I'm talking about starting up a firm. You know I'll have to pull eighty-hour weeks for a long time."

"We don't have that many clients yet," she pointed out. "You'll be lucky to pull a thirty-hour week unless you want to count launching stuff at young Lawless's head. His office is being redecorated and he's sitting at a desk in the cubes. He's so tall his head sticks up, making him a supereasy target. I take turns with the paralegals launching stuff at him. It's funny to watch him try to figure out where it came from. He's too polite to blame any of us."

It was good to know she was having a blast. "You know what I mean. I need to be here. I need to get our name out. I'm the one whose name is trashed. I have to make this right."

"Ah, there's the martyr I know so well," she said with a shake of her head. "It's not just you. We're practically the island of misfit lawyers. You married the wrong person and ended up in tabloid hell. Forgive yourself. You're not the only one who has trouble being taken seriously. David played defense in the NFL for three seasons. Do you think anyone wants a pro athlete lawyer? Especially with his history of concussions. He can get a meeting with almost anyone, but they want him to sign their memorabilia, not represent them. I'm a Latina who looks pretty good in heels. You have no idea how hard it is to be taken seriously. And Lawless . . . poor kid."

He would give her David and herself, but not Noah. "'Poor' is not the term I would use to describe Noah."

She shrugged. "Well, try being him for a day or two. Talk about a kid who was dragged through the tabloids. It's precisely why he decided to switch his major from technology to law. He wanted a place where he could make his own name, but no one lets him. No one thinks he's here on his own merits."

"He's not." He'd softened toward the kid, but it still rankled.

"He's actually quite brilliant," Margarita pointed out. "He's got a different way of thinking about things, and he could prove formidable in a courtroom if he's got the right influences."

"Aren't you the right influence?" There was zero question in his mind that Margarita was here to watch over Noah Lawless for his billionaire brother. She was here to nudge Noah this way or that and to make sure he had an advisor he could trust.

She turned, her eyes narrowing on him. "What is that supposed to mean?"

"It means I understand you have some intellectual interest in a start-up firm. Especially one with as many problems as this one has. I know you have a reputation for making things work even when they shouldn't, but there's no way you would waste your time vetting my real estate transactions if Drew Lawless wasn't paying you to watch over his brother."

"Or I would do it because I thought we were friends," she said, followed by a long sigh. "At least as much as you can be a friend. Not everyone views the world the way you do. Don't forget, Henry. I went to school with you. I know your tricks and you're distancing again. That's a dangerous thing. Call the woman. Tell her you want more than a summer fling."

He looked down at his desk, a little afraid he would give himself away. He had to get his game face back on. "Maybe I'm perfectly happy that it ended. How do you know I want more?"

"Woman's intuition," she shot back.

Maybe he did need to talk about it with a woman he trusted. He hadn't talked to anyone at all about Win and it was starting to get to him. Margarita was right. Distancing was a dangerous thing for him to do. Not talking about his problems put his sobriety at risk. "I've thought about calling her, but I decided that would be a mistake. I don't have anything to offer her."

"Offer her? I don't understand what you mean. Does she need a bank account balance before she'll date you?"

He frowned at the thought. He didn't want there to be some mistake about Win. "She's not like that. Not at all. I'm talking about how everything is going to be risky for the next few years. I've got to put all my energy into this business."

"Building this firm won't mean anything if you've got nothing to go home to, Henry. Haven't you figured that out? You have to have some kind of a life outside this building."

He gave her a faint smile. "I go to AA meetings. It's a real social scene."

"I'm sure it is. But you need more. You need balance and this woman might give you some. It might actually be good that she's not right here in the city. You can take it slow and easy and see each other when you can." It was apparent which side Margarita was on.

"I worry it will be different. I'll be different. You're right. We don't have a good client list, and we have to convince some of the most discerning people in the world to trust us with their very lives. It's not going to be easy, and I need to be more ruthless than the man she met on that island."

"It would be easier if you would let us sign some celebrity clients."

He could be reasonable and it was obvious his partners weren't going to let this go. "Yes to rock stars. Get me some rock stars or rappers. They get arrested all the time. We'll totally rep them. Athletes. Love athletes. Actors can kiss my ass. I hope they all go to jail."

Her head fell back on a groan. "You're so stubborn. Listen, I'm meeting with Bellamy Hughes tonight. That's why I'm going to the gala. He sent us an invitation and I wish you would go with us. He's a good man to know. You know how often that disgusting pig of a son of his gets into trouble. That kid is a gold mine. I've also heard he's had some corporate spying issues and wants to look into how to curb it."

"That's not what we do here."

"No, but we do get a finder's fee from McKay-Taggart if a client signs with them."

McKay-Taggart was a global security firm known for handling things like corporate spying and—if rumors were true—real, actual spying from time to time. Noah's only sister had married into the

Taggart clan, so 4L had deep ties with them and those ties crossed over to their new firm. McKay-Taggart would handle all their vetting of employees and would assist in investigations if needed. "I do see your point."

"It should also buy us some goodwill because you know that firm will handle things properly," she said. "If they're happy with the security firm, they're likely happy with us. Then we're standing right there when one of those privileged fuckers screws up again. Hell, it might not even be Hughes who hires us. He could refer us if we're in his orbit. He's got a wide range of friends who do some shady things."

"Are you talking about Hatch? Because I was hoping this one was the real thing." Noah Lawless strode into Henry's office. There was a pained expression on his face. "Tell me she didn't turn out to be crazy. I think Hatch honestly loves this woman. I might love her. She's the aunt I never had. Don't tell me she's horrible. You know this is why people hate lawyers. We always deliver bad news."

Bill Hatchard was Drew Lawless's partner in 4L. At least twenty-five years older than everyone in the Lawless clan, he served as the crazy uncle of the family. Hatch had proven to be an excellent sponsor in AA, even if he did get pissy when Henry called him at four in the morning.

Hatch also was looking for a lady to spend his twilight years with. Henry had been carefully vetting each potential bride. Unfortunately, Hatch liked ex-strippers. The first two he'd brought home had turned out to be gold diggers. This time was different. She was a nice woman closer to Hatch's age and with her own money and seemed to be the perfect match.

"Slow down, Noah. She's everything she said she is. Nothing came up in the reports except she has terrible taste in men. I think you'll have a wedding this time around." If someone like Bill Hatchard could find a partner, why couldn't he?

Noah smiled. "Excellent. That makes me happy. True love wins.

In that case, I'm heading over to Rikers to meet with a potential client. He's accused of drug trafficking, but the kid has no priors. I think he's being set up. The public defender is a whack job who didn't even contest the million-dollar bond for a first-time offense."

Henry felt his brow rise as he contemplated the young Lawless. "Does he have money? Obviously not if he can't make bail. You know you only need about ten percent to get a bondsman."

Noah went slightly pink. "You told me I could take pro bono cases."

Damn do-gooders. This was when he laid down the law and explained to Noah that their job was to make money, not waste everyone's time on a kid who was likely guilty anyway. They had to concentrate on people who could pay. If they couldn't bill hours, they shouldn't waste the time or the resources.

He sighed because he could guess what Win would say to that.

"All right. Make sure you know what you're doing. Get everything you can out of the cops and I'll go through it myself." He'd been so much better at this when he was a drunk.

Noah practically ran out the door, his enthusiasm near infectious. Like Win's.

"He's awfully excited. It must be his first time to go out to Rikers." The kid wouldn't be excited after he realized he was going into a dank hellhole and might need antibiotics. "Please go with him and make sure he doesn't touch anything."

"I will, but think about what I said." Margarita headed for the door. "Women need very little from men as long as they're honest. You might be surprised. She might be every bit as busy as you are and more than willing to take what time you have. You won't know until you try."

She left and he was alone with a ton of paperwork, and file after file of potential employees to go through, including a stack of applications to be his personal assistant.

He slumped into his chair. He hadn't wanted to deal with it to this point, but it kept coming up. She'd stopped texting when he hadn't replied. If he let it go another couple of weeks, she'd totally get the picture and move on with her life. He would become a memory, a few wild weeks she would forget about when she found a man who could take care of her properly, someone she could love and raise a family with.

Or he could call her and do exactly what Margarita had told him to do. Tell her the truth. Tell her he was kind of lost without her and wanted more. He could talk to her, explain what he could and couldn't give, and maybe that would be enough for her for now.

When he thought about it, they were both busy. Maybe a long-distance thing could work for them. They could see each other once a month. The Lawless kid believed in true love. He could pony up a private jet.

It might work.

He needed time to think about it. No more than a day or two. If he talked about it with his sponsor and thought about it, and it still seemed like something a doesn't-only-think-of-himself nonasshole would do, maybe he could call her.

Maybe they could see each other.

Maybe they could have a future.

He picked up the phone because anytime he had to make a hard decision, he wanted something more than time.

"Hey, Henry. You doing okay?" Bill Hatchard never failed to answer his calls. Not once.

It was good to have someone to rely on. Someone who had been where he'd been. "I'm thinking about Scotch."

"Ah, then you're worried about something. Let's talk," Hatch said.

Henry sank back into his chair and started that most important part of his therapy. Connection.

"You look lovely, dear," Uncle Bellamy said, handing Win a glass of champagne. He was resplendent in his tuxedo. Behind him, the lights of Manhattan sparkled like jewels against the velvet night. "The gala went beautifully. I hope you don't mind I invited a few more guests to our after-party. I made sure their names were on the list. Unfortunately, I couldn't get your lawyer friend here."

Win stopped, her heart threatening to pound out of her chest. She'd spent the entirety of the past two days in a state of near panic, but that was to be expected. She'd flown up from Durham, leaving behind her quiet town house because she had to be hands-on for an event like this. There was only so much she could leave to planners and assistants. Parties like the gala, where she'd entertained more than two thousand people, never ran smoothly. The key was to make it look like they did.

She'd expected that panic. She hadn't expected this. "You invited Henry?"

It might have been possible to avoid him at the gala. The ballroom had been massive and crowded. She'd mostly been behind the scenes, ensuring everything went well.

But here there would be only a hundred of the wealthiest donors, and a few of her close friends. There would be maybe twenty celebrities brought in to impress the big donors. There was no way she could miss him if he were here, and then he would have questions she had no idea how to answer.

Not that he cared. It was obvious, given his silence, that he'd been serious about not seeing her again.

Somehow, even though he'd explained it plainly to her, she had expected him to call. Or at least to reply to her. She wasn't angry with him, couldn't be. He'd been up-front and honest. But that didn't make her heart ache less.

"I did, but apparently he's got better things to do. He's a hard fellow to get hold of," her uncle said with a frown. "One would think he would want a connection with someone like me. Anyway, I'm meeting with one of his colleagues. She's got deep ties to 4L Software. Now, that's a family I wouldn't mind having connections to. Is it really over between you and the lawyer?"

She nodded but smiled, unwilling to let him know how much it hurt. "We agreed to a few weeks. Nothing more. I had a lovely time but I'm not going to see him again."

He stared at her for a moment, and she could practically feel the sympathy oozing off him. He finally sighed and reached out, patting her shoulder. "Well, he's a fool, then. I'm going to get another drink. Tell those idiot friends of yours that if they ever touch my Scotch again, I'll have them brutally murdered. I know people. I'm only tolerating them tonight for your sake."

She winced. "Yeah, I might have mentioned that you wouldn't take that well."

He shook his head, looking fatherly in the moment. "I'm glad you're putting some distance between yourself and that group. I know you've been friends with them for a long time, but you have to see you're on a different path from them. You have a future that doesn't involve being a washed-up half star. Quarter star, really. Why a person would want to be famous for being an idiot, I have no idea."

He'd made it plain that he hadn't liked her going on *Kendalmire's Way*. He'd even threatened to cut her off, but he'd finally decided the publicity would be bad for everyone. "Well, sometimes we have to make mistakes to know what we want in life."

"Yes, we do," he replied, more softly than before. "I'm quite proud of you, Winnie. Your parents would be, too. I blame myself for you falling in with that crowd. I should have paid more attention to you. I was far too busy trying to run the company. It was a choice I made. I'm good at running a company. I'm obviously not the world's most nurturing father."

"No, you aren't, are you?" Brie turned the corner. She'd changed from her elegant ball gown to a cocktail dress, one that barely covered her ass. It was her usual black, and she'd exchanged the diamonds she'd worn earlier for a harsh-looking black collar. There was nothing soft about her friend's look, but then she was playing a role—tough rock chick.

Brie was always playing a role, it seemed.

"Brie," her uncle said, with a dismissive nod. He looked Brie up and down. "I fear I preferred the dress you were wearing earlier. You looked less like a prostitute."

"Uncle Bell." Despite the fact that Brie's clothes were quite revealing, it was rude to point it out. Especially when Brie wasn't the only one dressed that way.

And everyone was suddenly watching them.

Brie shrugged it off. She was carrying a martini glass with casual ease, the very picture of decadent youth. "Don't worry about it, Win. Your uncle is an expert at pointing out whores. After all, he uses them so often himself."

Her uncle looked around, his eyes narrowing. "How much have you had to drink, dear? Should I cut you off?"

"There's isn't enough vodka in the world to make me forget some things. When you're done with the old man, I need a moment of your time, Win," Brie insisted before moving over to the stairs. She stayed out of earshot, looking out over the crowd below.

Bellamy stared at Brie for a moment, and he leaned in toward Win, his voice going low. "That is exactly what I'm talking about. Brie is a lost little girl. And sometimes lost and angry girls can try to drag everyone else down with them. I want you to be careful around her, and maybe next year you can leave her and the others off the list. You need to focus on people who truly have the same values you do."

She wasn't sure she would say she had a ton in common with the ridiculously wealthy people around her besides money and upbringing, but she got her uncle's point. And spending time with Henry had made it clear to her what she wanted out of her relationships. "I will think about it."

He nodded. "Ah, I see our vocalist is about to begin. I'll go look for my new friend. If you meet a woman named Margarita Reyes, tell her I'm looking for her."

She breathed a sigh of relief. She'd never met any of Henry's female coworkers, so she might be safe. Safe? It didn't matter now if he found out who she was, though she hated the idea that it could taint those weeks with him. He was a man who could use some peace, and while they'd been together, they'd both found some.

What would he say if he knew she'd bought his house? One day she would find a way to get it back to him.

She could hear the singer/songwriter she'd invited to play begin to tune up his guitar. He had a top-ten song right now, but she'd liked his music for years.

"Well, isn't it nice to see you and dear old Dad still getting along."

She forced a smile on her face when all she wanted to do was walk away as fast as she could, but then that would likely mean having to walk past Brie, and she didn't want another confrontation. She was going to have to talk to her at some point, but it could wait a few more minutes. "Hello, Trevor. I didn't know you were going to make it. I heard you were out of the country."

He gave her a leering once-over. There was nothing sexual about it, but she could feel him judging every inch of her appearance. It was what Trevor Hughes did. "I spent some time with my mother.

Learned a few things. You know my dad never allowed me close to her when I was younger. It's good to get to know her again."

From what she'd heard, her uncle and aunt's divorce had been incredibly acrimonious. They'd split shortly after Win's parents had died. She'd always wondered if it had been at least partially her fault. Her aunt had wanted nothing to do with raising another child. She would completely ignore Win when she came around. "I'm glad you're getting along."

Brie seemed to notice Win was no longer in her uncle's company. She breezed over. "Trevor? You look good."

"You, too, Brie. See, Win, I'm getting along with a lot of people these days. I met up with Brie while she was taping a couple of weeks ago," he said, arrogance in his tone.

"I wasn't aware you were out on the island." Not that she would have hung out with him.

"I thought I needed some quiet after that vacation in Europe with Mom," he explained. "The last thing I wanted to do was spend time with dear old Dad, so I went out to the island. You weren't staying at the house. It was perfect. I met up with Brie and I got to be on the show."

"At least someone appreciates what I can do for him," Brie said under her breath.

"You went on the show?" Somehow Win didn't think that would go well for her.

Brie finished off her cocktail. "Well, someone has to explain what's going on. You disappeared and now you're too good for the show and the fans."

Trevor's lips curled up in a smirk. "Yeah, Win. You're too good for the fans. One of us has to be pleasant or it could hurt our family name. You don't want that, do you? Don't worry. I didn't tell them the truth. I said you were exhausted, that you found you couldn't keep up with the pace of the show."

"I have a right to privacy. I don't owe anyone an explanation for why I left." Tension knotted her stomach at the thought of Trevor explaining her absence. The tabloids would read into every single word he said and twist it all for a story. She looked at Brie. "I thought you understood I don't want to be involved. It's not good for me or my health."

"You're so dramatic." Brie rolled her eyes. "It's not like you died."

Anger flared through her. She didn't care who was watching them at that moment. "I almost did."

"So you say."

"I want whatever Trevor said about me taken out of the show." She wasn't going to allow herself to get dragged back in.

Brie put a hand on her hip. "Oh, now we're not even allowed to talk about you? You can't control this. You can't stop me from talking about you."

"I bet I can." She wouldn't go after Brie. She would go straight for the producers. They would likely find a lawsuit reason enough to edit that episode.

Trevor's face had gone hard, his eyes slits as he stared down at her. "Fuck you, Win. You have to ruin everything for me. You think you're going to cut me out of the episode?"

"I only want to get rid of anything you said concerning me." She was sick of being the bad guy when all she was doing was standing up for herself.

"I think you're right, Trevor. I think she only wants her own success." Every word that came out of Brie's mouth was a nasty bullet. "She knows she can't make it in the entertainment world, so she's going to burn it all down around her and she doesn't care who she hurts."

"Stop with the drama." She wasn't going to have this fight in public, though she knew people were already whispering behind their hands. "There are no cameras here."

"But there are a few reporters," Brie threatened. "Maybe I should go find one."

Brie started to turn back toward the stairs, but stopped. Her whole attitude changed, and suddenly she was bubbly and light, her arms open to the newcomer. "Hello, Alicia. You are looking lovely tonight."

Win was ready for the night to end.

Alicia Kingman strode up, kissing Brie and Trevor on both cheeks in that vaguely European fashion. The actress was wearing a stunning sheath that showed her slender, elegant figure. Everything about the woman was perfect.

Yes, there was that hated word.

"Hello, Trevor." She glanced back, looking Win over with a vaguely sympathetic look. "Ah, this is your cousin, right? The Billion-Dollar Baby? I loved that movie on Lifetime. So tragic. Your parents were heroes. Giving their lives to save yours."

Both Brie and Trevor seemed to have flipped a switch the minute Alicia had shown up. Now they were all smiles and casual ease. It was like the tension of moments before had never happened, though Win had no thought that it wouldn't resurface. That fight was not over.

"That's right," Brie said with a laugh. "I'd forgotten all about that movie. *Love and Sacrifice on the High Seas*. What a terrible title. And they didn't even get a star to play Win."

Win bit back a groan. It had come out when she was a child. The film depicted her parents' final hours and how they'd valiantly sacrificed their own lives for their precious child. It was as overwrought as the title suggested. Her uncle had flipped out the one time he'd caught her watching it. He'd turned it off and made her promise to never watch that drivel again. "Well, I was only a baby."

Brie's nose wrinkled in distaste. "Still, they could have gotten a talented baby. The one they used was bland."

"I think that baby was very good at portraying Win at that age," Trevor replied. "She cried a lot and pooped her pants when she should have been potty-trained. She was a whiny thing."

Alicia frowned. "Well, she might have been a baby, but even babies can be affected by tragedy. And you have no idea how hard it can be to work with kids. Don't get me wrong. Some of them are great, but some are true brats of the highest order. I prefer working with dogs, to tell you the truth."

"As long as you don't marry another one," Trevor snarked. "Though you should know, apparently Win here is taking your sloppy seconds."

Brie gasped and slapped his arm. "You weren't supposed to talk about that."

So Brie had been gossiping behind her back. She was learning that the friendship of their childhood couldn't survive Brie's adult temper tantrums. Win had spent the last few years making excuses for her best friend, but her uncle was right. It was time to cut this off and move on with her life. Time to find new friends.

Trevor shrugged off the criticism. "Hey, Win is all about honesty, isn't she? Until it comes to her own life. It'll be good to see how she deals with it. See if she breaks, since she's so damn fragile."

He strode down the stairs.

Brie shook her head. "I should go and talk to him."

When had they gotten chummy? There had been a time in her life when Brie had been the one to hold her hand when Trevor made her cry. Now it looked like she'd switched sides.

Alicia flashed Brie a brilliant smile. "Please say hello to your father for me. He did such an amazing job on my last film."

Brie nodded. "I will. When I see him."

She raced off after Trevor, but she wasn't in such a hurry that she didn't stop to pick up another drink.

And Win was left with her summer fling's ex-wife. "I'm sorry if my friends caused you discomfort. I should get back to the party."

Alicia put a well-manicured hand on her arm. "Please don't think you have to rush off because your friends are idiots. The only reason I talk to Brie is because her father is an amazing musician. Now that he's left the coke-and-whores phase of his career, he's doing some brilliant soundtrack work."

"Yeah, that was a long phase for him," she admitted. "Most of my childhood. And Brie isn't normally like that." The excuse had worn terribly thin, but she felt like she needed to make it this one last time. "I can't say the same for Trevor. I'm surprised you've met him."

"I can't hear well in here. Let's go out to the balcony." Alicia took her hand and started to lead her outside. The balcony was lit up and there was a second bar. It was much quieter, though they weren't alone. "Hughes Corp has a television division, as you likely know, since technically it's your company." She gestured to the bartender. "Could I get a whiskey neat? Anything for you, dear?"

Oh, if she was going to get through what was likely going to be an uncomfortable conversation, she could use a drink. It would be her first of the evening. "A glass of white wine, please." She turned back to Alicia. "Our television division concentrates on documentaries and news. We don't do traditional movies or TV shows."

"The company does some fabulous programs. It's why I work with them often. Your cousin found out I was doing a voice-over for a documentary on child brides and he decided to take an interest in the project." She nodded and took the whiskey from the bartender. "He's disgusting, and I found the fact that a misogynist pig was the named producer of a film purporting to help women around the world to be quite ironic. Well, we all learn to take what we can get, but I'm not suing or anything. That's not what I want to talk to you about."

That was nice to hear, though Alicia wouldn't be the first to sue over Trevor being a groping ass. "All right. What do you want to talk about?"

She looked up from her drink, her eyes seeming to shine with tears. "Is he okay? Henry, that is?"

Damn, but the woman was good. Win decided to try honesty with her. "The last time I saw him, he was in good spirits. Look, Trevor made it sound like I'm dating Henry. I'm not. I spent some time with him when we were both on vacation. That was all."

"Oh, well, that might be for the best. I wish him no ill will," she began.

"Then why did you try to trash him in the media?" The question was out before she could think about the repercussions. The last thing she needed was more drama.

Alicia leaned in, as though she didn't want the drama either. "I didn't. I never mentioned his name. I was only trying to explain my method. When I realized the press thought I was talking about Henry, I immediately came out with a statement. I'm not the bad guy here. There are two sides to every story."

Win knew that well, but she also knew Alicia Kingman was an excellent actress and she obviously wanted something out of this conversation. "Like I said, it doesn't matter because I'm not seeing him again."

"Again, it's probably for the best. Henry is a charming man, but he's not what I would call forgiving. I'm actually surprised he would date you at all. He told me he would never again get involved with an overprivileged rich bitch. His words. Not mine. He hates old money. He can't stand anyone who didn't pull themselves up by their proverbial bootstraps."

"Well, I'm certainly not that girl." Had he found out her true identity and that was why he wasn't interested? Or had he been honest with her and all he'd wanted was a few weeks of distraction? It had been so much more to her.

"Aren't you, though? It's not like you haven't struggled. Money doesn't stop tragedy. That's what Henry doesn't understand." Alicia gave her a warm smile. "You know, I have caught an episode or two of *Kendalmire's Way*. Silly show, but it's mindless fun in its own way. I do enjoy watching Hoover try to figure out regular life skills."

"He struggles with those." They'd dedicated the majority of an episode to Hoover trying to open a can of beans without his housekeeper's help.

"I'm glad you got treatment," Alicia said. "Some people theorized that you took some mental health time or that you went to rehab, but I bet you had a different kind of therapy. You look good now and don't let anyone tell you otherwise. You look healthy and happy. Some people can handle this business. Some of us can maintain a balance and some of us can't. Don't think you're any less because you can't. Stand proud because you managed to get out. A lot of people don't."

Win shook her head because she was getting emotional, and the last person she'd expected praise to come from was Alicia Kingman. "I'm confused."

"Because I'm not the evil bitch goddess Henry told you I am?" She stared out over the city. "Oh, I can be. I certainly was to him, and maybe I'm not being completely honest with you about everything. Maybe I liked the idea that people were sympathetic to me after the divorce. After all, I've never had a man leave me before. He had his reasons, but I loved him. I'm simply not good at loving anything but my career."

"That's surprisingly honest of you."

"Yeah, I can be that, too," Alicia admitted. "Sometimes I need a good old jolt to the system, and Henry's new attack dog explaining how he can break me like an egg seems to have done the trick. I had already heard from Brie that you were seeing Henry. She called me a week ago. You're not supposed to know that, of course."

What the hell had Brie been doing? And why? "Why would she call you?"

"I believe she did it to cause some drama. Maybe she thought I would be closer with her if she told on her bestie, or I don't know. I have a movie coming up where the second-best part in the film is my younger sister. I know she's got an audition. She had some good gossip and she tried to use it to better her position. It's what we do. The problem is I actually loved that bastard, and when I'm reasonable, I know it was all my fault. I pushed him. I didn't see that he had a problem, so I wasn't supportive when he needed me to be."

"I thought you cheated on him."

She waved that off. "I cheat on all of them. Monogamy is not normal. We probably should have talked about that before we got married, but that would have been boring. Did you fall for him? It's okay. I would kind of think you're insane if you didn't."

"I came to care for him." She'd fallen utterly and madly in love with the man, but she wasn't going to admit that to a complete stranger.

Alicia nodded. "I know what that means. Be careful. He's incredibly narrow in his views. I wonder if any woman can truly please him. I wonder if he'll always find a way to put a woman in a box because he can't quite believe she's good enough. It's his mind-set. He's too cynical."

Too cynical to handle a woman who cheated on him? Win wasn't sure she knew many men uncynical enough to handle that. "I'll keep that in mind."

Alicia smiled. "You won't, but that's okay. I think you'll be all right with him or without him. If it starts to bug you and you don't have someone to talk to, call me. Or someone. I know you're going to be naturally reticent to talk to me, but I hate to lose a good female mind because some guy can't handle his shit. I have your number and I'm going to text you. Contact me whenever. And don't trust a damn thing Brie says to you. She's using you and can't stand the thought that you might move on from her."

Alicia started toward the door. She turned at the doorway. "And I'll be writing the foundation a hefty check. If you decide to take over some of those documentary projects, let me know. I would love to work with you, no matter what you decide to do with Henry. You know, the world could use your story. I'm sure right now it's too raw and you need some distance, but think about it. I would love to help with that. I need the karma, baby."

She walked through the door, and Win was left gawking after her. What the hell had happened? Should she believe a damn thing that woman said?

Was it possible someone could know herself that well and be honest about it?

She knew one thing. She was going to have a long talk with her best friend.

Win walked through the party, looking for Brie. She moved to the edge of the crowd. No sign of Brie or Trevor.

A nasty suspicion played through her brain.

Brie wasn't friends with guys. She didn't view men as friends. She viewed them as playthings, and playing around with Trevor would definitely be something Brie could do. It could cause a scandal that would drag them all through tabloid hell.

As quietly as she could, she moved toward the private residential portion of the penthouse. Win wouldn't put it past Brie to try to find something she could use to force Win's hand. Hell, at this point Brie might do it out of pure malice.

Sure enough, the light was on in her bedroom, the door open.

That bitch. She strode into the room and slipped on the marble floor. She fell forward, trying to catch herself. Win slammed into the floor and groaned. Her head hurt. Damn. Had she hit her head on the bedpost? The pain was crippling. What had happened?

She looked up and saw Brie. She looked weird though. Paler than usual. Why were her lips blue? That wasn't the shade of lipstick she wore. And why was she covered in red wine?

Had she spilled her drink? No, she didn't drink red. She'd been drinking vodka. The truth dawned, horror blooming.

Blood. She'd slipped in Brie's blood. It coated her dress. It was everywhere.

She was in a sea of blood.

Win heard someone screaming, but her vision faded and all went a blissful black.

SEVEN

The shrill ring of the phone shook him from his pleasant dream. Why didn't he turn that sucker off when he was sleeping? It's what he'd done on the island. He and Win would silence their phones at bedtime and not turn the ringers on again until the morning. They would shut the world out and sleep peacefully.

Henry sat up, looking at the clock.

He wasn't on the island, and there was no peace here.

Two in the morning.

Someone better be dead.

He ran a hand across his face, trying to wake up as he answered the cell. "This is Garrison."

"Henry, I need you to get dressed and come down to the Twentieth Precinct." David's voice sounded tinny over the line, like he was far away or there was a lot of noise he was trying to talk over. "I'm trying to get there right now but there's a traffic jam."

"At this time of night?" Henry tried to shake the sleep off. "What's going on? Is there an accident?"

"I don't have time to explain, but I need you." David sounded grave over the line. "Win needs you."

That name woke him up and fast. "What are you talking about? Win is in North Carolina."

"I meant what I said. I don't have time to explain. I'm almost there and I need to get in that building as quickly as possible. She's completely in shock. I don't want her talking to the police, but I think she might. She's scared. I don't know that she heard a word I said to her. They'll try to use every second they have to get her to admit to the murder."

He damn near dropped the phone. "Murder? David, you need to start talking. How the hell is Win in the city, and what murder are you talking about? Is this some kind of a joke?"

He rolled out of bed, slamming open the closet door. Win was in trouble. Apparently Win was here in New York and she'd gotten involved in something terrible. What had she witnessed? She'd talked about what had happened to her in Stockholm, but he'd thought that had been a random street crime.

What if someone was trying to hurt Win? He hadn't replied to her texts. She likely thought she was all alone. She hadn't called him. She'd called David. How the hell had she gotten David's number?

"It's not a joke. I'll fill you in when you get here," David was saying. "I have to go. Hurry."

"No. Don't you hang up on me."

But the line had gone dead.

He tried to get him back, but his call went straight to voice mail. He tried Win's number. Again, voice mail.

What the hell was going on?

He dressed as quickly as he could. He could walk to the station. Avoid the traffic. The Twentieth served the Upper West Side. He lived in the neighborhood. Had Win been coming to look for him?

Had something happened to her while she was trying to find him? But there weren't any phone calls. She had his number.

Nothing made sense.

His cell trilled again. He grimaced. Alicia. What the hell could she want?

He was irritated enough to answer. "I thought we agreed to never speak again. I'm sorry, but you decided to drunk dial your ex at the wrong time. Don't call me again. I have work to do."

A sigh came over the line. "Thank god. I thought you would leave that poor girl to rot. It's a nightmare over here. They've got us all locked up in the library, and they're insisting we stay and give statements. I don't know a lawyer in New York. I know you hate me, but I don't think I should say anything without a lawyer present."

It was turning into a surreal night. He kind of wondered if he was still asleep and this was all some kind of anxiety dream. "What are you talking about?"

"Brie Westerhaven's murder," she replied. "I'm at the party where she was killed. I watched them arrest Taylor Winston-Hughes. It's ridiculous. There's no way she killed anyone. You have to get to the station and help her, but please tell your friend to rep me. I saw David here earlier. Isn't that woman he was with a lawyer, too? She's here somewhere, but I can't find her. I think she's talking to Bellamy Hughes. Can you send someone? Please, Henry. It wasn't all bad. And I did what you asked me to a couple of weeks ago."

"Oh, gee, darling, thanks. I don't think you did that out of the kindness of your heart. You stopped spreading lies about me because my new law partner has contacts that could ruin your career." He picked up his wallet. He wasn't sure what was going on, but it looked like when it rained, it poured. Something had happened with Win, and it unluckily enough coincided with some famous person getting killed. At least he understood why there was a traffic jam. He was sure the reporters were everywhere. "Now explain why

I give a shit about you being at a party where someone I don't care about was murdered. I already got a call from David. If this is his way of getting us in the spotlight for representing some dumbass actress who got pissed another actress got her part, then I'm going back to bed."

What did Win have to do with any of this? Had she been working the party? Was it a fund-raiser for one of her causes? That would explain a lot.

There was silence for a second, and Henry thought about hanging up on her.

"Oh my god, Henry. You don't know who she is. She didn't tell you. Well, I did not suspect that."

A nasty thought twisted in his gut. He reached for the remote and flipped the television on to the twenty-four-hour news channel. If this was as big a story as Alicia made it out to be, there should already be news coverage. That was the joy of living in the city. No one had to wait for the press. The press was everywhere. They could mobilize in moments if the story happened in Manhattan. "Why don't you tell me who you're talking about, Alicia?"

There it was. The headline rushing across the screen was "Billion-Dollar Baby Accused of Murder." The picture showed a perfectly done up reporter standing outside one of the most expensive buildings on the Upper West Side. It wasn't that far from his own.

"I'm talking about Taylor Winston-Hughes," Alicia said, her voice calm. He thought of that particular tone as her "loving shrink" voice since she always used it to convey caring and understanding. "I know about your affair with her. A few days ago, Brie Westerhaven called me."

"The victim?" If Alicia had talked with the victim, then maybe she wasn't being overly dramatic.

"Yes, I know her father better than I know her, but I've come in contact with her enough that she has my number. She called on the grounds that she wanted me to know that she had an audition for a movie I'm doing and she would love my support. Normal actress shit. But at the end of the call, she said she had a little gossip for me that she thought I should hear before it hit the press. Brie told me that you were seeing Taylor Winston-Hughes. She stayed with you while you were on Martha's Vineyard. I know why you were there and I feel bad about it. That wasn't well-done of me, Henry. I was upset at the time, and I shouldn't have forced you to sell it."

He didn't give a damn about the house at that moment. No. He was far too angry about something else.

The reporter threw it back to the station, and they began running footage of a lovely blonde being carted out in handcuffs. She was wearing clean clothes, but there was blood in her hair. Dirty, mud-colored, but he knew what it was that marred her honey-blond hair.

Her eyes turned up and there was a hollow look there.

There was no doubt about who she was. Oh, she wore more makeup than he'd seen her in, and her hair—blood aside—had been expertly done, but it was Win.

His Win.

"Henry, are you there? They want to talk to me. The police, that is." Her voice went low. "Henry, I know Taylor and Brie fought earlier this evening. Should I say something about that? Do I have to? I don't want to make it sound like I think Taylor did it. I don't think she's capable of violence."

Oh, but she was capable of lying. Of deceit. Of betrayal.

Fuck. Fuck and fucking fuck. He took a deep breath. "I'll have Margarita find you, or I'll send Noah down. Don't say a thing until you've got one of those two at your side. Do you understand?"

Her relief came in loud and clear over the line. "Thank you. Thank you so much, Henry. And don't—"

He hung up. He dialed Margarita's number, and she picked up immediately.

"Henry? Are you at the police station yet? Have you seen her?"

So everyone knew but him. Nice. It was always good to be the last one to know. "I'm at home, taking in the fact that the lovely young woman I recently spent time with turns out to be a liar and a potential killer."

"I told David you didn't know." Her voice had gone low. She wouldn't want anyone listening in. "I told him he needed to handle this carefully. Tell me he didn't just call you down to the station."

Henry was sure David had meant well. Or David had realized getting him to the station could be rough if Henry had known who his lover had turned out to be. "It doesn't matter. I need you to find someone to rep Alicia. I know there's got to be twenty lawyers at that thing. Not you. I don't want her even associated with this firm, but she needs someone decent. Apparently she knows far more about what was going on between the accused and the victim than the police know at this point. Find someone to babysit her and make sure she doesn't turn this into one of her badly written scripts."

Margarita groaned. "Fine. I'll talk to Howard Klein. I saw him a few minutes ago. I wasn't going to let her talk to the cops alone anyway. They're being surprisingly nasty, by the way. I tried to get them to take Win out through a back way, but they paraded her right by the press. I think they're trying to use her to make themselves look good."

"Ms. Winston-Hughes, please." At least he knew where she'd gotten Win. It was a less ostentatious name than her real one. Taylor Winston-Hughes. She sounded exactly like the kind of woman he avoided. "Call the client—if she is the client—by her name."

"I've already told her uncle we would take the case."

"Then you can explain to him that you are not the senior partner and you don't manage this firm."

She was quiet for a moment and he could practically see her

standing there, trying to figure out how to handle him. "Henry, she's in trouble. She needs representation."

The trouble was he didn't want to be handled right now. Not by anyone. "And I'm sure she can find it. It appears she can certainly afford it." He stared at the screen in front of him. It was now showing pictures of the victim with Win, except this was a Win he'd never seen before. Her hair was dyed a platinum color that didn't suit her at all and she was far too thin. Scary thin. She was dressed in cutting-edge fashions and leaned into the dark-haired woman as though they'd practiced the pose.

The young woman on the screen had none of his Win's vibrant life in her eyes. She was pretty enough, but her skin was sallow, her body seeming to shrink in on itself.

This was Win before.

Who the fuck was she now? Besides a liar. Besides someone who had used him.

"Are you seriously going to let this case get by you?" Margarita asked. "Are you going to let her rot in jail when you're the one person who has a shot at getting her out? They found her covered in Brie Westerhaven's blood. The victim was murdered with Win . . . Taylor Winston-Hughes's letter opener. You can bet they'll get prints off it. Come on, Henry."

"Don't be so dramatic." He wasn't going to go back to bed. Not when he could confront the woman of his dreams and let her know she'd become a nightmare. Besides, Margarita was right. Taylor Winston-Hughes could pay and pay well. Representing her would likely put him and the firm back on the map. "You know any decent attorney would plead it out. It's likely her first offense, though for all I know she kills her friends all the time."

"She won't accept a plea." Margarita sounded serious. "I think she's innocent. You know they're going to tear her apart in the press.

They won't be able to seat a jury after all the coverage and the way the cops perp-walked her."

Could he let that chance go because he'd been a dumb shit and had terrible taste in women? Margarita was right. This would be the biggest case of the year. It would be complex and the strategy would be about so much more than merely the evidence.

"I'm leaving right now. Get Noah down there to help watch the cops and have him talk to the DA when he gets there. Believe me, the DA's going to be there for this one." It was going to be a major case, one that would keep the press fed for months, potentially years. "Tell the DA I'll call him in the morning and that I expect to have my client out on bail as soon as possible. If not, and he wants to play around, I'll go to the press."

It would be an intricate game. The DA would want to appear competent and thorough, and Henry would do his best to make the prosecutors look like they were bumbling fools intent on wrecking reputations because they couldn't solve a case to save their lives. He was already thinking about how he could make Taylor Winston-Hughes into a martyr of some kind. "Call me if you need anything."

He hung up with Margarita and sat down on the bed, unable to take his eyes off the girl on the TV screen.

It was Win and yet not.

Win had been a figment of his imagination. The young woman who made her "living" showing the world how rich and stupid she was on television was the real woman.

And she might have killed her friend.

Fuck, but he needed a drink. It was always there, but sometimes the need rushed up like a damn tidal wave. A drink would settle him. It would make him feel more powerful than he really was. A drink would relax him and he would think better.

Win had done that for him, too. Win had done all those things, and just like the fucking alcohol, she'd turned out to be one more addiction he couldn't afford.

He would settle for work. He stood in front of the mirror, making sure he looked perfect.

After all, if the Monster of Manhattan was back, the least he could do was look good.

~

The light made her head hurt, but then pretty much everything made her head hurt. She wanted to rub the back of her head, but her hands were still cuffed in front of her. They'd taken the cuffs off when they'd fingerprinted her but snapped them back on afterward, saying something about how dangerous those claws of hers obviously were.

She was still trying to figure out exactly what had happened. She glanced around the room. It was gray and utilitarian, with a mirror across from her. There was nothing else but a table and two metal chairs.

Win felt woozy, but a bit better now that she was sitting down. She'd thought she was going to pass out when they'd forced her through the booking procedure.

"You are going to have a lot of fun in lockup." The officer who had arrested her had handed her off to this man. She would guess his age at somewhere in the early fifties, and that he would be perfectly comfortable playing the bad cop.

She had yet to meet the good one.

"I would like to use my phone call. I need to call my uncle."

He pulled up a chair and sat down, the legs scraping across the linoleum in a way that made her ears hurt. "Your uncle already knows you're here. After all, you just murdered a girl in his house. I think he's aware of where you are."

"I didn't kill Brie." God, how was she saying the words? They didn't make sense. Brie couldn't be dead.

Why couldn't she remember what had happened? It was all fuzzy. The whole evening wasn't lost, but she couldn't remember those few moments. She'd walked into her room and then she remembered waking up and being covered in blood and then someone was screaming.

She'd been screaming. She'd looked down and seen the blank look on Brie's face and she'd screamed and screamed.

It was all so foggy. Her uncle had been there and then the police. They'd taken her clothes. A woman had come to help with that. Two, actually. One had been a police officer who had taken her clothes into evidence. She'd watched Win with a stern eye and let her know she didn't care how uncomfortable she was. She had wanted every piece of clothing, down to her underwear and her bra. The other lady had been kinder. She'd argued with the cop and watched carefully as they'd taken pictures of Win's body. They'd been concerned about a cut on her left hand. She'd tried to explain that she'd done that earlier in the evening when she'd helped open a crate of champagne. The caterers had been a little shorthanded.

Win was fairly certain they didn't believe her.

She kind of wished the other lady had come with her. Margarita? Or was that the name of the person her uncle had been meeting? She wasn't sure, but that name seemed right. Margarita had been extremely upset that the police wouldn't take her out the back way.

There had been all those lights and people screaming questions. Too many cameras. How had they gotten there so fast?

There was something she was supposed to ask for, but she couldn't remember what it was. Her head was killing her. Had she hit it? "Can I have some aspirin?"

"Sure, sweetheart. I'll get you all you like after you tell me how you killed Brie Westerhaven." He looked perfectly calm. Like he could stay here all night. "Once you explain what happened, you'll be able to get some aspirin and something to drink, if you like. You'll be able to rest, Taylor. Aren't you tired?"

She shook her head and then realized what a mistake that was. Nausea threatened to take over. *Don't move. Stay calm.* "I didn't kill Brie. I was looking for her. She was supposed to be at the party, but when I couldn't find her, I went to my room."

"You left the party to look for Miss Westerhaven?"

She started to nod and stopped, the nausea tuning up again. It was the truth. She'd gone looking for Brie because she'd found out all the crap Brie had been talking about her. "I did."

"Did Miss Westerhaven usually leave parties to go into the host's or hostess's private rooms?"

"Brie did a lot of things she probably shouldn't have." There had been something else. Something about Trevor. Trevor had been with Brie while she'd been filming. It had been exactly like her best friend to use her worst enemy to get what she wanted.

"That must have made you angry."

Had she been angry? Or disappointed? "She knew her way around my uncle's place. She's been there many times. We grew up together. When I was home, I lived at the penthouse. Brie would sometimes spend summers with me. She felt comfortable there. It's not surprising she would go to my room."

"Why were you looking for her?"

Her ears started ringing. It was brief but enough to make her head ache again. "I don't feel good."

"Did you slip when you were fighting Brie?" His voice had gone quiet, almost sympathetic. "Did you hit your head? Or did she strike you during the altercation?"

She was almost certain she had hit her head on something. Or someone had hit her. Had there been someone else there? Someone behind her? She couldn't remember. "I slipped."

He picked up his pen. "Was that before or after you fought with Brie?"

She had fought with Brie, but it hadn't been physical. Why did he keep trying to get her to admit to something she hadn't done?

He leaned in, his voice going low and soothing. "Maybe Brie started the fight. Taylor, you need to tell the truth. If she was doing something bad, maybe you tried to stop her. Maybe this was self-defense, but before we can investigate anything, you have to admit that you killed her."

Lawyer. She needed a lawyer. That's what the lady back at the penthouse had been. She'd been a lawyer.

Like Henry. She wanted Henry. She wanted him to walk through the door and put his arms around her and let her know everything would be okay.

This was a dream. A nightmare. She would wake up and be back in the little bungalow on the island. She would turn over and Henry would kiss her and make love to her and she would be all right. This time she would do what she should have in the first place. She would tell him she didn't want to leave him. She would ask him to rethink his plans to stay in touch. They could spend weekends together. She would explain her situation and that she could afford to fly into New York whenever she wanted to.

If only she would wake up.

"Taylor, I asked you a question. If you don't want to talk right now, I can take you to a cell. I think you'll find a lot of lovely people to talk to in there. We can take this up again in the morning after you've had some time to think about cooperating."

She hadn't been in a cell yet. Somehow she didn't think it would be a pleasant experience.

"I want to talk to my lawyer. I need a lawyer." She forced the words out. She was making a mistake by talking to the police by herself. They didn't believe her. They wanted her to confess to something she hadn't done.

She had to try to come out of this fog and start thinking.

His chair slid back, but before he could get a hand on her, the door came open.

"Detective, step back. My client asked for a lawyer. Unless you want to give me a reason to go to a judge tonight, I suggest you step away and allow my client to speak with her attorneys."

She gasped because she'd met this man before. David. Henry's partner. Why was he here? He was a big presence as he pressed through the door. Even though it was long after midnight, he was wearing a tuxedo, though he'd pulled the tie loose.

He looked like he'd come from a party. Had he been at her party?

Nothing made sense. Her head hurt so much.

The detective sighed and shook his head, looking back to her. "He can't save you. Admit what happened. This is going to go better for you if you leave the lawyers out. Tell us what you did, and maybe, just maybe, we can make a deal. You let a few days go by and there won't be a deal to be had."

A familiar voice caught her attention. "Detective, you've made your point clear. Now allow me to make mine. My client has invoked her right to counsel. Leave the room and turn off any cameras or devices you have recording. Understand that if I find out you've violated attorney-client privilege, I will have your job and your pension. Do I make myself clear?"

Henry. Oh god, Henry was here and her whole soul seemed to come back to life. Henry was here. He'd come to help her. He was dressed in a perfectly tailored suit and looked like power and authority and safety.

He was here.

The detective sneered Henry's way. "Yeah, I get it." He turned back to Win. "You need to understand that he can't save you. Once this evidence is processed, you'll be going to jail, little girl. You're going there tonight because no judge in the world is going to save you. Your privilege is over."

"Could we get the handcuffs off her?" David asked. "She's not running and she's not violent."

"The dead body in her bedroom tells me something different, Counselor," the detective replied.

"I would like to be alone with my client, Detective," Henry said, his teeth clenched.

She couldn't take her eyes off him. He was so big and strong. When he'd held her, she'd been safe and now he was here. She felt terrible, but it was okay because Henry was here and everything was going to be all right.

The detective turned and walked to the door. "You don't have all night. She's not going anywhere. There won't be a bail hearing for a while, so prepare your client for a nice long weekend. She's going to do well in the holding pen. Or hell, maybe we'll move her for a few days. Let her see how the other half lives."

The door closed behind him, and she was left alone with Henry and David.

"Henry?"

He turned to her, his eyes cold as ice. His suit was designer, custom-fit to his strong body. The shoes he was wearing had to cost a thousand dollars a pair. This wasn't the laid-back beach boy she remembered. This man was a professional. "Please call me Mr. Garrison. I'll call you Ms. Winston-Hughes, unless you prefer Taylor. No? Excellent. Ms. Winston-Hughes, your uncle has hired my firm to represent you in this case. Do you understand the charges against you?"

She kind of understood what the words meant, but there was still such confusion. He was so cold. And he knew her real name. He'd never called her anything but Win. People she didn't trust called her Taylor. Taylor was a different person. Taylor was a person she'd thought she'd left behind.

"Henry, I'm sorry. I didn't tell you about my family because they don't matter. I'm my own person," she said.

David sat down in front of her. "Hey, are you all right? You look very pale."

He'd asked a question. She was trying hard to concentrate. It was okay to answer these questions because they were lawyers. "My head hurts but they wouldn't give me anything for it."

"How much did you have to drink tonight?" Henry loomed over her.

There was so much judgment in that one question. "I had a glass of white wine a couple of hours ago. That's all I had this evening."

Henry stared down at her. "Funny. You look drunk. Your eyes aren't focused and you're slurring some of your words."

She felt woozy, but it couldn't be from booze. "I'm not drunk."

His lips curled up but there was nothing humorous about his smile. "Do you think I don't know a drunk when I see one? I would think you would remember. I told you a lot about me. Trust me. I know when a lady's had a little too much. Do you drink this way often? How often do you black out?"

Frustration welled inside her. Why wasn't he listening to her? "I am not drunk."

"Ms. Winston-Hughes, please don't think I'm asking because I'm worried or I care. I need to know because it could affect your case. Did they give you a sobriety test?" Henry asked. "Because the last thing we need is to have your blood alcohol level plastered all over the press."

"Henry, maybe you were right," David said, his eyes narrowed. "Maybe I should handle this one. Let me talk to her for a couple of minutes. You can wait outside."

"You're not the expert when it comes to getting privileged little debutantes out of jail," Henry replied, every word a bullet that peppered her skin. "I am. It's why you wanted me to take this case in the first place. You got what you wanted. Now deal with it."

"I didn't do it." That should be clear to him. How could he question that? He couldn't think she'd killed her best friend.

"I don't care," he replied.

"Henry, I didn't hurt anyone. You have to know that."

"Why would I know that? I have no idea who you are," he replied with ruthless candor. "Right now you're Taylor Winston-Hughes. You're a client and I need to know everything that happened tonight that could possibly lead the police to conclude you murdered the victim. They have to have found compelling evidence or they wouldn't have arrested you at the scene. The one thing I do not need to hear is whether or not you actually did it. Keep that knowledge to yourself."

"I'm innocent." The room was starting to spin a little.

"Again, I don't care."

How was this the same man she'd made love to? She'd known he would be upset with her, but she'd thought she could explain why she hadn't come out and been totally honest about her family. She'd thought they would have a few uncomfortable moments, but then he would understand.

He didn't care.

He didn't care that she was innocent. He didn't care that she could explain.

He didn't care about her.

That was why he hadn't texted her back, hadn't asked her to come visit him in New York. She'd fooled herself into thinking that he simply needed time, but he'd had all the time he'd wanted with her. He was done.

So why was he here?

Money. He was here because a case like this would likely be worth a lot of money.

"Start at the beginning. David, take notes." Henry began pacing. "You were the hostess for a gala, I take it. The killing took place at the after-party, but let's start with this morning. What did you do today? What does a hostess do? You can skip the parts where you get your hair and nails done, unless you and Miss Westerhaven were fighting over a hairdresser."

"Henry," David said, warning in his tone.

"I've seen it happen. These Hollywood types are damn serious about their hair and nails," Henry remarked.

He didn't see her as anything but a bimbo. Maybe he'd never seen her as anything beyond an easy lay. She'd fallen into bed with him fast enough. What man wouldn't take what she'd offered for a few weeks?

He wasn't different from the other men she'd known. He'd simply been better about hiding it.

"I think I would like a different lawyer," she said quietly. She wasn't sure she could take his rancor.

He rolled those gorgeous eyes of his. "Thank god. I can leave in good conscience. Good luck, Ms. Winston-Hughes. You're going to need it."

David stood up. "Are you fucking kidding me? You're going to leave her here? They mean to throw her in jail and not request a bond hearing until Monday."

Henry pointed her way. "You heard her. She wants another lawyer."

"Getting her another lawyer could take days," David insisted. "They're talking about locking her up over the weekend. How do you think she's going to fare in prison?"

Henry shrugged as if the answer meant nothing to him. "She'll probably find some nice lady to protect her. She's good at looking vulnerable. Find a nice prison wife, Taylor. You know how to keep a man occupied. I'm sure it won't be any different with another woman."

Her stomach rolled. David was saying something to Henry, but it didn't matter. She had to get to a trash can. There was one in the corner and she barely made it before she was sick.

So sick. Her vision blurred.

"Holy shit." Henry had dropped to his knees beside her. His hands were the only things holding her up. One arm was around her torso, and the other touched a place at the back of her head that made her moan in pain.

"Stop it. Don't touch it," she pleaded.

"David, get someone in here. She's got a massive contusion on the back of her head. It's covered by her hair, but the police should have damn well caught it."

She tried to push him away. She didn't want his help. He was a nasty, cold man. It had been stupid to think he could care about her.

"Stop it, Win." It was the first time he'd said her real name. It was the first time he'd sounded like the old Henry. "You've probably got a concussion. David's getting someone to help you. We'll get you to a hospital. And I'll get those damn cuffs off you."

She was shaky. Everything was cold, but he was warm. "It hurts."

He stood up, lifting her. "Yeah, it really fucking hurts, Win."

She was fairly certain he wasn't talking about her concussion, but the world blinked out for the second time.

At least this time she was safe in his arms.

EIGHT

Henry stared at the doctor and nodded. He did understand what he'd been told, but he felt numb. That was a good thing because there had been a few moments when the numbness had been stripped away and he'd worried she was going to die right there in his arms.

Now he stood in the hallway outside her hospital room, and the blessed numbness seemed to have taken over again.

The wound had been hidden by her hair, all the more dangerous because it had caved in instead of swelling out. The police had missed it, and no EMT had looked her over because she'd insisted she was fine and the police had been eager to get a confession out of her.

It had been a rough time getting her into an ambulance, the police insisting on escorting them every inch of the way, as though she could run away when she had a concussion and possible skull fracture. They'd refused to take her cuffs off. She was handcuffed to her hospital bed, an armed guard on her door with instructions that she could see no one but immediate family and her attorneys.

He'd been forced to catch a cab to the hospital. The look in her eyes as he'd left her still haunted him.

The doctor stood in front of Henry, looking over the chart in his hands. "She's responding well to the medication I gave her, but she still needs rest. The swelling is already coming down. She'll be fine, but her brain took a beating."

Yes, and that was a mystery he needed to solve. Had she been in a fight with Brie Westerhaven? "She thinks she fell and hit her head. That's what she told me while we were waiting for the ambulance."

The doctor frowned. "That wouldn't be my call on an injury like this. It looks more like blunt-force trauma to me, Mr. Garrison. I'll have the x-rays and photos sent to your office, but my feeling is this was done with something strong and slender. Something cylindrical, if that makes sense. Her skull looks like someone pressed a bar across it. And by pressed I mean struck with strong force. I would bet she was turning at the time, which is why she didn't take the blow straight to the back of her head. If that had happened, well, it could have been a killing blow."

That thought did nothing to settle his stomach. "You think it was a baton or something?"

"It's slender but that's definitely the shape I see . . . A fireplace tool, perhaps. The injury is consistent with the force hitting her, not the other way around."

So she'd been in a fight. His stomach threatened to turn. No matter what he'd said to her before, he was sick at the thought of her being in jail. He was stupid. So fucking stupid. She'd lied and betrayed him, and he couldn't stand the thought of her spending a single minute in jail. But the evidence was starting to stack up. She'd been found with the body. She'd been in a fight. Maybe it had been self-defense. He could work with that. "You think someone hit her."

"That would be my conclusion, but I'm sure you can find some forensic experts to make a case."

Unfortunately, there was always an expert somewhere willing to make whatever case a lawyer needed. They could take the thinnest of evidence and weave a tale. Often in court it was the battle to find the expert who was most relatable to the jury.

Still, it was a place to start, since it didn't look like Win would be explaining anything in the next few hours. The doctor had been firm about not forcing her memory while her brain was healing. She was supposed to rest. Because of the brain injury, she might never remember how she'd gotten hurt.

What would happen to her if he couldn't keep her out of jail? They might keep her in the infirmary for a day or two, but once she was out with the general population, anything could happen.

"I appreciate you keeping her overnight."

The doctor held out his hand. "Anything for that girl. She's responsible for a lot of good in the New York medical community. Everyone knows if you've got a sad story about your promising research or you need some cash to keep your clinic open, you go to Win Hughes. Her mother was active in helping the sick, and Win started following in her footsteps at a young age. I'll let the detective know she needs to stay here for a while and that any subsequent injury could prove deadly."

At least he had one ally. He would haul the doctor into court if it meant keeping Win out of jail. "She raises a lot of money for the hospital, huh?"

He placed the chart under his arm. "She's good at that but she donates her time, too. Whenever she's in the city, she comes up and brings presents for the children. She negotiates with some of the famous people she knows to bring them in and cheer up patients. Hell, when she was a teenager, she was the best candy striper we had."

Why had a debutante wanted to change bedpans? "You know her personally?"

The doctor was likely in his midfifties. Not the type he would expect a young reality TV star to hang around. "I've met her before, but we're not close. I respect the hell out of her though. Going through what she went through and coming out on the other side healthy isn't easy. I'll talk to her uncle because she needs someone to make sure she stays on track."

"On track?"

"With her eating. I'm sorry. I thought that was common knowledge." The doctor flushed as if he were embarrassed.

"I know she's been treated for anorexia," Henry assured him. "Is there something we should watch for?"

"Sometimes when traumatic things happen to a person with an eating disorder, it can lead to a regressive period," the doctor explained. "She can feel out of control and need to be in charge of the one thing she *can* take control of."

It was odd to think of the Win he knew as that shadow they'd shown on TV. The morning shows had been playing the story incessantly, and they'd used photos of Win at the height of her reality show success. Pictures of a haunted girl, one a stiff wind would have blown away. One who had nearly lost her life trying to fit in.

What had she said to him? *Alcohol isn't the only thing a person can get addicted to. Sometimes a person can get addicted to hurting herself.*

Would she go back to that comfortable denial if she found herself in a place like prison?

"And what happens if they won't grant her bail? Can you write up orders to ensure she eats?"

The doctor frowned. "I can ask for a psych evaluation but she's at a healthy weight right now. They won't do anything until she's already in too deep. I would keep her out of jail, Counselor. I think it

could kill her and that would be a shame. Call me if you need anything. I think I can convince the police to let her stay another night,
but then they'll want her in their infirmary."

Where they would make the decisions.

He thanked the doctor as David stepped up, Margarita at his
side. She was still dressed in her cocktail gown, looking lovely in
four-inch heels. How she managed to look like she'd just gotten
dressed he had no idea, especially when David looked like hell.

"Noah is trying to find a judge willing to set bail on the grounds
that she's far too sick to be in prison. I told him we're willing to give
up her passport and have her wear an ankle monitor," David explained with a yawn.

"She won't like it, but it's our best bet." Margarita glanced down
at her phone. "And I think David should make the argument. He's
the one with the most traumatic brain injuries."

"Gee, thanks," David said with a shake of his head, but he didn't
bother to hide his smile.

A flare of victory went across Margarita's face. "Yes. Noah managed to get Judge Davis to agree to an emergency bond hearing
tomorrow morning. He's a huge NFL fan."

"But he's also known to take a hard stance on accused murder-
ers," David murmured.

"We're going to twist this. We don't know everything that's gone
on, but Taylor Winston-Hughes is a victim. First someone tried to
kill her by striking her in the head with a blunt object, and then she
was victimized again by a police detective who was far too eager to
close a case without even investigating the facts. All we request is
that our client be given a chance to recover in her home under the
watchful eye of her uncle and her family. I'll put the monitor on her
myself if I have to." At least then he would know where she was at
all times.

"It's still not a knockout," David said. "But this is the first time she's been in trouble, and it's not like she can walk around in public. I'm worried about her going home, actually. There's already a huge memorial to Brie Westerhaven outside her building, and there are some crazy fans out there who are vowing to get back at her."

They could use that, too. Her celebrity could be used. She was in danger because of it. It would be difficult to control her health issues in prison. Did the police really want to have to deal with all the time and cost it would take to protect her when she could sit quietly and wait for her trial?

Of course, he might be able to keep her from going to jail now, but if he couldn't start building a case, she might end up there anyway. The news shows had gone wild, like predators thrown a bunch of red meat. The theories he'd seen this morning had run from mild—an accident had happened while both women were intoxicated—to the truly wild—Taylor was in love with her best friend and jealous that she might have started seeing someone else.

It would rage like this for weeks. How would she handle the scrutiny? She would be picked apart by a pack of hyenas, every fact of her life pulled apart like puzzle pieces that wouldn't fit back together after they were done. Someone would have to watch her to make sure she didn't read her own likely traumatic press.

Luckily, it wouldn't be up to him to take care of her. That's what she had an incredibly wealthy family for.

A family who'd allowed her to fall in with a crowd of people whose lifestyles had sent her to the hospital. A crowd of people who were turning their backs on her today.

He'd already seen the interviews given by her so-called friends. Several of them had gone on to explain that Taylor had always been jealous of Brie's vibrant personality. They talked about how fragile Taylor was and hinted that she couldn't handle pressure.

Not one of them talked about how kind and loving she could be, how when she smiled the world was suddenly a brighter place.

Henry squashed those thoughts. They would bring him nowhere good. "We have to have a solid plan in place to keep her safe and in the city for the judge to go along with it. Margarita, get the McKay-Taggart boys on the phone and have them send up two bodyguards. They can take shifts watching over her and coordinating with her building's security. I also want a team up here. We don't have an investigator on the payroll yet. I need dossiers on every single person who was in that building last night, and I want someone to examine all the security footage."

David's mouth thinned, and Henry knew whatever was coming out next wouldn't be something he would like. "They turned off the security cameras. Bellamy Hughes told me it was standard for parties with such high-level guests. We've got a list of everyone who came to the party, but there's no way for us to track the guests once they entered the building. We'll have to go on witness testimony as to where everyone was at what time."

That was bad, bad news for them. "And how many guests were there?"

Margarita winced. "As far as I can track, there were sixty-one guests there at the time of the murder. There were also twenty employees working the party."

His head was starting to hurt. "We have to talk to every single one of them. And again, we need dossiers on each one. I need someone to look into anyone else in that room who might have had reason to murder Brie Westerhaven."

"Good luck with that." Bellamy Hughes strode in wearing a designer suit that he obviously hadn't been in for twelve hours. He looked surprisingly well rested for a man whose family was in turmoil. "She wasn't the most pleasant of young ladies. I believe you'll find one of Brie's hobbies was starting feuds with the people around her for sport. You'll have no lack of suspects."

"Brie could be a bitch, but that doesn't mean she deserved to die." Trevor Hughes walked in beside his father. He looked more like Henry felt. The younger Hughes's eyes were rimmed with red, his shoulders slumped, as though he hadn't slept at all. "I've already given my statement to the police. I saw Brie and Win fight not an hour before Brie wound up dead. Win was angry because Brie and I were getting close. Brie was done with her. Win always was a jealous bitch."

"I wish you'd talked to me before giving that statement," Henry said before turning to Bellamy Hughes. "Do we have a problem?"

Bellamy shook his head. "We do not. I expect you to get Trevor's statements thrown out. He was drunk that night. He's always drunk. He doesn't know what he was talking about. After all, Alicia Kingman confirmed that she saw nothing out of the ordinary between Brie and Win."

Good old Alicia. She really could act. "Even with someone backing up Win's story, her own cousin testifying that he witnessed a fight between the two of them isn't going to help."

Bellamy turned to his son. "He would like to clarify his statement."

Trevor sighed and rolled his eyes. "Well, it wasn't like they were catfighting. Win was upset because I went on her old show and cleaned up her mess. She left the show without any kind of warning. I was going on to explain that she got sick and wouldn't be back. That was all."

"So she wanted her privacy and you wouldn't give it to her. Win was upset with you," David pointed out.

"Maybe, but Brie was the one who invited me on the show," Trevor admitted. "She was always looking to get under Win's skin. They were superclose when they were kids, but Brie always had to be in the spotlight. She had to be in control. When Win left the show, it threw Brie off. She doesn't like people walking away from her. She prefers to be the one to cut the friendship off."

"That sounds more like a reason for Brie to be upset with Win." Henry didn't like the fact that Win's cousin was so quick to throw Win under the bus. "I think we should definitely clarify his statement. The prosecution could come back with his original statement, but we can work around it if we can control what comes out of his mouth."

"He'll do as I say or he'll find himself on the street without a dime to his name," Bellamy threatened.

Trevor shook his head. "Of course I will, Father. You know me. Can't possibly survive on my own. I'll go tell my sweet cousin that she wins again."

He turned and strode toward Win's room. He was stopped by the officer there and forced to show ID before being allowed in.

So her family was wealthy and nasty. It shouldn't surprise him.

"Mr. Hughes, I'm going to need to assign bodyguards to Win once I get her out on bail," Henry said.

"Bodyguards?" Hughes looked a bit confused at the idea.

"There is a small but fervent group of Brie Westerhaven's fans that we're worried might try to hurt your niece," Margarita explained. "The show Brie was on was popular, and there are some fans who are far too invested in her life. There have already been a few death threats."

Henry had been monitoring Brie's social media. It appeared that Win had taken all of her personal social media down, but there was already a new page for her calling her Taylor Murderer Winston-Hughes. "We're looking into the situation, and we'll try to have anything incendiary investigated thoroughly. Having bodyguards will also help the judge see that we're serious about keeping her safe and in the city. She'll need someone with her."

Bellamy looked a little shocked by the death threats, but he seemed to shake it off. "Trevor will have to do. Her old nanny would come up but she broke her hip two days ago. She's staying in an assisted living facility while she rehabs. Hire whomever you need. I want my niece well taken care of. She's important to me."

"If she's important to you, then you should take care of her," Margarita pointed out.

"I can't and honestly, I'm not good at taking care of anyone. I'm better at taking care of the company that pays for everything. I'm leaving for Los Angeles in two hours. I have to get in front of the board of the company and assure them that Win's current status shouldn't affect the daily operations of the business. I'll likely need to stay a few weeks," he explained in a purely logical tone. "Of course, I've assured the detectives that I can be back here in New York at any time they need me. The same goes for you."

"Your niece is in serious trouble," David said, shock obvious in his tone. "How can you leave the city? If she doesn't have family support, we might not be able to get her out on bail."

Bellamy waved off that worry. "You'll get her out because that's what I pay you to do. I have a business to run and I won't be able to continue to pay for Win's incredibly expensive lawyers if that business loses profitability because of my niece's scandal. I have to deal with the real world, and her shenanigans could hurt our stock."

"Shenanigans? You call murder 'shenanigans'?" He shouldn't be shocked, but it was there. Maybe he'd been out of the game for too long. Or maybe the softness of the island and his childhood home and being with the Win he'd thought she'd been had changed him in some way.

Hughes simply straightened his suit coat. "I will call that ridiculous press coverage and the crowd that's forming outside whatever I like. I don't know what happened last night, but I know Brie has been pissing people off since she was a child. She was a desperate little girl who couldn't hold on to her fame and fortune, and she started looking for other ways to make a buck. Her own father cut her off six months ago because he found out she was the one leaking gossip about his new wife to the press. So this is all ridiculous and inevitable. That girl was going to wind up overdosing or being killed by one of her many victims."

"If you know of anyone else she was working with the press on stories about, I would love some names," Margarita requested.

"Like I said, she couldn't keep her mouth shut for her own father's sake. I would certainly look into those idiot boys she ran around with. Hoover and Kipton," Bellamy replied. "And everyone on that damn show of hers."

"What about you, Mr. Hughes?" Henry had to ask the question. There was a bitterness to Bellamy's tone that made Henry think this was personal.

Bellamy Hughes gave him a look that likely would have sent all his employees scrambling for cover. Luckily, Henry didn't intimidate easily.

"It's a fair question." He wasn't going to back down. "Where were you at the time of the murder? Were you one of those people Brie tried to use?"

Bellamy's lips curled in a smirk. "I was with your colleague."

Margarita nodded. "He was. He had just found me and asked me to come into his office for a chat when we heard the scream."

As alibis went it was a pretty good one. "And Trevor?"

"You'll have to ask my son, but know I can't conceive of a world where Trevor is smart enough to pull off a murder and pin it on someone else. He uses far too much cocaine to remember what his plans are at any point in time," Bellamy replied. "My son is an idiot who can't get his head out of his ass long enough to come up with a single original idea. Win is truly the only one in the family with any redeeming qualities, and now she's fucked up her future. I told her those friends of hers would bring her down and now they have. But she made that bed and she'll have to lie in it. I have a duty to our company."

"You have a duty to your niece."

"Yes, I do, and preserving the company her parents built from the ground up is my duty. What do you want me to do, Garrison? Hold her hand?"

"How about getting out there and telling people you stand behind her."

Bellamy shook his head. "That could hurt our stock. I'm staying in the background. Hopefully the company can stay out of the headlines that way. I know they'll mention she's an heiress, but in this case her stint on that dumb television show will be more interesting to the reporters. And I'm supporting her by paying your salary."

"It sounds to me like she's the one paying *your* salary," Henry shot back. "When does she come into her trust fund? When does the control of the company switch over to her?"

What would that mean to a man who was obviously serious about his job? He'd had to save the company after Win's parents had died. He'd been leading it for years and years. Would he want to turn it all over to his niece? Or would he fight her? Would he do whatever he could to ensure that she couldn't take his power away?

Putting her in jail might be a good way to do it. Henry would have to look into what would happen to the company and Win's inheritance if she were to be incarcerated.

Hughes's brows rose. "When Winnie turns thirty, she will have access to her trust, though I've never once in her life held money back from her. Not once. I've always known that I'm here to serve the company until Win could take over. It turns out Win has no interest in the company. That means it's my job to hold it for her children, which she might never have if you don't stop baiting me and do your damn job. I'm going to see my niece before I leave. If you can't get her out of this, let me know so I can find someone who can."

He turned and strode down the hall.

"You really do know how to piss off the clients, Henry," David said, shaking his head.

He stared after Bellamy Hughes, his mind turning. "It's a talent of mine. We need to get that conversation on paper. There were a lot of things he said that I think require looking into."

"Is anyone else curious about what would happen to the company if Win can't inherit?" David asked.

They thought along the same lines. It was why they worked well together. "It did cross my mind. And he never answered my question."

"The one about whether or not Brie Westerhaven tried to blackmail him?" Margarita looked thoughtful. "I noticed that. I'm also interested in how the housekeeper managed to break her hip just as Win needs her desperately. Probably nothing there, but I kind of want to look into it."

So many questions and so little time. "We need to sit down and plan for the bail hearing. I want to assign someone to digging into Brie Westerhaven and her connections to the Hughes family. We also need to hire someone to monitor social media. I want all the cloned pages of Win taken down immediately. She doesn't need to see that."

It would bother Win. She would hate to see herself that way.

David was staring at him like he was a toddler who'd recently taken his first steps.

It was weird. "What?"

He shrugged. "Nothing. It's good to see you getting back in the flow of things. You are trying to take care of the client in a way that's not merely legal. You're thinking of her well-being. It's refreshing for a change."

Because he wasn't known for giving a shit about the client, only the case. Yeah, he got that a lot. He didn't wear his humanity on his sleeve like some people. No one wanted a soft-centered defense attorney. "Don't read anything into it. She's got health issues and we don't get paid if she dies in prison."

"Of course," David agreed. "She's just another client. You carry them all when they're sick. I remember the time that accused arsonist had a tummy flu and you cradled him gently in your arms."

Sometimes it sucked to work with someone he knew so well. He couldn't intimidate David. David remembered when he'd been an idiot college kid worried about pledging a frat. But he needed to understand. "My personal relationship with Ms. Winston-Hughes is in the past."

"It has to stay that way, Henry," Margarita said softly. "How many people know you had an affair with her?"

"Outside of you and David and Noah? You would have to ask Win." He winced because he didn't want to admit the next bit, but his partners needed to know. "Alicia knew. She talked about it when she called. She said Brie had told her about the affair. We've got to think it's out there. But I don't have a relationship with her now. I cut off contact with her when I came back to Manhattan. I didn't talk to her again until this morning, and honestly, I had no idea what her real name was when we were seeing each other. I would never have slept with her if I'd known who she was."

"That's a little judgmental, isn't it?" Margarita looked at him, one brow raised.

He believed in putting it all out there. Margarita needed to understand the truth about him. "I would never have touched that woman had I known the types of people she was involved with. If that makes me judgmental in your eyes, so be it. I won't touch her again."

Unless she fell. He hadn't been able to stop himself. He'd picked her up and cradled her against him because he couldn't do anything else. It had been his instinct to save her, to comfort her. He'd never felt anything like it before. Even now it took all his willpower not to sit beside her hospital bed to make sure she got what she needed.

He hated that instinct. It needed to go.

"Still, we need to be prepared in case the rumor gets out there," Margarita mused. He could tell she was disappointed, but she wasn't going to push him. "I think David should go on the talk shows."

Henry held a hand up. "I would love to cede that to you, David. Go for it."

He hated doing interviews. He would likely hate it even more now because they would ask invasive questions about his divorce and his relationships. He preferred to keep his appearances to the court-room. If David got in front of the cameras, the worst personal ques-tions he would be asked would be about his former career and whether or not he was dating anyone.

David nodded. "I do agree I should do some of the press, but let's bring Noah in as well. His name alone will hold some weight with the press. I'll get our public relations firm to advise on strategy."

"We have a PR firm?" He hadn't been aware they'd hired one.

"As of two hours ago," Margarita explained. "Win needs a crisis-management specialist. I'll handle things from that end. You boys work on the judge." She smiled brilliantly. "This is so invigorating. Much more fun than contracts. No one murders each other at 4L. Well, if you don't count the Lawlesses' mom. I mean she killed a ton of people, but she didn't do it at the office. It's good to get out of the office."

It was easy to see that Margarita was going to be the bubbly, optimistic, every-murder-has-a-silver-lining cheerleader of the group. "All right, then. Tell Noah to get down here and let's see if we can find any decent coffee at all in this place and talk strategy."

He needed something to get his mind off the fact that Win

would be all alone in that big penthouse with a cousin who obviously hated her. If he could keep her out of jail at all.

The princess in the tower.

Too bad for her he was no one's prince.

They had just started down the hall when he heard a scream and all hell broke loose.

～

Win looked up as the door opened. She was hoping to see Henry, hoping for another shot at talking to him. Talking? She needed to explain. And maybe grovel a little.

She was feeling better now, but she could still remember how quickly he'd come to her aid, how he'd picked her up and looked down at her like he'd been hurt, too.

There had to be something left between them.

Unfortunately, the man who walked through the door was even less friendly than Henry.

"What are you doing here, Trevor?"

"I came by to see my cousin, of course." He stalked into the room, letting the door slam behind him. "It's fun to come see you now, cuz. I get a nice pat-down from that pretty officer. Lucky for me she wasn't some dude. So, you finding the accommodations to your liking? I like the new jewelry. You get it at Tiffany?"

He was going to be pleasant. Sarcasm dripped from his every word, but she had a comeback or two of her own. She'd found the only way to deal with Trevor was to pretend she didn't care. "New York's finest insisted I wear it." She was cuffed to a hospital bed. How surreal was that? "Have you checked in on Mary?"

Mary had been in a minor car accident, but she'd fractured her hip and required surgery. Apparently the Jeep had made out much better than Mary. Win hoped the woman who'd raised her hadn't spent the last few hours watching television. It would kill her.

Trevor rolled his eyes and sniffed. "Why would I check in on her? Dad shoved her in an old folks' home. I'm certainly not about to show my face at one of those so I can check in on an employee."

He was such a shit. "She raised you, too. After your mom left, she was the one who took care of you when you were home."

"Yeah, when I was at my dad's. That wasn't my home," he insisted. "And she didn't have time for me. She was always far too busy taking care of you and your friends. Also, my mom didn't leave. Dad kicked her out. I kind of blame you for that, too. After your parents died, all dear old Dad could think about was taking care of the heiress and making sure everything was sunshine and roses for you."

"He was a good uncle."

"Yeah, well, he was a shitty dad. But I didn't come here to revisit our childhood." Trevor stared at her for a moment. His face was pale, but his nose was bright red, an almost sure sign that he was high as a kite. "Did you kill her? I know you were pissed at Brie, but damn, Win. I didn't know you had that in you."

At least he'd actually asked the question. "Of course I didn't kill her."

"That's not what the cops think. You were found practically on top of her," he pointed out. "How am I supposed to believe you didn't get in a fight with her and it went wrong?"

"When was the last time I got into a physical fight? Never." She couldn't remember much, but she knew a few things. "I didn't fight with Brie. She was like that when I found her."

"She was dead in your bedroom. Why would she have gone there?" Trevor asked.

He asked it in a reasonable tone of voice, so she found herself answering. "I thought she might have gone into the residential section to look for you."

His jaw tightened. "Why would she look for me?"

"Tell me you didn't sleep with her. Tell me she didn't come on to you and start something while you were doing the show."

"We got close," he admitted.

For the first time in her life, she actually felt a little sorry for her cousin. He'd fallen for one of Brie's most common plays. "This is what Brie did when she got upset with her friends. She would sleep with someone who made us terribly uncomfortable, like a brother or some friend we'd always wanted more from. She would find a way to turn it all around so we were the bad guys. It was one more way to manipulate her friends."

"Of course she couldn't just want me."

"Maybe." Though Brie had hated Trevor for years. "Maybe I'm wrong, but I was looking for the two of you because I was going to tell you again that I didn't want anyone talking about me on the show. I want my privacy."

"If you wanted privacy, you shouldn't have gone after Brie," he insisted. "I don't believe you. I think she said something to you, something you didn't like, and you decided to try to take her out."

It was ridiculous. "Take her out? Am I some kind of assassin now? What would she have said?"

He suddenly wouldn't look at her. "I don't know. Maybe she knew a few things you wouldn't want her to know. Maybe you aren't as innocent as everyone thinks you are. You never liked me."

That was easy to answer. "You're an ass. It's hard to like someone who's constantly mean to you."

"Or maybe you know I deserve everything you have," Trevor shot back, his head coming up and righteous fervor in his eyes. "Maybe you know I'm the real heir to Hughes Corp. I'm the one who should take that company over."

What the hell was he playing at? Did he think because his father had taken care of the company for decades, that meant he should be the heir? Win wouldn't care if Trevor was at all easy to work with.

She would hand over a chunk to him if she thought for a second he wouldn't abuse it. "I'm not going to take over anytime soon. Honestly, I don't know if I want to do what your dad does. No one is trying to take away your job at Hughes."

"Hughes should be mine."

She was sick of his jealousy. "Well, then your father should have been the one to create the company. I'm sorry. It's not my fault you weren't my dad's son."

Trevor looked like he wanted to say something else, but he stopped. His face had gone a florid red. "You won't be able to enjoy the company while you're in jail. Have you thought about that? Maybe you should have before you took away something else I wanted."

She was trying to be tolerant. It was obvious Trevor had feelings for Brie. It made her wonder how far back they went. Sometimes an immature male showed his affection through bullying. Trevor had been excellent at bullying. "I'm sorry you miss Brie. I'm going to miss her, too."

"You haven't been her friend in years."

"I was trying to save myself and sometimes Brie can drag a person into deep water. I wasn't good at swimming, it seemed."

"You never were very strong."

Tolerance only went so far. "You should leave now, Trevor."

The door came open and her uncle walked in, frowning. "That girl put her hands places I didn't agree to. It was far less exciting than I thought it would be."

Her uncle had the prissiest look on his face. She bit back a laugh at the thought of her very proper uncle getting an overly thorough pat-down. "Sorry." She sobered. "Uncle Bellamy, I'm sorry to put you through this."

He moved in, laying a hand on hers. "Sweetheart, I know you didn't do this."

"How can you know that, Dad?" Trevor asked. "Are you even sad Brie's gone? You hated her."

"I don't hate anyone, Trev," he said softly. "I merely didn't like her influence on my kids. She was trouble from a young age, and I knew she would end up like this. I'm sorry for you if you got comfortable in that circle, son. I'm going to have to put my foot down. You won't see any of those people again. I was too indulgent with Winnie and it landed her here."

"I'm thirty years old," Trevor said with a roll of his eyes. "You can't tell me who I can or can't see."

"I can because I'm not merely your father. I'm your boss. And I know you've been irritating some of the talent in the media division. Your job is to run the division, not attempt to get in some actress's panties. I think I'll move you somewhere else. You haven't done a trip through accounting. Perhaps a management position there will ensure you don't get into more trouble."

Trevor's mouth dropped open. "I'll quit first."

"If that's how you want it, son."

"I am not your son. You have never been a father to me. You're nothing but a mistake my mother made." He pushed through the door and she was left alone with her uncle.

Bellamy shook his head. "He's been this way since he came back from spending time at his mother's. She always manages to poison him against me. I know I'm not the best of father figures, but he has no idea some of the things I've done to keep us together, to ensure that you kids get the things you need. You don't know what it's like to live without. You know your father and I grew up poor."

Her father had been responsible for inventing a chemical used to make rubber tougher and less vulnerable to punctures. He'd taken the millions from that patent and he and her mom had built Hughes Corp. Her mother had come from a wealthy family. She'd taught the Hughes brothers how to move in that world. "He was a smart man."

"Oh, darling, my brother was a genius. I was jealous of his mind, and certainly jealous of the fact that he managed to find a woman who could fund his brilliant brain. Hughes Corp would have been nothing if your mother's family hadn't funded it." He squeezed her hand. "Don't doubt for a second that I haven't done every single thing I've done to ensure you have a good life and you can make your own decisions. The company is yours if you want it."

"You know I'm happy having you run it."

"I do, and I can't thank you enough for your faith in me. You've had that since you were young. I know I wasn't a good father figure, but I did ensure that when I wasn't around you had Mary."

"She was wonderful." Win couldn't have picked a better mom. Sometimes she looked at pictures of the woman who had given birth to her and felt so distant. It wasn't fair. It wasn't like her mother had wanted her yacht to go down. She'd wanted a few days' vacation and ended up sacrificing her life to save her child's. "Mary was a great mom. Is she feeling okay? They won't let me call her."

It hurt not to be able to talk to the woman who had raised her.

"She had surgery this morning and they assure me she'll be fine. She's not a young woman anymore, and she's got fragile bones. She'll have the best care. I promise you that. I've talked to the police on the island, too. Mary can't remember much about the car that hit her. I'm going to make sure they find that bastard."

"You're a good man, Uncle Bell." He'd taken excellent care of Mary. She wasn't sure if it was simply because he cared for Win or because he wanted to reward a long-term employee, but he hadn't let Mary go even after Win no longer needed a nanny. He'd given her a job running the house on Martha's Vineyard and an allowance, though Win was the only one who visited more than twice a year. He'd paid Mary back for decades of love and affection and service.

"Your lawyer doesn't think so." He stepped away and walked to the small window. "He's upset that I'm going to Los Angeles."

Her heart constricted a little. She was going to be alone. Still, she could guess why he was going. "You have to assure the board that this is nothing more than a tabloid story or we'll lose value and quickly."

He glanced back, his lips curling slightly. "You always did understand."

"I know what you did when you dropped your own company to take care of my dad's." She'd been taught from a young age that family sacrificed.

"Sometimes I wonder what would have happened if your father and mother had lived, if you hadn't been the only one to survive," he mused. "I wonder if I would have been his competitor. That would have been fun. Two brothers fighting it out. I miss him, Win."

"I wish I missed him. It's not that I don't. I think I'll always feel like I lost something, but I wish I could miss them by thinking of something other than their pictures. Though I'll admit today I'm glad they don't have to see what's happened to me."

He moved back to her. "Your father would stand beside you and I will as well. I'm unfortunately going to have to do it from L.A. for a week or so. If you want me to stay, I will. I know I don't say it often, but I love you. We might have started out rough, but if I could have picked a daughter, she would have looked a lot like you. It's funny how things work out. I think that's what you learn as you get older. You make plans and follow through and never think about what the consequences might be years down the road."

"You're thinking about the company you left behind?" She couldn't remember ever seeing her uncle so contemplative. It worried her. Uncle Bellamy was a take-charge guy. He made decisions quickly and then plowed ahead with single-minded intent.

"No," he said. "I was wondering what your life would have been like if that yacht hadn't gone down. I wonder if you would be here or if you would have already finished grad school and started on your life. I know how hard it's been to be you, Winnie."

Because of the press. Because she'd been famous before she'd understood what the word meant. "I know who I am now. I know what I want. I'm not going to fall into a hole again."

"See that you don't."

He'd started to lean over when the door flew open and a woman entered.

The girl was wearing scrubs, but Win hadn't seen her before. She looked far too young to be a nurse. And she had a nose ring. Not that a nurse couldn't have one, but it seemed odd. That was when she lifted something no nurse making her rounds would have. Win saw a gun waved in front of her face. "You bitch. You killed her. You killed my friend. She was all I had."

Win couldn't move. She couldn't defend herself or do anything except scream. Her uncle started to say something, and then just as she was sure the young woman would fire that gun her way, the door opened again and Henry was there.

The young woman turned and Win realized it would be so much worse if Henry took a bullet. She struggled against the cuffs that held her to the bed.

"Hey, no. It's me you want," she shouted. "Not him."

Henry's hands were out. "Come on. You don't want to do this. You don't want to ruin your life."

The young woman's hands shook, but she held the gun up. "I do. She killed Brie. I've seen every episode. Every single one. I go to all the clubs Brie goes to. We were going to be friends. I can't let Taylor get away with it. You're so fake, Taylor. Everyone sees through you. You faked the anorexia thing so you could take camera time away from Brie. I hate you."

It was true. Win could see that plainly. This young woman hated her. Though she'd never met the woman with the gun, there was such rage in her eyes, all of it directed toward Win.

Tears pierced Win's eyes. Why would someone hate her like that? This woman had never met her. She'd never laid eyes on her, but it was clear she thought she knew who Win was, and all because of a television show.

"Put the gun down now." The police officer had made her way inside and stepped in front of Henry.

"It's not fair that she's alive when Brie is gone." The hand holding the gun started shaking.

The officer held her ground. "You have three seconds before I shoot. Am I understood?"

"It's not loaded." The young woman dropped the gun, tears streaming down her face. "I only wanted her to know how horrible she is. Everyone hates you. Why did you have to kill her?"

"Where the hell were you, Officer?" Henry moved into the room, his hand on his cell phone.

The officer had the young woman cuffed in seconds. "I'm sorry. We had a disturbance down the hall. I walked away for a second. Someone yelled for help, but when I got there he was gone."

Win's hands were shaking. "It was a setup to let her in."

"Probably." The officer hauled the young woman up. "I'm going to get my ass handed to me for this. Come on. I think you're going to spend some time in the psych ward, you freak."

"I hate you!" the girl screamed as she was hauled out.

"Noah, we're moving that timeline up," Henry was saying into his phone. "After what happened a few moments ago, there's no way I'm allowing her to even go to the prison infirmary. I want those bodyguards up here now."

"You're in good hands," her uncle said quietly, his voice shaking a bit. "You'll see. This is all going to blow over and we'll go back to normal. It's going to be fine, Winnie."

"No, I'm not sending her to her place," Henry said. "It's too dangerous for her. I'll take responsibility. We'll move her to my building, and I'll let the judge know that I'll personally ensure that she doesn't go anywhere."

She looked up at him, his words seemingly sweet to her ears. But then she saw the way he was glaring at her.

It was a little like the woman with the gun.

Win lay back, too weary to even cry.

NINE

"You understand all the conditions of your release, Ms. Winston-Hughes?"

Two days later, Win signed the paperwork and passed it back to the woman speaking. She was an older woman dressed in a nice suit and comfortable shoes. She had a badge around her neck, identifying her as a representative of the court.

She'd had several court employees in her hospital room over the last forty-eight hours. She'd gotten to listen to the DA argue that she needed to be placed in jail or she would flee the country and live like a queen. He'd made her sound like some crazed tyrant, killing her opponents and using her money to get away.

David Cormack had quietly made the case that she was a young woman with no record and deep ties to the community. He'd talked about how dangerous it would be for her to have another brain injury, pointing out how heated the case had already gotten in the media. Did the judge want to put a young woman in jail with those who would likely view harming her as a way to make a name?

The judge had asked her a few questions, and she'd promised she wouldn't leave and would comply with all court dates.

The judge had seemed relieved to be able to wash his hands of the whole thing.

One million dollars' worth of bail and she was going home.

Not home. She was going to Henry's place, and she wasn't sure why. He hadn't come to see her since that first day. One of the other lawyers checked in on her every day, but she hadn't seen Henry once. He wasn't here now. A man named Noah Lawless was here, and they were waiting for her bodyguards to bring the car around.

She was wearing actual clothes for the first time in days and her head was clear. That was good because she wasn't in pain, and bad because she remembered she'd been arrested for murder and her life was in the toilet.

Yeah, she was taking the good with the bad.

"I do understand," she replied to the court rep. "I thank His Honor for not forcing me to wear an ankle monitor."

The woman gave her a sympathetic smile. "Not many people have the kinds of community ties you do. It was brilliant of your lawyer to have all those letters introduced. Oddly enough, I don't think it was the mayor's praise that swayed the judge. It was all those nurses and doctors."

Hearing that was bittersweet. "I think my mom would have been happy being a doctor or a nurse. She lived to help people. My mom was a big proponent of helping New York's hospitals. I suppose I followed in her footsteps as a way of feeling close to her. Though now I kind of wished she'd done the same for the NYPD."

The court rep laughed and handed her a copy of the paperwork.

She'd managed to avoid the ankle monitor, but she knew this fight was far from over. She moved to the window as the door closed and she was left alone with Noah Lawless. She glanced down and saw there was still a crowd. Reporters and "fans." She could barely think the word. "Do I have to go out the front way?"

"No," Noah replied, moving toward her. He had blond hair and blue eyes that would catch any woman's attention. Well, any woman who hadn't seen Henry. "We've got a car in the underground parking garage. David is going to give the press a statement and we'll take you out then. It's Henry's favorite sleight of hand. They're looking one way. We're going another."

She deeply appreciated that, but she was confused on a couple of fronts. "Why am I not going home? I'm not leaving the country. I swear. I really want to fight this out. I didn't do anything wrong, so there's zero reason for me to leave."

"I think Henry's worried about you being alone."

"The building is secure." Although it hadn't been for Brie.

"No building is perfectly secure."

"I've got two large bodyguards," she argued. "I assume they're there to keep me in as much as they are to keep others out. Does he really believe I would run and leave everyone high and dry?"

"It could happen," a familiar voice said. Henry stepped into the room. "You wouldn't be the first wealthy person to use your money and privilege to attempt to escape the justice system. I believe the only reason we managed to avoid the ankle monitor was how pathetic you looked in that hospital bed. That was excellent, by the way. I couldn't have coached you better. With the addition of all those upstanding citizens willing to speak for you, it was a one-two punch. It doesn't hurt that you look a little like the judge's granddaughter. It was excellent theater."

Who was he? This wasn't the man who'd shown up in her bedroom the night of the storm. This man was cold as ice. "It wasn't theater. I *was* miserable and pathetic."

He glanced around the room. "I suppose being stuck in a plain old regular hospital room would be considered one of the worst things that could happen to you. I suspect you would normally have a suite of rooms they reserve for their wealthiest clients."

She was done with that ass. Two days she'd sat in this room, hoping and praying he would show up and be the Henry she'd fallen in love with. She wasn't even going to pretend that wasn't what it had been. She'd fallen for him and he'd been an illusion. There was no question that he could have felt the same way. He couldn't talk to her like this if he had felt even a tenth of what she'd felt for him.

She turned back to Noah because at least he seemed reasonable. "I would very much like to go home. I'll take the ankle monitor."

Noah sighed. "That's a bad idea. The minute the press gets a picture of that, it'll go viral. It could prejudice potential jury members against you."

"Do you intend to call some of your hacker friends?" Henry asked the question as though he didn't care about the answer but was merely curious. "You think one of those kids you've been hanging out with in Durham can manage to get the monitor off you?"

"What are you talking about?"

He glanced down at his phone. "I'm talking about Colin Knapp and Harley Prior. Your new friends. They've left several messages on your cell phone."

She wasn't sure where he was going with this. "I've made a lot of friends down in North Carolina. Colin and Harley are in one of my classes. We're in a study group together. Why do you know about them?"

He gave her a chilly smile. "I'm going to know everything about you and anyone you come in contact with. Did you know that Colin Knapp has some ties to a couple of ideological groups on the web?"

"I met him a few weeks ago, Hen . . . Mr. Garrison." It was a good way to distance. Henry had been her lover. The man in front of her was definitely Mr. Garrison. "No. I don't know what his web habits are."

"He's been involved with a group of hackers. Hacktivists, I believe they call themselves," he continued. "Though law enforcement hasn't been able to prove anything yet. Your friend Harley has been arrested several times."

"For political protests." She did know that. "He was arrested for peacefully protesting."

"Of course he was peaceful," he remarked dismissively. "Both men have knowledge of mechanics. I suppose you could invite either one up and perhaps get the monitor off you. Hackers tend to be good at those types of things. You know what they say. Judge a man by who he hangs out with."

Noah cleared his throat. "Yes, you'll come out well in that case, Henry. I assure you I've had far worse connections to the hacker world than any kid from Duke. Would you like for me to leave, or do you suspect I'll help her run, too?"

"That's not what I said and you know it. It's not the same. You left that life behind."

"And yet it's still a part of me. You need to remember that you're not the prosecutor on this case. You're supposed to be on her side." Noah's eyes were squarely on Henry.

"I can't be on her side if she flees the country," Henry replied. "And it's a good thing for me to think like the prosecutor in this case."

The idea of Henry standing over her, interrogating her, made her sick inside. "I don't want a lawyer who is constantly questioning me."

"That, my dear, is what a lawyer does." He looked through the window. "You're coming home with me. I don't like the situation any more than you do, but I think it's for the best. If you go home, you'll be subjected to your cousin, who despite all my best efforts has gone on several talk shows stating he can't be sure you didn't kill his beloved Brie."

"What? They hooked up a couple of times. It only lasted a few weeks, and it was more about making me uncomfortable than Brie being in love." Why was Trevor such a massive ass?

"I believe your uncle now has him on a tight leash," Noah explained. "But some damage was done, and I agree with Henry that you don't need to be close to him. I'm still not sure it wasn't Trevor who distracted the officer that day."

"We have him on a security camera talking to some of the . . . I don't know what to call them. Protestors? Fans? People with way too much time on their hands? Anyway, Trevor spent about fifteen minutes talking to some of the young women outside before he joined your uncle and came up here to see you," Henry explained. "It would have been easy for him to set something up. Why does he hate you so much?"

Why did everyone hate her? "Because I breathe, Mr. Garrison. He didn't want a sibling. Trevor likely would have hated anyone who took attention away from him. There was also the fact that apparently my aunt wasn't happy with having to take care of me. They fought a lot about how to deal with me and then my aunt divorced my uncle and took off for Europe. Trevor blames me."

"But you were an orphan." Noah looked at her like he didn't quite understand her words. "Of course your uncle would take you in. I don't understand why your aunt would have had a problem with it. You were her niece."

Win sighed and sat back down on the bed. So weary. She'd lain in bed for days. How could she be so damn tired? "She didn't see it that way. I don't think she liked my mother much, and she thought my dad held Uncle Bellamy back or something. There was some jealousy in there. I don't know, but that's why Trevor hates me. I don't think he'll kill me. He's more into annoying the hell out of me and trying to make me feel small. I've dealt with that all my life. And now I have two bodyguards to watch over me."

Remy Guidry and Wade Rycroft. They were massive hunky men

who had rings on their fingers and loved to talk about their wives, who had come up to stay with them while they were working here. They were the kind of men she could look at for hours. Gorgeous and majorly in love with their wives, so they were perfectly safe.

"Yes, two guards who need to stay close to you," Henry pointed out. "I've already gotten a place for them in my building. There's no place in yours. They would have to stay in a hotel to remain nearby. This could be a long-term assignment. Do you know how much more comfortable they would be in an apartment? Is your comfort worth more than theirs? I guess you probably don't care."

"Yep, I'm a vicious monster who uses everyone around me. I would keep them chained on the street if it meant I could have all my luxuries." She was sick of listening to it on TV. She didn't need it from her lawyer.

"Damn it, Win." Henry stood over her. "I don't want you in that house right now. Have you thought about the fact that you would be staying in the same room where she died? I'm not trying to be an asshole."

"But he's doing a fabulous job of it anyway," Noah offered.

Henry ignored him. "This is the best scenario. David's place is far too small. Margarita is in and out of the city all month. And Noah's place has a revolving door for the women he sleeps with. I'm worried I could get an STD just walking into it."

"Hey," Noah said.

Henry shook his head. "You've got a horrible reputation with women."

A bright smile suddenly lit Noah's face. "It's actually quite a good reputation. I promise. They all leave satisfied."

"See. You would seriously cramp his lifestyle." Henry turned again and began to pace, as though it helped him to think. "We'll be able to work on your case in relative peace, since as far as anyone knows, David is your attorney. So far we've been able to keep our personal indiscretions off the press's radar, so they shouldn't come looking for you at my place."

Indiscretions? It hadn't felt indiscreet. It had felt right and good. "I still think this is a mistake."

"I can leave," Henry offered, his demeanor going back to positively arctic in a second. "If you don't want me to represent you, all you have to do is say the word and I'll walk away. You can find your own way home and make your own decisions. You're a big girl, after all. If you want to call an Uber and see how you fare, feel free."

He was such a bastard. And he was right. She couldn't argue about that. She was alone right now, and she wouldn't know how to start to look for another lawyer. All her so-called friends had abandoned her. Her uncle was trying to save the company and didn't need to hear her sob story about how staying close to Henry hurt too much.

"Can we go now?" She would survive it. That was all she could do. She would put a wall between the two of them and slowly she would learn not to care about him anymore. "I signed all the paperwork."

"Of course. Where are your bags?" Henry asked.

She picked up the plastic bag they'd placed her medications in. She had a few days' worth of antibiotics left to take. "I'm a light packer."

His jaw tightened. "I didn't think to send someone to get you clothes."

She waved it off. "I'll order some off the Internet. If you send someone to get my things, the press could follow them back. As far as I can tell it hasn't died down yet. I need to see if the university will let me finish the semester remotely."

Noah cleared his throat, and when she looked at him, she realized she wouldn't like what he was going to say next. "They've put you on suspension. I'm afraid they don't like the press coverage. If you're cleared, they'll allow you back in the spring semester."

Her stomach dropped. "I don't understand. How can they suspend me?"

"Because I'm sure they have a student code of conduct that includes not murdering people," Henry said.

"But I'm not guilty." She stopped. He'd made himself perfectly clear on that point. "I know. You don't care."

He was quiet for a moment. "I can look through their student code of conduct and see what I can do. There's probably a loophole. I can force your way back in."

She shook her head. She didn't want to force herself on anyone. "No. It's fine. If I manage to survive this, I'll make some decisions about the future. I'd like to leave now."

She was numb and that was good. If she let herself feel anything, she might break down. One foot in front of the other. At least when she got to Henry's, she could be alone. That had been so hard, knowing she wasn't alone, that someone was always watching her.

She could shut out the world and cry for a while. But not until she closed the door. Not until she was alone.

"Ms. Win, are you ready to head out?" The big Cajun god of a man had a smile for her as Henry opened the door. "Wade's got the car ready."

At least someone smiled at her. She gave him a tepid smile back. "Thank you, Mr. Guidry."

He winked her way. "Nah. You call me Remy. I heard you've got some problems with packing light. Give me a list of what you need and your size, and I bet I could convince Lisa and Genny to go do some shopping."

"Thank you. Tomorrow is soon enough. Tonight I want to actually get some sleep." She followed him to the staff elevator. "But I appreciate the offer. I can give your wife some tips on where to shop. Though she might not want to drop my name now."

She knew tons of salespeople who lit up when she walked in the room. Would they do that now? Would Sandra at Bergdorf still smile and hold back the prettiest boots for her? Would the staff at Chanel bring her champagne and ask about her life? Or would she be a persona non grata there, too?

"Have you eaten?" Henry asked as the elevator doors closed and they began their descent to the parking garage.

She hated that question. It took her right back to a shitty time in her life. Though she had to admit, this one might be worse. "I'm good. I'm not hungry."

"I didn't ask if you were hungry. I asked if you had eaten," he insisted.

"I had a lovely bowl of oatmeal this morning." She'd forced it down, though she hadn't wanted to. She lost her appetite when she got emotional. She knew she was already floating against her danger zone, but she didn't want to talk about it here.

"It's almost three in the afternoon. They didn't bring you lunch?"

"It wasn't anything I wanted." She hadn't been able to force herself to eat the mystery meat.

Henry looked to Remy. "Tell Wade we'll need to stop somewhere and get her lunch."

"I'll be fine." She wanted to get where she was going, not stop for lunch. Alone. She wanted so badly to be alone.

"I don't think you understand how this is going to go, Ms. Winston-Hughes. You're going to be staying at my house. I will be in charge of you. You will not leave without my approval. You do not talk to anyone I don't approve of. I don't care if you're talking to a cat you met on the street. You don't say anything at all to anything with ears without first getting it vetted by me. And you will eat three meals a day. I don't care if you're not hungry. I don't care if the thought of eating makes you a little sick. You will eat."

"Jeez, Garrison." Remy looked at Henry, a frown on his face. "I thought I was supposed to protect her from crazy fans. Am I going to have to protect her from you, too? Maybe it's because I'm from the South and we're taught to be polite to ladies, but I don't much care for how you're talking to my client."

"I'm your client," Henry insisted. "I hired you to watch over her and I'm who you report to. And I'm not on a power trip. I need you to watch her. If after a meal she stays too long in the bathroom, I would like to be notified. If you see her exercising excessively, I would like to be notified. Regular exercise is fine, but she might try to overdo it."

"She's not a child," Remy argued.

"No, but I am a recovering anorexic and I might try to take control again," she said, her voice completely toneless. "I already feel like it. I want to. It would feel good to have one thing in my life that I could control. I'll eat three meals a day, and I promise not to make anyone work purge patrol. I wasn't a big purger. I preferred to practice discipline. That's what I called it. It really was oblivion. Addiction. It was my drug. I'll try hard to stay on the wagon."

It was humiliating that all these big gorgeous men knew how weak she'd been, how little she'd once thought of herself. The silence was filled with her shame.

"And I will try hard not to drink every bottle of liquor in Manhattan," Henry said. "We'll keep each other on the wagon. No falling off on either side. And I'll let you order some groceries. I want you to eat so you don't get sick again, Win. And if you want revenge on me, well, I'm not fond of beets."

The doors opened. He hadn't had to put himself out there in front of Remy and Noah. He could have kept his mouth shut and not outed himself as an alcoholic. She wouldn't have said anything.

He was a frustrating man.

She started out of the elevator, but Henry's hand came out, stopping her.

"You go nowhere until he's checked it out." His hand stayed on her arm as though he was worried she would try to walk forward anyway. "Unless you're safely locked up in the apartment, he or Wade goes first."

She didn't like the sound of that. "Henry, a few days ago someone waved a gun in my face. Maybe this isn't such a good idea. Those men are married."

"And they're good at their jobs. They've stayed alive so far," Noah said. "I've learned those McKay-Taggart boys are tough to kill."

She took a deep breath as Remy touched his earpiece and said something she couldn't hear. "Well, the good news is that crazy chick's gun wasn't actually loaded. She merely wanted to scare me."

"There are people out there who do want to hurt you," Henry said under his breath. "I don't want you to pretend like everything is all right. I've spent the last few days looking into the past year of your life. You mentioned the attack in Sweden, but you didn't tell me about the car that tried to drive you off the road three months ago."

"It was some drunk asshole." The only reason she'd reported it to the police was the fact that she'd had some damage to her car. She'd needed the report for the insurance company.

"And then someone keyed your car while we were on the island," Henry pointed out. He'd seen that damage himself. He'd been angry, but Win hadn't even filed a report on that incident.

"That's a lot of near misses for one year," Noah commented as a big black SUV with heavily tinted windows pulled up. "No one can see in the windows, but I think I would rather have you in the middle seat between us."

Remy opened the door for her, but Henry moved into his space, offering her a hand up. She stepped on the running board and got into the car.

Were they right? She hadn't thought the incidents had anything at all to do with one another. One happened in Europe and the other was nothing more than bad timing and being on the wrong road. "Why would someone follow me from Sweden?"

"I have no idea," Henry replied. "But I want to find out if anyone who knows you was in Sweden at the time when you were attacked."

"It was the weekend before I came home. Everyone was there. Brie and Hoover came out. My uncle came to bring me back to New York. Trevor was there because he'd heard it would be a party. Everyone was at the club that night except my uncle. He went back to the hotel after dinner."

"Well, that's helpful." Henry settled himself in beside her. "I don't love the fact that Trevor was there."

Noah sat on the other side of her. "Why would someone want to kill Win? I know she's got a shit-ton of money waiting for her, but I would assume Bellamy Hughes would desperately want to keep her alive. If Win dies before the age of thirty, the company would revert to the foundation they originally bequeathed it to. There was a codicil written in after the pregnancy was discovered that allowed everything to pass to a child of their blood. I assume they simply hadn't taken the time to go in and name Win after she was born. They would have at some point, but she was a baby. They weren't thinking about dying. Trust me. I've gone over that will a hundred times now. I wanted to see if there was any way that douchebag Trevor could get his hands on the prize if Win died."

"He wouldn't. I don't think. My parents originally wanted the company to be sold and all of the money to go into the Winston-Hughes Foundation," she explained. "The money that originally funded my father's company came from my maternal grandfather. The Winstons were old-school money, but they lost most of it over time. Basically, when my mom married my dad, my grandfather scraped together everything they had and backed Dad's company. It paid off, obviously. But one of the promises my father made him was that if they didn't have children to pass it down to, he would memorialize the Winston name by funding the foundation for decades to come. Dad agreed. My own will is written in the same way. If I die before I have kids, the company becomes property of the foundation. Not my uncle or my cousin. They shouldn't want me to die. They would lose everything."

"It doesn't make a lot of sense," Noah mused. "From everything I've gathered, Brie was trying desperately to get Win back on the show. She wouldn't have wanted Win dead either. I know you have excellent instincts, but this feels more like bad luck and coincidence."

"I want to investigate all of it," Henry said as Remy got into the passenger seat.

"Mr. Garrison," Wade said, "you should know that while I can avoid walking her out in front of that crowd, I can't avoid the crowd altogether. We'll have to drive by, but they won't have any idea who's in the car. I can't make a left turn, so I have to drive by."

"Go as quickly as you can." Henry's voice sounded tight.

Wade turned out onto the street, and they went from darkness into the bright sunshine of the New York day.

How was she here? A few days before, her main worry had been a test in statistics, and now she didn't even have a school to go back to.

She heard the shouts before she saw the crowd. As they started to move down the street in front of the hospital, she could see the mass of humanity that had gathered. News reporters were out talking to the groups of young women, most dressed a lot like Brie. There was also a group of youngish men holding signs.

JUSTICE FOR BRIE

NO MERCY FOR THE 1%

BURN THE BITCH

Well, the crazy chick had been right about one thing. Everyone seemed to hate her. Would it matter if Henry found a way to win her case? Or would everyone think she'd gotten away with it because she was rich? Would she spend the rest of her life with people looking at her like she was a circus sideshow freak?

Or would some judge decide to make an example of her? To show the 99 percent that not all wealthy people got away with it. She could spend the rest of her life rotting away in prison.

"Damn it, Win," Henry said. "Don't cry. They don't mean anything. They're utterly meaningless."

Maybe they were to him, but to her they were a symbol of what she had to look forward to. Her name dragged through the mud. A million stories on how the baby her parents had sacrificed their lives for turned out to be one more entitled bitch.

She stared straight forward and tried to stop the tears.

"Damn it." Henry's arm went around her, pulling her in close. "Don't look. Don't watch them. They don't matter."

She let him hold her, closing her eyes.

But the image would be there forever.

⁓

Henry watched her move through his apartment, her hand running over the spines of his books. If she was looking for some fiction, she was in the wrong place. This was his office and it had law books and not a lot else.

She stopped at the picture of the bungalow on Martha's Vineyard. It was one of the things he'd brought with him. It was a picture of him and his grandfather sitting on the porch. His grandmother had taken it. He'd been five or so, and his grandfather had been teaching him how to tie fishing lures.

God, but he wished his grandfather had taught him how to deal with women. It was late and Win had changed into the only sleep clothes available to her—one of his old T-shirts. It hung down to her knees and was perfectly shapeless, but she looked so sexy in it he felt a physical ache.

"I got you a toothbrush and some other things you might need." He'd run down to the drugstore at the end of the block and bought her a few things. Hairbrush, shampoo and conditioner, and a whole lot of mini travel things she might or might not use.

She walked out of the office, though it was more of a space than a true office. There were no doors. The majority of this part of the apartment was open space. It had a loftlike vibe that she looked right at home in. "Thanks. I thought you'd left for the evening after your duty was done."

He was sure she was talking about the duty of watching her eat. She'd ordered groceries and set herself up in his kitchen. She'd made a delicious chicken parm and salad for the entire group. David and Noah had spent the afternoon with them, along with the body-guards and their wives.

He would be eternally grateful to Lisa Guidry and Genny Rycroft for getting Win to smile again. She'd been so quiet for much of the afternoon as he'd worked with David and Noah, going over strategy. She'd puttered around the kitchen until the two women had shown up, and they'd been so friendly and kind that he'd watched Win open up and smile.

It had been nice to sit and have dinner with people. It had been nice to see her across the table.

What the hell was wrong with him?

"Where would I have gone?" He handed her the bag.

She shrugged. "I don't know. You could have had a date."

He chuckled but there was nothing funny about it. "I don't date, Win."

This was the time of night when he used to pour himself a glass of Scotch and watch the news. It had been months since he'd indulged in Scotch. He had to avoid both tonight.

She held the bag close and glanced around the room. "Okay, well, you should know that I don't want to disrupt your normal life. If you need to go out, you should. I won't try to run."

"You don't want to disrupt my normal life?" It was a ridiculous statement.

She stared at him for a moment as though trying to figure out what hole she was about to step in. "No, I don't."

How could she think for a single second that bus hadn't already left the station? "You've already ruined my normal life, Win. You did that the minute you came into it."

He watched the color drain from her face. Her shoulders straightened. "Well, on that lovely note, I'll go to bed. Good night, Mr. Garrison."

He hadn't meant to start this with her. The whole time he'd been in the drugstore, he'd been thinking about how he had to back off. He had to find a way to be less angry with her, and part of that was viewing her merely as a client he was helping out. And one who could do magical shit for his new firm. He needed to treat her with the courtesy she should expect.

As she started to walk past him, he intended to tell her good night and that he would see her in the morning. He did not intend to reach out and grab her arm. He didn't mean to growl her way.

"What did you expect, Win? Did you expect me to thank you for lying to me? Did you think I would be thrilled you made a fool of me?"

Her eyes flashed with fire. "I expected you to not care. It was a brief affair. You made that clear. Why should I bare my soul to a man who doesn't want anything but a couple of weeks of sex from me?"

He felt his hand tighten around her arm. He had to stop himself from squeezing too tight. "It was more than that and you know it."

"Do I? I thought it was at the time. I thought it meant something, but when you left, you left. No messages. No replies. I texted you several times. I tried to continue any kind of connection with you. Tell me something. Were you ever going to reply?"

"No." He wasn't about to tell her the truth. He couldn't tell her that he'd kept every text, and it had only been the fact that he hadn't had anything to offer her that had kept him from begging her to come with him. He couldn't let her know that he'd forced himself to walk away from her. "I wasn't going to reply. I meant what I said. I wanted to spend those weeks with you and nothing more."

She pulled her arm out of his grip, her hair swinging. "Then I don't get why it matters and how the hell you can say it meant anything at all to you."

"It did. It meant a lot to me. Just because something is finite doesn't make it meaningless." That was what killed him. Those two weeks with her had been some of the most peaceful of his life. He held them close as some of the best memories he'd had. Now he had to question every second he'd spent with her.

"No," she insisted. "If you cared about me at all, you wouldn't be able to look at me like I'm some piece of trash you wish you could sweep up and toss out."

She didn't understand him at all. He looked at her like she was a temptation he shouldn't give into. That was why he'd stayed away for days, dreaded having her in his home. And yet he hadn't really tried all that hard to find another place for her. He'd managed to shoot down every decent proposal David or Noah had come up with. "You lied to me, Win. You lied to me about something as simple as your damn name. How am I supposed to handle that? I thought I knew you."

She stopped, crossing her arms over her chest as though she needed protection from him. "You did know me. You knew the me

I want to be. And I didn't lie about my name. Everyone who actually knows me calls me Win."

It was what her uncle called her. "Why Win? For Winston?"

For a moment he thought she wouldn't reply, but she sighed and finally gave in. "My mother hated her first name. At least that's what everyone tells me. She was named after her grandmother Prudence. Mom was a bit of a free spirit and she didn't like the word 'prudence' or what it meant. She started calling herself Win when she was in high school. I read some of her diaries. She thought Win better fit her spirit. When I was a kid, I wanted to feel close to her, so I called myself Winnie and it felt right. It felt like it fit me."

There was a problem with that. "Yet you decided to go with your full name for that show of yours."

"Because it wasn't really me," she argued. "Brie convinced me to go on. She made it sound like it would be this grand adventure. I'd finished college and I was a little at loose ends. I suppose in some ways it was a rebellion. I don't get access to my trust fund until I turn thirty. I know why my parents did that. I get it, but having to ask my uncle for everything bugged me. This was real money that I would make."

"A regular job would have worked, too."

"Brie made it seem so exciting," she admitted. "She said I could find myself, and I was a little lost, so that sounded like a good thing to do. Besides, we hadn't spent a ton of time together while I was in college. I missed her at the time. So I agreed to be Taylor Winston-Hughes. The producers liked the name, said it sounded more sophisticated. In the end I was glad they went that way. I needed to keep something of myself private."

"How about not doing a damn reality show in the first place?" He couldn't quite keep the nastiness out of his tone. "That might have helped you with privacy."

She flushed. "I'm sorry, Henry. I'm sorry I made mistakes and that fucked up the precious two-week affair you didn't intend to do anything about in the first place. I'm sorry I didn't walk up to you that first day and lay out my whole life to you. I should have sat down with a stranger I'd just met and told him my life story from beginning to end."

He didn't like how rational she sounded. Logic didn't matter. He'd opened himself up to her and she'd lied. "We didn't merely have sex, Win. We spent two whole weeks together. We sat and talked. We really talked."

"Yes, we did. And I didn't lie to you about anything I said during those talks. I didn't lie to you when we walked on the beach together. I didn't lie when we went to bed. It was all me."

He couldn't accept it. "I told you pretty much everything about myself. You might have mentioned a few facts about your life."

"Like my plans for the future? Because we went over those incessantly. You helped me make sure I had the classes I needed. Not a lie. Like the fact that I love soap operas and romance novels, and everyone makes fun of me for watching and reading them? You sat there and watched me do both. Not lies. Like the fact that I am so scared I'll get back to that place where I can't see myself in the mirror without wondering how long it's going to be before I fade away? I told you that in the middle of the night and you held me and made me feel better. I wasn't lying. Those things are the real me."

She was willfully missing the point. "I'm talking about your family. I'm talking about your money and lifestyle. I'm talking about your history and the fact that you were on a reality show."

"But those things aren't really me." She said the words quietly, as though she didn't expect him to believe her. "They might be facts about me, but it's all trivia. You got to know the real me. I got to know the real you. You're more than a lawyer. You're more than how and where you were born."

"You should have told me." She was good with words. He would give her that, but he had the high moral ground and he'd learned to never give that up.

Her eyes narrowed. "Fine. We should start over again. My name is Taylor Winston-Hughes. I was born into an incredibly wealthy family and it was awesome. It was awesome to lose my parents. I didn't notice they were gone because there was all that money to love me. My uncle was kind but distant because he had to take care of all that money that made life worth living. He sent me to plenty of amazing boarding schools, but it was okay because he made sure the money was there to hold me and make sure I was loved."

He put a hand up. "I get it. I don't need more of your sarcasm. You knew who I was. It didn't occur to you that I wouldn't want to get involved with a woman who had ties to the entertainment industry?"

"I don't anymore. I left that life and I won't go back."

That was where he had her. No one really left that life. They always went back for seconds. "Sure you will. Women like you always go back. You won't be able to help yourself. You need the attention. It's like you said: You didn't get enough of it as a child and now you need it from everyone around you. You need someone filming you twenty-four–seven so your life feels meaningful."

It was the only reason he could think of to explain why someone would do that to themselves, would open their lives up like that.

"Women like me?"

He was being an ass again. He was getting riled up when he needed to calm down. "You know what I'm saying."

Win shook her head. "I don't. I would love for you to describe a woman like me. Get your story straight, Counselor. Either you know me because you've reduced me to some cartoonish stereotype, or you don't know me because I'm some evil woman who stole your precious sex for some crazy reason. Decide and stick with one or the other."

He took a deep breath. This wasn't how he'd wanted the evening to go at all. Hell, he wasn't sure how he'd expected it to go, but it wasn't like this. "I don't understand why you lied to me."

"I lied because I'm just like all the rest, Henry. I'm selfish and wanton, and I don't think of anyone but myself. I lied because I thought sleeping with you would make an excellent story for me to sell to the tabloids because I can't get enough attention from them. I lied because I could and I wanted to and I'll do it again to the next precious, naive man who comes along." She spat out the words with a bile he wouldn't have considered her capable of. "So you should feel good about dumping me. Your instincts were all correct. You're good. I'm bad. That's the way the world is, so consider yourself safe."

"I simply want to know. I want to understand." He wasn't sure why he couldn't seem to move on without a reasonable explanation. "Why?"

"Because I wanted those two weeks to be real." He moved in because he knew how he'd wanted the evening to go. It was the single stupidest thing he could do, but being close to her was bringing out the idiot in him. Being close to her made him forget all his good intentions. His intellect and all his plans went right out the window the minute he caught sight of her.

Win backed up, but not far. Her back found the wall and she stared up at him as he invaded her space. "They were real."

"How can I be sure?"

She was staring at his mouth, her own opening slightly as though her body knew what it wanted. "You have to have some faith. You have to believe in something. I still don't understand why you care. You weren't coming back for me."

"I read those texts a hundred times. I read them and stopped myself from replying because I thought I wasn't good enough for you. Because you were young and shiny and I would do nothing but drag you into the mud. I don't think I would have lasted another week without calling you." He was so close he could feel her body heat. How long had he been cold? He was so fucking cold when she wasn't around. "I missed you. I missed you so fucking much."

"I don't think I should believe you."

But he could show her. There was one way he could show her. "Believe this."

Why had he bothered to talk to her? He couldn't believe a word she said, but this . . . oh, they could have this. There was no way to lie to him when he was kissing her.

He lowered his head down, brushing his lips over hers. "I missed you."

Not a lie. Not even close to a lie. He kissed her, softly at first, and wished there was even the tiniest hint of deception in his words. He wished he could qualify it by saying he missed her body, missed how good it felt to sink himself inside her.

He let his hands find her hair, gently pulling it out of the band that held it up and letting it flow over him. He deepened the kiss, letting his body pin hers to the wall. Her tongue rubbed against his and he knew he had her.

She couldn't deny this. This was too good, too right.

He still couldn't bring himself to tell her that her body wasn't all he'd missed. He'd missed waking up next to her, listening to her hum while she cooked. He'd missed walking on the beach with her. They hadn't even talked, simply held hands, and he'd let the beauty of the beach and the quiet companionship bring him peace.

Even in the midst of his anger, he was starting to see that a lying Win was better than no Win. She said she wanted to leave that part of her life behind her? He could help her with that. She could be exactly what she'd promised. She could transfer her studies up here to New York, settle in with him, and he would watch her every freaking move. He would ensure she didn't fall in with that crowd again. She would stay in line and he would keep her out of trouble. There would be no more ridiculous television shows or crowds of crazy fans.

It could work.

He lifted her shirt and let his hands move on her warm flesh. This was what they needed.

That was when he felt something on his cheek. Something wet and warm.

He pulled away because she was crying.

He practically fell on his ass getting away from her. "I thought that was consensual. I'm sorry. I thought you wanted that."

"You don't even like me, Henry." She sounded very small. She looked small. Her shoulders slumped, her body curving in on itself like she needed protection. "You don't like me, but I'm still ready to fall into bed with you because there's a part of me that wants you any way I can have you. Even if all you want is sex. There's this voice inside me saying it doesn't matter. I can pretend you care about me. I'll know it's all fake, but isn't that what everything is? Isn't that the world?"

The words came out of her mouth with such hopelessness that he felt lost.

She stared at him for a moment and then sighed, an endlessly weary sound. "I'm not going to accuse you of anything. No sexual harassment case here. You're safe. I'm going to bed."

She turned and walked down the hall.

He followed.

What the hell was he doing? He'd dodged a bullet, but here he was following it so it had another shot at hitting him square in the chest.

Something had happened to him that day he'd met her. Something terrible and incomprehensible and it was all her fault.

He didn't want to feel this way. He didn't want to want her, and more than anything else, he didn't want to feel like someone had opened up his chest and exposed every single part of him.

That was how she made him feel. No one else had done that. Ever.

It made him angry. It made him restless. And when she looked at him with those tears in her eyes, it turned him into a completely different human being than the one he'd been before.

She made his breath catch, his heart seize. The world seemed softer than it had been before and he owed her. It was right there, the bond between them. He wasn't sure why. Maybe it had been that day when she'd taken the bottle away, as though she'd known she might never see him again, but she couldn't leave him alone with his demons. So she'd carried them away.

He couldn't leave her alone with hers.

He reached for her hand. Tears were already streaming down her face.

"Please, Henry. Just let me go to bed. I'll answer all your questions tomorrow. I'll be a good client, but I need to be alone tonight."

If he left her alone, she would cry and edge ever closer to that pit that lived inside her. He knew because it lived inside him, too. No one was truly bright and shiny. Every human soul held secrets. "I only have one question, but I need you to answer it for me."

Her eyes closed as though prepping herself for something horrible. When she opened them, she was calm and centered, and he wondered what that had cost her. "All right. What's the question?"

There was one thing he could give her that he'd never given anyone else. "Did you kill Brie Westerhaven, Win?"

Her eyes flared as though she understood what he was asking. He never asked. He never cared. He couldn't afford to and still do his job. But she needed someone who believed in her.

"I didn't, Henry. I didn't kill her." There was relief in her voice, something deep and soothing to her tone.

"I believe you." It was like jumping into the deep end of the ocean without a single lesson in how to swim, but he had no choice. He'd just realized there was something worse than Win's lies.

Her pain. He couldn't accept it, couldn't see her broken and weary.

He pulled her into his arms. "Let me stay with you. No sex. Only this. I did miss you. I don't know what to do or how to move past it. I don't know if I can. I only know that I can't leave you alone like this. Don't make me leave you alone."

She took his hand and led him to bed. It was silly because this was the small bed, the one David used when they worked late into the night and he was too tired to catch a cab home. It was barely a queen, but he didn't want to move her into his room. He wanted to be in her space.

He wanted to be the Henry he'd been when they'd been together on the island.

Just for a night.

He undressed in silence and when he was down to his boxers, he turned off the light and crawled into bed beside her.

He was awkward. Should he move to her? Did she need to be held? He'd never gotten into bed with a woman simply to comfort her.

She rolled over and laid her head on his chest. She was quiet for a moment, but then her tears began again. It was like she'd been waiting until she was safe so she could let go.

She thought she was safe with him. It was a stupid thing to think. Or she could be playing him. This would be a good way to soften him up.

Yet even with all the suspicions running through his head, he held her close.

Sometime, deep in the night, she fell asleep. They hadn't talked, merely held on.

As she slept in his arms, he had to wonder if he was in entirely too deep.

TEN

Two days later, Win stared at the thick stack of files on the dining room table. "This is my life? Is this what the investigators found on me? Because I didn't think I'd done that much. That's a lot of paperwork for a twenty-nine-year-old. Did you dig up my old report cards?"

She wouldn't put it past him. Henry Garrison was a thorough man.

Henry glanced up and adjusted his glasses. He was dressed in what she'd come to think of as his casual chic. Slacks and loafers with a button-down, but he could easily strap on a tie and jacket and change into SuperLawyer. When he put those nerdy, hot glasses on, he was right back to Clark Kent. "This is what I've had McKay-Taggart working on. Did you meet the investigators?"

She shook her head and leaned against the table. "I was in a meeting with Margarita when they came up yesterday. I was laying out the murder scene. She has this software that re-creates the space. Which is my childhood bedroom, so it was a little freaky, but we got it done. Right down to where Mr. Bear was sitting when the action went down. I think he's going to need some serious therapy."

His lips curled up, a tiny hint of his amusement. "You're the one who needs therapy. And I thank you for doing that with her. I want to know if anything in that room was moved prior to you walking into it."

"I sort of slid, actually," she admitted. "Blood on marble is slippery."

He put the file down. "When did your sense of humor go so dark?"

She sighed and sank into the chair across from him. "I can laugh or cry, and I think I'm cried out. The good news is, we did find something that's missing. It would have been easier if I'd been able to go back in, but I noticed that the fireplace poker thing is gone. The sweeper and the pan are there, but the poker is missing. I almost never used that fireplace, but it was part of the original house, so we left it in during the remodel. That fireplace set has been sitting there completely unused for probably fifteen years."

"That works in our favor," he said, nodding. "You wouldn't have had time to hide it, and if we can find it, we can compare it to the wound you took that night. I can hope and pray there's fingerprints on it."

"They shouldn't be mine. Like I said, I haven't used the fireplace. The central heat works fine and while I call it my childhood bedroom, I've never truly lived in it. It was a place to stay when I wasn't traveling or working."

"I'm going to ask NYPD if they've found it and if they haven't, I'll request a full search of the house. This could be exactly what we need." He slid the glasses off, staring at her for a moment. "How are you sleeping?"

Not as well as she had that first night when he'd held her. That night she'd slept like a baby, listening to the steady sound of his heartbeat. But they'd woken up the next day and still had to face all the problems they had in front of them. They'd sat down and agreed to try to find that easy companionship they'd experienced on the island. It had been a brief, awkward conversation, but they were working on it.

She missed him, too.

Unfortunately, they hadn't had a ton of time alone in the last forty-eight hours. Working a big murder case was tough on a lawyer.

"I'm good, Henry," she replied. "How about you? I can't tell if you sleep at all. You came in so late last night."

Not that she hadn't had company. She was rapidly coming to love Lisa and Genny. They'd brought her clothes and makeup, and more importantly, they hadn't let her feel alone. While their husbands watched her back, these two women had been important in bringing her hope.

"I was working on a couple of things. We have your grand jury hearing in two weeks, and then we'll start with discovery and a ton of pretrial hearings to decide what evidence will and won't be allowed in," he said.

"Have you found any evidence you'll try to get thrown out?"

"I'll try to throw everything out, Win," he admitted. "I'll bury the DA in minutiae until I can find what I need."

"What do you need?"

"I need to prove someone else did this," he explained. "You see, the shitty thing about believing that your client is truly innocent is the fact that I can't be the one who lets you go to jail, and jury trials are a crapshoot. If I can't find another explanation, even without concrete evidence, the truth is, juries walk into a trial wanting to punish someone in a case like this. I can file for a change of venue, but there's not going to be a single person out there who hasn't read the story or seen the TV coverage."

Yeah, it sucked. She hadn't been able to watch TV for days because every time she turned the channel, her face popped up. "So your plan is to find the actual killer? Is that what you would normally do?"

"There is nothing normal about this case." He sat back, frowning.

Because she'd made him break his rule of not caring about the guilt or innocence of his client. Because this case wasn't merely a puzzle to be solved.

She decided to give him a pass because he wasn't particularly good with emotions. It was one of the things she'd pondered while she'd begun the shut-in phase of her life. She knew she wanted Henry, but she couldn't be sure which Henry she would get.

It was past time to stuff those thoughts away. She'd promised him she would work on their friendship. Whatever it was they had when they weren't going at it like rabbits.

She missed sex. That was a revelation because she'd never missed sex before. It was something she'd talked about with her new friends and something she was going to handle on her own because she was a modern woman and she could use the Internet.

It would be better if she didn't have to use the Internet for that particular problem. She would rather handle it the natural way, with Henry's hands on her body.

She turned back to the files because that was some seriously dangerous ground. "So if these aren't all on me, who are they on?"

He relaxed and put his glasses back on, obviously happy to be talking about something less touchy-feely. "These are files on every single person who came in contact with you or Brie Westerhaven that night. They're dossiers on everyone who attended the party. I'm going to interview a couple of them. This pile is the people I find interesting. The middle I'm on the fence about, and the last one is everyone I've cleared. Somehow I don't see Mr. and Mrs. Condiment King waiting in your bedroom to take out a reality TV star."

The Hanovers were a lovely couple who had built their fortune off tiny packets of ketchup and mayo. They were definitely not the murdering type. "I talked to her that night. She'd recently had a hip replacement. I think murder would have been too much exercise for her."

"That was my assessment as well. None of the people in pile number three had any links or ties to Brie, and no meaningful ties to you."

"Meaningful ties to me?"

"None of those people have any reason to hurt you," he explained.

"It was Brie they hurt."

"Oh, I disagree. They've certainly ruined the last few days of your life, and if you go to jail, I would say you owed it all to whoever killed Brie. I've got three working theories of this crime. One, Brie was killed over something she did or said or by someone she trespassed against, and I mean that in the biblical sense."

Brie's crowd wasn't into forgiving those who trespassed against them. "I can see that. Brie could certainly rub people the wrong way. And the other theories?"

She was fascinated by watching him work, listening to him talk his way through some legal issue.

The Monster of Manhattan was an incredibly smart man. She wished he wasn't so damn sexy.

"Theory two is that this has something to do with you. That the person who killed Brie was actually waiting for you to walk into that room. It's mere coincidence that you weren't killed yourself."

The thought sent a shudder through her and took her right back to that horrible night in Stockholm when she'd felt those hands around her throat, had known she was going to die. "The police still think I tripped or that I was injured while I was fighting with Brie. Have they gotten back any of the report things yet?"

A single brow arched. Yep. That was his "dumbass said what?" face. "By 'report things,' I suppose you mean forensics?"

Such an intellectual snob, and yet it was incredibly fun to tease him. She kept a perfectly straight face. "Forensics. Got it. Have those things come back yet?"

He stared through her as though trying to figure out if she was serious or not and then gave up. "No. Those tests take time. Well, except the fingerprints on the murder weapon. That was simple enough."

She could guess from his sourpuss face the fingerprint report hadn't gone well. "It was my letter opener. I used it a lot. I would pry open stuff that didn't want to come open with it. I would scratch my back with it from time to time. It served to hold my bun in place at the back of my head when I couldn't find a set of chopsticks or a pen. So yes, very useful, though I never once stabbed anyone with it."

"Obviously your fingerprints are on it, but I can maybe deal with that. Especially given your creative uses for it. Did you ever open a letter with it?"

She shrugged. "I opened a lot of DVDs. Letters aren't that hard to open and I mostly get email. The letter opener was a high school graduation present from an elderly relative. Like a second cousin or something. Who gives an eighteen-year-old girl a Tiffany letter opener?"

His lips curled up. "Probably the same kind who gave an eighteen-year-old boy an expensive pen set. Even when *I* went to college we had laptops."

She glanced down, looking at the names on the files of the people he really wanted to talk to—the ones he thought might have something to do with the killing. She felt her eyes widen. "Alicia Kingman? Your ex-wife? What would she have to do with anything?"

"She was right there, front and center, and she knew about our affair. While Alicia never loved me, she was quite possessive and didn't like her territory being infringed on. She also doesn't take it well when someone puts her in a box. I did that a few weeks before the murder. This could be part of my third theory, the one in which you were the target, or hurting you was the object, even if it was only to get to another person. In this theory, Brie either walked in at the wrong time or was set up in a way that would make you look like the guilty party. In this version, the point is to send you to jail for something you didn't do."

"That's a very convoluted theory, Henry." It would be a spectacularly hard sell to a jury, too. Even she could see that.

He sat back, his frustration evident in the way his shoulders slumped. "Well, money is out, and that's my usual go-to. When incredibly wealthy people get murdered, it's almost always over money. But you're right. Your parents' will was airtight. Without you, the money, the company, and everything in between goes straight to charity. Your uncle has zero reason to want you killed."

"He wouldn't hurt me." At least they could cross her uncle off the list.

"Though it occurs to me that getting you put in jail would leave all those assets in his hands. As long as you're alive, the assets remain in play. There's no clause for your going to jail or being incapacitated. Bellamy Hughes would continue to run everything."

Crap. She didn't need him running down leads on her uncle. "Why would he do that? I could die in prison and then it would all go to hell for him. He should want me right where I am. I don't want the headache of running Hughes. I never have. That's the sad part about it. My parents left me this enormous birthright most people would kill for and I never wanted it. It's why I didn't go into the business after college. I couldn't stand the thought of being a cog in a wheel, of sitting through meeting after meeting and making choices that hurt people. I could never agree to a layoff. And yet I know they're sometimes necessary."

"So what are you planning on doing with your master's degree?"

"Run the foundation. That's what I want to do. I told you I wanted to work for a charity group."

His eyes dimmed, and she knew she'd made a mistake by mentioning anything from their past. "Yes, you did tell me that. You failed to mention that you already had a multibillion-dollar one waiting for you."

She stood up. "I did fail to mention that. Be happy you phrased it that way and didn't say the word 'lie' or 'liar,' because I swear every single time you throw that word at me from now on, I'm going to find the first newspaper I can, roll it up, and swat you on the nose with it."

She turned to walk away because she wasn't going to spend the afternoon fighting with him. Nope. No way. She would go back to her room and read a book. Lisa had brought her some romances. They were a good way to forget her troubles.

A hand wrapped around her arm and she was pulled back toward him. To her surprise, he was smiling down at her. "You going to train me like a wayward puppy?"

"I'm sick of the lying thing, Henry." She wasn't going to back down from that. "I can't let you use it anytime you want me to feel guilty. I know you don't understand why I did what I did, but I don't think any amount of explanation from me is going to work."

"No use of the word 'lie' or 'liar,'" he said, his hand drifting down to hers. "I don't want to make you feel guilty. I'm sorry. I really do want to understand."

But she feared it was something he couldn't do, and that that lie—even if he never said the word around her again—would always sit between them. It was precisely why she'd kept her distance the last few days. She knew he would break her heart in the end. "I wish I could explain it better than I have."

His fingers tangled with hers. "Win, trials like this can take years. In fact, until I'm sure I've got what I need, my intention is to push this as far out as I possibly can. Have you thought about what it would mean to stay here for a long period of time?"

"How long?" She'd known it would be weeks. Maybe a month. "At some point it's got to be safe to go back to my own place."

"I don't think that's a good idea. I think this is the kind of story that will stay in people's minds."

"I can go quietly." She didn't like how soft her body got the moment he touched her. It was like she had a button only he could push. "Once my uncle is home, I should be safe with the bodyguards around."

"Your uncle travels constantly. He isn't home more than a few days out of the month. You would be alone in that house with Trevor," he pointed out. "I don't think that's a good idea."

"I could find a place of my own." She hadn't wanted to because she'd been planning on living in Durham for a few years.

"I think you should stay here."

"Even if it takes a year?"

"However long it takes."

"You know why that's a bad idea."

"Because we're going to end up in bed together? That's inevitable." He stared down at her hand and the place where their fingers entwined. "It's a matter of time and proximity. I've had to work late the last few nights. Hell, I forced myself to work at the office because I knew what would happen."

"And you don't want it to happen." Somehow, even as the words were coming out of her mouth, she found herself closer to him.

"Don't I? I wanted it to happen the minute I saw you again, but it would have been an ugly thing. I needed time to process. I still don't think I have anything to offer you, but I also know that if we're stuck together, we might as well enjoy it."

"So I should have sex with you because we don't have anything better to do? That's an offer I can refuse."

He winced and held her hand as she tried to walk away. "I'm bad at this part. I don't know what to say to you. I know that when I make the proper decision to stay away from you, thirty minutes later I want to touch you again. I'm not as angry as I was. I'm more sad than anything, and not kissing you is killing me."

"Kissing me, making love to me, won't solve our problems. I'll still be me when you wake up in the morning."

"But I don't know that I'll be me. I can't seem to stay me around you."

And it bothered him. "I don't want to cause you stress, Henry."

His lips curled up in the sexiest smirk. "You know what's good for stress?"

He killed her when he softened like that. He was probably right and she wouldn't be able to hold out. "You should do what I did. I went on the Internet and bought a . . . Well, it's going to prove helpful."

The smirk left his face, replaced with the most prudish frown she'd ever seen on a man with that filthy a mind. He dropped her hand in favor of putting both of his on his hips, like an outraged priest or something. "You bought a vibrator?"

She felt her face flush. "Well, I thought it would help with stress, and there's not a lot to do around here except sit and worry about going to jail. Also, Lisa really recommended this brand. She says it's long-lasting and gets the job done."

He stopped for a minute and then his head fell forward on a booming laugh. When he looked back up, he was pulling his glasses off and wiping tears away. He reached for her again, pulling her in. "I forgot how funny you are."

It felt so good to be in his arms and feel genuine warmth from him. It almost made her forget all their problems. Still, it was a moment and she allowed them to have it. She let her arms wrap around him. "I haven't had much to laugh about lately."

His hand stroked her hair but whatever he was about to say was interrupted by the door to his apartment opening. His hands relaxed and he stepped back.

"Mr. Guidry, I would appreciate it if your wife would refrain from selling my client sex toys," he said.

"Henry!" She couldn't believe he'd simply put it out there. It hadn't been like the big Cajun bodyguard had been around when they'd had their girl talk.

"Well, if you can order it, I can complain bitterly about it," Henry replied.

If the bodyguard was shocked, he didn't show it. Remy simply shrugged. "If you're talking about the Pleasure Wand 5000, that thing is worth the money. Good call, Win. But right now you have other company."

Two men were behind Remy. One was tall with sandy-blond hair and the other was . . . Her heart clenched at the sight of him.

"Win, these are our investigators." Henry gestured to the men. "Case Taggart and his partner—"

"Michael Malone." She teared up and hoped she could hold it together. "Yes, I know him. Our families were close when we were younger. Michael, it's good to see you again. I didn't realize you were working on the case."

The big, gorgeous Texan stared at her. "Winnie, don't you dare hold back on me. It's been too long. Don't think for a single second I'm still mad at you. Come here and give me a hug."

Oh, that dark-haired billionaire's son looked like happiness and home, and he was one of the people she'd cut out of her life because he'd been far too reasonable. She ran to him, throwing her arms around her childhood friend. When they were children, her uncle and his father had been on several corporate boards together.

He was a piece of the old Win that she wasn't ashamed of.

"Don't you worry, girl. I'm going to make sure you're okay," he whispered, his arms holding her close. "I'm not going to stop until I figure out who did this because I know damn straight that it wasn't you."

"Uhm, Mike, I think you should let the girl go or her lawyer might murder you," Case Taggart said with a smirk. "He's got those crazy eyes my brother is always going on about."

With a chuckle, Michael released her, looking over at Henry. "Sorry, Counselor. No one told you Winnie and I grew up together? My father and twin brother run Malone Oil. I got sick of being covered in crude, and honestly I was never good at board meetings, so I joined the navy and eventually ended up at McKay-Taggart."

"I ordered an investigator, not another bodyguard," Henry replied.

What the hell was going on? Henry was looking at Michael like he was going to attack at any moment. "I'm sure he's good. And he knows me. I'm thrilled to see someone who knows me."

"Knows you?" Henry's eyes had narrowed.

Was he jealous? It was her turn to put her hands on her hips and sound a little prudish. "Yes. He knows me in the we-used-to-throw-mud-pies-at-each-other way, not in the biblical sense."

"Though you look good, girl," Michael said in his deep Texas twang. "We could rethink that whole thing. You know I'm still single after all these years."

"That's because you're a picky bastard," Case said. "And you're going to get taken out by Crazy Eyes if you don't watch it. That dude likely knows how to get away with murder."

"This *dude*, as you so eloquently put it, knows what a truly great investigative team looks like, and it's not based on childhood friend-ships." The words came out of Henry's mouth in a positively arctic tone. "I need to talk to Taggart because I thought he recruited ex–special forces, not rich boys who like to play at investigating."

"Henry, that was rude." She was shocked.

He really was an idiot when it came to the whole emotional thing. Men. Not a one of them could be reasonable. She either got idiot men-children or superhot passionate cavemen with brilliant IQs when it came to all things intellectual, and nothing when it came to how to handle themselves emotionally.

If this was all about sex, he wouldn't have held her and asked her if she was innocent. He wouldn't have broken that sacred rule of his for a fun lay. He wouldn't have spent the last few days skulking around because he didn't know what to do. He'd said he'd forgotten how funny she could be. Well, she really hadn't been herself the last few days. That might be part of the problem. He'd been faced with the fact that he thought he didn't know her, and all his evidence pointed to that conclusion because she'd been a teary, weepy, needy mess.

She was starting to feel like herself again. Maybe it was time to let that happen.

Michael started to explain his many qualifications for the job, but she suspected Henry only needed one thing in order to feel com-fortable with her old friend investigating.

She moved to his side and slid her hand into his. He stiffened for a moment, and then his fingers curled around her and he pulled her closer to his side.

"Better?" Win asked. "You feeling less like a Neanderthal?"

She could have sworn he blushed, but he simply cleared his throat. "I'm sorry, gentlemen. Of course McKay-Taggart sent their best. If you'll join Win and me, we can go over some of the reports."

He moved to the big dining room table, pulling back a seat for her and then immediately taking the one closest to hers.

When he sat down, he was right back to the competent, professional Henry she'd always known.

"You do have crazy eyes, you know," she said with a shake of her head.

He picked up a folder, but under the table his leg touched hers, rubbing against it in a way that was more about connection than sex. "Only for you," he said under his breath before looking back to the investigators. "So what have we found out?"

She settled back, wondering what the hell she was going to do with that man.

~

"Would you like the good news or the bad news?" Case Taggart asked.

Henry hated bad news, but he was definitely a rip-the-bandage-off kind of man. "What's happened?"

Besides him making an idiot of himself? He knew he'd been tremendously unprofessional and yet he couldn't make himself take it back. It was nice to sit beside her. It was completely inevitable that they would sleep together and he didn't want to fight it anymore. He'd spent days staying away from her because he didn't want to hurt her again, but he knew he was failing.

And lying. He was staying away from her because he didn't want to get hurt again. Because he was still completely unsure of what to do.

"I'm afraid a couple of the tabloids will be running stories claiming that Taylor Winston-Hughes is sleeping with her lawyer in the next couple of days," Malone said. "I've got some lawyers trying to shut the articles down, but you know how this is going to go."

Win's eyes widened and she gasped. "Oh no. I thought we could keep it quiet. We had a relationship but it was before we started working together. He's not breaking any rules. We haven't slept together since he became my attorney."

He could feel her panic and knew it wasn't about her own fears. She was scared for him, that she was going to ruin his career. He needed to put all of that to rest. He reached out and put a hand on her arm. "It doesn't matter. It's one more scandal and it will blow over after they've taken it to its natural conclusion."

She looked a bit sick. "Natural conclusion?"

Oh, he knew exactly where they would take it. "That you might be the real reason Alicia and I broke up, and Brie Westerhaven got caught in the middle. It's going to get messy and we should try to get ahead of it. Does my ex-wife know about the tabloid stories?"

"I didn't want to contact her without talking to you first," Case explained.

"Call her. I've heard she's filming in Toronto. I need a meeting set up with her. I want to go over everything she remembers about that night. As for the story, it's going to hit no matter what. I'm sure they'll have all kinds of unnamed sources. We can sue, but the truth is we did have a relationship. We need to mitigate the damage. I want it made plain that I am not the lead lawyer on Win's case. I'm her boyfriend and she trusts my firm to handle this, as many lawyers' loved ones would trust close advisors. David Cormack is her attorney, with Noah Lawless and Margarita Reyes as seconds. Ms. Winston-Hughes has slept with none of those people. Right, sweetheart?"

She turned to him, ignoring his final, slightly snarky question. "Boyfriend? How did we go from we're staying in separate rooms to avoid the inevitable to you're now my boyfriend?"

Ah, but how things changed. This situation was completely fluid, and he was excellent at changing tactics when the circumstances called for it. The circumstances had changed. They had to evolve with it. "We release a brief statement to the press about our personal relationship and that it did not begin until after the termination of my marriage. Alicia will back this up with a statement of her own. She will also state that she supports both the relationship and Win herself. Then we will go silent unless we need to strike back because of gross maliciousness." He looked to Win. "And avoiding the inevitable is an oxymoron. You understand that, right?"

She was so confusing to him, but it was clearer when she seemed to be the woman he'd spent those two weeks with. When she was bold and assertive and didn't take crap from him, he could see her again.

Was he looking at her in the wrong way? Was he being too hard on her?

She turned to him, her breasts pressed against the V-neck of her shirt. "Who said it was inevitable, Garrison? I assure you, I could hold out a long time, especially when you're mean. After all, I have a present coming."

There she was. There was the woman who challenged him and made him crazy, and got his dick so damn hard he couldn't think about anything except her. It wasn't just the sass that got to him. It was the combination of strength and sweetness. Of brains and that rich vein of kindness everyone who knew her talked about.

He leaned over. "You haven't even seen mean yet, sweetheart. I can intercept that present, but you should know that I'm excellent stress relief. You don't need double-A batteries."

Her lips curled up. "It's a plug-in, Henry. Very powerful."

His whole soul responded to her. What the fuck was he doing? He didn't care. "I'm more powerful. I don't need to be plugged in and I do more than mere orgasms."

"Yeah, well, we'll have to see about that." She turned to their guests. "Yes, a nicely worded public statement about the status of our relationship would be lovely. Please put in there something about how taken the counselor is with me and how hard he's working to ensure my safe status."

Bitch. Gorgeous, sexy, smart bitch. And if he was a monster, didn't he need a bitch?

Don't ever settle for a simple woman, Henry. Simple comes easy. You want something worth fighting for and that's never simple, son.

Why did he hear his grandfather so clearly now? After he'd gone out into the world, his grandfather had been a photograph he'd carried with him, but then he'd died and Henry had gone butt-fuck crazy for years and now the world had somehow realigned and become something . . . beautiful.

When he was still, when he put aside the alcohol and ego, the insecurity and arrogance—that was when the world drew down, simplifying into the lessons of his childhood.

Work was honorable. Love wasn't simple. People were meaningful.

He'd forgotten that for so long, and it had really taken Win Hughes to remind him.

"I think we can work with your publicist to handle that," Case said.

Michael was silent and that was super–all right with Henry. He was too young and apparently loaded with cash, and he did not like how that asshole looked at Win. Like she was something precious.

She'd lied. She'd lied to him.

Did that mean she wasn't precious? Did that mean he couldn't forgive her?

He pulled back his hand, noting the frown she sent him. It made him wonder if she could hear his thoughts. She'd promised to newspaper-strike him if he said the word *lie*. He needed to ensure all the papers and magazines were locked up. Would she switch to a water spritzer? He'd heard that was a way to train bad puppies.

Damn but he liked her.

"Excellent. I think that's the proper way to deal with the tabloids. Make it a nonstory. Happy couples are boring." He needed to move on or he would be the idiot declaring his undying love or something. "What else did you find out? I asked the forensic accountant to try to pull up anything interesting."

Michael held up a hand. "The accountant found two things I was interested in. One, did you know that Mary Hannigan spent over five thousand dollars on a recent trip to Los Angeles?"

Win sat up straight. "You're investigating my nanny?"

"Damn straight," Case shot back. "She's got an odd history. I can't find records of her before 1989. Do you not find that interesting?"

"I was born in 1989," Win said.

Yes, he found that interesting. "You think she was brought in as an illegal?"

"With your permission, we'll go out and have a talk with her," Michael replied.

Win was shaking her head. "No. My nana did not murder Brie. First off, she wasn't even there that night. She was stuck in a hospital on the island, recovering from surgery. She was in a car accident."

Case worked the tablet he'd brought in. "Yes, I've got the police report on that. Were you aware she was driving your vehicle?"

A fine chill made the hair on Henry's neck stand up. "She was driving Win's Jeep? The same one that someone tried to run off the road a few months back?"

"Yes," Michael replied. "She was driving the Jeep. This was roughly forty-eight hours after she got back from Los Angeles."

"Do we have any idea what she was doing in L.A.?" Henry asked.

"I'll ask her," Win offered. "I'm sure she was taking a vacation or something."

"Or going to have a talk with Brie Westerhaven." Case turned the tablet around. "I've been combing through banking records. I find it interesting that Brie Westerhaven deposited five thousand dollars the same day Mary Hannigan pulled five thousand dollars out of her account. Coincidence? I think not."

"I think I'll go out and talk to Nana Mary myself." He wasn't leaving that to the investigators. Something was up with the nanny, and there was no way Win would believe it if he didn't have airtight proof against her. "What else?"

"Dear Uncle Bellamy has a mistress." Michael winced a little as he made the announcement. "Sorry, Win."

She waved him off. "Is it still Amber or did she get too old for him? I'm not an idiot. I'm fairly certain he's always had a woman on the side. Even when he was married. I caught him one time at a Broadway show and he tried to pass her off as a coworker who had won a company-wide contest to attend with him. Sure she was. They're always roughly twenty-five and always brunette and flashy. Henry, Mary had nothing to do with this."

He put his hand on hers. "Sweetheart, have you thought about the fact that she loves you and if she found out someone was trying to hurt you, she might put herself in harm's way to protect you?"

That was the way to get her on his side. Oh, he didn't necessarily believe it, but Win wouldn't accept that her precious Nana could do wrong. So he had to flip it around until he had proof.

Win could be naive. She needed someone to protect her.

Or she was a liar who was good at getting people to protect her. His cynical self wouldn't go away, but it was easier and easier to push him back. Maybe he could have held on to all his righteous anger if she weren't here, but it was hard when he saw her every day. It was hard to reconcile the woman who had lied to him about her past with the vibrant, loving woman she was when he was around her.

"I need to talk to her," Win said. "She might have tried to do something to protect me. I know she didn't want me to go back on the show and she knew Brie was pushing. I can't believe Brie would blackmail her like that. And for five grand? Brie comes from money. She can't buy a handbag for that."

"Brie Westerhaven's father cut her off six months ago," Michael pointed out. "He stopped putting money in her trust fund and stopped paying her bills. I do believe that had something to do with his new wife and the fact that she's having a baby, and Brie was quite upset by all accounts."

Win's mouth had dropped open. "She didn't say anything to me. I mean, not about the money. She said horrible things about the baby, but she didn't mean them. Or maybe she did. I didn't realize how desperate she was. She can't live without money. She would have no idea how to live a regular life."

Yes, that was his thought exactly. Brie Westerhaven wouldn't know how to live without plenty of cash, and she would need to find alternative sources of income. "Would her salary from the show make up for it?"

Win shook her head. "Not at all. She made maybe fifty thousand a show. I know that sounds like a lot, but it's not to a woman who drinks five-hundred-dollar bottles of champagne without blinking and who can't buy a car for less than a hundred K. We were different in that way. My uncle didn't grow up rich and he was a frugal man. Trev hated it, but he put us on a budget while we were in school. I learned how to make my money last. Brie's dad was a rock star and spent much of his time high on coke. He gave Brie whatever she wanted, whenever she wanted it."

At least now they had some kind of a lead. "Are there other deposits? Ones we can't account for?"

Case nodded. "There were three cash deposits in the last four months. Nothing at all before that cashwise. Everything else is direct deposit or check."

"How much cash are we talking about?" Henry asked.

"Thirty thousand dollars," Case replied.

That was a nice amount. The day was looking up. "It sounds like she's got a nice side business going. And we're sure this isn't from Mary?"

"Mary wouldn't have that kind of money," Win said quickly.

Michael cleared his throat and sent Win a sympathetic look. "Mary Hannigan is worth almost two million dollars, according to her accounts. That's liquid and her stock in Hughes Corp."

Win shook her head as though trying to clear it. "She bought stock?"

Case flipped through the file. "Not that I can tell. There are some complex dealings, but it looks like part of her employment package included vesting in stock every five years or so. She even received another round of shares three years ago. It's like clockwork. Your uncle has taken good care of that woman."

They needed to talk to Mary. He would have to find a way to do it without involving Win because he wasn't sure she could handle finding out her precious Nana was hiding something. Had she had an affair with Bellamy?

Win sat back, obviously thinking the problem through. "I think some of the extravagant payment comes from my uncle's sense of guilt. He wanted to make sure I didn't go through a long line of nannies, like some kids do. Because he knew he wasn't going to be there the way my parents would have, he felt like he needed to buy me a mom. Could they have had an affair? I don't know. Mary wasn't my uncle's type even when she was younger. If they did and Brie found out about it, they might have been embarrassed enough to pay her off, but that doesn't mean my uncle murdered Brie."

"His alibi has held up so far," Henry conceded. "Margarita was with him when you screamed. But she'd just met with him and we know you were knocked unconscious. The question is how long? I still haven't gotten the ME's report so I don't have a time of death. Until I have that and can confirm where everyone was, they're all still on my radar. Anything else?"

Case and Michael looked at each other and seemed to have some kind of silent discussion. Finally, Case shrugged and Michael leaned forward.

"Do you have any idea why Brie would be so fascinated with DNA and ancestry all of a sudden?" Michael asked. "She spent roughly twenty-five hundred dollars in the last six months on books and Internet programs about tracing ancestry. She also paid for three separate DNA tests. The who's-the-daddy kind."

Win frowned. "I think I can put two and two together. Damn her. No wonder her dad kicked her off the family accounts. She was probably trying to prove that her stepmom, Jackie, was cheating on her dad. You have to understand. Jackie is only two years older than Brie is. Was. Brie hated her and she was very likely trying to find a way to oust her. Proving Jackie's baby girl wasn't fathered by Brie's dad would be one way to do it."

Michael frowned. "I don't know. I've got a feeling about it. And neither Jackie nor Brie's father was in New York the night of the murder."

Case sat back. "Michael's been like a dog with a bone about the DNA stuff. I thought she was just playing around with her ancestry for that show of hers. You know, if she'd found out she was mainly Irish, they would go to Ireland and do a special: 'Brie Finds Her Heritage.' But I like Win's explanation more. I'm going to look into Brie's family. See if they might have hired anyone questionable lately."

Henry liked the lead as well. If Brie had been blackmailing people left and right and trying to break up her stepmother's marriage, there were a lot of suspects out there. "Excellent work, gentlemen. Follow up on those leads and check into Trevor Hughes."

He was satisfied that Win didn't even blink.

"Sweetheart, could you get our guests some water?" He needed a moment alone with them.

She stood up. "Of course, but I totally know you're going to say a bunch of stuff to them you don't want me to hear."

Well, he'd never said she was stupid. "I appreciate your discretion."

She walked into the kitchen.

Henry leaned in. "I want to know everything you can dig up about the nanny."

"That's the problem," Case argued. "There's nothing before 1989."

"There's always something. Find the thread and pull that sucker." Something about the nanny wasn't right. "I want to know if she has a will and who all that stock goes to when she dies. I want to know everything about her connection to Bellamy Hughes."

"We can do that," Michael promised. "But I want to know how serious you are about Win."

Case shot his partner a what-the-hell look. "Hey, we talked about this."

"We disagreed about this," Michael shot back. "Win's been through a lot and the last thing she needs is some cold-ass bastard using her for sex."

"Did anyone think about the fact that *she* might be using *me* for sex?" Why did he always have to be the bad guy? Not that he would turn her down. He was getting to the point that he could handle being used for sex. By her.

Only her.

Fuck, what the hell was he going to do? He didn't want anyone else, but he couldn't quite forgive her, couldn't quite believe her.

Michael's green eyes rolled. "Sure she is. Winnie's not like that. It's why I knew she was getting into trouble when Brie talked her into doing that show."

"You knew Brie and that crew?" Henry asked.

Michael shook his head. "That's a totally different crowd. I've probably met Brie twice, but we've never done more than exchange pleasantries. I never understood how she was Win's best friend. She was always . . . 'sneaky' might be the right word. Anyway, I could tell she was in it for herself. And by *it* I mean everything. But I suspect you might be like Brie, too, Garrison."

"How so?" He'd been called so many names it didn't bug him. Not at all.

Maybe because this was Win's friend, but mostly it didn't bug him.

"You're cold and you've got a reputation for not giving a shit. You've recently come out of a relationship where you made quite a few scandalous headlines of your own. Win needs out of that life. It nearly killed her."

"I didn't see you trying to save her."

Michael huffed. "I did. I flew to the set because it was obvious she was in trouble. I could see her wasting away. She kicked me out. Told me I was crazy and jealous. What did I have to be jealous of?"

"It wasn't really her by then, I suspect. Not the Win you knew. By then she was too far in and the disease had taken over. She was trying to protect the habit," he explained quietly. "When you get to a spot like that, the addiction is all that keeps you going, in a way. So you protect it. You protect it from your friends and your better self, and all those facts and obvious realities. You shove them aside and hold on to the one thing that makes you feel good."

"You sound like you know something about it," Michael said.

"I'm a recovering alcoholic." He wasn't going to hide anything. "You should put that in my con column. I'm too old for Win. I'm too hard. I've got a job that keeps me working all the time, a job that many people view as nothing more than a highly paid ambulance chaser. I don't tend to care about anything or anyone. I'm neither shiny nor optimistic. I'm not a good bet for her."

"Then maybe she should come and stay with me," Michael offered. "My father has a penthouse on the Upper East Side. She'll be safe and protected and we can keep her spirits up."

"I'm staying here, Michael." Win's face was grim as she handed the investigators two bottles of water.

Michael stood up. "I'm merely offering you a choice."

"She's made her choice." Henry found himself staring out the window so he didn't look at either of them. The younger man was starting to irritate him. The whole talk had made him emotional. He didn't like being emotional.

They were right. He was cold and unforgiving.

So why couldn't he send her away?

"All you need to do is call and I'll be here," Michael promised.

"We'll be in touch, Mr. Garrison," Case said as they started toward the door. "If we're not kicked off the case. Nice to meet you, Win."

Henry heard her follow them to the elevator that would take them past Remy and down to the lobby. He turned back to the folders in front of him.

Of course she knew billionaires' sons. She was a billionaire. Or she would be in a few months. Hoover Kendalmire hadn't bothered him. Michael Malone did. Michael Malone was an actual functional human being.

Did she wish she'd stayed close to him? Had she had a crush on Malone?

It didn't matter. He needed to focus on the case at hand, and that included dealing with the gossip that was about to hit.

Would it be smarter to let her move to Malone's and work the case that way? Malone would likely jump at the chance to play the white knight and save the lady from the horrors of having her name attached to a washed-up alcoholic lawyer who'd lost everything and was using her case to lift himself back up.

If Malone was seen escorting her around, was willing to give an interview about how they'd reconnected after all these years, it would probably look good for her.

It would be good for her case.

Warm hands touched his shoulders, rubbing across them. "I'm not going anywhere, Henry."

Why could this one woman practically read his fucking thoughts? "Maybe it would be for the best."

Her fingers worked their way up his neck as though she knew exactly where all his tension was. "You think they would even buy the story? I don't know. Michael and I haven't seen each other in forever. Not since he tried to talk sense into me. I kind of thought he hated me."

"I don't think anyone can hate you, Win. I hate everything and everyone, and I can't seem to do it." He couldn't help himself. He was relaxing under her touch. He didn't even want to fight it. He was sick of fighting her.

"Oh, I think you're wrong. I'm definitely beginning to believe Brie hated me," she said softly. "But as to all the ideas that are whirling around in that big brain of yours about changing the story line, stop. The truth is best."

He reached up and took her hand, pulling her so he could see her. "But my story wasn't the truth, either. We're not lovers now."

She stared down at him, but the soft look on her face made him feel good. "I thought it was inevitable."

"I thought you had a vibrator now and didn't need me."

She reached out and smoothed his hair back. "I don't know what to do with you, Henry. You scare the hell out of me."

"I know you won't believe me, but I feel the same way. You are the single scariest thing I've ever come up against. I hate that man. I don't even know Michael Malone but I hate him because you lit up when you looked at him. I'm not a possessive asshole."

"I don't like knowing you slept with Alicia Kingman. I stared at myself in the mirror for the longest time today, trying to see if there was anything about me that was prettier than her."

He wasn't going to have her do that. He tugged on her hand, pulling her into his lap. "There is nothing she has that even comes close to how gorgeous you are to me. Don't you dare question that."

"I don't like the way I feel right now," she admitted. "My chest feels tight, and I'm tense because I'm starting to understand that so much has been kept from me. There's only one person I know who understands, really understands, what I went through. Everyone else thinks I flipped a switch at the institute and now I'm cured. They never understood why I did what I did. Why I starved myself."

He knew. "Because it felt good. Because you were so out of control everywhere else that you needed to ruthlessly control that part of your life. Mine was the opposite. I was so in control and hated what I saw and felt. When I drank, I could let go. I could pretend I was this other person. The problem was I would relax and start to enjoy myself and then wake up from getting blackout drunk and find out I'd turned into Mr. Hyde. I do understand that part of you, Win."

How could the simple act of touching her calm him?

"Then maybe you could help me." She put her hands on his shoulders. "I'm tired of sleeping alone. What I really mean is, I'm tired of not having you in bed with me. I can joke all I want, but I need you. I need you now."

It was a mistake he was happy to make. All he had to do was lean forward to bring his mouth to hers, and he suddenly didn't care about the case or the past. He didn't care about the future or what anyone would think.

All that mattered was her.

ELEVEN

Win knew it was a mistake. She knew it the minute she put her hands on him. She'd felt him exhale, and there had been no question in her mind where this ended. Still, she couldn't let him be alone. Hell, *she* didn't want to be alone. Seeing Michael again and hearing about all the things Brie had done, all the lies and truths that had been kept from her . . . she needed to breathe, and lately the only place she felt perfectly comfortable was in Henry's arms.

She needed to get back to that place they'd been to before. Before he'd found out her full name. Before she'd been accused of murder. Before she'd realized how much more he meant to her than she did to him.

One perfect hour was all she needed. She wouldn't push him. She wouldn't ask for more.

All she could ask was that he took her out of herself, took her to that place where she was more than just Win.

His mouth came down on hers. Soft, sweet. He took his time, moving his lips over hers, warming her up. He kissed her that way for what felt like forever. Every slow caress of his mouth made her feel precious and wanted.

"God, I missed you, Win." The words rumbled over her lips as his tongue made its first appearance.

Heat flashed through her. He hadn't called her Taylor in days. He was back to calling her Win. His anger was still simmering under the surface, but he'd softened.

Time. They both needed it, but that didn't mean they couldn't have moments like these. Moments of respite. A brief time of sanctuary from all the bad.

His hands found their way under her T-shirt and she sighed at the contact. Skin on skin. It was what she needed. Nothing in between them. His hands flattened on her back, warming her everywhere he touched as his tongue slid against hers.

She gave over, letting him lead her with slow, drugging kisses that made her brain pleasantly fuzzy.

Everything else seemed to fall away when he touched her.

"I dream about this every single damn night," he whispered. "I want to get you out of my head but I can't."

"Do you think you can fuck me out of your system?" She had to ask. It was a dangerous question because she wasn't sure she could walk away, even if he answered the way she thought he would.

His arms tightened around her, pulling her close even as his head moved back and he looked right into her eyes. "Never. I don't think I could ever fuck you enough that I won't want you. Win, it's only been a few weeks, but I don't want anyone else. I was going to call. I was fighting it, but I was going to call you. I couldn't help myself."

He was so gorgeous. Sometimes his beauty seemed like a cold thing, like a work of art, but when his eyes were hot and his voice deep and dark, his beauty was infinitely warm. She'd only ever seen him look that way at her. A little voice played in the back of her head. How many other women had seen that look in Henry Garrison's eyes?

Why did it matter as long as he was true to her? She was letting her insecurity come between them. It didn't matter if he'd cared about a woman before. That woman had been crazy to let him go. What did matter was the fact that the right woman would get the Henry Garrison she'd met on that island.

She cupped his face, loving how straight his jawline was. "I would have answered. I would have picked up that phone and pretended like you hadn't made me wait because I know what's wrong with you."

"Do you?"

She nodded and leaned over, kissing the bridge of his nose. "I do. You think you know everything, but you've never met me. You have no idea how to handle me, but I can teach you."

He pulled the T-shirt over her head, tossing it aside, challenge plain in his eyes. "Oh, I know exactly how to handle you. You think I've forgotten?"

His fingers twisted, unclasping her bra, and it joined the shirt. Cool air hit her skin and she felt her nipples tighten to hard buds. She hadn't been talking about handling her sexually, but she couldn't seem to find the will to argue with him. Not when he lifted her up with nothing but his upper body strength and ordered her to straddle him. She found herself with her legs spread, his cock rubbing against her core.

It was like a lap dance except there would be no money exchanged, and they were definitely going to do more than tease each other.

All that stood between her and that rock-hard cock of his were a few thin layers of clothing.

Damn but she was pretty sure if those layers weren't there, he would have already found her aching and ready and she would be riding him right then and there.

His hands cupped her ass, pulling her in closer. "I might have fucked up a lot in the last couple of years, but I can do this."

He leaned forward and sucked a nipple into his mouth.

She gasped, trying to get air into her lungs as she felt the bare edge of his teeth on her breast. She went perfectly still, letting the sensation flow over her. He nibbled and sucked, every now and then lighting up her system with a bit of a bite. Nothing that would truly hurt, but it reminded her that he was excellent at handling her.

"See, I remember exactly how to touch you." The words rumbled along her skin. "You respond to me like no other woman. You respond like you were made for me, like these nipples were meant for my mouth. I know how and where to touch you because I spent hour after hour learning this gorgeous body."

He moved to her other breast, sucking and tonguing her in a way that gave truth to his every word. He did know exactly where to touch her.

And he knew what to say to her.

"No one ever moved me the way you do." The words came out shaky, but she felt like he needed to hear them. He was so good at telling her how much he wanted her, but he needed to know, too. "I've had a few guys I slept with, a couple of boyfriends, but they weren't anything like you."

His hands tightened on her hips. "Malone?"

Michael was still on his mind? She needed to get Henry out of that headspace. She cupped his head, running her fingers through the silk of his hair. Her big predatory cat liked to be petted. She'd found stroking Henry got him to calm down. "Not even a kiss. We were only friends. I didn't have much of a chance to date because of the all-girls-boarding-school thing, but I would travel with my uncle sometimes during the summer, and I spent a couple of weeks most years out on the Malone ranch. I was a kid sister to him and his twin brother."

"See that it stays that way," Henry grumbled. His hips flexed, rubbing his cock against her clitoris with a perfection that made her whimper. "I know he's some badass ex–special forces dude, but I can be mean, too."

"I'll make sure he knows we're just friends."

It wasn't like she had a ton of men begging to date her. Of course, the problem was she didn't want anyone except Henry. Stubborn, irritating, sexy, and smart Henry Garrison.

"See that you do." He dragged her down, kissing her again, his tongue dancing against hers.

He ground up against her, running that thick cock over her clit and making her moan.

She let him take the lead, moving her body in time with his. They'd fought this for days and it had been stupid. He'd been right. Inevitable.

It felt like it, but she knew things weren't always as they seemed.

"Don't leave me," he rasped against her lips. His hands slid under her jeans to find warm flesh. "Stay with me. Whatever you're thinking about, it can wait. Stay here with me for a few hours."

She looked down into those clear blue eyes of his. "I'm going to be here for more than a few hours. I'm worried about it. I can't stay away from you. How bad is it going to get if I'm here for months?"

"This doesn't feel bad." He pressed up against her, his jaw tightening. "It feels pretty fucking good to me."

He was willfully misunderstanding her. "I'm crazy about you."

He went still for a moment and then she saw pure stubborn resolve light his eyes. "Good. There's nothing wrong with that. That can work in our favor. It's obvious there's something between us. We need to be a happy couple for the press. Why can't we make it work personally?"

Not the most romantic thing a man had ever said, but then he wasn't the most romantic of men. She had to be careful. "You could break my heart."

"Don't give me a reason to," he ground out. "Don't lie to me again. Don't go back to that world. Stay in mine. Stay with me, and we'll be fine. It's simple."

But it wasn't. It was so complex because she had to deal with the fact that Henry had been burned before, and in a way that had wrecked his life. Maybe if they'd met at some other time he might have pushed past some of his fear, but her very name compounded the problem.

She had to make a choice. He couldn't keep her here. If she wanted to, she could pack up and be in her uncle's home in fifteen minutes.

And leave Henry all alone. He could be surrounded by people and still be alone. He could have all the friends in the world, but without someone who truly understood him, he was alone behind walls so high and strong she wasn't sure anyone could get through them.

He'd bent for her and not in some shallow way. He'd broken his number one rule, and didn't that mean something?

"I'll stay with you." She couldn't stand the thought of Henry being alone with all his dark thoughts. He needed someone to force him into the light.

She was in love with him and it was stupid and she was going to get so hurt, and she couldn't stop herself.

Inevitable.

"You won't regret it," he whispered before taking her lips again. "I'll take care of you. You won't need anything else."

Oh, she would need so much more from him, but she wasn't sure he was capable of giving it to her. Love. She wasn't sure he would ever allow himself to do that again, but she had to take the chance. It was the most important gamble of her life.

Because she was betting everything on him. Her heart. Her freedom. Her life. They were all in this man's hands.

"Take off those jeans. Do it now." His voice had gone low and deep, all his patience dissolved.

She scrambled off his lap and worked the fly of her jeans, watching him the whole time. His eyes were on her, his whole body and being seemingly wrapped up in what she was doing. Like a predator who had a nice, fluffy bunny in his sights. He was still, waiting for the moment when he would pounce.

If she didn't know how damn good it felt when he made a meal of her, she might have been wary. In this, she trusted him implicitly. She eased her jeans over her hips and drew her undies with them, finally standing naked in front of him.

How could she feel so comfortable with him? She'd spent so much of her life struggling with her body. She'd come to peace with it, but sex was still hard. Not with him. "Somehow I know when you look at me you're not judging me."

"I'm far too busy having my breath taken away," he replied. "I don't want to ever make you feel less than beautiful, sweetheart. That's not our problem. Our problem is I think you're too good to be true. I want you to be real. I want you to be everything you seem to be, but I can't quite make myself believe. Make me believe, Win."

If she thought for a second he was truly asking her to prove herself to him, she could have walked away. But she heard the real plea under his words. Time. He needed time and intimacy. He needed her to stay. No words were going to prove anything to either one of them. They had to roll the dice and bet on each other.

"I can't make you believe anything as long as you're wearing pants, babe." For now this had to be the language of their love. He didn't know how to say the words, but she could see his affection in his actions. He worked day and night on her case. He cared that she was innocent. He was willing to try.

His eyes never left hers as he unbuckled his belt and undid the fly of his slacks. He reached into his pocket and came back with a small packet. "You've turned me into an optimist. Well, at least about one thing. I want to be ready to fuck you. I want to walk through my day thinking that at any moment I might be able to have you. I've gotten obsessed with the thought. You might not like what you've unleashed."

Oh, she liked what *he'd* just unleashed quite a bit. He sat back in his chair, stroking his cock. Her whole body was ready for him, needed to connect with him in the most intimate way possible. "Give it to me, Henry."

His eyes flashed and for a second she thought he would refuse her, but he passed her the condom and his whole body tightened as she dropped to her knees in front of him. She pressed in between his legs, taking his cock in her hand.

"God, you make me crazy. I can't . . . I can't stay away. No more pretending. This isn't for the freaking press. This is for us. You and me."

It was all she could ask from him right now. "You and me."

She stroked him, loving the silky feel of his skin. How could something so damn hard be soft against her skin? She couldn't hold out. This wasn't going to be some exploratory session. They'd been apart for far too long. But she wanted another taste.

She heard him growl as she sucked the head of his cock, flattening her tongue against the bottom and drawing him inside.

"Not long, Win," he warned. "I'm too close and I don't want to come in your mouth. Not this time."

He wanted them together and connected. She wanted the same.

One long pass, and then two. She could feel how ready he was and she couldn't wait another second. She opened the condom and rolled it on, stroking him and never giving him a moment to rest.

"Come up here. Just like this," he commanded, reaching out to help her up.

He wasn't moving. He wanted her to ride him, and the idea made her heart race. She got to her feet, and a thought occurred. "I'll ruin those slacks."

He tugged on her hand. "Ride me. I don't give a damn about the slacks. They can be cleaned, and I don't care what the dry cleaner thinks any more than I care about the fact that your bodyguard is right outside that door. I want you. No one else fucking matters."

She had completely forgotten about Remy. "He could walk in at any minute."

Henry shook his head. "I assure you, he'll be discreet. He's not about to walk in unless there's some danger to you, and then he can shoot the bad guy and leave us alone again because no one is going to stop me from having you."

How was she supposed to respond to that? His single-minded will worked wonders on her inhibitions. No one had ever wanted her like Henry did. She gave in, letting him guide her down. The feel of his slacks against her naked skin reminded her that he was still dressed, still in his slacks and a button-down. Still looked like a proper lawyer except he had a woman about to ride his cock. A naked, wanton woman who no longer cared who heard her.

She groaned at the feel of that big cock against her pussy. Slow. She eased down slowly, wanting the moment to last. Every inch of him was pure pleasure as he stretched her wide.

"Look at me," he demanded. "Tell me how it feels. I don't want to hurt you."

She brought her eyes to meet his, hoping her passion and pleasure showed through. "You only hurt me when you push me away. This doesn't hurt. This is what I've needed for days. I needed it about two minutes after you left me."

He pressed up, forcing her to take more of him, his face contorting in pleasure. "That was a mistake. I should have made you come home with me. I would have found out and been mad, but the damage would have been done. I wouldn't have kicked you out. I would have taken out all my anger on this pretty flesh and we would have been through this by now."

She wasn't so sure about that. He made it sound easy. His issues were far more complex and wide-reaching than her mere name. She clutched at him as she started to move. "No more talk about the past. Be with me. Here and now."

He dragged her close and kissed her as she started to ride him in earnest.

It was too good to last and before she was ready, she felt his cock slide over that place of pure perfection deep inside her and she shouted out his name. He clutched her, holding her tight as he pumped himself in over and over again. He shuddered as he held her, giving her everything he had.

She slumped over, all energy gone. All the stress and worry had floated away. They would come back undoubtedly, but for now she could be at peace and she was taking it moment by moment.

His arms tightened around her. "I'll take care of you. You won't regret being with me while the case is going on. You'll see that it's for the best."

She rested her head on his shoulder. He would take care of her for now, but what about after? She let the thought go because thinking about the future had become a dangerous thing.

TWELVE

"Are you sure you know what you're doing?" David asked, sinking into the chair at the conference table. The table was set up for three, as Margarita was back in Texas for a few days.

Henry looked up from the file he'd been studying. Trevor's banking records were interesting, to say the least. He took out a whole lot of cash. "Are you commenting on the fact that I have an appointment with my ex-wife in thirty minutes and I haven't gotten into my body armor yet?"

David frowned his way. "I'm talking about the fact that you're living with Win."

"I thought you were aware she was staying with me."

"Staying with you is one thing. Sleeping with you is another."

He sighed. "I'm not her attorney. You are."

"That's bullshit and you know it. Tell me you aren't planning on micromanaging every single piece of this case."

He wasn't going to bother to lie to his best friend. "Of course I am. I'm the lawyer with the most experience. It would be wrong if I didn't oversee you. How many murder cases have you won, David?"

The door came open and Noah stepped in. The kid was wearing a tailored suit, his hair slightly longer than it should be to be considered professional. He smiled, showing perfect, even white teeth. "Morning, guys. How was your evening? I had an interesting one."

He'd probably hit a club and trolled for women. Was that what Win should be doing? Not the trolling part, but going out and dancing. She'd spent the whole night curled up on the couch with him. She'd watched some silly TV show about doctors in love while he'd gone over his notes for today.

When the time had come to call it a night, she'd kissed him without reservation and let him lead her to bed.

David's face flushed, but he held his ground. It was obvious that the inclusion of Noah wasn't going to make him back down. "My experience with murder cases is not the problem and you know it."

Noah's eyes went wide, but he sank into his chair anyway. Henry wanted to order the kid out, but Noah's name was on the door, too. If David wanted to have this out in front of the partners, he could do it.

"Noah, David has some issues with how I'm handling the Winston-Hughes case. So, David, what is the problem?" He didn't see a problem at all. It had been five days since he and Win had given in, and his world seemed to work much better than it had before. He woke up every morning with her wrapped around him, and most mornings he got inside her and started the day right. She would make breakfast while he got ready for work and they would enjoy the morning together. She'd taken to kissing him before he got on the elevator. It had felt far too domestic that first day, but this morning when she'd gotten caught up in some book she was reading, he found her and demanded it.

It was such an easy trap to fall into.

"The problem is that the world now thinks you're Win's boyfriend," David pointed out.

"I thought we all agreed to that," Noah said, confusion on his face. "We brought in a publicist and everything. It seems to be working. After the announcement Henry made and Alicia Kingman going on record saying she totally supported the both of you, we haven't heard any other rumors. In fact, a lot of the tabloid crap has turned against Brie Westerhaven because a couple of people she tried to blackmail have come out to talk about her. What's wrong?"

David sent Noah a pointed look. "I'm not concerned about some tabloid. I'm pretty sure Win thinks Henry is serious about her, too."

"Well, that probably has to do with the fact that they're fucking like rabbits," Noah replied.

Henry was going to try to ignore Noah. "Win knows what she's doing. I haven't lied to her about anything." Well, almost anything. "I haven't lied to her about anything personal. I have kept a few things about the case to myself, but she doesn't need to worry until I'm sure."

Noah leaned in. "Is this about the nanny?"

Maybe they could finally get around to some of the important points he needed to make this morning. "Yes, I've told her the hospital Mary Hannigan is supposed to be recuperating at is still dealing with the storm from three nights ago. There was a big one out on the island and their phone lines are having problems. The patients were evacuated to higher ground and Mary didn't bring her cell phone with her. Win is worried, but her uncle assured her he's talked to Mary via the hospital's director and she's fine. I'm feeling quite lucky that Win can't leave Manhattan or she would be caught up in all this."

David frowned. "So she has no idea we can't locate Mary Hannigan? Win doesn't know that Noah went to the nursing home and there was no record of Mary Hannigan being there?"

"That's what I mean." The woman seemed to have vanished off the face of the earth. They could trace her through the emergency room she'd been taken to directly after the accident. They'd reset her hip in a noninvasive surgical procedure and then released her to the rehab/assisted living facility to heal for a few weeks.

She'd never shown up.

"Why is Bellamy Hughes lying about talking to her?" Noah asked.

That was something he needed to figure out. "We don't know that he's lying about talking to her. He could know exactly where she is and be in touch with her. He comes back to New York tonight. I want a tail on him. I want to know everything that man does and everywhere he goes. I don't like this. He's hiding something and it has to do with Mary Hannigan."

"I agree," David replied. "Win's uncle is lying to her. So do you think she needs the added pressure of an impending breakup with the man who's supposed to take care of her? Who's supposed to have her best interests at heart? I think we should consider moving her out of your place. I understand that one of the investigators is a childhood friend of Win's and has a place where she can stay. Getting some space might help her understand what kind of game you're playing."

He sent David his most arctic stare. "My personal relationship with Win Hughes is none of your business, and I would advise you, for the sake of our friendship and this partnership, to stay out of it. She's not going anywhere."

Noah sat back and David rolled his eyes.

"Told you," Noah said. "That's twenty."

David pulled out his wallet and slid a twenty Noah's way. "I don't understand. He's been my best friend for years. I thought I would know."

Henry bit back his irritation. "You thought you would know

what? And I'd like an explanation of what you were betting on and when you turned into a frat boy, betting on your friend's future."

Noah held up his hands. "Damn, man. You've got the angry-dad thing down. And, David, he might have been your friend for a long time, but I watched my oldest brother fight the love thing and then give in to it. At first it was all 'Shelby's just around for sex and the job we're doing,' and the next thing you know, bam, I'm standing around wearing the world's most uncomfortable tuxedo and watching him marry the woman who was supposed to be around only for sex."

"I never said she was only around for sex." Henry didn't like them talking about his sex life, much less betting on it. "She's also staying at my place for protection and because it makes it easier to work on the case when she's close. I don't have to worry about where she is or who's got access to her."

Noah nodded. "Sure, man. That's it. And you're both healthy people with sexual needs, so you've talked about it and why not have sex while she's here? It only makes logical sense, right? What's her ring size? Because women like rings to go with their marriages."

David chuckled a little. "What's the over/under on a quickie Vegas wedding?"

Henry frowned. "I'm not getting married."

"Wanna bet?" Noah asked with a smirk. "Because even the paralegals think this won't take more than six weeks."

He'd completely lost control. When he'd had a solo practice, he hadn't had to worry about any of this shit. He'd been the overlord and everyone had fallen in line. No one would have gossiped about his love life. Not that he'd had one for years, and then he'd had a train wreck. But no one would have dared gossip then. Not where he could have heard it. That would have led to someone getting their ass handed to them and potentially being blackballed in the legal community.

David had told him he was making a mistake with Alicia. And then Henry had cut him out of his life for a year and a half. It had been David who'd picked up the phone when Henry had needed a friend.

He'd been sure he'd known what he was doing back then. He'd known that he and Alicia could rule the fucking world together.

All he wanted from Win was to have her by his side. He didn't want to rule the world anymore, but he might want to build a world, a private world with her.

"Am I making a mistake, David?"

He couldn't miss the way his best friend's jaw dropped before he covered his shock. David sat up, his elbows on the conference table. "I don't think giving Win a second chance is a mistake. I think the mistake you'll make is putting a time limit on it. This case is starting to fall into place. We're going to have several possible alternative suspects, and the forensics aren't as solid as the DA would have everyone believe. This case could be over before we expected it to, and then what are you going to do?"

He didn't like thinking about it, but David was right. Every single person who came forward talking about some of the bad shit Brie had been involved in brought them closer and closer to potentially getting the case thrown out due to lack of evidence.

Even the time of death had come out in their favor. According to the ME, Brie Westerhaven had died around eleven P.M. The body wasn't found until midnight. That put Trevor and Bellamy Hughes back into play and it just might take Win out of contention if Henry's meeting with Alicia went well.

What would he do if he got Win's arrest thrown out? If she was free to go back to Durham and continue her life?

"I don't know," he admitted. "I haven't thought about it. We've tried to stay in the now."

"I don't think it's working for you," Noah pointed out. "You got crazy eyes when David mentioned Michael Malone. Crazy eyes don't lie. My brother's eyes right before he gave in and married Shelby? Yep, they were crazy. I don't get what's so hard about it. Win's awesome. I like the hell out of her."

"I don't want to get involved in that lifestyle again," Henry explained. "Even if she never goes back to television, there will always be celebrity associated with her name."

"You're afraid you'll slip up," David said, his eyes narrowing. "This isn't about Win. It's about you."

He was saved by a knock on the door. The receptionist poked her head in. "Mr. Garrison, Alicia Kingman is here to see you."

He never thought he'd be happy to see her. He stood up and gathered his file. "Show her to my office, please." He turned back to his partners. "I need someone looking into those cash transactions on Trevor's accounts."

"I've got a phone conference with the forensic accountant from McKay-Taggart," Noah replied. "She says she's got some interesting info for us. I'll let you know what she's found."

David watched as Henry moved to the door. "Think about what I said. You were saved by the bell this time, but we'll talk again."

"When did you get all chatty? You know, you were more fun when you made your living hitting other people and trying to hold on to a football." NFL pro David would never have tried to turn a conference into a relationship discussion.

David stared at him, his eyes serious. "Ever since I realized my best friend wasn't superhuman and that there was way more to life than money."

Henry stopped because the memory of the day David was talking about was clearly etched in his brain. David had already started his transition from pro athlete to lawyer. He'd been working as a first-year when Henry had called. It had been his rock bottom and David had flown across the country, picked him out of the dive bar he'd been holed up in, and gotten him into rehab.

He owed David. "I will think about it."

He walked into the hall. He wasn't sure he could think about anything else.

~

"Hello, Henry," Alicia said, settling into the chair across from him. "I heard a whole lot about how I ruined you financially, but this place is pretty sweet. Nice view."

She was looking out the floor-to-ceiling windows with a spectacular view of the Hudson. It was a ridiculously expensive piece of real estate, but it didn't prove anything.

"Yes, I can't take credit for that. Drew Lawless owns the building." It wouldn't hurt to remind her who he was in business with. "He was kind enough to allow us a floor for our offices."

But he had to be careful because he needed Alicia to cooperate. The last thing he needed was to get into some crazy war with his ex-wife that could land his current girlfriend in the big house for a murder she didn't commit.

Alicia sat back, looking utterly perfect for the part. He could see what she was going for. Femme fatale. The witness who might be able to bring the whole investigation to a close or who could throw the heroine of the piece straight in the slammer. Alicia was wearing a retro-looking sheath dress, her hair in a perfectly Hitchcockian updo. She'd likely had her makeup professionally done in case she couldn't avoid the paparazzi. The woman did know how to look good on camera. She crossed her legs and sat back. "Yes, I know all about your silent partner. Mr. Lawless is an intimidating man. If he wasn't already married, I might be intrigued. Hell, who cares that he's married. I'm definitely intrigued."

"You should try it." Henry had met Shelby Lawless. He would have no problem representing her after she took Alicia apart.

Alicia laughed. "Ah, you think the wife can take me. You know I've been taking Krav Maga classes for my new movie. I might surprise you. It's all about one of the first female spies. Very interesting. The director is yummy, too."

He was sure the man was. The only thing as important to Alicia as a director's credentials were his looks. "Well, we all know you live to fuck your directors."

"There's the Henry I know. See, darling, I told you. You can be perfectly evil without a drop to drink. You didn't need to stop. The liquor made you quite entertaining at times."

He closed his eyes, taking a deep breath. He wasn't going to order her out. He wasn't going to strangle her. He was going to maintain control of his temper for Win's sake. Because Win needed Alicia and he needed Win.

He opened his eyes and Alicia was staring at him, an almost-concerned look on her face. "I need to talk to you about the night of the murder."

Alicia went silent for a moment before she replied. "You care about her."

He was not getting into this with her. "I know you had a conversation with both Taylor Winston-Hughes and the victim at the party."

She leaned forward, putting one perfectly manicured hand on his desk. "Oh, Henry, I'm sorry. You really care about her. It's the only reason you're not shouting at me. I thought I could come in here and rattle your cage a bit, but you're not going to let that happen, are you?"

"I need to know how firm you are on the time you talked to Win alone. I need to know if anyone else would remember that you were out there on the balcony with her."

She looked softer than he could remember. "Wow. I did not expect that. I like the girl. She's very kind. She doesn't know this, but I have a reason to care about her. When I was a young actress, nineteen, actually, my first husband had an aggressive form of cancer. I married him because I knew how much he loved me and I knew he wouldn't live long. He was my high school sweetheart. The funny thing is, I would never have married him if he'd been healthy. I knew I needed more, but when Brad was given six months to live, I took him with me to L.A."

"What does Win have to do with this?" He knew her first husband had died. The tabloids claimed Brad Kingman had been her only true love and she'd never gotten over him, so she chose a string of losers who couldn't capture her heart. He'd been one of those losers.

"We didn't have any money. When he got bad and I couldn't take care of him, I applied for special housing that would let me stay with him. I got turned down by everyone. Win was maybe fifteen, but she was already active in the foundation. I'd read about her, knew her story, and I'd heard she could get things done despite her age. I got a job as a cater waiter at one of her fund-raisers and when I could get that girl alone, I gave her my sob story."

"And you had housing the next day." He knew what Win would do.

Alicia nodded. "I got two months with him because of Win." She stood up and walked to the windows, her fingers brushing away tears. "Believe it or not, I thought I might be protecting her from you. I thought you might have decided the best way to get back what you lost was to marry into some serious money."

"I did that when I started the new firm, though it was more of a business marriage." It wasn't something he was proud of, but it did seem to be working out nicely. Despite the whole betting-on-his-love-life thing, it wasn't horrible to have partners.

"The Lawless boy," she surmised. "So you don't have any interest in the billion dollars Win's going to come into in a few months?"

This was where Alicia didn't know him at all. "I prefer to make my own money. When I met Win, I thought she was a townie working her way through grad school."

"That must have come as quite a shock."

"Can you help me with the timeline or not, Alicia?"

She turned back, looking at him. "Ah, so you didn't handle it well, then. What did you do when you found out? You know you can say some truly terrible things. Henry, you have to see that she's not the little nitwit they showed on television. They call it reality TV, but there's nothing at all real about it. Not only did they likely give her scenes to play, but there's also editing, and believe me, they can make a person look like a complete moron with the right editing."

He wasn't sure why she cared. He knew he shouldn't get pulled into talk, shouldn't give her any room at all. "I've never seen her show."

"Good. Don't watch it because it doesn't mean a thing," Alicia replied. "I have no idea why she did that stupid show, but I would bet Brie Westerhaven talked her into it."

At least they were close to being on the subject. "What do you know about their relationship?"

"It's gossip mostly, though I did recently spend some time with Wes Westerhaven. He speaks quite highly of his daughter's friend. Thinks Brie would have done better if she'd gone to college with Taylor. Anyway, the gossip was mixed and mostly kinder to Brie than Taylor because Brie has deeper ties," Alicia explained. "Though you can always read the truth under gossip, and it's usually one of the people involved who starts the gossip in the first place."

"What do you mean 'kinder to Brie'?" He couldn't think of why anyone would be kinder to Brie. Apparently she'd spent a lot of time blackmailing people.

"Some people thought Taylor . . . sorry, you call her Win. Anyway, a lot of people in the beginning thought Win was nothing but a hanger-on. Making money off something Brie had built, though she didn't really build anything. That's a big thing in Hollywood—the hangers-on. After the show went big, Win joined, and that looked like jumping on board without taking any risk. And some people think the whole getting-too-thin thing was all about attention."

Henry felt himself flush with rage. "She was anorexic. It wasn't about fucking attention. She nearly died."

"Well, darling, you didn't ask me to tell you the truth," Alicia said with a shake of her head. "You wanted the gossip, and you should know that if this goes to trial, it will likely come up. It's not fair, but it's true. And by true, I mean anything but the truth. They'll drag up all kinds of old rumors about Win fighting with Brie over Hoover. It's completely ridiculous because he's a moron, but it was good for the show."

He found the entire idea of the show distasteful. He couldn't help himself. He was already fielding calls from producers who wanted to know who Win's agent was because they wanted first rights to her story. So far, she'd told him she didn't want to talk to anyone, but how long would she hold out? "I don't care about the show."

"Oh, you care about it. That's plain. You hate the thought of her doing it, of her opening herself up like that." Sometimes Alicia could be like a mind reader. Sometimes she could look into his freaking soul and pull things out that disturbed him. "You'll sit around and wonder how long it will be before she needs that kind of attention again because you don't understand why she did it the first time. So in your head, it's something that can happen again, something that will happen again. But I don't think it's like that. Not for her. I think Win had just gotten out of college and she was looking at going to work or having some fun with her friends. She got sucked in. I've seen it happen before. She's out now and I don't think she'll ever go back. Not in that capacity."

"What does that mean?"

She sighed, the sound a bit weary. "It means she'll never truly be out of the public eye and you should think about that. She's the Billion-Dollar Baby. Do you understand what a miracle it was that she lived? They never found any of the other bodies, but that baby lived. How amazing is that? No one can explain it. She's a living, breathing miracle. *People* magazine will run a story on her every now and then simply because she's incredibly wealthy and tragic. No matter how quietly she tries to live, they'll find her and write about her. They'll make movies about this case. I can assure you of that. And when she decides to settle down, all that press will be about the man she's chosen."

It turned his stomach. He didn't want that scrutiny. Not in his personal life. He could handle it in his professional life, but he wanted his family to be private. Family. Was he thinking that way? He never had before. Now he was wondering what it would be like to have a couple of kids with Win.

"You need to toughen up or let that girl go." Alicia leaned over, both hands flat on his desk. "You know, you didn't mind the press in the beginning."

"I didn't realize what sharks they were."

"No, you were the shark back then. You were the biggest, baddest predator in the ocean, and that was exactly what I loved about you. Yeah, I said love. I might not be good at being in love, and my love might not mean as much as someone like Win's, but I loved you, Henry."

"None of this matters. I'm certainly not going to change my mind. We're done. I won't ever go back to you."

"But you won't move forward either," she replied. "I know it was a mistake for us to marry. We're oil and water. You got caught up with the sex and the power, and then you were in a spiral. I was angry that I wasn't enough. You were supposed to marry me and show everyone how worthy I was. Because if a man that smart and successful wanted me, how could I be anything else? Turns out I'm exactly what you said. I thought you could lift me up, but all that happened was I managed to drag you down."

"We seem to have two different versions of the story. We should never have gotten married in the first place. I was drunk and we were in Vegas. The sex had been good and I wasn't getting any younger. I thought you would come back to New York, but again, I don't think properly when I drink that much. And none of this has anything to do with the case at hand. I don't want to go over our divorce again."

"But it's important," she replied. "Do you know why I was so damn mean in the divorce when I didn't have to be?"

"I have some theories." Coldheartedness was one of them. Greed was another.

"Because the minute you called David and he took you to rehab, you were done with me."

"I was done with you the minute I found you in bed with your costar," he explained.

"I didn't even like him. I wanted you to notice me again. Once the sex had worn off, you were more about your work than our marriage, and I couldn't handle being second in your life. So I acted out like a child. I do get that. When I couldn't even get you to talk to me, I forced your hand."

"No, you forced me to pay." That was what bugged him the most. He hadn't wanted a thing from her. No cash. No connections. And she'd found a way to make him give up everything that meant something to him.

"I did. I thought maybe you would rethink the matter if you realized how far I was willing to go, but I was wrong. Once you're done with something or someone, you don't look back."

He'd gone back to Win. He couldn't seem to help himself. How would he handle it if she gave in to the vultures and wanted some of that fame and social power back?

Was it better to let her go now?

None of this was helping him. All this talk was doing was making his gut clench at the thought of all the mistakes he'd made before. Win seemed like calm in a storm, but he knew how quickly that could change.

He'd fallen back into the trap and he wasn't sure he would be able to get out this time. What would happen if Win changed her mind? If he gave her everything he had and then she decided to go back to that lifestyle? Hell, even if she didn't, could he handle the one she had? Alicia was right. Win would always be a story. Whoever was with her would always deal with reporters and the extravagance of her lifestyle.

She would have endless parties and tons of people who would try to get close to her to use her connections.

"Henry, are you all right?"

He hated the fact that Alicia was the one pointing out his vulnerabilities. "I'm fine. I'll deal with Win when the time comes. For now, the best place for her to be is with me."

Alicia sat back down and reached into her bag. "I hope it stays that way because I think she could be good for you if you let her. I hope you don't let the fact that you chose poorly once mean you won't ever choose again. Now, you wanted to ask me some questions."

Thank god. Yes, he wanted to focus on something, anything that wasn't his relationship with Win and the fact that they probably had an expiration date. "What do you think of Trevor Hughes? I saw in my reports that you recently worked with him."

Her eyes rolled in perfect disdain. "He's a massive ass, but he's also the head of a major entertainment wing, though I've heard Bellamy Hughes is moving him. Good for the old man. Anyway, yes, I recently spent some time with the moron. Now, there's a man who could use some therapy. When he's drunk, he talks up a storm."

"What does he talk about?"

"The normal male chest-pounding crap. We were at a party together in L.A. a few months ago and he was wasted. He told me he would be taking over Hughes Corp, and I should start dating him then to get in on that action."

"Why would he think he's taking over Hughes? Technically the company belongs to Win."

"He said something about how he had a plan. He'd learned a secret or something, and when the time was right, he would spring it on Win and she wouldn't see it coming. Like I said, he was wasted. I didn't take it seriously."

But sometimes alcohol could lower inhibitions just enough that the truths one didn't want out slipped away more easily. He would have to take a longer look at Trevor. "Do you remember approximately when you spoke to Trevor at the party at Win's place? If you can give me the time, that would be helpful."

"It was before I talked to Win. I wanted to avoid Trevor. I planned on leaving after I had my talk with Win, especially since the real object of my quest wasn't there." She had her phone in hand. "I'd hoped you would be there since Brie had gone out of her way to let me know you were seeing Win. Now, of course, I know you wouldn't have come."

He didn't like that Brie had known all about him when Win had never once mentioned Brie to him. It didn't seem fair. "Win wouldn't have wanted me there. I had no idea at the time that she was the head of the foundation. So you planned on going home after the discussion with Win. Do you remember what time you began that conversation?"

She groaned. "No. I didn't keep minutes of my evening out. I know it was late."

"I need more than that." The jury would want precision. "Did anyone witness your conversation with Win?"

She thought about that for a moment. "There was a bartender working on the balcony. He might remember something. People tend to remember me." She sat up a little straighter. "And I realized I have something. I know that I took this video after I talked to Win and before all the craziness happened. Teddy Seeran played the party. He's such a cutie. I'm crazy about his new album. I recorded his last two songs and I realized Win's in this video. You can see her walking around the edges of the crowd. I think that was when she was looking for Brie. Does this help?"

She tapped the screen and turned the phone his way.

She'd had video footage and she hadn't bothered to tell anyone? He thought about explaining the idea of withholding evidence to her, but he was too busy watching the DA's whole case fall apart. The video on the phone was time-stamped. Sure, there were ways to screw with that, but Alicia wouldn't know how. This was what every defense attorney dreamed of. His client on tape, walking around and talking at precisely the time of death.

Win was innocent. He'd known it deep down in his bones, but here was the absolute proof.

"Is it good, Henry? I've got some selfies with Teddy. Those have a time on them, too. I also uploaded them to social media. Will that help?" Alicia asked, eagerness plain in her voice.

He reached out and clicked a button on his desk phone. "Could you have Noah join us?"

His secretary agreed and he hung up. Noah was the only one he knew who would be able to figure out how to safely dupe Alicia's phone. The evidence needed to be unquestionable. He had to find out if anyone else had video of that performance.

"It helps, right?" Alicia wasn't giving up.

It wasn't as hard as he thought to give her a little praise. After all, she'd made it easy to ensure that Win didn't go to jail. "This blows the case wide open." He kept watching the screen. Win walked up to an elderly couple, smiling in the background, and she spoke quietly to them. "Why didn't you give it to the cops the first night?"

"I didn't think about it," she admitted. "I do so much social media I didn't even consider that I could have anything valuable there. I do mini selfie interviews all the time. It's a part of my business plan. You're the only one who wouldn't allow me to post them."

It had been a massive fight between the two of them. Every aspect of Alicia's life was ruled by her career.

It wasn't the same with Win—at least he didn't think so—but it would always haunt her. She'd gone through something terrible. Would she come out on the other side and realize how much she missed her old lifestyle and all it had to offer her?

He looked up. "There was zero reason to post that crap. It was our private life."

"Nothing is really private in my world."

"Because you won't let it be," he retorted, the phone still in his hand. He glanced over and saw Noah making his way down the hall. Henry could still hear Teddy Seeran wailing about love and his hair or something. He didn't listen to that shit. It was annoying. "You have a psychopathic need for approval."

She shrugged. "Attention. I actually don't care what people think as long as they're paying attention."

Noah poked his head in. "You wanted me?"

"Can you pull this video off Ms. Kingman's phone in a way the

DA can't question? Because we're going to have to turn the entire thing over to the police. She's got proof that Win wasn't in her room at the time of death."

Noah's eyes widened. "Are you fucking kidding me? We have proof?"

He wished he felt more satisfaction than he did. He was thrilled that he could save Win's life, but he had to make a decision and it might have just been made for him. He wanted more time. He wanted weeks and months where she needed him. But it wasn't going to happen because he wasn't about to let this chance get by. Her life was precious.

Noah took the phone. "Yeah, I can do it. Holy shit. We're going to be so fucking famous. They'll all come to us now."

Alicia turned to the youngest Lawless sibling. "So I did good?"

There was no way to miss the way Noah glanced down at those well-paid-for breasts. "You did, ma'am."

Henry was surprised to find he didn't care. He was actually feeling a little magnanimous toward her. "Noah, this is my ex-wife, Alicia Kingman. She's incapable of monogamy and will eat you alive in the sack. As long as you understand that you would be utterly insane to want anything more than a purely sexual relationship with her, she could be a good friend. She's quite intelligent and she can be fun to be around, but she's not the woman you want to lose your heart to. If you understand that, you should ask her out."

Alicia looked back at him, and he was shocked to see tears in her eyes. "Really? You're giving me a billionaire to play with?"

He shrugged. "As long as he knows what he's getting into. I did, Alicia. I didn't realize it would change me. I don't think it would change him."

"Ms. Kingman?" Noah offered his hand and he was smiling like he'd just gotten a present. "If you would come with me, I'll help make you the heroine of this whole case."

She stood up and turned to Henry. "I liked you then, Henry. But this man you are now? If Win helped you be this man, then don't let her go. And keep that fucker Trevor away from her. He's such a prick. He talked about sending an assassin to take her out in Sweden. Who even jokes that way?"

Henry's blood went cold, and out of the corner of his eye he saw Noah go still. "What did he say?"

Alicia waved it off. "When he was drunk at that party a couple of months ago, he talked about taking care of his problem. Said he knew assassins. Sure he does. Is there such a thing as a Swedish assassin? Isn't that an oxymoron? Swedes are massage therapists."

Noah's eyes had gone wide. "Two weeks before the attack on Win in Stockholm, he took out twenty thousand cash. I have the records. I was just going over them. Customs records don't have him bringing back anything even close to that value."

"There's no line on the customs form for hiring a killer." Henry didn't like the way his heart had started racing. "Why would he do it? If Win dies, he and his father lose the company."

Alicia put a hand to her mouth in obvious shock. "You mean he wasn't kidding? Someone tried to hurt her?"

"It was kept quiet in the press, but while she was in Sweden an unknown assailant followed her into an alley and nearly strangled her to death. He would have killed her had a couple of club kids not been taking a shortcut to their car. At the time Trevor was with a group of Win's friends who'd come to bring her back to the States. Perfect alibi, but if he hired someone, he wouldn't need to be there."

"I'll get someone in Europe to try to run the assassin down," Noah said. "I don't know. This doesn't add up unless Trevor's just trying to burn the whole place down."

It didn't. Trevor got nothing if Win died. It was actually much better for him and Bellamy Hughes if she rotted in prison. Legally, she wouldn't be dead, and the money hadn't come from her crime, so it couldn't be seized by the government. All that money and power would stay right where it had been—in the Hughes men's hands. They lost it if she died.

Something played through his brain. Something someone had said earlier. It was a lead, a clue that might start to form the core of a theory.

The theory of the crime. It was where he would normally start building a case, but not with this one. He'd been thinking on an emotional level.

A crime usually had several theories he could attach to it, stories that, when played out to logical conclusions, led to the dead body and gave reason for the crime.

Why would Trevor Hughes kill Brie Westerhaven? Perhaps that wasn't the question he needed to ask. Why would he kill his cousin?

"Uhm, do you want me to wait?" Noah asked.

Henry heard Alicia hush him. "Shhh, he's thinking. That's the look he gets when he's finally putting the threads together. He's found one and he's going to pull it."

Well, at least a year's worth of marriage had taught her something about him. He let the noise fall away. She was right. It was often like he had a messy box of yarn and thread, like the one his grandmother would keep by her rocking chair. He had to find the right one. Sometimes he would pull and it would come up short. It wasn't right.

Rage. Trevor Hughes hated his cousin, but rage wasn't the reason for this crime.

Money was still the reason. He could feel it.

But the money was locked away. He couldn't get to the money if Win was dead.

"What did the will say?" Henry said, opening his eyes to find David had joined them. Noah, David, and Alicia were all looking at him intently.

"The will? The Winston-Hughes will?" David asked.

"What's the line of succession when it comes to the company? Win wasn't named in the will, correct?" This went back further than Brie Westerhaven. Much further. Brie's murder might have been incidental. She'd been in the wrong place at the wrong time, or she'd learned something she shouldn't have. Yes. Yes. She'd been the one Trevor had turned to.

"No." Noah was busy pulling up notes on his tablet. Thank god for geeks. Henry himself would have been forced to go find his handwritten notes amid the files. "The will was actually written before Win was born, and they hadn't gotten around to naming her specifically. It states that the company should go to any natural children of the couple or any children the couple adopted in the future. The company would be divided equally among those children."

"And what if one or the other died first? Any provisions for children that might come from a second marriage or relationship?" He was onto something. It was right there. All he had to do was keep asking the right questions and it would fall together. Not the truth, but a theory. The truth would be harder. It had to be proven, but he could work from a theory.

Noah scrolled down. "Yes, if either spouse died, the other was the direct heir and any children would have been secondary heirs."

"What did Brie Westerhaven spend several thousand dollars on a few weeks before her death?"

"It was probably cocaine," Alicia quipped. "That girl liked her blow."

He stared at his ex-wife.

She frowned his way. "You know that look is one of the reasons I married you. I think it's kind of hot, but now it's a little scary."

"Are you talking about the weird DNA ancestry stuff?" David asked.

Alicia paced behind David. "Why would she do that? The show

did an entire episode on Brie's ancestry last season. They delved deep into her history. Brought in a team of experts for it. It was one of the lowest-rated shows, probably because you could actually learn something from it. She and Hoover went to a testing facility and everything. Hoover was an idiot, of course. They even did a whole breakdown about Brie's parents. It was quite fascinating. The next episode was about Hoover trying to figure out how to program his remote."

"Why would she want to do more testing on herself?" Noah asked. "It's one of those things you only really need to do once."

And there it was. When logic failed, the answer was incorrect and another, more reasonable answer must be applied to the theory. "She wasn't testing herself. She was testing Trevor. What do we know about his mother? Besides the fact that she bailed shortly after Bellamy took Win in?"

David shrugged. "She hasn't come up in any of the investigations. We know she was in Paris at the time of the murder. She hasn't been back to the States in years."

"But Trevor visits her regularly," Noah pointed out.

"She was the girl next door," Alicia said.

"What do you mean? And how would you know anything about this?" He wasn't discounting her. The devil often knew things normal humans didn't.

"I told you. I've always been fascinated by the story. Billionaires die in a storm at sea and the only thing left is a baby wrapped in a life vest, found floating and half-dead by two fishermen a day and a half later. Win was a miracle. I've read books about the family and watched all the movies and TV specials. A lot of people are fascinated by her and her family."

Okay, he could buy that. "Tell me about the girl next door."

"Trevor's mother's parents lived next to the Hughes family, upstate. This was long before Win's father made his fortune and created

Hughes Corp. She was friendly with both of the brothers. There were rumors that she dated Win's dad before settling down with Bellamy."

"He thinks he's Win's brother, not her cousin." It fell neatly into place. "He had Brie try to run tests. It's why she turned up on the island that week I met Win. They hadn't seen each other in months, and I don't think Win had any intention to see her."

"She would have had access to both Win and Bellamy." David clapped his hands together. "She could have stolen hairbrushes or toothbrushes and sent them off along with Trevor's DNA. Win would have gotten suspicious if she'd found Trevor in her bathroom, but not Brie."

"Oh, I get first dibs on this, Henry," Alicia insisted. "I helped. First dibs on the film rights because this is going to be juicy."

Henry stood up. "Can I talk to Win before I sell off her rights?"

"Of course," Alicia agreed.

He needed to do this in person. "David, find someone who can check Brie's mail. I want those DNA results as soon as possible, and Noah, call the DA. I want the charges dropped on Win. Tell them they can put that video out and look like heroes or I can put it out and sue them for false arrest. I'm serious. I want a press conference this afternoon with the DA and NYPD admitting that Win Hughes is an innocent woman."

Noah gave him a salute. "Will do, boss."

Henry strode out the door. Win would be free by this afternoon, but he might have to blow up her world to do it.

Would she walk out the door or hold on to him?

Either way, they had decisions to make, decisions he wasn't ready for.

THIRTEEN

Win looked up from her book, glancing at the clock. It was barely ten A.M. Henry had left a little over an hour before. By now he would be sitting down for his morning conference with David and Noah. They'd gone over his schedule for the day. He had the conference first thing and an interview with Alicia shortly after that.

An interview with his gorgeous, sexy ex-wife. It was hard to think about the fact that he'd been married to someone magazines hailed as one of the most beautiful women in America.

She tried not to go down that path, but it was impossible not to think about it.

Of course, it was way easier to forget it when Henry was actually here. When he had his mouth on her, she wasn't thinking of his past. She was only thinking about him.

Would she think about him for the rest of her life?

"Hey, Win, you have company." Wade Rycroft stood in the doorway. He was dressed in his normal uniform of jeans, T-shirt, and boots. He would likely wear the same thing to the fanciest restaurant in town if his wife would let him. Win had to admit that the cowboy looked good in them. "It's the douchebag. He's still down in the lobby. I can tell him you're not here."

She frowned. There was only one person her bodyguards would say that about. And only one they called "the douchebag."

"Trevor's here?"

"Yep," Wade replied with a frown. "He's downstairs, and he says he has something he needs to talk to you about. He's on the family list. According to Henry, he's been cleared, but I can still make him go away. He says he's got contracts for you to sign, but again, he can leave them here. Or I can go down and get them for you."

And then Trevor would whine about how she wouldn't even let him do his job. She'd talked to her uncle and he'd mentioned some contracts she needed to sign. There were always things about the foundation that required her signature—even if she was hanging around waiting to be convicted of a murder she didn't commit. She sighed and hoped this would be a conversation she could get out of quickly. "No, you better let him up. I don't want him going to the press about how I can't be bothered to do my job. It could be bad for the foundation. Some of those checks haven't cleared yet. I've got to try to salvage as much as I can."

Wade nodded and walked back to the front room.

Win put on a pot of tea. She would need it. Usually she'd reach for a glass of wine to relax, but that was a no-no here, and she was finding she didn't mind. She'd switched her nightly pinot for Earl Grey. She'd even gotten Henry to switch from coffee to tea at night after dinner.

He was a man who needed rituals and routines. He responded best to a firmly kept schedule.

Even for his kisses. She smiled at the thought of how he'd come looking for her earlier. She'd gotten caught up in something she was reading and had forgotten to walk him to the elevator and kiss him goodbye. She'd kind of thought it was something he simply put up with, but he'd proven her wrong. He'd wanted that kiss because she'd gotten him used to it.

Now if she could just get him used to her. It was a good plan. Get him so used to their schedule that he wouldn't order her to leave the minute he could.

The more time they had, the more time Henry had to put some distance between their relationship and his fears.

She heard the elevator doors open and the heavy thud of loafers moving across the hardwood floors. Trevor stepped into the kitchen looking way worse for wear. "What happened to you?"

His clothes were wrinkled, dark circles around his eyes. "I had a late night and then Daddy dearest ordered me to get on a plane and bring these to the princess of Hughes Corp ASAP. No time to sleep. I need your signature on all of those so I can get back to L.A. Hurry it up. I don't have long before my flight leaves."

"Somehow I think it won't take off without you." She took the folder out of his hands. The paperwork was a mess. "What is all of this? Is this a whole contract?"

He groaned. "It's three contracts and two banking updates that require your signature. The lawyers have already vetted everything. Do you not see the sticky arrow things? That's where you sign your name and then I can leave. And the plane isn't waiting for me. I had to fly commercial."

She gasped at the thought. Her cousin hadn't flown commercial in years. "What?"

"Again, Daddy dearest seems to think I need to learn a lesson," he spat back, hopping on the barstool. "I don't suppose you have any beer in this place?"

Her teapot started whistling. "Nope, just tea. Would you like some of that?"

He made a gagging sound. "Absolutely not. Why doesn't His

Highness have beer? Is it too cheap for his tastes? We all know Garrison has expensive tastes."

She settled the bag in her mug and poured out the water. Naturally there were a couple of meanings to what Trevor was saying, but he likely meant the nastiest possible one. Where was a pen? She glanced around, looking for one. "It's not about expense. Henry doesn't drink at all."

"How funny. He doesn't drink and you don't eat. No wonder he can afford this place." Trevor was looking out the windows at the amazing view. "I thought he was supposed to be all poor and shit. He whined enough about his divorce. Can you imagine giving up a woman like Alicia? God, I can't. He's a moron."

She caught the supersubtle edge of his question. Could she imagine a man giving up Alicia and ending up saddled with a woman like Win? "Well, not every marriage works out."

"And not every marriage is as perfect as it looks on paper," he shot back. "How do you feel about that?"

"What are you trying to say?" She didn't like playing his games. He often tried to trap her into saying something he could use against her later. He'd done it all their lives. "Could you just come on out and say it? You know you're not going to be happy until you do."

He shrugged. "I've heard a rumor someone's planning a new book about your parents."

That was the last thing she needed. Henry would hate that. He would hate all the press that came with it. "Why would anyone do that?"

"I don't know. Maybe the scandal of you killing poor Brie is causing them to relook at the sainted pair. You know how it is. The Billion-Dollar Miracle Baby grows up to be a killer. It's made a lot of people think. I think it makes a person ask some hard questions, you know. Would it have been better if you'd drowned with the rest of them? Your survival meant that later on a beautiful woman would meet her end."

It made her a little nauseous. Was there someone out there actually asking that question and putting it in print? Would there be whole talk shows devoted to whether or not it would have been better for the world if she hadn't survived? "I didn't kill Brie and you know it."

He ran a hand through his hair, brushing it back. "How would I know that, Win? How would I honestly know what you're capable of? I know what you want the world to believe, but there's always another side to the story. I think you're really good at manipulating everyone around you. You know I was close to her in the end."

They were getting into this again? "No one was really close to Brie. Not any man I ever met."

"You didn't see her with me. She kept it secret because she knew what you would do. She knew you would try to break us up. You were always a jealous bitch. I knew it, but after some of the stories she told me, I can't believe she managed to stay friends with you."

"She lied," Win shot back. It was useless, but defending herself had become a habit. "She lied a lot and she made up stories to make herself look good. I'm sure she told you all about how I tried to take Hoover from her. Why would I want Hoover? Don't get me wrong. We were friends, but never once did I want to touch that man. He wasn't my type."

"He's rich," Trevor pointed out. "That's everyone's type."

"I don't need his money. Look, I don't know what Brie told you, but I didn't have any reason to hurt her. I was getting out of the whole scene. I didn't want to get pulled back in." They'd been going their separate ways for years. If only she hadn't gotten pulled back in that last time, she would likely be a happy grad student in North Carolina.

But then she would never have met Henry.

Trevor pointed her way. "See, you know all the right things to say and you say them with such conviction. And you claim you're not a good actress. I think you're better than the critics give you credit for."

"Is there a problem here?" Wade stepped in, letting his massive presence be known. His arms were crossed over his chest, but that left the gun attached to his belt on full display. "I can take out the trash if you need me to. It's all part of the service."

"Ah, the big bad bodyguard is going to protect poor little Win. Like I've never seen that before," Trevor said with a roll of his eyes. "What if the rest of us need protecting from her?"

"Don't bother engaging, Wade," she said with a sigh. "He's in one of his moods. I'll sign the contracts and he'll leave. It's really okay."

Wade tipped his head slightly her way. "All right, but I'm close. Don't you forget it."

"Guess dear old Dad is paying for him," Trevor remarked. "I wonder how much that's costing the company."

"Well, it is my company, so I would say I'm paying for him." She was sick of Trevor's attitude. She didn't pull out the "mine" card often, but then, Trevor didn't bring out the best in her.

She grabbed the gorgeous Montblanc pen off Henry's desk, ready to be rid of her cousin. Her cell phone vibrated in her pocket, notifying her of a text.

She hoped it was Henry. A few times in the weeks she'd been living with him he would text her asking if she wanted some company for lunch. She loved those times. Dinner they often spent with the bodyguards and their wives, or one of the lawyers would come with Henry, but breakfasts and lunches tended to be the two of them.

No luck. It was her uncle.

Sending a courier with some paperwork for you to sign in a few hours. Be home tomorrow but I thought I'd head out to Martha's Vineyard for a few days to check on Mary.

Good. She'd been worried when Henry had told her Mary had been moved around. The news that she would be coming home soon was such a relief.

She texted back.

Your "courier" came early. Trevor's here with the paperwork. No problem. Please tell Mary I love her and hope to see her soon.

If she wasn't in jail. It might be a good thing Mary had been out of touch. It meant she might not have heard all the horrible crap people were saying.

She shoved her phone into her pocket and walked back to the bar with the pen. "I'll take those."

He hesitated and then handed the folders to her. "I want to know why you did it."

She rolled her eyes. "I didn't, if you are asking about Brie's death. Let me state plainly and for the record that I did not kill Brie. If you've got a recorder or something and you're planning on taking this to a reporter, don't bother. I didn't kill her. I'm innocent."

She glanced down at the papers. The first was authority for the foundation to pay its bills. She signed that one on the line indicated.

"You went looking for her that night, didn't you?"

She signed a second contract allowing the foundation to release the funds to buy mammography machines for the ten clinics selected. But hadn't she seen this one before? She could have sworn she'd signed it already. "I did look for her. I thought we should talk. Trevor, we've been over all this. Why are we going over it again?

And I think I signed this paperwork before. I released these funds weeks ago."

"You know how shit like this works," Trevor replied, smooth as glass. "Gotta have ten copies of everything. And we're going over it again because I'm trying to understand. I know the two of you had been fighting. You know no one would blame you. Brie could be mean at times."

"I thought you were her biggest fan now." Her cell vibrated again. She pulled it out and glanced down.

"I cared about her. She helped me out when no one else would," Trevor was saying. "I would do a lot for her."

Trevor? He's in L.A. I didn't send him. I wouldn't send him on an errand like that.

She stopped. Why would Trevor lie? Why would he bring her a bunch of contracts and forms she'd already signed?

Why would Trevor ask her questions he already knew the answer to?

"So you went looking for Brie that night? To talk to her? Or to fight with her?" Trevor pressed.

She placed the phone facedown on the bar, her instincts on edge. She looked through the rest of the paperwork, trying to figure out what his game was. "I just wanted to talk."

Every single contract he'd brought was a copy of something she'd already signed. All but one. She found a form slipped into the rest of the contracts.

"Could you hurry it up, Win?" Trevor stood up, starting to come around the bar. "Not all of us can sit around all day. Some of us have work to do."

"I have to read them." She got the feeling reading the contracts would make Trevor nervous.

He suddenly looked far more predatory than he had before. His eyes narrowed as he glanced at her cell sitting on the bar. "But our lawyers have already gone through them. You don't trust your own lawyers anymore? Is that what Garrison is teaching you? He's the only one you can trust?"

She held her ground even as she looked to her left to see if Wade was still watching. He wasn't there. He'd done what she'd told him to do. He'd left her alone with her cousin. Still, this was Trevor. He was an ass but he wouldn't physically hurt her. Why would he ever do that? She couldn't let the jerk intimidate her. "I like to know what I'm signing, Trevor. I've already signed all of these with the exception of one. You want to explain it to me?"

His lips curled into a cruel imitation of a smile. "All right. I suppose I can explain it to you, but we should make one thing clear. I've got a gun and I'm going to use it on that bodyguard of yours if you make this difficult on me. Do you want your bodyguard dead, Win?"

The room seemed to have gone cold. She was as still as she could be. He had to be joking, but she couldn't take the chance. "Of course not. Why would you bring a gun?"

"Because I knew you would find a way to fuck this up. You always do. If I have to shoot the bodyguard, I'll take you out, too. Do you think I haven't gone over this in my head?"

His eyes had gone a little hazy, his jaw tight. She needed to keep him calm. "I'm sure you have."

"By the time I'm done manipulating this story, the police will believe I was only defending myself. Everyone will believe me. I've got the best reason for you to try to kill me. I think you know what I'm talking about. It's why you killed Brie. You found out my secret." His voice had gone low, but there was no way to miss how he'd eased his hand into his jacket. No way to pretend her cousin didn't suddenly have a gun in his hand. "I won't let you take this away from me."

"Take what away?" The question came out quietly because she believed him about her bodyguard. She didn't want Wade turning a corner and taking a bullet.

"Sign the paper, Win. Sign it and I'll go away quietly," Trevor promised, "because that's all I want. I want that paper signed and then I'll have what I need. I wanted you to admit that you killed Brie, but you're too stupid to even remember properly. One little tap to the head and Win goes down. You're pathetic and you'll still go to prison in the end. Now sign or I'll go looking for him."

She pulled out the paper he wanted her to sign. She signed her name and handed it back to him. She wasn't even sure what she'd signed, but it didn't matter. She wasn't about to start pointing out all the flaws in Trevor's plan. "There you go. You should leave now."

He tucked it into his jacket. "Don't even need to know what it was, do you? That's what I thought."

"I don't care." She just wanted him gone. The minute he left she would tell Wade, and two seconds afterward she would get Henry on the phone because there was no one in the world she wanted to see more than Henry. She wanted his arms around her.

"Did you know that idiot left you as her emergency contact?" Trevor ignored the rest of the documents. "I suspect you did and you thought you could find a way to get to her mail before I could. Well, sister, let me tell you, you don't win this time. This time I win, and wait until you see what I have in store for you and Daddy dearest."

"I'm going to need for you to drop the weapon," a deep voice said.

Before she could take a breath, Trevor was on her. He wrapped his arm around her waist and she could feel the hard press of the gun against her side.

Wade Rycroft was standing in front of her, the gun in his hand up and aimed directly at Trevor's head. "This is not going to go well for you, son."

"Put the gun down or I'll shoot her," Trevor said, but his voice was shaking.

Henry walked in, dropping his briefcase to the floor when he realized what was happening. "Wade, I think you should put the gun down. Win, baby, I need you to stay calm."

Wade kept the gun level. "Where do you think you're going, Mr. Hughes?"

She could feel Trevor behind her. He was shaking, but his arm tightened.

"I think I'll take my cousin here and figure that out in a bit," he said. "Now you two fuckers move back or I'll put a hole in her gut. She won't be worth much to you then, Garrison."

"I've already called the police, Trevor," Henry said.

"You're lying," Trevor shot back.

"Your father called me." Henry spoke calmly, his hands still in the air. "He's been texting with Win. When he found out you were here, he thought you might be up to something. I know you've tried to kill Win before."

"What?" She couldn't believe the words he was saying. Trevor was an ass but he'd never been violent around her.

Henry stood his ground. "You paid an assassin twenty thousand dollars to kill her while she was in Sweden."

"You can't prove that." The gun Trevor was holding bit into her side.

"What are you on, Trevor? Coke? Did you take a little to get you ready for this particular job?" Henry asked. "I hope that gun's not loaded because then maybe the cops will go easy on you. And I'll be able to prove it the same way I'm going to prove you've tried to kill Win several times. You didn't bother even waiting for the DNA test to come back, did you? That wasn't smart."

"DNA test?" She had no idea what Henry was talking about.

"That's right, bitch," Trevor said in her ear. "Turns out my mom and your dad didn't care about marriage vows. I'm not Bellamy Hughes's son. I'm Matt Hughes's son. That makes me his heir. Hughes Corp belongs to me, and I'm not sharing it with my sniveling, whiny baby sister."

Sister? Trevor was her brother?

But that wasn't the worst. No, all those secrets and lies were rolling through her head now. He'd tried to kill her. He'd been the one to send that man to Sweden, the one who'd looked into her eyes and shown her how cold a person could be.

"You thought you could have the whole company? The company is huge, Trevor. Even half of it would be worth more money than you could ever spend." Her voice was shaking, her world upending again. She'd known Trevor hated her, but she hadn't expected this.

"I knew you wouldn't let me have it. My mother told me you would try to find a way. Brie told me you would never let me have it. She hated you. You wouldn't believe how she talked about you. Why would she leave everything she had to you?"

Win hadn't heard anything about Brie's will. She hadn't known she was Brie's emergency contact. "I don't know. But you can have it. You can have the company. You can have the name. You can have it all. I don't care anymore. I never wanted any of it in the first place."

In the distance, she could hear the wail of sirens.

"I'll tell them that you were all in on it." Trevor's voice shook. "You all knew that I was about to take the company and you were ready to kill me. I was just defending myself. I can make that work. Cops hate you, Garrison."

"Or you could run," Henry offered. "Just let Win go and get out of here."

She could feel Trevor shaking his head and heard a choking sob.

"No, it's over. They won't believe me. Fucking Win. You fuck up everything," he said.

"Trevor, that's the coke talking," Henry said calmly. "You're coming down. I've seen it happen. There's a paranoia that sets in and everything seems dark. It's okay. You need to rest and everything is going to look better in a few hours. Let Win go and we'll talk. I can defend you. Do you have any idea how good I am? You won't spend any time in jail."

"You're a liar," Trevor screamed. The gun came away from her waist as he lifted it up toward Henry.

Oh god, he was going to shoot Henry. He was going to kill Henry and she would have nothing at all left. She loved him. In that moment, she realized that she'd been fooling herself. She didn't want an affair. She didn't want to pass some time and keep her mind off things with him. She wanted a life with him.

She kicked back, trying to ensure his shot went wide, but the world was suddenly filled with the roar of gunfire. Trevor stiffened behind her, his gun falling away.

When she turned, her cousin—her brother—was standing there, a neat hole in his forehead. He stared at her dumbly for a moment before his knees buckled and he started to fall toward her.

Henry rushed in, sweeping her away from the body. He picked her up and carried her out into the living room. "Are you all right? I've got EMTs on the way, too. Did he hurt you? Did the bullet graze you?"

"That was a perfect shot, Garrison," Wade explained. "It didn't even come close, but I had to take it because he was too shaky to trust. He had a good line on you. I couldn't risk losing you or a ricochet hitting Win."

Henry clutched her in his arms, even tighter than Trevor had. "You could have hit her."

He was in shock. She wrapped her arms around his neck. "I'm fine, Henry. I'm fine."

Those sirens were coming closer. Henry just stood there with her in his arms.

"I figured it out," he said, his voice hollow. "I figured out that he thought he was your brother. I figured out that he'd been the one to try to kill you, but I didn't think he would come here today. When Bellamy called me—"

"Mr. Garrison, I'm going to need you to put Win down and you're going to have to show your hands to the officers," Wade said. "They're coming into a situation with no knowledge of who's who. They need to see that you're not a threat."

"I don't want to let you go," he whispered.

But he had to. She kissed him and pulled away. "It's going to be okay."

He let her down and joined Wade, raising his hands as the elevator door opened and the police swarmed in. She tried not to look at the body on the ground. She stayed focused on Henry.

Win saw the lost look in Henry's eyes and prayed she was right.

⁓

"He's here, Henry." Noah opened the conference room door and let Bellamy Hughes in.

Win got up and ran to her uncle, who welcomed her with open arms. Bellamy looked like a man who'd had his whole life turned upside down. Henry had never seen him without a perfectly pressed suit, but this one was wrinkled, and the older man's eyes were red-rimmed.

Henry paced the floor, knowing this particular interview wasn't going to be pleasant. Telling someone the truth about a loved one never was, but he had even more to say than anyone else knew. The whole thing turned his stomach because he knew what it meant. It was almost over.

Twenty-four hours had passed in a wave of police interviews and long sessions with the DA. He and Win had mostly been kept apart except for that moment when they'd been allowed to leave the police station and had been inundated with reporters.

They were everywhere. He couldn't leave his building without someone shoving a camera in his face.

He'd tried to take Win to a hotel because the crime scene unit was still working in his place. They'd been followed by paparazzi.

They'd ended up at Noah's penthouse, where Win had fallen asleep in her clothes and he'd had to put her in bed.

He'd sat up most of the night wishing he could find the bar. A place as nice as Noah's would have a bar. A nice one. He wouldn't have to settle. He'd been absolutely sure Noah would have a middle-aged Scotch sitting there, waiting for him. Not even Win's sweet presence had calmed him. He'd stayed awake, her head resting against his chest while she slept.

Because he'd almost lost her.

Because he didn't think he deserved her.

"So I'm not Trevor's father?" Bellamy Hughes paced the floor of the conference room.

Not a question Henry could answer yet. "I have no idea. I suspect that's what Trevor believed. Have you been able to talk to his mother?"

Bellamy sank into one of the chairs. "No. She told me to go to hell and hung up on me. Not before she'd explained that I was a bastard and Trevor was dead because of me. He was my son. I raised him."

Win put a hand on her uncle's shoulder. "Of course you did. We don't know anything at all yet."

"We know that Trevor had some sort of reason to suspect that he was Matt Hughes's son," David explained.

The gang was here. Noah and David had joined him every step of the way. Margarita was flying up from Austin, but she'd missed all the good stuff. She would miss the end of the case because that sucker had already been written. He had it all in his hands and he almost wished he didn't.

He had everything he wanted. The phones were ringing again. He'd brought in a couple of wealthy clients since it had come out that Garrison, Cormack, and Lawless was representing Taylor Winston-Hughes. After this evening's press conference, there would be many, many more. This was why he'd taken on the case to begin with. He would again take his place as the Monster of Manhattan—the go-to lawyer when all looked bleak. But only if you had the cash. Justice was expensive.

Yes, he was getting everything he'd hoped for when he'd started over. So why did he feel so fucking hollow?

"I think Aunt Pamela told Trevor that Uncle Bellamy wasn't his dad." Win looked pretty, sitting there in tailored slacks and a silk blouse, her hair and makeup done in a way he'd never seen before. This was the Win the rest of the world saw, the Win she'd been raised to be. Manicured to perfection for the cameras.

It should make her less lovely. He preferred her with no makeup, her skin glowing in the early morning sunlight. But even with the makeup and perfectly done hair, she still had that glow he'd come to realize was simply a part of who she was.

But so were those reporters. She would always be in the public eye.

"Here's what we know," Henry began. He'd put a bunch of clues together once he had access to some of Trevor's information. Once the cops figured out Trevor was the bad guy, they'd been more than happy to hear Henry's theories and look at the information his investigators had gathered. "Roughly a year ago, Trevor began an affair with Brie Westerhaven. He regularly showed up where she was filming and was a guest at her home on many occasions."

"So right after I left the show they started sleeping together?" Win asked, her voice tight.

There had been betrayal all around her and it wasn't over yet. He felt for her. "Yes, I think given Ms. Westerhaven's personality, we can deduce that getting close to someone who hated you was a form of revenge on you for leaving her behind."

Noah shook his head. "I don't understand. Win was sick. She wasn't trying to hurt Brie. She didn't leave Brie behind. She went to get help."

David sighed. "I believe the technical term for what Brie was is 'narcissist.' Brie was incapable of understanding or empathizing with anyone but herself. She would view Win's defection as a shot across her bow, so to speak. It's also how she could hate and love Win at the same time."

Noah's eyes went grim. "All right. I might have known someone like that."

He might have been raised by someone like that. As far as Henry could tell, Iris Lawless had been a monster who made Brie look happy and shiny. "At some point in time, Trevor got it in his head that Bellamy might not be his father."

Bellamy ran a weary hand over his forehead. "Win's right. I'm sure it was Pamela. My ex-wife is always looking for ways to make my life hell. She would use Trevor to do it."

"Is it possible it could be true?" He had to ask the question.

"I suppose," Bellamy admitted. "Matt, Pam, and I grew up together. I guess deep down I always knew my brother was the one she wanted and I was the one she settled for. Did Trevor do a DNA test?"

"We think he did several, or rather, he had Brie do them for him," Henry explained.

"Brie decided she was some kind of expert after filming the episode that looked into her ancestry." Win sat up, her body stiff in the chair. "They did it for all of us, but they didn't have time to spend filming the rest of us. Brie and Hoover were the only ones featured."

Bellamy turned to her. "They did what? They took your DNA?"

Win waved him off. "It was one of those spit-in-a-jar things that tells you what your DNA makeup is. Mine was a whole lot of European. It was deemed boring. Apparently our ancestors didn't go anywhere or do anyone interesting."

Bellamy put a hand on hers. "Well, perhaps not. Apparently my ex-wife might have done my brother. Can't say I'm happy about that. Would that DNA test they did for the show prove something like who's related to whom?"

If only it were that easy. "No," Henry said. "We'll need new tests. The one Win did for the show was very specific and they weren't comparing her DNA to anyone. Trevor wasn't on the show, so Brie did the testing herself. From what we can tell, she bought several kits. You can buy them at a drugstore these days. These are tests meant to prove paternity. I'm sure at some point she stole some hair from Win's brush or something and sent that in alongside some of Trevor's DNA. That's how they would be able to tell you weren't his father, though a familial relationship would still show up in the DNA. I believe they likely did DNA tests on all of you in an attempt to prove Trevor was Matt's son and Win's half sibling."

"My toothbrush went missing several weeks ago," Bellamy admitted. "I had to go buy a new one. Unbelievable. Brie was trying to prove that Trevor was my brother's heir and he should have half of Hughes Corp. That would have been a disaster. But why try to kill Win? She's never done anything to him. Half of Hughes Corp would have been more than enough to keep him in cocaine for the rest of his life. That was all he really cared about."

"I managed to read some of the text messages from Brie to

Trevor." Once he'd produced the video that absolved Win of the crime, the police were more than eager to take a look at Trevor. "Brie truly poisoned him against her."

"Not that we were close before." Win had gone a little pale. "What did she say? Trevor could be easy to manipulate if you knew how to do it. He had thin skin, but anyone who stroked his ego could do no wrong."

He was never going to let her read those texts. They'd shown a terribly nasty side to the woman Win had called her friend. Still, he could give her some consolation. "She was pushing him to take half the company, not to kill you. From what I can tell, Brie didn't realize he'd hired people to hurt you. In fact, that was the whole reason Trevor showed up yesterday. You're Brie Westerhaven's heir. She had a will, and everything is supposed to go to you. Now, you wouldn't have been able to remain her heir if you had been convicted, but everything was frozen. Including her mail. That document he got you to sign gave him the right to pick up her mail."

"He wanted the DNA results," Noah surmised. "I'll get right on that, by the way. Unless NYPD wants it."

This was the rough part. "NYPD has a new theory on Brie's murder."

"They believe my son did it," Bellamy said, his tone grave. "I rather worried about that myself."

"Apparently DNA was found under Brie's nails and she'd had intercourse earlier that evening." Henry didn't want to go over all the nasty details, but he needed Win to understand that her part of this case was over. She was safe and she could move on with her life. "They believe it's likely Trevor's, and that Brie pushed him too far. Trevor apparently had quite a cocaine habit, and he could be violent when he was using. The police are theorizing that he got angry with her and stabbed her with the letter opener. They believe he was still in the room when Win walked in and he knocked her out using the fireplace tool. They're going to search his property for it, but even if they don't find it, they likely have enough to close the case."

Bellamy's eyes shut, but he held on to Win's hand. "So this new tape you found exonerates my niece completely? They can't keep her any longer?"

"The DA and I are holding a press conference in a couple of hours to explain that given the new evidence, Taylor Winston-Hughes has been exonerated and is free to go on with her life as she sees fit. All charges have been dropped."

Bellamy stood up, his face still grim but his hand out. "Garrison, I can't tell you how much I appreciate the work. I only wish someone had been able to save my son from himself. Nephew. I don't know what to call him now."

Win stood beside her uncle. "We don't know anything yet. And it doesn't really matter, does it? You raised him, Uncle Bellamy. That's all that matters. You raised him and you loved him."

"I think some people would say I did a poor job of it," he said sadly. "I think I'll skip the press conference. I want to go out to the island for a few weeks. Mary's coming home. I'll keep her company for a while. Winnie, I'd love for you to come home while we make arrangements."

David held up a hand. "I still have some questions. I know the police think they've got this wrapped up, but I'm not so sure."

"I agree." Noah leaned in. "Why did Mary give Brie five grand?"

Bellamy frowned. "She did it to try to spare me. I didn't know about this until I spoke with her this morning. Brie intended to blackmail me. She was going to use me against my son to see how much money she could get out of me before turning the evidence over to Trevor. She promised Mary if the money kept coming, maybe that DNA test never managed to make it back from the lab."

He wasn't sure how Brie had thought she could keep that up for long, but it likely didn't matter. It was obvious Brie had been desperate for money and had tried to get it any way she could. Now she was gone and the police would pin the murder on Trevor. He wasn't sure Trevor had been the one to kill Brie, but Trevor was convenient and he checked off all the boxes.

Trevor *had* been the one who tried to kill Win. Of that he was certain. Win was safe. That was what mattered. Everything else was noise.

"And would you like to tell me why you've kept Mary hidden from me?" That was another question he wanted cleared up.

Bellamy's eyes met his. "I certainly did not hide her. There was a storm and the facility she was in flooded. You know how the storms can get this time of year. She had to be moved and it was chaotic for a while. She's home now and it's time to take care of her. If you would like to speak with her, you're certainly welcome. You have our address out on the island. Feel free to stop by. I'm sure my niece would love to see you."

"Oh, Uncle Bell, I was planning on staying here for a few days," Win said, looking to Henry.

Yes, here was the bad part. "I think you should go with your uncle."

The color drained from her face.

"Could we have the room for a moment?" He shouldn't do this in front of an audience. It would be bad enough without everyone watching.

David stood up and came in close. "Don't do this."

"I've thought this through. It's for the best," he whispered back.

"It's not best for her." David shook his head and walked to the door. "And you know what, it's not best for you either, but you're going to be a stubborn bastard, aren't you?"

Noah reached a hand out to Win, taking hers. "If you need anything, anything at all, call me. We're still here for you no matter what he says. He's being an idiot. I should know. I've seen it happen before."

"Noah, your opinion is not required," Henry shot back.

"And yet it's still true." Noah squeezed her hand and escorted Bellamy out, promising to call for a car.

And then they were finally alone.

"I've had your things packed up and they've been sent to the plane. It's going to take you out to the island in an hour." He forced himself to go cold.

If he kept her here, he exposed her to more scrutiny. She would feel the need to look perfect for the cameras, and that had proven dangerous once before. He couldn't do it to her again. She needed to go back to her proper life track: grad student and all-around do-gooder. He didn't do good. He made money and that was his proper track.

"Why?" Win asked, the question tinged with the ache he could plainly see she felt.

It was better for her to ache now than later. She needed to find a nice man and settle down, a man who'd never fucked up his entire life, a man who could love her with a whole heart. A man who could stand beside her and hold his head high. "I told you in the beginning this was a temporary thing."

"Yes, you also told me you would have called me," she pointed out.

He wished he'd been strong enough to have not told her that particular truth. "I would have, perhaps. We are good in bed together and I don't have a ton of time to find women I'm compatible with."

She stared for a moment, the silence becoming uncomfortable.

That was not the response he'd expected.

"Is this the part where you tell me I was nothing but a good lay, Henry?"

"I didn't say that." He wasn't sure how to handle her. He'd expected her to retreat, to cry a bit and make him feel like the world's biggest bully. He'd been counting on it because he needed her to see that they had no place in each other's worlds.

"Oh, I think that's exactly what you said, Counselor." She put her hands on her hips, facing him down. "I'm supposed to believe that you've gotten everything you could want or need out of me and so now I'm some piece of trash to throw away."

"Again, not the words I said." He held his ground. He was the bad guy here, but somehow he couldn't let her think he was that bad.

"They were implied. Look, I'm not a victim here. You did tell me it would last two weeks. I tried to stay in touch because I did want more. When you didn't reply, I let it go. When you took me into your home, you're the one who said we were inevitable."

"I said having sex with you was inevitable."

"You coward. That wasn't sex. You're old enough to know the difference," she said with a disappointed shake of her head. "I get it. You came out of a bad marriage and you're still a little singed from that fire, but we don't get to choose when the right one comes along. Fate or the universe or pure coincidence decides that for us. I'm the right one for you. You're the right one for me. I love you. I'm not ashamed to say it and you can't make me ashamed. No words that come out of your mouth are going to make me go hide in a corner and cry. I'm not a fairy-tale princess who needs you to save me from my lonely castle. But we could save each other. No woman alive is going to understand you the way I do, is going to see you the way I do, and I'm never going to meet a man who can make me believe in myself the way you do. So you have a choice. Take the love and affection and companionship I'm offering you or let your past win."

He wanted to take it all. This Win, oh, this Win was exciting, and she'd been there all the while, bubbling under the surface. This was the Win who couldn't be beaten, who'd looked her disease in the face and made the hard choice to survive. This was the Win who would stand beside him no matter what.

He didn't deserve her. She was right. His past was too much.

"It won't work. Do you think I want to get back to the place where I'm some rich girl's arm candy?" He could do this. He had a whole spiel that was guaranteed to send her running. Once he was done, she wouldn't want him. She would be free. "Do you think—"

She put up a hand. "Really? You're going with the 'rich bitch couldn't possibly love an actual person' theme? Do you know how many times I've heard that? That's the bottom of the barrel and truly unworthy of you. You're supposed to be better at making your arguments, but I see through every single one. You're scared. Stop being scared and be a man, Henry. Nothing is guaranteed. The world doesn't work that way. All we can do is love as hard as we can for as long as we have."

She moved in, her body nearly brushing his.

He might be shit at making this argument, but she was good. Damn good.

She put a hand on his chest. "Please. Give us some time. We need to get through a couple of days and you'll see that life will go back to normal. I know what you're scared of. You think it will always be like this, with all the reporters and all the lights and scrutiny. You're scared we'll both slip back into those dark places, and this time we'll have to watch each other disintegrate. But it's not like that. I'm really the girl you met on the beach. Once they have another story, we'll be nothing more than a boring couple trying to make it work. Once a year you'll put on a tux and smile for the cameras at the foundation benefit. The other three hundred and sixty-four days, you'll be the star of the family, known for your brain and not your gorgeous looks."

She made it sound so reasonable. He hadn't counted on her fighting him.

Fighting for him.

She was fighting him for him.

"I can't, Win." He wanted to be stronger. Or weaker. He wasn't sure. She'd thrown him for a loop and he wasn't sure how to handle it. He'd spent his whole life knowing what he wanted, knowing how to get it. He'd never stopped.

Until he had, and he wasn't sure how to get himself going again.

Her eyes softened. "I love you, Henry. I can see that you have no idea how to handle that right now. I'm going with my uncle so you can take a couple of days. I'll text you and if you like, we can start slow. But I love you and I won't not love you because you're scared. If you can't love me back, that's something else entirely."

"I didn't say that." He couldn't. He just couldn't. Couldn't quit her even though it was for the best. If she'd cried and run out like he was a monster, he might have been able to carry through, but the resilient, strong woman in front of him wasn't going to make it easy.

She went up on her toes and kissed his cheek. "Take some time. Think about it. I'll contact you in a few days and if you reply back, I'll know we're not completely lost."

"And if I don't reply?"

A ghost of a smile lifted her lips. "I don't know. I'll figure it out then, but I think you should expect a fight."

She turned and walked out of the room, and Henry was left alone.

He stared out over the city and wished he were a better man.

FOURTEEN

Win watched the clouds rolling in from the Atlantic. The storm was still hours away but it looked like it would be a doozy.

She couldn't help but think about the last storm she'd been through. She'd had Henry to hold her, wrapping his arms around her and making her forget all about the chaos outside.

It had only been a few days and she felt the loss of him as an actual ache in her heart.

She'd watched his press conference. He'd seemed so strong, authoritative in his suit. He'd carried himself perfectly, explaining all the aspects of the case and how he'd found the evidence that exonerated his client.

She hadn't been able to stop herself. She knew she'd told him she would wait a few days, but she'd texted him.

You looked good out there, Counselor.

She'd left it at that and hadn't expected anything from him.

You know I do work out from time to time. Stay safe, Win. Give
me time. Don't give up on me.

She'd texted back a single word. Never.

And then nothing but silence for days. She had to let him figure
this out. Patience.

"It looks like a bad one." Mary sat in a lounge chair, her knitting
in her hands. She was moving better, maneuvering around the house
with her new walker.

"Yeah, it does." She moved back, sitting across from Mary.
They'd tiptoed around certain subjects, but Win was discovering she
could only be patient with one person at a time. "Why didn't you tell
me about Brie?"

Mary's hands stopped working the yarn. "I didn't want to upset
you. Especially if there was no reason to. We don't know anything
for certain yet. But I was worried it might be true, and I didn't want
to upset you. It can be hard to realize that your parents are only human, you know. I suppose I wanted to keep them perfect in your
mind."

"No one's perfect. You can't do that again. I'm an adult now. I
know you protected me before, and you can't even begin to understand how much I appreciate it, but I'm strong now. I have to face
these things head-on. I can't help but wonder if I'd found out about
what was going on if I could have stopped it. I was good at talking
Brie out of the stupid crap she did." That was what haunted the hell
out of her. Despite the fact that Brie and Trevor had been horrible
to her, they'd been family. Brie had been in a bad place and done
terrible things, but she wouldn't have a chance to redeem herself.

"I don't think she would have allowed it," Mary said, her accent
a bit thicker than normal. Her Polish accent came out when she was
emotional. "Brianna was determined to destroy everything. She
wasn't going to back off. I knew she would come back. I wanted to

buy some time in order to find a solution to the problem, but then the accident happened."

The one where Mary had been driving her Jeep. "Do you really think Trevor tried to kill you that night?"

She shook her head. "No, I think he wanted to kill you. You were supposed to come back that day, remember?"

Win grimaced, the reality punching into her. "Yes, I was going to come spend the night out here and then head to the city the next day, but I had to cancel at the last minute because of a problem with the gala. Trevor knew I was coming. I told him. He thought you were me. Mary, I'm sorry."

She laid the knitting down, her eyes finding Win's. "Don't you be sorry. I'm happy it was me in that car. I wouldn't have you hurt for anything in the world, don't you know that? You're my . . . Well, let's just say I think of you as a daughter. I would do anything for you, my baby. From the moment they put you in my arms, I knew I would do anything for you."

Tears pierced her vision, and she reached out to the woman who had been a mother to her. "And I would do anything for you, but I'm not a baby anymore."

"Don't you know daughters are always babies in their mother's eyes?" Mary cleared her throat. "You know what I'm saying. When you raise a child, the child becomes important to you. I know your real mother would have done anything for you, too. She would have looked at you and always been able to see your father. You have his eyes."

"You're joking, right?" Win had to laugh. "My father's eyes were brown. I must have been the result of some very recessive genes since Mom's were hazel and mine are blue."

Mary picked her knitting back up. "I don't understand all that scientific stuff. It all seems like nonsense to me. Could you go down to the shop and ask your uncle to make a run to the store before the storm comes in? I need broth to make the stew."

"I can cook tonight, Nana." She stood up, glancing down to the shop where her uncle kept the boat he worked on when he was in town. He'd been working on that boat for years. "Though I'll still need broth."

"Don't you go," she said. "There are still some reporters running around. They'll be gone soon, but I don't want them bugging you. Send your uncle."

Sometimes Mary truly did sound like a mom. "I'll see what I can do."

She helped Mary up, putting her walker in front of her. Mary straightened up. "I'll get started on the vegetables. Tell your uncle not to take too long. That storm will be bad."

She wasn't about to send her uncle out. Despite what Mary might think, those reporters would know who Bellamy Hughes was, and they wouldn't leave him alone simply because he was grieving the loss of his son. She could handle a couple of questions.

Ms. Winston-Hughes, how did it feel to finally get your freedom back?

Crappy because my man didn't come with me. I bought a vibrator, but I can't work up the will to use that sucker. Thanks for asking, CNN.

Why do you think your cousin wanted to murder you?

Well, MSNBC, he was a coked-up asshat who didn't care who he hurt as long as he got his precious proof that he was the heir.

Yes, she could handle a few questions.

She passed the wall of photos. Her family history in pictures. She stopped, looking them over. They went back to her great-great-grandparents. Now she was the last one left.

How sad it was to think that there was no one to reach out to, no one to work with to carry on the family name. Her uncle had many good years ahead of him, but eventually she would have to decide what to do.

All those generations, counting on her.

She sighed because she didn't even look like a Hughes. It was one of those twists of DNA. The Hughes family were all tall, stately looking brunettes. Of course, she didn't look much like her Winston side either. The Winstons tended to be tall and slender as well. She was a petite blonde with blue eyes.

Did anyone else in her family have blue eyes? She peered at the photos. It was hard to tell.

She stared at a picture of her mother and father. They were smiling at the camera and holding their baby girl. There weren't many pictures of her as a baby. She'd always thought it odd since most new parents took tons of baby pictures. This portrait was the only one of her. Her uncle had made sure there was money for regular portraits after they'd died.

How old was she in that picture? Her parents looked happy together. It was hard to think that her father had been unfaithful. He held her like a proud father. She was dressed in a pink jumper, smiling at the camera, her brown eyes wide.

Win blinked. Brown eyes. The baby in the picture had brown eyes. The baby in the picture looked a lot like her father.

Win shook her head. It must have been a trick of the light. Something had gone wrong with the photo and a shadow had changed her eye color. Because blue eyes might turn brown, but never the other way around.

It was weird.

She picked up the keys to her Jeep and tried to forget the eerie feeling that something was very wrong.

⁓

Henry stared down at the files. "Is there a reason I've got files on my desk for a case that is no longer active?"

His admin frowned down at him. She was a seasoned legal secretary with more knowledge than a lot of lawyers possessed. Sharon didn't take his crap even though she'd only recently been hired. It was one of the reasons they worked well together. "Those files came in yesterday and you should have seen them. Someone said there was interesting information in there. I thought you might look at the reports before I filed them. Also, Margarita requested a few moments of your time. I think she's going to come in here and try to save the firm from the fire-breathing dragon in the main office. That's you, by the way."

He hadn't been that bad. Well, maybe he had. Maybe he'd been a little irritable the last few days. He might have yelled more than once when a tersely worded email could have worked as well. "I suppose David and Noah are avoiding me?"

He'd noticed that the room tended to clear out the minute he walked into it. Talking ceased and the clacking of keys on laptops would be the only sound as he crossed through the associates' communal workroom. He was turning into Scrooge or something.

"Anyone who can is avoiding you," Sharon pointed out. "Now, I'll go file those reports that we paid for and you didn't read."

He put a hand on the folders. "Fine, I'll look through them, though it's going to be a waste of time. And let me know when the courier with Brie Westerhaven's mail gets here."

He hoped that would contain the DNA test results they were looking for.

She walked back to the door that led to the outer office. "I got a message that it's been signed for. I'll go get it from reception and bring it back to you. We're all eager to see who the daddy is."

"If there's a betting pool, I don't want to hear about it." It wasn't so odd that the staff would be interested, but he couldn't help but think about the fact that this was Win's life and family.

Everything was easier when he didn't care.

The trouble was he didn't think he could stop caring about Win.

She was right. She was the one. He'd thought the ache would ease with time and distance, but every minute he put between them seemed to refine his misery.

"I hear you're being very difficult, Henry," Margarita said in a soothing tone as she walked in the room. "You know what might help? A short vacation. I hear Martha's Vineyard is lovely this time of year."

"It's hurricane season." He glanced down at the folders. It looked like McKay-Taggart had been very thorough. They'd come through with full dossiers on all the important players. He flipped through them until he found the only one he was truly interested in: Mary Hannigan.

Yeah, he still would like to solve that mystery.

Margarita looked down at him, her eyes warm. "Sometimes riding out the storm with someone you care about can be a good thing."

Win didn't sleep well during storms. Who would hold her when she woke up and the thunder and lightning was cracking all around her? She would be alone out there on the island. If he was there, he could distract her. He would make love to her over and over again until she was so tired not even the storm could keep her awake. Then he would cuddle up and sleep against her and start all over again in the morning.

"Henry, what are you doing?" Margarita asked. "You want that woman, and she wants you. Go after her."

"I thought it would be smart to give us some time," he explained. "Our relationship was built on some pretty heavy trauma. The time isn't just for me. It's for her. She's young and it's very reasonable for her to fall for the man who saved her life. You know those types of relationships almost never work."

"But you met her before, when there wasn't any stress. You were too stubborn to call her then."

"I was going to." Henry sat back. He wasn't going to lie about that a second longer. He'd been ready to call and set up some way to see her. "I want to now, but I don't know if I have the right to. I'm too old for her. I'm an alcoholic, a workaholic."

"You haven't been too much of a workaholic lately," Margarita said nonchalantly. "In fact, before the last couple of days, some of the associates were complaining because they'd heard you were a hard-ass who never left the office. They started clocking when you left work. I believe on average they had you walking out the door a little before five. Not quite the usual hours for the Monster of Manhattan."

His associates needed more to do. "I had to make sure I got home at a reasonable hour because . . ." He was such an idiot. Margarita had led him right into her trap. "I wanted to spend time with Win, so I made her a priority."

"See, you can do it." Margarita sat down in the chair across from him. "You're totally trainable. Tell me how she did it. It was food and sex, right? She worked quickly."

He frowned. "She certainly didn't train me. She merely made it clear that dinner was served at a specific time and it would be rude to leave her alone after she cooked. And then she would come and sit in my lap for dessert." He thought about that for a moment. "Damn it. She used food and sex to train me."

He laughed for the first time in days.

He'd been worried about taking advantage of her while she'd been quietly working to mold him into a good boyfriend. Not perfect. She didn't want perfect. She wanted healthy and good and right.

"I love her," he admitted. It was good to say the words.

"Excellent because I asked Noah to get the plane ready." She stood up, a happy look on her face. "I also had a bag packed for you. You leave in forty minutes and you can't be late or you might get grounded because apparently there's another storm. You're right. It is storm season."

He could see Win in less than two hours. He could show up on her doorstep and she would welcome him. She would open her arms—not asking him any questions, merely making him glad to be there.

He was tired of being without her. Not alone. He could be alone, but now being alone meant being without her. If he stood up and got on that plane, Win would gently mold him, and slowly his career would become less important and she would likely talk him into marriage and he would wake up one morning a poor schmo idiot who spent more time on his wife and kids than he did on his stellar career. He wouldn't be excellent because he wouldn't have time to make his career the way he'd dreamed of. He would be ordinary. An ordinary man who loved his wife and kids. An ordinary life. Not perfect. Merely right and good.

Henry stood up because he was done with perfection forever. "I need David to take the Jameson case."

"Already done." David was standing in the doorway, a smile on his face. "And your bag is waiting in the car. Go get your girl. You're probably going to have to grovel though. Do you remember how?"

Win wouldn't make him. She'd given him time and she would likely reward him for not taking too long to come to his senses. She'd probably been ready to give him another few weeks before she got mad at him.

Noah stepped up beside David. "Let's get going. I'm going to be your pilot today."

"You don't have to do that. I can hop on a commuter plane."

Noah shook his head. "And not take the company jet? Oh, sure it says 4L Software on the side, but I consider it ours. Let's head out. I've got a date."

Henry felt lighter. Younger. Less stupid. More stupid. He didn't care because he was going to see Win. "You have a date?"

David shook his head. "When we went out to the island to make sure you were alive a few weeks ago, he met a woman. Apparently she's very open to accommodating his busy schedule. He's going to fly you out, spend the night, and come back in the morning. You and Win can come with him or hang out for a couple of days. Margarita and I will hold down the fort."

He was going to Win. Why had it been hard to make that decision? Because having made it, he felt so damn good. Being with Win was the best decision he'd ever made.

"Let's go." Nothing else mattered. Only Win. Getting Win in his arms was the most important thing in the world.

Sharon stepped in. "Who wants this?"

The DNA report. He pulled the folder out of her hands. It didn't matter, but he wanted to be able to go over it with Win and her uncle. They could settle everything. And while he was at it . . .

He jogged back and grabbed the intelligence Sharon had put on his desk earlier. He could read the files while he was in flight. It wasn't like they would tell him anything interesting. It would tell him things like Trevor had a coke problem and Win had control issues. There would be reports on how Win should dump her reality TV show friends.

Some people would read the latest thriller. Henry liked to read reports on people he found suspicious.

"Let's go. I want to touch down long before that storm hits," Noah said.

Henry didn't argue. He wanted Win in his arms before the first thunder shook the house.

An hour later he stared down at the report, a chill going over his skin.

"You're quiet," Noah said, walking out into the cabin.

"Shouldn't you be flying the plane?" He didn't look up. He couldn't quite manage to process the words on the page. He shouldn't have ducked Big Tag's call earlier this afternoon. He hadn't wanted to deal with the head of McKay-Taggart—Case's older brother, Ian, was known for his sarcasm—but now he realized what the man had been calling about.

"It's on autopilot," Noah replied. "This sucker pretty much flies itself. I just sit in the seat for takeoff and landing. We've got smooth skies on this side. Are those the final reports on Win's case?"

Now he wasn't absolutely sure Win's case was over. Not by a long shot. A sick feeling had opened in the pit of his stomach. "I asked the investigators to find out everything they could on Mary Hannigan."

"The nanny? Wasn't there some issue with her immigration status?"

Immigration was the least of their problems. "No. There was an issue with her existing at all before she shows up on the tax records thirty years ago. Apparently she changed her name after her husband died, when the yacht he was piloting went down."

Noah frowned. "That's weird. Didn't Win's parents die in a yachting accident?"

"Yes, they died during a storm. The boat was captained by a man named Milo Jarvisch. His wife was named Mary."

Noah huffed, looking down at the names on the files. "Are you fucking with me? Mary Hannigan was married to the captain of the yacht Win's parents died on? How did we not know that? Shouldn't that have been all over the initial reports? I read a bunch of background on the accident and that was never once mentioned. They mentioned the captain's name, but not that he had a wife."

The fact that he'd been married wasn't even the bad part. "And child. Milo and Mary Jarvisch had a child. A daughter."

Taylor Winston-Hughes had been called the Miracle Baby. How

did a baby survive when the adults hadn't? When the storm had been so bad it had broken a million-dollar yacht apart and they'd never found the bodies?

Only one living baby strapped into a life vest. She'd been saved from the ocean's dangers by a fishing boat twenty-four hours later and miles from where she should have been. That baby had managed to survive in ten-foot waves, in the frigid water for hours and hours.

Her uncle had been called to identify her.

A miracle.

Or a very clever way to keep a billion-dollar fortune in the family.

Noah went still. "What are you thinking? Because that would be terrible. If you're thinking what I'm thinking. What happened to the Jarvisch daughter? Where is she now?"

"There are no records of the child beyond her birth certificate. She would have been almost the same age as the Winston-Hughes baby. There are no school records or immunization records. It's like Mary dumped the baby and continued on with her life. Or she's been with her baby girl all along. I think I know exactly where she is." He turned to the envelope with the DNA tests and opened it. There it was. Not one test but two. One of the envelopes was marked *TWH*.

Taylor Winston-Hughes.

"Oh, shit. Brie figured it out." Noah moved back to the pilot's chair. "I'll have us down on the ground as soon as I can."

Yes, Brie had figured out a decades-old con. That was why she'd died. And that was why he had to get on the damn ground, because Win was with the real killer.

FIFTEEN

Win pulled the Jeep into the garage, her mind still on that picture. She'd seen it a million times, but this time it had disturbed her. She stepped out of the garage, closing it behind her. She delivered the cans of stock to Mary, who was cutting up vegetables.

"Thank you, sweetheart." She shook her head. "Though I told you not to go yourself."

"The grocery store was completely paparazzi-free." In a few weeks no one would even want to talk to her. There would be a new scandal and everyone would move on.

"I'm happy to hear it." Mary glanced out over the yard toward the shop. "Could you go and ask your uncle to make sure the generator has gas? I don't like those skies."

"Sure." She started toward the door but turned, asking a question she'd always wanted to ask. "Do you ever wish you'd had kids of your own?"

Mary looked up, a sad smile on her face. "I did. I had you, my love. Never think I don't love you as my own. You are my own. Sending you to those boarding schools was the hardest thing I ever had to do. I fought with your uncle, but he convinced me it was for the best. If I could do it over again, I would have kept you at home and maybe you wouldn't have fallen in with that terrible girl."

When she thought about it, her uncle and Mary had functioned as her parents. Right down to fighting over what was best for her.

"I would have found other trouble," Win replied. "Things tend to work out the way they should. At least I hope so. I hope fate is kind this time around and Henry calls."

Mary's eyes met hers. "Sometimes you have to take control of fate. Sometimes you have to make hard decisions and never back down from them. If you want that man, if he's the one for you, don't give up on him."

The first clap of thunder shook the house. They were running out of time. "I'll remember that. I'll go and talk to Uncle Bell. He'll get stuck in the shop if I don't make him come in."

It wouldn't be the first time. She jogged across the yard, the scent of the storm rolling over her senses. It was like the ocean air, only with an extra charge to it. The sky was dark, with flashes of light making it seem like one big show. Nature's mighty entertainment.

The first raindrops hit her forehead and she raced into the shop.

Music filled the space. Chopin. It was soothing, along with the soft light that filled the building. Uncle Bellamy's shop was neat and well kept. For much of her life, it had been off limits because of the tools. She and Trevor had been locked out after Trevor had played around with a saw and nearly lost a finger.

"Is that you, Win?" Her uncle's voice was muffled, and she could see his feet sticking out from under the boat he was restoring.

"Yeah, the storm's moving in. Mary wanted to make sure the generator is ready in case we lose power," she said over the music.

"I already checked it this afternoon." He didn't move from under the boat. "Give me a few minutes and I'll walk back to the house with you. I'm almost done here. Can you pass me the sander?"

She moved around the shop to where her uncle kept the tools and picked up the triangular sander he used on small jobs. Her uncle's hand came out and she could see he was working with a light wrapped around his forehead. "Here you go."

"Thanks." He took the sander. "I'll only be a few minutes."

"No problem." She glanced around the shop. She knew why her uncle was hiding out here. It was soothing for him after the chaos of Trevor's death. He could come here and work in peace and quiet and try to forget that the police still hadn't released his son's body for burial.

That was something she would have to get him through. A funeral for his son. Who might be his nephew.

If her father had cheated, could her mother have cheated, too? With a man who had blue eyes and light-colored hair? Would that explain why she didn't look like anyone in the family? She wasn't sure why, but that picture was still bothering her. "Do you think my mother cheated the way my dad did?"

The sander stopped. "What did you say, dear?"

This wasn't the time or the place. "Nothing. Just commenting about the rain. It's starting to come down now."

"I think there's an umbrella in one of the bins by the front door." The sander sounded again, the whirl oddly peaceful.

She moved around the shop, brushing her hands over the neatly kept tools. Maybe she needed a hobby to take her mind off things. She couldn't start school again until the next semester and she wasn't sure she would go back to Duke. It was too far from Henry. NYU would work. Maybe Columbia.

Maybe he wouldn't call at all and she would really need a hobby and that wand she'd ordered.

Umbrella. She needed to concentrate on finding one because it was coming down hard now, the sound competing with the music and the sander.

There were several containers near the door. One of them was a box for the wood her uncle used. The other seemed to be a catchall. There were a couple of umbrellas and the walking stick her uncle took with him when he walked along the beach. She reached in and pulled out the umbrella. It caught on something, pulling it along.

Something heavy and metal had caught on the fabric. She pulled it free and then stopped.

It was a fireplace tool.

She stared at it dumbly for a moment, trying to understand why it was here. It was supposed to be back in her bedroom in Manhattan. That was where it had been for years. Until it had gone missing the night of Brie's murder, the night she'd been hit on the back of the head.

That was when she realized no one had cleaned it. There was blood and strands of blond hair clinging to it.

Her blood. Her hair.

"I should have gotten rid of that," a deep voice said from behind her.

She turned and faced her uncle, fear beginning to rise. "Why? Why would you kill Brie? Why would you nearly kill me?"

He looked odd in his shop clothes. He was always so perfectly pressed, but he looked older, more timeworn in the denim coveralls he wore when he worked here. "I wasn't trying to kill you, Win. That would have made everything I've done in the last twenty-nine years meaningless. As for that bitch friend of yours, she figured it all out. She knew I would pay to keep the secret, but she didn't understand that I couldn't trust her. Can't trust anyone but Mary. It was why I had the fishermen killed a few years later. I couldn't risk them talking."

"Fishermen?" Why was he talking about fishing when she was holding the evidence that could send him to jail? "Brie knew that Trevor was my dad's son? Why would you kill her over that? I know it's got to be a blow to your ego, but . . ."

"I didn't care about that stupid son of a bitch. I don't care if he's my child. Hell, I hope he was my brother's. My brother was a selfish bastard. I told him not to go that night. I told him not to get on that boat, but he was always smarter than the rest of us. He said he had a captain who could get around the storm."

She was so confused. "The night they died?"

"Matt fucked everything up. I always had to clean up after him. Yes, he was the brilliant mind, but I was the one who had to keep everything together. Who leaves their billion-dollar company to charity? Who fucking does that? What was I supposed to do? He got his whole family killed and I was supposed to let the company go to some hippie-dippie organization that would run it into the ground?"

Her stomach turned as she realized what he was saying. Was he saying that? She couldn't quite make herself believe it. "But his whole family wasn't killed."

Her uncle stopped, his face clearing and becoming calm again. "That's right, sweetheart. You lived. You saved us all. You were a miracle."

What had Mary said? *Sometimes you have to take control of fate.*

She'd also said she loved her like a daughter. *You are my own.*

Mary had blue eyes. Her hair was gray now, but at one time it had been a honey blond. It was all about DNA. Brie had started out trying to discover if Trevor might be heir to half of the Hughes fortune. She'd attempted to prove that Trevor was Win's half brother. How surprised had Brie been to discover Win shared no DNA at all with either Trevor or Bellamy Hughes? Was that when she'd gone to Mary and made the first threat?

"How did you find me?" The words felt dumb on her lips, like she couldn't believe she was saying them, but still they came. "Did Mary sell me to you?"

Her uncle's jaw tightened. "Don't open this up, Win. It's done and everyone who could hurt us is gone. We're going to be fine now."

"Did she sell me to you?" She had to know.

"Your mother knew a good deal. We made a bargain. Mary lost her husband in that wreck. I gave her a way to have a good life for her daughter and herself," he said, the words harsh out of his mouth. "She came to me when she couldn't reach him on the radio, and we knew we had to have a plan in place."

A plan in place. She'd been the plan. "So Mary was married to the captain of the yacht. She knew it had gone down before anyone else."

"Yes. She came to me, but I was the one who knew what to do. She didn't want to put you in the water, but we had to make it look good. I was surprised the papers couldn't see the truth, but they didn't even question it. You were a miracle and everyone wanted that."

"I'm not Taylor Winston-Hughes." Her whole life had flipped.

"You are. No one will question it now." He moved toward her. "All you have to do is keep your mouth shut."

"The company isn't mine. Now I know why you kept Mary away from Henry. Mary knew Brie had run a test on me and she knew what the results were. I know when Brie did it. She took my brush a month ago, and when I asked for it back she said she couldn't find it. She tested me to see if I was Trevor's half sister, and guess what she found out. You think keeping my mouth shut will fix things? Have you thought about Henry? Henry is waiting for the last of the DNA tests to come in. According to him, Brie had multiples done from different labs. I don't know what happened to the others, but he will get those final results and he will open them."

"He's your lawyer. Garrison can't talk," her uncle said with confidence. "He'll be disbarred if he talks."

"Not if he knows his client is committing an ongoing crime. It's fraud. Billions of dollars' worth of fraud." How had he gotten away with it for all those years? How had he managed to keep this secret?

She wasn't Taylor Winston-Hughes. She was someone else. Her mother was alive and had spent her whole life lying to her.

She didn't own the company. She didn't own anything. Her whole life was a scam.

Her uncle stared at her like they were in some kind of standoff. "Win, put that down and we'll go talk to Mary."

"You mean my mother." Mary was her mom.

"You can't call her that. We have to keep everything the same. No slipups. And I'll handle the lawyers. Don't worry about that."

"Like you handled Brie?" Her uncle had killed Brie. That was hard to imagine. Her urbane, sophisticated uncle had taken a letter opener and stabbed Brie. Then he'd gone back to the party, even found Margarita so he would have an ironclad alibi.

"She left me no choice."

"You had a choice. You have one now. Come clean. Make things right."

"Right? You think it was right to let that company slip out of my fingers? You're an ungrateful little bitch, you know that? You should be kissing my feet, not standing there looking at me like I'm some kind of monster." He stepped closer, causing Win to take a step back. "If I hadn't come along, you would be living in some crap hole with a mother who would have worked all day for a pittance. She was an uneducated immigrant when I made my deal with her. She would have had nothing. You would be nothing without me, so you start paying me a little respect."

For the first time, it occurred to her that she was truly standing in the same room with a man who had killed before.

She backed up toward the door.

The whole shop shook with the force of thunder.

"Where are you going, Win? You can't go out in a storm like this," he said, sounding so reasonable. "We'll run back to the house together and sit down and talk this out like the family we are now. Blood isn't important, Win. Family is about who you can depend on when times get tough."

"You don't care about any of us." She wasn't going to be fooled by his words ever again. "All you ever cared about was that company. What are you going to do, Uncle Bell? If I die, you lose it all. You could kill Brie. You could set up Trevor to take the fall. There's nothing you can do to me. If I die, you lose. If I tell, you lose."

His face fell. "Yes, I'm afraid I had to plan for that, too. I've always known something like this could happen. You seemed so reasonable, but I've always been ready. It's funny that it's going down here, where I keep all my secrets. I suppose it really is meant to be."

"Ready?" She felt her back come up against the door as her uncle turned and reached out, grabbing a leather bag.

He reached in and pulled out a gun. It was black with a wood-paneled handle. "Don't worry, dear. It's not filled with bullets. Just tranquilizer darts. I don't intend to kill you. You'll spend the rest of your life in a very nice mental facility."

Win pulled back the metal tool in her hand and hit him with all the force she had. She caught him in the side and the gun dropped to the floor. Bellamy cursed and reached for the gun. He brought it up, but Win was already running.

Something sizzled against her leg, fire brushing her skin. She ran for the main house, rain pelting down on her.

"You can't hide, Win," he shouted. "I'll have a dozen men looking for you within the hour. There's nowhere to go."

Her feet pounding against the sand, she ran even as the sky above her flashed with lightning.

She did have somewhere to go. Home wasn't an option. Her mother was there and she couldn't be sure Mary wouldn't go along with Bellamy Hughes's plan. After all, she'd sold her daughter once before.

But she had another home.

If she could make it across. The rain had only just started. It might not be flooded yet. If she could get across to Chappaquiddick and into Henry's old house, she knew where he kept a rifle. He'd sold the whole place as is.

What he didn't know was that he'd sold it to her.

She had to get there. The path was up ahead, the way illuminated by flashes of lightning. She had to make it. Her lungs burned as she ran, the rain nearly blinding her.

And then she saw the lights across the beach. She'd set the lights to come on at night as a security measure. She could see them glowing in the darkness, like a beacon to guide her.

She stepped out into the water. The beach was starting to flood, but she could make it. It would be one more barrier between her and her insane uncle.

The water reached her calf. It was impossible to tell how deep it went. Hands shaking, she moved into it.

"Win!"

She started running again because he was still behind her. It couldn't be too deep. She had to make it.

She had to see Henry again. She had to tell him she loved him again. This time she would say it until he knew she meant it. This time she wouldn't let him go.

Something hit her back, a stinging, burning sensation.

She reached around, finding the dart and pulling it out.

It was too late. The world was going hazy and she couldn't seem to make her feet work. She hit her knees, heard someone shouting in the background, but it was far away. The rain kept coming but she couldn't feel it anymore. There was only cold.

She slipped into the water. How odd to go out as she'd come in. She thought of that poor baby, drowning and never found. Taylor Winston-Hughes.

She didn't even know her real name.

The water was all around her and Win floated away.

~

Henry was happy Noah was apparently a paranoid bastard, or came from a paranoid family, because the airplane had come equipped with more than a gourmet kitchen. Noah had handed him a .45 after asking if he knew how to use it.

"I'm not paranoid," Noah said as they turned down the long drive that led to Win's house. The rain was starting, a fine mist across the windshield. "My brothers and sisters are from Texas. They don't feel comfortable unless there are a couple of guns stashed around. Given the fact that at one point every single one of them has been shot at, it's more like self-preservation than paranoia. Speaking of paranoia, we're not going in guns a-blazing, right?"

He'd thought about it. "Of course not. We're going to walk in, casually get Win out to the car, and then we leave as quickly as possible. I'll let the cops deal with Bellamy Hughes. He's obviously far more dangerous than I gave him credit for. That's it, up ahead. But I don't see Win's Jeep."

His heart wasn't going to stop pounding until she was safely away from here. He was going to walk in, sweep her off her feet, and before Bellamy or Mary knew what he was really doing, she would be well on her way to . . .

"Where are we taking her? We can't fly back to the city in this." The sky didn't look bad now, but Henry had been through enough storms to know it would get worse very quickly.

"I've got a hotel room," Noah assured him. "I like to cover all my bases. In case the date goes bad, I want a place to go. Also, I don't sleep well with others."

"Women don't like it when you sneak out of bed." He needed something to take his mind off the fact that Win was likely sitting down to dinner with a man who had killed to protect his secret before.

"That's probably why I don't have a girlfriend." Noah parked in front of the gorgeous beach house. It had to be three times the size of the one Henry had grown up in. This was one of the historic houses Martha's Vineyard was known for. It had beach access and several outer buildings.

"Well, let's try to save mine." Girlfriend. It was a silly thing to call Win. Girlfriends were things for high school kids who held hands, not for a man who held on to a woman like she was a lifeline. Not for a man who couldn't think of spending another minute without one particular woman at his side. There was only one word for that: *wife*.

The minute Noah parked the car, Henry was out and rushing to the front door. The weight of the gun in his pocket was calming.

He wouldn't need it. He would get Win out and explain everything to her. God, he was going to have to rip her world out from under her, but he would be there to pick up the pieces. She was strong. She could handle all of it as long as she had someone beside her, someone who never betrayed her. Someone who would never leave her again.

She was about to find out she didn't have a name. He would give her his.

He would give her his everything, including his struggle. That was what he'd realized. People in love didn't merely share the good times. They shared it all. The good, the bad, the horrific. The joy. The sorrow.

He wanted to share it all with her. He could have it all *because* of her.

He knocked on the door and hoped he didn't look like a crazy person.

"Smile," Noah said, stepping up next to him. He brushed the rain off his suit coat. It was starting to come down a bit heavier, but not too badly yet. "Be charming."

The door came open and Mary Hannigan stood there, leaning on her walker.

Damn but she looked like Win. Her hair had grayed, but it was right there in her smile and the way her eyes crinkled. It was in the line of her jaw and the petite shape of her body.

There was no doubt in his mind that this was Win's mother.

He wasn't sure how to feel about that because she'd been willing to let Win be used. Had she done it out of desperation? Had she known she would likely be sent back to Poland without a dime to her name and a baby to take care of?

What would he have done if it had been his child?

"Mr. Garrison?"

He'd thought it would be hard to deal with her. He needed to view her through the filter of a woman desperate to save her baby. Without a husband, without money or a place in society, how would she have raised her daughter? He knew, perhaps more than many, that desperate people did desperate things. They did them out of self-preservation, but often they also did them out of love.

It was easy to soften his tone. "Hello, Ms. Hannigan. It's good to meet you. Yes. I'm Henry Garrison and I've come to see Win."

Her face brightened and she opened the door wide. "I knew you were a smart one. No one can resist my Win. She's entirely too sweet. Come in. Come in. She should be back momentarily."

He followed her inside, Noah on his heels. He took a deep breath, smelling a familiar scent. "Ah, that's where she got the stew recipe. It smells delicious."

Mary moved with her walker. "She learned how to cook from me. She liked to spend time in the kitchen when she was home. I think it's part of her personality to want to please those around her. Cooking is the purest form of showing you care."

Even when one couldn't express her love, a mother could cook for her daughter. "It must have been hard for you when she wouldn't eat."

Her eyes closed briefly and tears shone there when she opened them again. "It was horrible. She got so small and I thought I would lose her. I don't want her ever in that position again. How could she not see how beautiful she was?"

"I won't let her see herself as anything less than beautiful again." No matter what happened, he could see she loved her daughter. "I promise you I will take care of Win from now on. I love her very much."

Mary stopped, her face falling as she looked them both over. "This feels far more serious than it should."

"I'm very serious about Win." He smiled to try to throw her off. "Where is she? We decided to take a little time, but I'm through with that. I know what I want and I want her."

Mary looked back and forth between him and Noah. "That's good because she deserves someone who loves her. I meant to thank you for all your help with the recent problems. Both of you. Actually, the whole firm. Expect a shipment of my special cookies very soon."

Noah gave her a smooth smile. "It was our pleasure."

Where's Win? Where's Win? Where the fuck is Win? The question pounded through his brain, but he needed to stay calm. He had no idea what Bellamy Hughes would do if he knew they'd figured out his secret. "I was more than happy to help her, obviously. But I also was very foolish to think we needed time apart. I've come here to-night to see her because I want to spend my life with her."

He was saying the right words. Mary calmed considerably, her face flushing with obvious pleasure. All the while his brain was whirling, going through all the options. How would he handle Bellamy if he knew Henry had learned the truth? He could tell Bellamy he would play along. Of course he would never tell. Why would he? He loved Win. He meant to marry Win and he would never betray his future family.

Lies, but he could be convincing when he wanted to be.

"So you've got good intentions toward my girl, have you?" Mary asked with a smile.

"Only the best." He glanced around. "I didn't see her Jeep. Is she out? The storm coming in is supposed to be bad."

Mary wheeled her walker back toward the kitchen. "She got home a few minutes ago. The Jeep should be in the garage. She went out to the shop to bring her uncle in for supper. He gets lost out there sometimes. I swear he's been working on that boat for years. One of these days he has to finish it, though I don't like the thought of anyone being out on the water."

Because she'd lost her husband on the water. "Point me in the right direction and I'll go meet her."

Mary waved that off. "Oh, she'll be along. I'm sure Bellamy is simply finishing up, and they probably only have the one umbrella out there. You don't want to get wet, do you? I've been through many of these storms. But then you grew up here. You know how it goes."

"Yes, storms can be very dangerous this time of year." Which was precisely why he needed to get her back to the hotel as soon as possible. "How much rain have you had in the last few weeks? I know Norton Point can flood quite easily."

Which would mean sticking to the main roads when he was getting away.

"Oh, it's been bad this season," she admitted. "I'm sure that beach is several inches underwater. I should warn Win about that. She likes to hike through there. She's been sticking close to home because of what happened with her cousin. Such a bad business, but then that's what happens when you get involved with people like Brie." Her shoulders stiffened with her disdain. "I'm not sad that one is gone. I won't admit it to Win, but the world is a better place without her. But I did have a question. If Win was Brie's heir, does that mean she needs to go through her things? I don't think that's such a good idea. We should just have it all thrown out."

"We can't do that. There are a lot of procedures and paperwork that go along with an estate. I don't think there's a ton of money left in Brie's, but there was property and that will have to be dealt with," Noah explained. "We can advise Win on all of that."

"Who goes through the everyday things?" Mary's tone had gone cautious, a bit stilted, as though she was trying to sound casual. It wasn't working. "Like who would get Brie's mail?"

Henry saw the immediate danger but before he could reply, Noah answered.

"Oh, that all comes to us," Noah admitted. "Win wanted that to come to us. We'll go through all the mail and paperwork and ensure everything gets done. No problem."

The color drained from Mary's face as she looked up at Henry. She stared for a moment and he realized the ruse was over.

"I would never do anything to hurt Win," he said quietly.

"You know." The spoon she'd been holding clattered to the floor. "You know."

"Damn it." Noah flushed. "I shouldn't have said anything. I'm sorry, Henry."

Mary's face contorted as tears formed in her eyes. "I always knew it couldn't last forever."

"I need to know where your daughter is," Henry said quietly. "You do understand that Bellamy killed Brie Westerhaven."

"She was threatening us, threatening Win. She came to me with the first of those terrible tests and told me she would send us all to jail," Mary argued. "That terrible girl was going to take away everything we worked for. Win doesn't know."

"I understand that." He was absolutely certain Win had nothing to do with what happened years ago and that she would be devastated to learn the truth.

He also knew she would want to make things right. There was no question in his mind that Win would give it all up. She would do it without blinking an eye.

He trusted her. He believed in her.

But he needed to find out whether Mary Hannigan would choose her child or the life she'd become accustomed to. "If you know that Bellamy murdered Brie, you must know what he did to Win."

How much did Mary know about what had happened? Bellamy had been very careful to keep her far from the investigation. There was a chance she didn't understand how close Win had come to dying.

Mary's eyes widened. "He wouldn't do anything to Win. He loves Win. He loves her like she's his own. What we did, we did so we could salvage one thing from tragedy. I lost my Milo, and my baby lost her father. Bellamy was going to lose the company. We would have had nothing. It didn't hurt anyone. It gave them hope. It made some people believe in miracles."

The rain had started to pound on the roof.

"Ms. Hannigan, I don't think you understand. The night Brie was killed, Win nearly died, too," Noah explained, his voice calm and soothing. "The killer hit her with a fireplace tool. She spent days in the hospital recovering. We think he was trying to make sure she didn't see him, but it was a brutal blow to the back of her head."

"He hit her?" Mary held on to the walker like she would fall without it.

Now he had her. This was what he needed. "Where is the shop? Let me take her away from here before Bellamy finds out we know. Let me make sure she's safe."

"But he wouldn't hurt her," she insisted.

"I've got the medical documents that say differently," Noah replied. "Why don't you come with us, too. I think it's time for you to tell Win everything. We can go somewhere safe and sit and talk. It's going to be okay."

"But I need to get Win," Henry insisted. "He can't kill her, but I don't know what he'll do if he thinks she knows. He'll have to do something because you know as well as I do that Win won't go along with this."

"The shop is the building to the west. Please get my daughter," she said, her eyes tearing.

Noah moved in. "I'll get you out to the car. We'll be ready to go."

They would drive away from Bellamy Hughes. They wouldn't be subtle about it, and he was probably declaring war on a man with more resources than Henry could count, but it didn't matter. He would do it for Win.

He raced outside, the wind blasting against him. Damn, the storm had picked up. The rain was coming down in sheets. He was immediately soaked through, but it didn't matter. The gun was safe in the pocket of his trench coat. He took comfort in that. He needed to be able to defend Win if things went poorly.

He jogged toward the outer buildings. He could see the warmth of lights coming from the shop. It would be all right. He had zero reason for Bellamy Hughes to have figured out that someone else knew. As far as Hughes knew, they hadn't gotten the final tests back and he would assume the others were with Brie's estate, ready to be tossed out with the rest of the trash. Henry was sure the man had a plan in place, but he hadn't realized Win was letting her lawyers handle the estate.

So he would go in that shop and find Win and everything would be fine. Bellamy wouldn't realize something was wrong until they were driving away.

He realized that plan had gone to hell when he saw the door had been left open.

He rushed into the shop. "Win?"

Nothing. No one was here. He ran a hand through his hair, slicking it back. Where the hell was she?

And then he saw it. His heart threatened to stop. There on the ground was the fireplace tool taken from her room. Fuck. Fuck. Fuck.

She'd found it and Bellamy Hughes had been here. He knew Win knew he'd killed Brie.

Pure panic threatened to overtake his system. She hadn't run back to the house. He would have seen her.

He ran back out. There were footprints in the sand, though they were faint because of the rain.

Where would she run?

The answer hit him like a kick to the gut. She would go where she felt safe. She would go where she knew she could get away.

She would have run toward his place. When she'd stayed with him the first time, she'd gotten to know some of the neighbors. They would take her in. That's where she would go, but she didn't realize the beach was flooded.

She could drown.

He sprinted or tried to. The sand sucked at his feet, but he wasn't about to give up. The wind whipped around him as he made his way toward the point. The trails were hard to navigate, but he could see them when the lightning flashed and the world around him cracked.

He heard a shout and then saw a figure in front of him. It was a shadow against the night sky. Henry watched in horror as the shadow raised a gun and shot.

That wasn't Win. The figure was far too large, and that meant Bellamy was trying to hurt her. Henry drew the gun Noah had given him and prayed he remembered how to use it.

He leveled the gun and fired. He saw the figure stiffen and then drop out of sight.

Had he hit Bellamy? Where was Win? Was she down? He raced over the dune, losing his footing. He slipped, the gun lost as he scrambled to find some traction. He landed in a thud against something in the water.

Henry rolled, trying not to get drawn out further into the water that was flooding the beach. Here it was only an inch or two, but even a few feet away it would go deep and there would be a current taking it all back out to sea.

"Win!"

"Help her," a ragged voice said.

Henry looked down and realized what had stopped his fall. Bellamy Hughes was lying in the water, a hole in his chest.

He looked up at Henry, blood on his lips. "Didn't know what to do."

He knelt down. "Where is Win?"

"She . . . Damn it. Never meant to hurt the girl. Shot her but it was only a tranquilizer. Didn't think about what would happen. Meant to get her back home so we could figure out what to do."

"Where is she?" It was obvious Henry's shot had been a good one. Bellamy Hughes wouldn't be around for long. Where was Win? She'd taken a tranq dart? How much had been in it? Was she passed out in the sand somewhere?

Bellamy's eyes glanced over. "In the water. She went down in the water. We were worried the first time we put her in. Had to make it look good."

She was in the water? She was unconscious in a current that could go anywhere?

Henry threw off his coat and waded in. Where was she?

Please. Please. He prayed to anyone who would listen. *Please don't let her be dead.* Not when he could see home. His home was close. If she'd just made it fifty yards more, she could have been on his porch.

Where they'd met.

Close. They'd come so fucking close.

He strode in farther, the water rushing around his knees. It didn't matter how deep it got because he was going to find her or die trying. He would let the current take him to wherever she was. They would find out together.

Lightning flashed and he caught sight of something in the water. It was moving ahead to his right, caught on something.

Henry rushed to get there. Win. She was floating, her jeans caught on a log that had been left behind. His sweet Win was floating facedown, her hair a halo in the dark water.

He picked her up. Pure dead weight. She didn't move as he flipped her over and started to make his way to the other side. They were closer to Chappaquiddick now. He had to get her somewhere dry.

If she was dead, he might lie down beside her and wait. Just wait because he couldn't go on without her.

He forced his way to the other side, the water beating at him. Win looked pale in the moonlight. He hit sand and ran, shouting for help. The lights were on in the bungalow he'd grown up in. He laid Win on the porch and pounded on the door. There was no time to wait. Every second was taking her further and further from him. There was no life in her body, no warmth, and she was always so warm.

CPR. He had to give her CPR. He had to stop the panic in his brain long enough to save her. Nothing was more important than saving Win.

He felt for a pulse. Nothing. Her skin was smooth and chilled, but there was no discernible pulse. No spark of life. She was cold from the water. Her lips were blue.

No. He couldn't give up.

"Don't leave me." He felt for her xiphoid process and moved up two fingers. Calm. He had to stay calm. One. Two. Three. Four. Five compressions.

"Please, Win."

Her eyes came open. He rolled her on her side as her lungs released what had to be a gallon of seawater. She shuddered and shook as she came back to life.

She turned her eyes to him. "Henry?"

"You were drugged, baby. Try to stay with me. I know it's hard. I'm going to get some help. The cell service is out. I have to find a landline." He couldn't leave her. How was he going to leave her here to go find help?

She sagged in his arms. "Where are we? Are we at your house? I was running for your house."

She sounded stronger, but he wouldn't feel safe until an ambulance came. "We're on the porch, but the bastard who bought it won't open the fucking door."

Her lips curled slightly. "Key's under the mat. Who do you think bought it? Meant to tempt you back with it. I'm tired, Henry. Oh god, he's after us. Henry, you have to run."

Relief poured through him as he found the key.

"Never again." He wouldn't ever run from her. He lifted her up and took her inside.

He wouldn't ever run from home again.

EPILOGUE

SEVEN MONTHS LATER

Win closed the door on the last of their guests. It was almost midnight, but she wasn't tired. She was ready to get to the good part of the day. Not that it hadn't been pretty spectacular up to this point.

The bungalow and yard had been covered with twinkle lights, and a band had played while she and Henry and their guests had danced the night away.

She may have given up the big house on the island, the Manhattan penthouse, and all the other properties, but this bungalow had been bought with funds from her reality show. It was hers and Henry's. She hadn't come out of it with nothing.

She'd gotten the best prize of all.

"So, Daisy Jarvisch, how do you like your new name?" Henry had taken off the bow tie and shrugged out of the jacket to his tuxedo. Though they'd been married on the beach, she'd wanted a formal wedding. After all, she was only doing this once.

She smiled. "I think I'll stick with Win Garrison. I never got used to Daisy."

Daisy, she'd learned, was her real name. It was the one on her birth certificate, but she was too far from that baby who'd been chosen to replace the lost heiress.

She'd never really been Daisy and never truly been Taylor Winston-Hughes, but she thought she would be a spectacular Win Garrison.

Henry smiled as he crowded her. "Have I told you how gorgeous you are, Mrs. Garrison?"

Seven months of living with that man had made her comfortable with a lot of things, mostly with how intimate he needed to be. If he was in a room with her, he wanted to touch her, even if it was simply her leaning against him as they sat and watched TV. "You might have mentioned it. Did I thank you for getting the trial pushed out so my mother could come? Actually, I should simply thank you for letting Margarita handle her case."

He kissed her forehead. "No need. You know we always handle family cases. And I think we can expect leniency. She was in a desperate position and your mother didn't commit any acts of violence. The DA is getting anxious about it. He knows he could lose. We might get him to plead down. After all, you're considered something of a miracle."

She shook her head. "I was definitely not a miracle."

"I don't know, sweetheart. What do you call a woman who has everything and decides to give it all up to make things right for a group of people who died long ago? I think the hospitals and charities that have money flooding in think you're quite the miracle."

She wasn't sure about that. There were angry people, too, but she was dealing with it. She'd found not being the heiress to a billion-dollar corporation was incredibly freeing.

Especially since she was still employed. The foundation wasn't going anywhere, and she'd been shocked to discover the board didn't care what her name was. They wanted her running the same charity she'd worked at since she was a child. Between her job and getting her MBA, she was going to be a busy lady. Though she was transferring to NYU because there was no way she was going to be apart from Henry.

"Well, I think we should enjoy the calm before the storm." She wrinkled her nose because she'd kind of hoped she wouldn't be the one to tell him. "Uhm, I got the news tonight."

Henry groaned. "I know. Noah told me. They're making a new movie about you. I don't even want to know what that script is going to look like. I could sue Alicia if you want me to. It would be fun."

The weird part was she kind of liked Henry's ex-wife. Alicia Kingman was a force of nature but she could also be quite kind. And she knew a good story when she saw it. "I couldn't turn her down. It's too much money and it's all going straight into your pro bono fund. Now that I know what it means to worry about money, I think I should help out people in trouble, like I was. After all, not everyone has an amazing lawyer for a husband."

He pulled her close. "If she didn't do it, someone would. Tell her she better get someone incredibly handsome to play my role."

"Only the best will do." She went up on her toes and kissed him. "But he still won't hold a candle to you. I love you, Henry."

He hauled her up into his arms. "I love you, Win. I think I knew it the minute you fell into my arms that first day."

Such a liar. "You did not."

He shrugged. "That's not how I remember it. I remember clearly falling for you then and there. That's my testimony and I'm sticking to it."

Revisionist history. She could handle that. "Well, you are an expert witness. Who am I to question you?"

"Remember that." He cuddled her close and started for the bedroom. "It's going to get better. One day, I'll buy your house back."

She shook her head. "Absolutely not. This is our house. This is where we'll bring our kids. I love this house. I don't need the other one."

"Our house," he said as he took her into the bedroom. "Our history. Our kids. I like the sound of all of that, my wife."

He kissed her and eased her onto their bed. The house was small, but it was good and right. It was theirs, with no tragic ties.

She'd given up a fortune, but she'd found a future.

Win lay back and welcomed her new husband home.